Resounding praise for the

Inspecto

ROBE

D0807309

"Lovers of historical thrillers will be shocked, stunned, beaten to hell, and, most importantly, riveted. . . . Robert Walker is a master craftsman and this is the series he was born to create."

Jay Bonansinga, author of *Frozen*

"Walker's taken on Caleb Carr's territory, with a superb haunted protagonist with a graveyard on his back. Ransom your soul for this one; it's that mesmerizing."

Ken Bruen, Macavity Award winner for *The Killing of the Tinkers*

"His prose cuts like a garrote, transporting us back to the Chicago of yesteryear with panache and style to spare."

J.A. Konrath

"Vivid and passionate."

Barbara D'Amato

"Walker writes . . . entertaining stories filled with surprises, clever twists, and wonderfully drawn characters."

Daytona Beach News-Journal

"Robert W. Walker has enjoyed a solid reputation for his unique concoctions of twisted crimes, colorful characters, dark humor, and solid plotting. The Walker brew is as bubbly as ever. . . . I'm hooked!"

Raymond Benson

By Robert W. Walker

CITY OF THE ABSENT
SHADOWS IN THE WHITE CITY
CITY FOR RANSOM

CITY
OF THE
ABSENT

ROBERT W. WALKER

HARPER

An Imprint of HarperCollins Publishers

This is a work of fiction. Names, characters, places, and incidents are drawn from the author's imagination or are used fictitiously and are not to be construed as real. Any resemblance to actual events, locales, organizations, or persons, living or dead, is entirely coincidental.

HARPER

An Imprint of HarperCollins*Publishers*
10 East 53rd Street
New York, New York 10022-5299

Copyright © 2007 by Robert W. Walker
ISBN: 978-0-06-074012-2
ISBN-10: 0-06-074012-4

First Harper paperback printing: December 2007

HarperCollins® and Harper® are registered trademarks of Harper-Collins Publishers.

Printed in the United States of America

Visit Harper paperbacks on the World Wide Web
at www.harpercollins.com

10 9 8 7 6 5 4 3 2 1

I pay respectable homage to all the authors that've come before me, and from whom I've learned so much. We all build on those who've preceded us.

ACKNOWLEDGMENTS

My great and abiding thanks to Lyssa Keusch, who guided my hand over many a rough spot and opened my eyes to what I couldn't/shouldn't do to my own hero, heroine, and story. She has been the "constant" on the project, and she deserves an award as One Great Editor. A series such as *City for Ransom*, *Shadows in the White City*, and now *City of the Absent* does not get written in a vacuum, and I remain indebted to Lyssa, May Chen, and Danielle Bartlett for all their help. I would also like to thank artist Debra Lill for the wonderful, moving artwork evoking the gaslight mystery-noir appearing on all the covers.

Robert W. Walker

CITY
OF THE
ABSENT

CHAPTER 1

October 28, 1893, Chicago, Illinois, on the last night of the World's Fair

Mayor of Chicago, Carter Harrison, a politician who split families and lovers over the issues of the day, a man both beloved and despised, lay dying of an assassin's bullet. The murderer's three consecutive shots left Harrison writhing in agony on his own Ashland Avenue lawn. His last thoughts for his family faded in and out with his pride in Chicago on this special night, as it had been a night of celebration. Harrison had presided over the closing ceremonies of the Great Chicago World's Fair.

Across the city, Inspector Alastair Ransom and Dr. Jane Francis Tewes lay curled in one another's arms. Alastair, sleepless, contemplated Jane's outward ladylike appearance and demeanor, her inner beauty, her caring, giving nature, and her magical lovemaking.

Jane also lay awake, contemplating and fearing that she might love this man, fearing what her own heart kept telling her—that it wanted him. That it wanted whatever Ransom wanted.

She'd even said so; out loud, she feared. She now whispered, "World be damned if things aren't right between us, Alastair."

"What?" he'd sleepily replied.

"No matter, I will do whatever you ask . . . "

He liked the sound and beat and counterpoint she'd found.

" . . . Alastair . . . whatever you ask me to . . . "

"Jane, you needn't make promises that—"

" . . . even if you finally ask me . . . in the end . . . to leave . . . "

"Jane, you must not—"

"I must do what you ask me to."

He was unsure where that had come from; likely some deep wellspring of desire within her? Something in her deepest recesses? A need to wholly, completely give herself over to someone she believed in? In a love she might trust above all things—or rather, dreamed of in childhood along with castles and fairy-tale worlds? Else she was truly in love with him on a level he had no prior experience with, save in his own imaginings with Polly Pete before her death.

But how was he to take this? Coming from Jane? An emotional rock up till now. How to play it?

Their lovemaking had been extreme and pleasurable, lights going off inside his head like those in the sky over Chicago's Lake Michigan on this, the last night of the World's Fair commemorating Columbus and worldwide progress since Columbus. *Isn't that enough in and of itself*, he silently asked, furled in her arms, her heart beating against his. Pleasurable beyond measure, in fact . . . it'd been remarkably pleasurable; he'd thought such spiritual elation impossible in any physical bonding, yet both the hardened detective and the seasoned lady surgeon had transcended this ground, this room, this city, and this plane.

Still, perhaps that was not enough for Jane, and perhaps she wanted more of him—*far more of him*. Perhaps she wanted him to repeat her words. Words she'd spoken to entice words from him? To join her as in a mantra—a chant they should together adopt when addressing one another, and next she'd convince him that the two should marry, and God forbid, have children at his age. These rampant thoughts flitted through his mind along with an even more terrifying idea—his loss of freedom. Just as marriage to her must end the career of one Dr. James Phineas Tewes—her other self—it could end the career of one Inspector Alastair Ransom, should she, as a wife, demand he take a safer, cushier job, say that of a store clerk or haberdasher.

It'd never work. Besides, given his proclivities, his life-style, his set ways, he'd be doing her no favor whatsoever tying the knot; in fact, it'd be like tying her to a raging bull. This, in his mind, must be the end of it.

Bells began to toll all across Ransom's city and outside Jane's window. Then came the thundering of horses pulling police wagons. Aside from the fracas, something deep within, in the nature of self-preservation, roused Alastair from Jane's caress. The admixture of tumultuous questions and passions assailing Ransom with the staccato alarms created a strange wave of panic. A panic rivaling his most lovely moment; he just knew something awful had happened.

"Is it a fire?" Jane asked.

"Dunno. Could be." *A fire on the final night of the fair*, he thought. *This could be disastrous.*

The bells and whistles sounded like a wailing, wounded animal. Again Alastair felt shaken by whatever it might be that'd occurred *outside* his inner storm—the eruption of passion ending in confusion. From what he could tell from the limited perspective of Jane's window on Belmont, the disturbance must be uptown. Somewhere near the fair, perhaps along Michigan Avenue. The two locations police in Chicago were sworn to protect above all else.

Ransom continued to peek out through lace curtains, his action sending a shaft of diffused gaslight into the room and over the bed, where Jane's reclining figure became silhouettelike, even fairylike.

"Damn . . . this can't be good," he commented, ignoring her unconscious call for him to return to her bed. "I'd best go have a look."

Jane climbed from her own wakeful dream, joined him at the window and wrapped her arms about Alastair, hardly capable of the reach. She was dwarfed beside him. "Whatever the problem, they may need my medical assistance, too," she groggily muttered.

"Yours or Dr. Tewes's?" He turned as he said this, his eyes accusing. He'd long argued for an end to her dressing as a male doctor in order to attract patients to her clinic—or rather, the clinic below the shingle reading: DR. JAMES PHINEAS TEWES.

Jane squeezed him to her. "This is no time for old arguments, Alastair."

"When the devil're you going to respect me on this? Give up this masquerade, Jane, please! It's seriously troubling, this . . . this situation, more so now than ever."

"And why more so than ever, Alastair? Tell me. Say it aloud."

She spent so much time trying to get him to speak about his emotions that it'd become a full-time job, and he knew this, and he knew what she wanted to hear, but a reluctant, thick ball of uncertainty sat lodged in his throat. "Because I am seen with you daily now. Everyone thinks I am seeing Dr. Tewes's sister, and it is growing increasingly difficult."

"I couldn't agree with you more, but circumstances continue to dictate that Dr. Tewes be, *ahhh* . . . kept alive, at least for the time being. His bank account alone has to be dealt with, not to mention the practice, the rent, and there's Gabby's tuition at Rush College; her lab fees alone are draining me, and—and—"

"And indeed . . . and there's always another rationalization for your being an impostor, placing me in an impossible situation, yet whispering promises in my ear all the while."

"It's not entirely about you, Alastair."

"It affects me, and it is increasingly more difficult for me to—"

"Heavens! Why is it men always find the *'me'* in everything? What's in it for *me*? How much trouble is it for *me*! We should enforce a new law, Alastair!"

"What new law?" He took the bait.

"That no male can ever end a sentence with *me*!"

"Look here, I'm thinking of Gabby, too! This is not easy on her."

"Leave my daughter out of this." At the same time, Jane realized that she'd herself used Gabby as an excuse. And as her voice rose along with her ire, she recalled the peace and strength she'd found in this man's arms. She had never felt such power stirring within her by anyone's touch once he'd gotten over how daring she could be. She guessed he'd been absolutely stupefied to learn how sexually imaginative, bold, knowledgeable, and naughty Dr. Jane Francis Tewes could be.

He broke into her thoughts. "How is it you can whisper unconditional love in one breath, love that dictates you do my every bidding, and the next you care not a whit for my opinion on important matters?"

"We're speaking of one matter here. Just this one matter," she defended.

"And a large matter it is, especially if it comes to light."

"I grant as much, but Alastair—"

"All right, Dr. Tewes, but I haven't time to sit about while you don your mustache and ascot and coat and remember your pipe and imported French absinthe-flavored tobacco. Or have you taken to snuff or chaw these days?"

"Don't be silly!"

"Look, Jane, something's happened out there," he pointed to the window, "and I am duty bound to find out what."

She realized from his tone that he wanted to escape her bedroom far more than he wanted to investigate another incident. "Of course, duty calls."

Her facetious coy smile made Ransom grit his teeth. "Yes, duty calls."

"Since when does Alastair Ransom put duty before a night of pleasure?"

"I think you know less about me than you think, Jane."

She heard him stomp like a buffalo down the hallway and

out the front door, gone. "Damn it!" She hadn't wanted him leaving in a state of anger. Still, she lowered the window and helplessly shouted after him. "Duty is just an excuse to escape! You're drawing at straws!"

But it was no use. Alastair flinched but kept moving. He was gone in an instant, disappearing into the Chicago night after latching onto a hansom cab.

Jane Francis felt a definite chill at the night wind rushing in until she slammed the window down. She then looked down at her perspiration-soaked nightshirt, thought how remarkable the sex had been, and then growled, "God how that man infuriates me!"

CHAPTER 2

"Really, Mother!" Jane had thought herself alone, but her grown daughter, Gabby, stood in the doorway. "The two of you are like children! And that racket outside gave me such a start!"

"Go back to bed, darling."

"I thought sure that madman of a preacher at the Episcopal church had come crashing through our door with torches and ropes to drag us out and hang us from the nearest flagpole as sinners and heretics. To flay our skins, to burn us at the stake, to make us walk the city with a scarlet letter 'round our necks!"

"Don't be foolish!"

"To drag us bodily into the street and excommunicate the lot of us!" Gabby continued unabated.

"I think I'd prefer that Reverend Hobart Jabes excommunicate me than to have me sit for another of his sermons."

"Three hours last time!" Gabby shouted.

"Wields a helluva brimstone hammer over our heads!"

"And that nonsense trash about the evils of the woman's suffrage movement!"

"Yes, peculiar notion: that granting women the vote will let loose the 'hounds of Hades'!"

"Ahhhhhh!" Gabby screamed. "I'll not go back to hear another single word from that man!"

Jane stared out at their next to nearest neighbor, the Episcopal church and parsonage, wishing again that she'd taken the house across the street instead of this place. *"Shhh . . .* you'll wake the parsonage, and then God save us from more of his blather!" Jane crossed the room and sat before her brightly lit mirror. She began dressing as the male doctor, James Phineas Tewes, applying makeup. As she did so, she mumbled, "I just keep asking myself, is this man worth it?"

"Which man're you meaning, Ransom or Tewes or the minister?"

"Very funny." Jane applied the oily base to change her very skin color.

"You love him, Mother." It was not a question.

"Nonsense!"

"Shakespeare tells us it is so, that love is nonsense, insanity, madness."

"Shakespeare was a man ahead of us all," she agreed, continuing to apply her makeup. "He held more knowledge of the human mind and heart than . . . than all the medical books together."

"So why not admit your love for Alastair?"

"Don't be foolish, child!"

"If to no one else than to yourself?"

"Stop it with the Socratic dialogue! It won't work here!"

"But what *do* you feel for Alastair?" Gabby persisted.

"It's so awkward, and it's not how I feel so often as how I think I feel, and I'm always thinking he makes me angry! I'm so . . . so . . . "

"Confused? Join the rest of us poor feminine creatures who know naught of our own minds or how our minds work, Mother! Have ya not listen't to Rev-run Jabes at all, ma'am?"

"Don't be facetious. It will leave wrinkles!"

"I've read all 'bout us poor dear li'l weak creatures, Mother! Repeatedly!"

"Enough, child."

"In every medical text at the college, Mother, whole chapters on the frail and easily confounded of the sexes, and—"

"I know about the medical texts!"

"And Mr. Jabes must've read the same books."

"Agreed, Gabby, now go away." Jane continued at her makeup.

Gabby did not go away. "And—And apparently, we are *it*, Mother, you and I."

"*It?*"

"The living *embodiment*. You with your Inspector Ransom, and I with Jere Swift, the cad."

"Please heed my advice, Gabby. Keep your eye on one goal—your medical studies—and steer clear of men! They have but one aim in mind, to bed you like a mare! They fear a woman of intelligence, and this Swift boy, isn't his father a common butcher? Mr. Armour's chief rival?"

"Well yes, the Swift Company's bigger than Armour, but please, while the family is rich from the slaughter, my Jeremiah, his eyes are set on human anatomy and surgery. He wants none of the business."

"That'll change should his father fall ill, should the family business need him."

"You've become cynical, Mother. Why, Jere has a sensitive soul, I believe, and—and—"

"We'll take this up later. For now, I must catch up with Alastair . . . see what all the fuss is about."

Gabby came closer, blocking her mother's way. "Why don't you wait to see if there is a call for Dr. Tewes before you further upset Alastair?"

"Upset Alastair? I don't run my life round that man's fulminations!"

"Oh . . . I see, but Mother, do you really see him as an explosion?"

"One ready to detonate, yes." She applied a few finishing touches.

"I suppose he can be, *ahhh* . . . fulminating, but more so with you and Dr. Tewes than with me."

"Smart aleck. Listen to me, if that man can inspire anything, it is fumes and fiery damnations, so allow me this much."

"Fine, Mother, but he has a point."

"I'll thank you to back away and allow me to stand!"

Jane had transformed herself into a male doctor before the looking glass. Gabby thought her transformation remarkable—as complete as the actor Herrick changing from Dr. Jekyll to Mr. Hyde at the Lyceum theater a few nights ago. Suppressing the Jekyll and Hyde comparison, Gabby instead asked, "What do you suppose all the alarms are about? Here on the last night of the great fair?"

"I haven't the faintest."

"I pray it's not another dreadful fire."

"If city officials don't enforce the fire laws, and allow the building codes to be sold to the highest bidder, one day we're sure to have another major tragedy here."

But Gabby spoke of tonight's sirens. "It's likely one of those warehouses along the wharves."

"Or a sweatshop, or a dance hall, or a theater."

"Or a factory over on Hubbard."

"Or all of the above."

The telephone rang, its patter in ominous harmony with the cacophony going on in the streets.

"Who at this hour?" asked Jane.

"Perhaps it's to do with the alarm?" asked Gabby.

"I suspect so, yes. Calling for Dr. Tewes."

"Rather regularly these days."

The phone continued its jarring alarm. As she went for it on the foyer wall, Jane, trying out her baritone voice, asked Gabby, "Do you recall what Mr. Oscar Wilde said at the Garden Theater about the telly?"

"No, refresh me."

"The value of the phone is *only* the value of what two people have to say to one another."

Gabby laughed but stopped short when she read her mother's face as Jane responded to the news that Mayor Carter Harrison had been assassinated in front of his home and would Dr. James Tewes come to comfort Mrs. Harrison.

"Murdered, our mayor?" Gabby had gone white at the suggestion. She could hardly take it as news, as fact, as in her mind it must be some nasty, awful joke someone was pulling on Dr. Tewes. It simply must be.

"But Mother, why . . . why call Tewes? I mean, if the mayor is indeed dead, murdered? What can you or your Dr. Tewes possibly do for a dead mayor?"

"It's not for the mayor I am called, but for his wife."

"The mayor's wife?"

"In her grief, she's called for Dr. Tewes, and she wants him—*me*—immediately. Lock the door behind me, and I'll return as soon as I can."

"But what does the sudden widow want with Dr. Tewes?" asked Gabby, her words cut off as the heavy front door closed between them.

CHAPTER 3

When Alastair came on the scene of the shooting death of Mayor Carter Harrison, he immediately saw the crowd milling around the mayor's porch, lawn, and gate. Quickening his step, his cane firing against the bricks, he next saw the body lying below a bloodstained sheet on flagstones between house and gate. Ransom froze. He stared in disbelief, uncomprehending, not wanting it to be true—the report he'd heard all along the way. But it appeared horribly so.

At his feet lay what had been a vibrant man with a spring in his step, a wave and a smile for all of Chicago, and a strong personality and a vision for the city's future, a man who'd believed himself destined to drag Chicago, kicking and screaming, into the next century—only seven years away. Mayor Harrison'd had plans for what he termed "my city." In fact, Ransom had learned of the mayor's burning desire to be reelected again, despite having served for two consecutive terms. Harrison had quietly been working to alter the election law that prohibited him from running for a third term. He so wanted to be mayor at the turn of the century.

It hardly would be the worst law that'd been "altered" in Chicago for reasons of expediency. But now Harrison lay dead. He'd never see the twentieth century, not as mayor, not as husband, not as a father.

"He died instantly," said the tall, blond-headed Officer Darren Callahan, one of the first police on scene, a friend to Ransom. "The assassin placed the gun through the bars." Callahan pushed the gate closed behind Ransom. "And the sick bastard shoved it into the mayor's heart and fired three successive shots."

"Witnesses?"

"Harold Baumgartner."

"Who is?"

"The butler." Callahan pointed to a man with his head in his hands, half collapsed on the mayor's steps. "Baumgartner was looking on from the open doorway," he continued. "The assassin had been bathed in light flooding from the open door, easily recognized."

"The butler's identified the shooter?"

"The man made no attempt to conceal his identity. Bell rang. As was his habit, Mr. Mayor comes out to answer it personally."

Harrison, who had a great love of the city and its people, made it his habit to confer with any concerned citizen, or anyone with a scheme to bring jobs to the city, and by extension, his constituency. This time the habit proved fatal. All had happened in the blink of an eye.

"Damn you, Carter," muttered Ransom. "Why didn't you let the butler handle it?"

Callahan gauged Ransom's pained features and realized he was a personal friend to the mayor.

Ransom began telling Callahan what he already knew. "The mayor's bell gate was well used. He'd had it installed for anyone in the city to ring to answer the least question."

Callahan nodded. The story of how accessible Chicago's mayor was had long become legend. "Baumgartner says this madman had been hanging about all day, waiting for the mayor's return. Told him he'd be busy with the fair closing, so he disappeared, and the butler thought nothing of it again until he saw the mayor go out to the gate."

"Damn fool bell," muttered Ransom. "I suspect Carter was still excited over the closing ceremonies."

"Baumgartner said the mayor knew the man, his killer. Called him by his first name. Obviously thought him harmless."

"Is he in custody?"

"Not as yet, but we know who he is and where he lives."

"Name, then, and address."

"It's taken care of, Inspector."

"Who was the guy?" Ransom stomped the fieldstone he stood on.

"Seems he was an irate election official who believed Mr. Harrison owed him a government job."

"You're determined not to tell me the man's whereabouts and name, Darren?"

"I am. For your own good, Inspector, sir."

The young officer was polite, concerned, and infuriating.

And still Ransom couldn't believe events had led to Carter Harrison's murder. Even now as he again stared in blank, dumbfound confusion at the prone mayor at his feet.

Some fool at the gate behind him began ringing the offending bell. His rage getting the best of him, Ransom shouted to no one in particular, "Stop ringing that bloody bell!"

He straightened his shoulders, and his eyes fixed now on the mayor's home, a small plush mansion compared to all the more pretentious homes surrounding the mayor's manor.

Ransom, a man who thrived on instant gratification, wanted to murder the murderer, here and now. To this end, he rushed the butler, Baumgartner, asking the killer's name, frightening the demoralized man as he took hold of him.

Callahan pulled Ransom away, surprising Alastair with his strength. Ransom stepped off but felt sick to his stomach over the assassination.

"Harrison didn't deserve an end like this," he muttered to those standing around.

"Three shots! He took three bullets at point-blank range!"

the cry had gone out to be repeated like a mantra throughout the growing crowd.

"Who killed Carter and why?" asked Thom Carmichael of the *Herald News,* who'd bribed his way into the crime scene and now stood in shock over the body. "Why, Alastair?"

The deputy mayor, Leland Crawford, stepped up to Ransom and Carmichael, his eyes tear-stained. "There's been a man coming 'round City Hall, repeatedly threatening us all, but chiefly the mayor."

"Why the hell wasn't he arrested? Why the hell didn't I hear of it?" asked Ransom, teeth grinding.

"He *was* arrested—repeatedly so!"

"Not at Des Plaines station."

"No, elsewhere. Does it matter? He was released, only to do this filthy, cowardly deed."

"Give me his name."

"What'll you do with the information, Ransom?" asked Carmichael, ever fascinated with the things he'd heard Alastair capable of, and the things he'd witnessed first-hand.

"I will have every inch of 'im before they hang 'im."

"Then I can be no part of it," said Crawford.

"Just a name is all I ask."

"The man's a lunatic, and he's hallucinating!"

"Doesn't matter. Not to me! A name, sir!"

"The fool was under the mistaken notion that the mayor made promises to him," continued Crawford. "He's off his head."

"Off his head?" asked Carmichael. "A candidate for the asylum?"

"Mentally off, yes."

"What sort of promises did he believe the mayor made him?" pressed the reporter, Carmichael.

"Says the mayor should've crowned him corporation counsel to the city!"

"Corporate counsel? Then he's a lawyer?"

"No! Only a foolish accountant who thinks he could fake it."

"A bean counter?" asked Ransom, listening in. "A bean counter killed Carter Harrison?"

"Yes, a bean counter nutcase."

"His name, damn it!" Alastair's rage looked as if it might send him into the deputy mayor.

"He's already under lock and key, Alastair," came a voice from behind him. It was big Mike O'Malley, no longer in a Chicago blue uniform, now a plainclothes detective. "Some of the boys got hold of 'im and bloodied him up good, you needn't worry on that score."

"How many people knew about this lunatic?" asked Ransom. "And why didn't I know about him?"

"Everyone who works out of the Hall," said the deputy mayor.

"And that includes the cops who work the Hall," added O'Malley. "You may's well stand down, Alastair."

"And the mayor? He knew this creep might be dangerous, and yet he walks straight out to him?" asked Ransom.

"You know Carter," said Crawford. "He believed he could talk a mad dog or a bull into a peaceful resolution."

Ransom looked at the bulging shape below the shroud. "A peaceful resolution indeed."

"The surgeon, Dr. Fenger, was called," replied Deputy Mayor Crawford, "but Carter succumbed instantly to his wounds. The whole thing happened no more'n fifteen, twenty minutes ago."

"How do we know this isn't some conspiracy? That this lunatic wasn't put up to it?" asked Ransom.

"Not everything bad that happens in Chicago is a conspiracy, Inspector."

Ransom heaved a sigh and gave a thought to precisely where he had been—in Jane's warm embrace—when the mayor had sustained the mortal wounds that took him from this place. He turned to see the swelling crowd as it pushed in against the mayor's wrought-iron fence here on wide Ashland Avenue. The crowd felt like a single animal, threatening to topple the delicate decorative metalwork displaying leaves and birds at play in a world as black as coal. The pushing and shoving caused the gate bell to ring on and off, further upsetting Ransom.

The crowd shrugged this way and that, its weight and girth building, growing, swelling to ominous proportion. Ransom thought the crowd a well-fed heifer and about as mindless. Still, he had a gentler thought about the mob here, for all in the crowd mourned and wailed, some calling the dead man's name, others calling him the King of Chicago . . . "Long live the King." Still others cried out, "The work of *our* Carter is done!"

Then additional disturbing news began filtering about the crowd. One, that it had been a well-planned, well-executed assassination, the work of savage, armed-to-the-teeth, militant union men spurred by bloodthirsty anarchists who disagreed with Harrison's politics, ways, and means. Two, that he was killed to end talk of an investigation into Chicago police corruption from Haymarket Riot days to present. And three, that he was killed by a jealous suitor for his beautiful wife's hand. Rumors piled themselves thick as they came out of the mouth of the mob.

A police line was hastily thrown up to guard the shaking fence and house. The mayor's body, which had lain out on the flagstones next to the front lawn so indecorously for the past hour, was now lifted by four able men looking the part of pallbearers as they moved Harrison's remains to the interior, where his son and wife looked on in stunned terror. The mob, too, remained in stunned disbelief and terror; they wanted to see Harrison, as if still in denial, as if expecting it all to be a big mistake or final element of the carnival atmosphere tonight, a joke in the worst imaginable Chicago taste.

Others, late arrivals in particular, wanted to see the body with their own eyes, and this circulating group, rowdy and boisterous from drink, felt cheated to learn that the mayor's corpse had been removed from view—from the street.

News of this made its way through the police barricade and into the mayor's home, where his wife made a conscious effort to deal with this strange problem atop her husband's murder before things should get out of hand. She ordered the body placed on a dining room table at a window so the remains could be seen from the other side of lacy, see-through curtains.

A precursor to lying in state, Ransom thought.

He merely shook his head at the beast before him, the demanding mob. He then realized that Thom Carmichael had disappeared from his side, and the reporter now awkwardly pushed and pulled his way through the maddening crowd where he'd gone "to get the pulse of the city," as he'd put it. So wrecked did Carmichael appear once he managed to get back to this side of the fence, Ransom thought he'd been in a brawl. In fact, he appeared dizzy from having been hit in the head or trampled, his clothes in disarray. Ransom found the reporter on his right and O'Malley on his left, when Carmichael asked, "Didja hear what's afoot on the Midway, Alastair?"

"No more than what has been afoot there since the mayor and the bigwigs decided to *have* a White City."

"Never been pure white, has it, now?" asked the journalist.

"Whoever imagined it a fairyland didn't have the sense God gave a turnip," suggested O'Malley, drawing a laugh from Carmichael.

"No, they just live in another world, men like Burnham." Alastair gave a moment's thought to the architect of the fair, and then lit a pipe. He'd stopped and started smoking so many times, he'd lost count. Smoke curled about his features when he exhaled. "People with so much ready money, they dream of a place like something out of Dante's rendition of heaven, and they begin to think they've enough money and imagination to recreate it on Earth."

"Like the Palmer House." Thom nodded. "And they think it'll change men . . . change the bedrock of all mankind, along with the arts, and how people think. But when you're hungry, who has time for the ballet?"

"Turn us all into dreamers, heh, Thom?"

"Dreamers, politicians, philosophers, land developers, saloon owners, shopkeepers, and architects, I suppose." Thom laughed. "Tell it to the jackals and rats among us." He sneered. "H-H-Here . . . in Chicago of all places," he ended, sputtering, as if spitting hair from his teeth.

But Ransom's thoughts were on Thom's remarks about the Midway. The fairway had been rampant with thefts, hoaxes, even murders since the inception of the fair. The "low-downs" as some called the thugs, prostitutes, pimps, and petty thieves, had quickly moved in to fill every conceivable void, which only led to territorial squabbles, gang activity, terrible knife and fistfights, and, too often, murder that went unwitnessed in a city that once knew no such violence, at least not on this scale.

Every knowledgeable cop in Chicago had predicted as much when first learning of a gigantic months-long world's fair in the name of mankind's progress since Christopher Columbus to be raised and held in the city. Immediately, every rat and snake within the city limits and beyond had gone into the plan-making stage of how best to make big bucks off the fair and fairgoers. How to build a machine, for instance, that could convert ordinary sandstone to gold after a year's processing; a device to change air to water, and water to dirt, and dirt to electric power. Sure . . . why not? Why not make human advancement and science and art and human endeavors—all celebrated by the fair exhibits—pay out in green? *God made man, and man made money*, Alastair silently reasoned.

"Make it pay . . . make it pay well," said Thom Carmichael in his ear, like some mind reader, but it was a common enough saying here. "Word has it that Bathhouse John and the Dink have armed themselves and their men," he continued, pulling on a fistful of chewing tobacco. "Armed whole regiments of rabble."

Ransom gave a thought to Bathhouse John Coughlin and Mike Kenna—also known as Hinky Dink Kenna, two former tavern owners, now aldermen, who'd made their fortunes by being in the right place at the right time, and with their hands at the right controls. The pair had separately risen to influence by backing the right candidates and purchasing the right properties after various questionable fires, as land prices had skyrocketed. They'd wisely bought out those who were burned out.

Nowadays, the saying went, Bathhouse John and the Dink ran Chicago as they ran City Hall. And the pair of them represented success stories in Chicago and Chicago politics, one a former bathhouse operator in whose tubs people consumed more liquor and cigars than soap, the other a former saloonkeeper who came into money when both his wife and mother-in-law caught a scurrilous fever and died under his care. Hinky Dink Kenna had the foresight to take out large insurance policies on both ladies, whose untimely departure left no one to clean out spittoons, but enough money had rained down on Dink that he simply now rented out the place. Being a landlord suited his personality, especially when his cousin took care of the day-to-day while he raked in sixty percent of all proceeds.

"Coughlin and Dink've armed their men?" asked Ransom. "But why?"

"You of all people can ask that? After seeing Mayor Harrison gunned down tonight?"

"OK, all right, but tell me, what trouble do they expect?"

"Truth be told, the two of 'em fully expect to have assassins coming after them."

"Panicked, did they?"

"Yes, why not, on hearin' their 'beloved' mayor'd fallen to a murderer?" The two scoundrels had maintained a close, working relationship with the mayor they'd engineered into office.

O'Malley, overhearing this, grunted. "Expected that lunatic Prendergast to hunt them down and kill 'em like he did Harrison?"

"That's the killer's name, Prendergast?"

In Alastair's estimation, while Harrison was by no means perfect or without corruption when circumstances called for corruption, the man had done more for Chicago than all the previous mayors combined. And tonight at the close of the Great World's Fair, October 28, 1893,

Carter Harrison had been proclaimed the man of the hour, showered with accolades in speech after speech. Former President Benjamin Harrison had shared the stage with him, alongside Little Egypt and Wild Bill Cody, but the real man of the hour this night had been Mr. Chicago, the Mayor Himself.

In fact, tiring of the speeches, it'd been near 10:00 P.M. that Ransom had made off with Jane for her cozy home on Belmont, where they had to sneak inside so as not to outrage the pastor at the Episcopal church next door.

"God, how I'd like to have strangled the man who did this," muttered Ransom, taking a final look at the inert body now laid out on a table under the half-light through the window back of Alastair. Below the sheet someone had laid over the mayor, all that remained of the lively, vivacious, loud, complex man amounted to a corpse. "Killed by some useless idiot coward," muttered Ransom, his eyes fixed on the scene around the table, where the mayor's closest relatives had gathered to give support to his widow.

"Prendergast," said the thin-lipped deputy mayor, "will be hung for sure."

"Unless he is proved insane by some shrewd lawyer like Malachi Quintin McCumbler," said Carmichael. "In which case Prendergast may wind up one of Dr. Christian Fenger's pet projects," he added, ending with a hiccup.

The noise of the crowd and the continual bells of more and more people riding up on bicycles added to the general noise of horse-drawn fire and police wagons.

Amid the chaos and the now hundreds of standing mourners outside the Harrison home, Dr. James Phineas Tewes suddenly appeared. Jane, dressed as James, moved to Ransom's side. "I came as soon as I heard."

"Too late . . . we're all too late, *sirrr*." Ransom made the *sir* sound like a slur.

"We must do all we can for the family, for Mrs. Harrison," Jane as Tewes said.

"Prepare for the biggest funeral in the city's history," Ransom replied.

"When you were so badly injured, and lying in pain of your injuries from the Leather Apron killers, Mayor Harrison asked for his congregation to pray for you, Alastair."

Alastair had heard this before from other sources, but it made him uncomfortable and he'd turn it into a joke, but not now. "He was a good man, when all is added up—a good man, despite what others think."

In Tewes's deep voice, Jane firmly said, "Harrison'd want you to pray for the man who shot him."

"I'd as soon pray for the devil."

"Pray for the devil then!" Jane said and stormed off toward the Harrison residence.

Alastair gave chase and stopped her. "They'll want their privacy now, Dr. Tewes."

"Mrs. Harrison called for me; she wants Dr. Tewes at her side."

"Really?"

"She and her son . . . they wish to attempt to reach him."

"Him? Him who? Reach who?"

"Their husband and father, of course—before his spirit flies."

"Jane, you're a medical professional. You can't believe in spiritualism. Fraud is cause for arrest, you know."

She laughed at this. "Fraud in Chicago an arrest offense?" She pulled her arm from his hold. "I'll do all I can to comfort Mrs. Harrison inside there." She indicated the semidarkened window. "I can do no more."

Ransom grabbed her arm again, drawing attention to them, saying, "Don't be a fool, Ja—James!"

"Let go!" She again pulled away.

Alastair was unaware he'd again taken hold of her, so upset was he with the notion of Jane conducting a séance for an orphan and a widow. It made him wonder, *How cold can Jane be?*

It seemed every last police and fire wagon and official had turned out for this sad spontaneous gathering made up of human and mechanical cries. Alastair Ransom thought of the World's Columbian Exposition as a thing that had set so much else in motion, and now it represented the first stone thrown into the pool as the causative factor in the mayor's death. He gave some thought to this lunatic named Prendergast: likely alone and lonely, living apart, a Grendel creature holed up in some urban cave. The man was perhaps bedazzled by the cityscape, the cold streets, and finally the fantastically huge Grecian edifices created for the fair. He'd likely become both enchanted by it all and mad as hell by it all. As it all may well have combined to give him a false faith—the kind of obsession of an Ahab. An obsession that had convinced Prendergast that he deserved a seat at the table alongside Benjamin Harrison, Wild Bill Cody, Little Egypt, and Mayor Carter Harrison.

Perhaps like so many thousands, the city itself had whispered promises in his ear, convincing Prendergast to never again take no for an answer, and that he should not be disenfranchised or alienated, not by man nor machine—*and politics in Chicago was indeed a machine*.

Alastair became instantly angry with himself for rationalizing the assassin's monstrous act. To shake it off, he relit his pipe, and he uselessly shouted for the mob that'd gathered at the mayor's house to break up and move along. He may as well have been asking the trees lining Ashland Avenue to move along.

The grand fair had brought greatness to the city, had brought refinery, had even brought world renown, establishing Chicago as a contender for trade and commerce around the world, able to compete with London, Paris, Moscow, and all across the globe. CHICAGO BEDEVILS NEW YORK AS AN UPSTART CITY had been a recent wishful *Tribune* headline, the subtitle: JOBS GALORE HERE. The grand fair had gotten Chicago a big head of steam and pride up.

However, the same fair had now ended in colossal tragedy and shame.

How would the murder of the mayor play in the national press? What would it say about Chicago? That it remained a rough and tumble pioneer city and no safe place for women and children?

Ransom told his own troubled mind that he didn't even want to get into how the damnable fair had changed people he knew personally, how it had changed their politics and their perceptions of the world. Sure, he could accept the fact that he was no longer at ease with his city, and he could make adjustments as required, but others could not, while still others only wanted what they considered their "share" of the spoils. And make no mistake about it, Chicago crawling from the muck and mire of a mosquito-infested backwoods hovel to a world leader was a war, a war of economics and geography. And God help the poor sots who got in the way of progress, development, land speculation, growth, and the making of money hand over fist. Beneath the sheen and gilded exterior of the city, another world existed—a world as grim and poverty-stricken as Calcutta, Shanghai, or portions of New Orleans and New York from which men like Prendergast sought to save themselves, a world ignored by the rich and powerful. Perhaps one day poverty and illiteracy would be a thing of the past. Ransom certainly hoped so.

The chief architect of the fair, Daniel H. Burnham, had become famous for the beautiful structures he'd built to grace the lakefront, and for his now famous quote, repeated on the lips of every Chicago businessman: "Make no little plans . . . as they have no magic."

CHAPTER 4

As Alastair watched Dr. Tewes—*Jane Francis*—go off to mesmerize the grieving son, widow, and close-knit friends and family in another show of magic, he stooped to pick up one of the World's Fair brochures off the dead man's lawn. The pamphlets dotted the streets nowadays like leaves after a storm. This one was blood-splattered. Perhaps thrown into the mayor's face moments before Prendergast pulled the trigger. Ransom even imagined the mayor clutching it as his last act in this life.

The little brochure, handed to everyone at the fair entrances, seemed a sad and eerie tribute to Mayor Harrison's sudden demise, and in Ransom's hands, like a hymnal. The thin brochure recalled how, as a child in church, he'd collect the catechisms left in array and in all manner of places by people leaving after the final prayer, and how as a child he'd wondered at the hollowness of many people, and many things of this world.

His grip tightened around the fair bill, but after a moment, with little to do and feeling useless where he stood on the mayor's lawn, he opened the brochure and gazed down at it without reading the words he knew by heart:

Visitor's Guide to the World's Columbian Exposition

In the City of Chicago, State of Illinois, May 1 to October 26, 1893.

BY AUTHORITY OF THE UNITED STATES OF AMERICA.

~~~~~~

**Issued under authority of the World's Columbian Exposition
[HAND BOOK EDITION.]**

~~~~~~

CHICAGO

Ransom had read the brochure more than once, and now he absently turned a page, remembering the whole of it by his photographic memory. The brochure read in part:

> The first duty of the visitor who is desirous of obtaining the best possible results from a visit to the World's Columbian Exposition, be his time brief or unlimited, is carefully to study the accompanying map. This is an absolute necessity to one who would not travel aimlessly over the grounds and who has a purpose beyond that of a mere curiosity hunter. It is presumed at the outset that the great majority of visitors are those who seek to enlighten themselves regarding the progress which the world has made in the arts, sciences, and industries. To him who enters upon an examination of the external and internal exhibit of this the greatest of all world's fairs, a liberal education is assured. It is the aim of this volume to aid in such endeavor—to clear the way of obstacles—to make the pathway broad and pleasant.
>
> It has not been attempted to point out or to describe everything within the World's Fair grounds. Such an attempt of necessity would prove futile. The visitor will

*find ample directions on all sides, nor will he suffer for
want of information of a general or of a specific nature.
Directing signs and placards will be found on the
grounds as well as within the buildings. The employees
of the exposition are instructed to answer pertinent
questions, promptly and civilly. Guides may be employed by the hour or by the day. The Columbian
Guard, acting as a semimilitary police force, provides
against unusual or uncomfortable blockades.*

*The Visitor's Guide is an adjunct to all of the other
wise provisions made by the exposition management,
and with proper regard for the suggestions it makes,
and the information it contains, the visitor cannot fail,
it is hoped, in obtaining comprehensive and satisfac-
tory results.*

"What sorta dribble're you reading, Ransom?" asked Carmichael, at his side again. The reporter'd had a few too many
whiskeys for one night, and he looked old to Ransom. The
cynic amid a cynical city, Thom Carmichael found nothing
lovely in the world, and in fact had remarked often in his
paper that "a most innocent child at her cotillion—*Chicago*—
is marked for ugly reality to befall her once the big party is
over and the chips counted."

"It's not the *Her-Herald,* I hope you're readin'," Carmichael now said, slurring his words. The man had been toasting the mayor's death once too often.

"Are you hallucinating, Thom?"

"I've too much respect for you to believe you'd read that rag."

"You're insulting your own rag, Thom, and you're drunk.
Best go home, sleep it off."

"Sleep it off, heh? Indeed, but it'll be there tomorrow,
Rance, and you know it *as-well-as* I." Even drunk and slurring, Thom remained ever the proper grammarian.

"Are you meaning the newspaper or the evil tales you
typically cover?"

"Tell enough crime stories and, and . . . well, it becomes a
crime in itself perhaps."

This remark seemed far too philosophical to get into at the moment, Ransom thought. Perhaps over cigars, when the other man was sober. Most definitely another time.

"It's not safe being about here," Ransom said now, "with so many pickpockets and thieves that'd kill you for the change in your pocket, Thom. Not in your condition."

"Nor sober as old Reverend Jabes either, I warrant!" Thom slapped his knee and laughed like a screeching banshee, drawing stares. "And how safe was ol' Carter inside his little Ashland Avenue mansion?"

"He's dead, now you can call him by his first name."

"I never treated him ill unless he had it comin', Rance. You know that."

"All the same, let's get you a cab to haul your wobbly behind home."

"Home? Where is home for a man like me, Rance?"

"Your place is on Byron Street, isn't it?"

"Fitting address for a man of letters, heh? Byron." Thom's laugh now came out hollow. "I can't leave, Rance. Too much going on. Got to get the story."

"It's cooled here, Thom. Nothing hot here."

"Ahhh . . . not here at the mayor's, but you must've heard what's on at the Plaisance."

"The Midway? What're you talking about?"

"Looting and rioting is the word. All hell's broke loose since the mayor's been shot dead."

"Just what we need." Even as Ransom said it, he heard the deafening sound of bells on a number of police wagons dispatched to the fairway, where a French-styled, open-air beer garden sat amid exhibitors displaying and celebrating diversity in culture, dress, and color. Called the Plaisance, this huge area of the fair had become the gathering place of rowdy hoodlums and gangs of roving men. *White City's not so white*, Carmichael had said, and he couldn't have be more correct. A special police force called the Columbian Guard, acting as a semimilitary unit, had their hands full to overflowing tonight.

"Are you going to investigate, Inspector?" asked Thom, sputtering now. "Isn't it what you inspectors do, *inspect*?"

Ransom looked from Thom, who truly needed putting to bed, back to the window where Jane's séance continued, and he knew he must get quickly to the Midway and the Plaisance.

CHAPTER 5

Ransom grabbed a sunken-eyed scarecrow of a man leaning against the mayor's fence and made him an offer. "I've a job for you. Could you use some coin?"

The sunken eyes lit up. "Sure could." The man looked as if he'd not eaten in days.

"Look here, friend, if you'll hail a cab for Mr. Carmichael here and see he gets in it, there's two bits in it for you. More than enough for a good meal at Rayburn's or at the fair."

"Fifty cents," the man haggled, "and I'll do it right, sir."

Ransom frowned at the ante but nodded, doling out one recently minted quarter, explaining that the second would come once the job was done. Now the stranger frowned, but he rushed off to find Carmichael's ride home.

"Get yourself indoors, Thom. Else I'll be reading about you in that rag of yours."

"It's not my rag anymore."

"What?"

"Fired . . . boss got orders from above."

"Mayor Harrison?"

"Ironic, isn't it? He as much as kills me. A political writer who can't harangue and bluster as he sees fit is as useless as a corpse! No disrespect to the dead!"

"I'm sure none taken."

The crowd around the mayor's home had quelled in its desires, some singing mournful dirges, others beginning to leave the area. A grim pall cast a lead heavy sadness over those remaining, candles lit and waving as they sang "Amazing Grace," followed by "Leaning on the Everlasting" and other hymns, led in prayer and song now by Father O'Bannion and Reverend Jabes, the two religious leaders taking polite turns.

With a hansom cab secured, Alastair and the scarecrow forcibly placed Thom into it. Alastair had to pinch his nose against the stench coming off the homeless helper. He next paid the driver in advance and shelled out the second of two bits to the seedy-looking, sad-eyed fellow who'd jumped at the chance to earn it.

The city is full of such blokes, he thought, and dug deeper for another five cents. Overhead, a public gaslight flickered as if to go out, followed by another and another, yet the night was still, windless, the trees limp. Orders perhaps from authorities? Shut off the lights and people might disperse? The gas lamps were covered, protected from the wind, and the flow of gas controlled. When the lights flickered out for the final time, it threw the remaining mourners into darkness.

Against all reason, this Chicago crowd began to shout that it'd been Mayor Harrison's doing, shutting down the lights so magically, although it occurred every morning come twilight. This crowd wanted to believe that Carter Harrison's spirit still had a hand on the controls. As if the mayor's own spirit had blown past the lamps and over the crowd. But of course Alastair reasoned that this was but a ludicrous fantasy, like something out of a romance novel like *Jane Eyre*.

He looked up at the mayor's house, where he made out Jane's silhouette as Dr. Tewes going about the parlor, and in a moment he saw her hugging Mrs. Harrison, whose own silhouette shivered and sobbed behind the lace curtains.

Alastair quietly counseled himself. "Perhaps Jane can do some good in there after all."

* * *

Ransom made his way to the Plaisance at the Midway in
White City. On a good day, a balmy day, with wind and sun
filtering through the lakefront at Jackson Park, this large
open air garden for food and drink looked like a combina-
tion of an August Renoir painting and one of Mr. Edison's
new moving pictures, which had enjoyed so much attention
at the fair. Renoir right down to the sailboats in the harbor,
but recently the Plaisance had become more a haven for every kind of insect, vermin, lowlife, and foul bastard found in
the city. All manner of underworld activities, once reserved
for back alleys and places like Mother Gatz's Parlor, Moose
Muldoon's Bar, or Mike Hinky Dink Kenna's "back o' the
yards" saloon were being played out here, often in plain
view of the fairgoers, the most outrageous being the pimps
who'd dressed some local addict like Lulu Lee, Ugly French
Mary, Lizzie Allen, or Lottie Maynard up as a Little Egypt
or a Lillian Russell and touted "fair" prices for such tarts!

Tonight the usually pleasant Midway had become a hot-
bed of new sedition and rantings. Men who felt disenfranchised, and men who *were* disenfranchised, got up on
soapboxes and began politicizing about the *"Unfair!"*

The only ones getting wealthy off the fair appeared those
who least needed it. This fact had had a long-smoldering ef-
fect on many displaced small-time merchants and vendors,
and their cry had been building all summer long. Others
shouted about the shabby state of affairs in the city in general. Some began to sound a lot like the arsonists and the
anarchists of Haymarket days. In fact, the situation and its
potential for violence reminded Ransom just how perilous
circumstances in his city were, regardless of the laws passed
since the Haymarket Square labor riot and bombing that'd
left him physically and psychologically scarred. For many
Chicagoans, not a lot of change had come about, and they'd
grown impatient this sultry night that had taken the mayor
from their midst. *When leaders die*, *chaos reigns*, Ransom
thought; that much, even a casual reading of Shakespeare or
the Bible warned.

Ransom had caught one of the police wagons going from

the mayor's Ashland Avenue home to the fairgrounds at the lake. Leaving the night's greatest tragedy in more capable hands, he now found himself pushing past people bent on rebellion and mayhem in the wake of the assassination. He also found a small army of brown-uniformed police in formation—the Columbian Guard—slowly, cautiously, but forcibly guiding the revelers from the area.

The semimilitary unit of coppers moved in mass, every face a stern admonition even if silent; in fact, their silence was the more frightful and perhaps their strongest weapon, along with upraised night sticks. Orders had been given by Chief Agustus Pyles, head of the guard, to clear the fair and close it down for good and all this night, despite what the mob wanted.

Already the fair had been held open two days over the original closing date to accommodate a visit from former President Benjamin Harrison, who, as visiting dignitary, had been whisked from the city by rail the moment word of the mayor's assassination had reached William Pinkerton of the famous and infamous Pinkerton Detective Agency. President Harrison was guided by Pinkerton out of the Chicago area to an undisclosed location. Word filtering through the blue grapevine said that Pinkerton had indeed handled the matter personally.

Ransom knew Bill Pinkerton, the eldest son of the famous Alan Pinkerton, President Lincoln's bodyguard on the now legendary, dangerous trip to the White House days after Lincoln's election. Out of the services provided Lincoln throughout the Civil War, the Pinkerton Agency had become the model for the U.S. Secret Service. Ransom believed the Pinkerton Agency set the standard for criminal detection. Many a police program had been designed in the same fashion.

After Alan Pinkerton died in the summer of 1884, Bill had taken over operation of the Chicago branch of the agency, while brother Robert did the same from the New York home office. The brothers now co-partnered the business they'd been raised on. Ransom had recently read that the brothers captured bank robber Giant Jack Phillips—whose modus operandi was to carry out a bank safe on his back! He recalled hearing that the Pinkertons had opened new branches in Seattle, Denver, Kansas City, and Boston.

For once, Ransom found himself in complete agreement with the Columbian Guard chief and, most likely, Nathan Kohler, who, if rumor proved true, had conferred with Agustus Pyles. It always felt strange to Ransom to come down on the same side of an issue as the brass. But this made sense— *shut down the fair immediately*. Set and enforce curfew, an effective method used by Pinkerton agents during labor disputes and strikes.

Chief of Police Kohler had in fact ordered a citywide curfew, and when a copper, whether a guard or a flatfoot, did let out a cry, it was a simple declarative sentence: *"Curfew is past! Curfew is past, you men!"*

"Off with you now, lads!" another added.

"The fair's come to an end."

"A bad end!" shouted a crone among the men in the crowd. "I warned it would, and it did!"

"Go home! Fair's come to an end," went the mantra.

"The fair, yes, but not the drinking!" shouted one reveler. "You can't stop us drinking!"

"We got a right to celebrate the death of that bastard mayor!" came another as he toasted Harrison's death.

"He were never no friend to the working man!" came another, lifting his bottle to his lips.

Next a bottle was thrown, hitting one officer across the bridge of his nose, cutting him badly. Then a half-crushed brick flew at the police, leaving a gash in another officer's cheek.

"That's enough!" shouted Ransom. "Curfew is on! To your homes, now! Every runt and mother's child of you! Else you've me to deal with!"

The grumbling continued but more subdued now, and no one dared stand against Alastair Ransom. No one wanted to be in his jail, under his glare, or interrogated by him, as most knew his reputation and the stories circulated about him, and those who did not know the latest tales were shushed and quickly told.

There lived few within the city limits who had not heard the urban "truths" that swirled about Ransom, how it was his city, how he had killed more than one man who'd challenged the fact. People spoke in whispers about how he had "cleaned" the city of the worst sort of gutter life imaginable. That he had taken "bloody good" care of the Phantom of the Fair, quietly and discreetly and completely when the wheels of justice had turned the murderer loose to kill again. Other tales told of Ransom's having put an end to the career of the butcher commonly known as Leather Apron. Still others maintained that Inspector Alastair Ransom had occasion to once burn a man alive, and was anxious to repeat it with any man daring to stand in his way or refusing to level with him.

In fact, such grandiose legend had grown up around this bear of a man that others went silent when he stepped up onto one of their upturned apple crates, and when he shouted for them to disperse, they grumbled and sputtered and made out as if it meant nothing as they thinned out.

The men of the Columbian Guard watched in awe as the crowd began to slowly disintegrate, first at the edges and soon at the seams.

Ransom stepped from the crate and rejoined the humanity around him, almost as a dare, certainly as a man unafraid, and drawing the respect of men on both sides of the situation here at the Plaisance on the Midway.

When it became sufficiently clear that no one in the mob was going to dare knife or otherwise attack Ransom, and that indeed the worst instigators and most wretched rabble had scurried off into the city proper like a horde of rats for their sewer homes, the brown and blue uniformed police surrounded Alastair and began patting him on the back and shouting, "Buy that man a pint!"

The cheers and camaraderie of the gathered officers made

Alastair feel, if for only a moment, part of something larger than himself. And this felt good; in fact, this notion floated spiritlike through him.

Several firemen on hand joined in his praise. By now he'd begun shouting for them to stop with this foolishness. "Enough of it! Off with youse!"

"You averted a sure riot, Inspector," said one of the firemen.

"We all know that," added a Columbian guard.

"Then we celebrate at Muldoon's in an hour, lads!" railed Ransom. "My second office, where we'll hold a barroom wake for Carter Harrison."

This remark broke the comrades into separate camps, those pro-mayor, those against Harrison.

"Come on, you men!" shouted Alastair. "Whatever your leanings, the mayor died on duty, a captain of this whaleboat we call Chicago."

"Yeah, a regular Ahab he was!" blustered another guardsman.

"Treated this bloody fair like the White Whale, he did," said another.

"Show a little generosity and respect," countered Ransom.

"The man—like all the bigwigs—put this blasted carnival ahead of everything," commented one of the firemen. "Including the homeless and starving folk!"

"And why not?" asked Ransom. "Whatever ills it brought, fellas, it's brought a boon to the city as well! Hell, it's given a lot of you jobs!"

"Jobs gone now," lamented one guard.

Ransom pleaded, "Lads . . . lads, in the end, it brought fame to our city." He was surprised at himself for taking so strong a stand on the matter. He'd never voiced it before, and wondered why he was doing so now. In fact, he'd always been the first to condemn the extravagance of it all.

Someone pointed this out to him.

"I guess I don't know what I think until I hear it come out

here!" He indicated his mouth, making the men laugh. "Or out my arse!" he added, creating more laughter.

Still, the assembled police and firemen began slouching off now, and Alastair was left standing with a handful of Irish cops who'd agreed with him from the beginning.

Then a shot rang out in the darkness. The cop beside Alastair fell wounded and bleeding out badly, others rushing to his aid. Ransom, meanwhile, instinctively pulled his weapon and went to his knee, aimed and fired, killing the assailant instantly: one of the drunken revelers who'd quietly returned.

"Damn you, man! Damn you!" he shouted at the man he'd been forced to kill, wondering if it were a hired job or a second lunatic at work, and if a Columbian guardsman would die only because he'd stood too close to Alastair Ransom. He knew there was many a man in the city who would pay to see him as dead as Mayor Harrison this final night of the World's Fair, not the least being his own chief and arch nemesis, Nathan Kohler. *Could it've been a contract hit on me?* he wondered.

The shots had brought the horde of police racing back, all either shouting the name of the killed policeman, Burt Menealaus, or asking, "Who did it? Who is he?"

No one recognized the dead shooter except for Ransom. It was the man he'd paid fifty-five cents to hail Thom's cab. Other than that, the man was a total stranger. His turned out pockets revealed the fifty-five cents and a workman's card proclaiming him Johnathan Noicki of the Netherlands.

One cop in blue held a young, dead cop in brown uniform to his chest. Muttering epitaphs under his breath, this older copper, named Cantebury Nuebauer, was a German Englisher and friend to young Menealaus, a Greek. Nuebauer had beaten the odds many years ago to gain a place on the largely Irish police force, while Menealaus had held his job with the Columbian Guard for mere months. Who wanted to police a fair the size of Chicago's?

Nuebauer said over Menealaus, "Never a healthy idea to stand too close to Ransom."

"You'll think twice, then, comin' for a drink at Muldoon's!" shouted Ransom, stalking off. As he stormed away, he thought about it, and the truth hit him. Yes, people near him, people in his orbit, did indeed travel in danger just by association, just by standing at his shoulder, and it made him think how vulnerable he'd become since falling in love with Jane and Gabby, and then he thought: *Me with my foolish thoughts of having a real family someday.*

Unsure how long Jane as the mesmerizing Dr. Tewes might be at the mayor's home, Alastair waved down a passing cab, the sound of the horse's hooves beating out a rhythmic *cloppity-clop* that went now with the quiet reigning over the Plaisance. As he climbed into the plush Fischer interior, he felt a pang of remorse at being Alastair Ransom. Laying his cane aside, grimacing with the pain in his bad leg, he thought how he'd allowed the scars of his past to determine his years since Haymarket, seven years now, and how that night obsessed him. Just a fortnight ago he had conferred with Mayor Harrison to attempt a meeting of the minds on the matter, but the mayor, like every Chicagoan, simply wanted the whole matter buried, and promised him that if he did not "get off it," he'd find his badge and his title gone and himself on the street. The mayor would not listen to a word of Ransom's theory that Nathan Kohler had orchestrated the entire event, making puppets of both the workers and his own fellow officers.

"Kohler was a beat officer then, same as you!" Harrison had lit a cigar in tandem with his shouting. "If he orchestrated the riot as you say, he couldn't've acted alone. There'd have to've been a conspiracy involving men at the highest levels."

"I'm aware of that, sir, but I think it Kohler's idea from the start, perhaps with help from the then chief."

"Why stop at slandering Kohler's immediate supervisor? Look, Ransom, you're a valuable fellow. You've proven it time and time, but this witch hunt you insist on must go! Too many people could be hurt, daughters, sons, grandchildren. Bury it with the dead here, now."

"Has Nathan Kohler got to you, too?"

"What?"

"Has he got something on you?"

"Don't be ridiculous!"

"He's asked you to step on me."

"All right, Nathan's come to me about the situation, of course, yes."

"I knew it."

"Why, you've bedeviled the man. So let me warn you, Alastair, if you persist—"

"But sir—"

"*If* you persist, Alastair, in your secret investigation, then you're going to feel the full weight of a huge shoe come down."

"I see."

"Don't do that, Ransom! You see nothing, and you won't see it coming. Not the next time."

"Is that a warning, sir, or a threat?"

"It's a Chicago tip."

For no accountable reason, the familiar phrase made Ransom think of the Henry Vaughn poem, the lines that ran, "I saw eternity last night . . . "

And now, alone, abandoned by his own kind, who'd thought to have a beer with him before Burt Menealaus was shot dead beside him, Ransom sat in the cab trundling off toward Muldoon's.

He felt a wave of loneliness wash over him like long faded, trailing clouds of glory, and wondered if anyone would remember Carter Harrison for the good he did Chicago. Then he wondered if anyone would remember Inspector Alastair Ransom for the good he did Chicago. Or would they remember only the bad decisions and actions of both men? Or worse yet, recall nothing at all of them?

CHAPTER 6

"Daaa night grew dark, da sky went bluuue, an-an-and down da alley a shhh-shit-wagon flew," twenty-eight-year-old, hunchbacked Vander Rolsky sang to himself to pass time, and to feel less lonely in the night, although his twin brother waved at him from just down the street. In his big, childish voice, Vander intoned the street rhyme he'd heard repeatedly from children playing jacks or hopscotch as he moved about Chicago's various ethnic neighborhoods. "A scream was heard, the man was killed by a flying turd." He laughed hyena fashion through his pushed-in nose, and a passing pair of gentlemen in cloaks, taking him for a simpleton down on his luck, each pushed pennies and one nickel into his pawlike hands.

"The wagon overturned, see?" he said, stepping after the nice men, laughing more, pocketing the coins, certain his twin brother Philander had seen the exchange and would take it all from him. *For your own good,* Philander would tell him. *Everything is for my own good*, he thought now as the two gents rushed off, their steps wider, faster, increasing the distance between him and them.

Looking up and down the street, there was a pattern of light and dark from the well-spaced gas lamps.

It was past ten, and all but the lewd houses and saloons were shut down and asleep below signs that designated a millinery shop here, a grocer there, a wainwright, a smithy, a bakery, and a reader of palms. The street stood alone, solitary; silent but for the onerous low growl of Chicago, the by-product of the myriad gas lamps and hum of concentrated animal and human life here, the stockyards not far off. Still, small sounds carried down the streets and alleyways, as did Vander's voice, reaching his brother, who had Vander's height but not his heft nor his gargoyle features. Philander didn't have Vander's hunched back either, as he'd been the lucky one at birth and looked normal by everyday standards.

Philander now gesticulated like a wild baboon at his brother to *Shut up and back up into the shadows!*

Domestic sounds from the windows of houses warmed by a hearth on either side floated on the air. And the hint of anyone who rode past in a cab came to the ear immediately and with such force as to spin Philander Rolsky, a man of instinct, to the next sound and the next opportunity.

The report of approaching footfalls again seemed shockingly vivid to Philander's ear. The sound of even the slightest, thinnest vermin could be heard as a result of so crisp a night.

Philander settled in for a long watch below the shadows of McCumbler and Hurley's law offices, old-world Polish or Austrian castlelike turrets forming overhanging window facings. Chicago's architecture proved as varied and multifaceted as its population.

Philander looked at the list again, his eyes and mind ticking off the anonymous names—people the good doctor had targeted for harvesting, people the good doctor felt contributed nothing to their families, their neighborhoods, their city, their world. Disposable people. People that Philander and his brother could watch and in a vulnerable moment snatch.

From his vantage point, Philander—the smart twin—watched for a victim from the list, a Mr. Burbach, who fre-

quented this street each night about this time to go through
the garbage set out by the grocery and the restaurant beside
the attorney's office. Philander grimaced now, disapproving
of Vander's pacing, singing of all things, drawing attention
to himself, while the men who'd dropped Vander coin had
not even known that a second man was here. They'd gone
right past him and never knew.

His teeth began to hurt from the grinding caused by wor-
ries brought on by Vander. "My counterpart," he muttered,
"the one of us without patience or cunning or boldness. My
broken, timid other self." He flailed with both hands again to
signal his disgust at his brother for being under a light and
easily seen and recognized.

"Let the fool be arrested and tossed into the Cook County
loony bin," he muttered to himself. "Deserves nothing better. Fool will get me caught as well."

The dead, Alexander, could've been me, he thought, *else
the thought was forced on me from my second and dead
brother. Just as I could've been born Vander, and Vander
could've been me. Just barely escaped being stillborn, then
being Vander, and in a sense, I've not escaped either. Not at
all.*

"Vander, oh . . . Vander," he muttered. "He'll never fly."

His dead brother's creaky voice sounded a reply. "Yes, b-
but he makes a g-good diversion t-to the real show." Philander had become so accustomed to his third self, speaking
from inside his head, that it never shocked or surprised him.

They were born triplets, a rarity if only the third born had
not died and the second hadn't come out a brain-dented fool.
So their mother had lamented all their lives. Who knows?
Perhaps the trio *might've* been celebrated as a rarity. *Perhaps mama wasn't exaggerating, but what kind of a freak
did that make him?* Philander wondered.

The dead one was Alexander, but even dead, Alex still had
a voice—a sepulchral voice to be sure, but clear as a bell
inside Philander's head. The other one, across the street,
surveying another direction for prey, Vander, couldn't hear
Alex's voice. He hadn't the imagination or element of empa-

thy, Philander had decided years before. Mama had called the dead one simply *It* or *Number Three*, adding, *Though it'd come out after Philander and before Vander.*

The stillborn one was never christened, except by his first-born brother years later when it made itself known inside him like a phantom limb or phantom frontal lobe.

It was in fact a welcome entity, a welcome possession, and Philander knew that Alex wanted him, something he could not say of his mother and father.

Strangely, oddly, Alex often told him that he wanted Vander to die off, even as children, warning that the big fool could come to harm in this world, that he'd ever be a burden to Philander, and that Vander would indeed be safer inside him, like Alex . . . safe and close as close gets.

Guilt. It's all just guilt, he told himself. *Ignore it,* he'd been telling himself for years. But Alex never gave up petitioning for Vander to join them, in a sense reuniting as one whole instead of three disparate parts.

"How long've you asked for Vander to join you?" Philander muttered.

"T-Too long."

"Since childhood."

"And tonight bears me out—yet again . . . " Philander, the normal one, had a wild imagination and bizarre, meaningless, chaotic dreams, all filled with horrors and curious creatures, and he imagined such things often. He decided it was due to his upbringing in the back woods of Germany—the Black Forest region—where as children he and his Polish brother were beaten until Alexander's urgings that he kill his parents in their sleep came to pass. He'd placed a brick in a burlap sack, knocking his father and mother unconscious with two quick blows. Seeing the blood ooze over their pillows made the rest of the blows come easy, and he rained his anger on them until their faces were no longer recognizable as human. After that, he'd taken his slow-witted twin in hand and come to America—land of the free, where no one knew them, where they could all three begin life anew.

They'd boarded a merchant marine ship, working their

way to America. Once in the United States in a place called Boston, they'd drifted to Chicago by way of Syracuse, New York; Pittsburgh, Pennsylvania; to Cleveland and Columbus, Ohio; finally, Indianapolis, Indiana, riding the rails into Chicago in the company of hobos, whose existence meant nothing to anyone—and one whose death had meant nothing to anyone either. Philander had killed for a piece of bread and a scrap of potato for himself and Vander.

Vander, Philander, and Alexander had all found Chicago a frightful place, huge as a monster and just as uncaring. Philander had never seen such tall buildings, reaching to twenty stories and beyond, with news of even taller ones in the works. He'd tried to find work in the brickyards, the stockyards, the cemeteries. Nothing, nothing, and nothing. He'd tried to find work in the garbage collection business. Nothing. His accent, he knew, held him back; he'd have to perfect talking like an Irishman to get anywhere in Chicago.

He'd never seen such rampant community growth, and so much money in one place, and he unable to tap into the least of it. Still, he'd determined to have whatever share he could get. To this end, he began to watch things closely, to learn how things worked in the city. He hit upon a plan to make large sums by going into profitable business with a medical man in need of corpses. Garbage collection of another sort.

With the help of Vander, he arranged nowadays to fill the doctor's every needful prescription. This sent them out nightly and sometimes by day to stalk and eventually trap and harvest fresh bodies, and the fresher the body or organ, the more Doc paid for it. *Disposable people*, he'd called them. "I only want disposable people."

"Ahhh . . . disposable, sir?"

"In the sense they contribute nothing to society, are a burden on the public trust fund, have no purpose, and . . . "

"I understand your meaning, sir."

" . . . and they've no ties whatsoever."

"Ties, sir?"

Vander piped in, repeating the question, "Ties? Neckties?"

"No familial ties."

"Familial?" asked Philander.

"No bloody family, no one who's going to be filing a missing persons report."

"*Ahhh . . .* clever, sir, most clever."

"Then you do understand?"

"I do, sir."

"And your hunchback strongman? What of him?"

"Oh, not to worry, Doc, as I'll drill it in his head."

"See that you do. Should you begin indiscriminately, *ahhh . . .* harvesting, then we're all three sent to the gallows."

So here they were, continuing their hunt for the people on the list, who, once killed, went absolutely unmissed.

"No ties . . . no ties . . . " Vander chanted during each hunt.

"Jump 'em, mug 'em, rob 'em, kill 'em, transport 'em, and collect a second fee," Philander had told him. "It's all too easy. And it's good pay."

"No ties . . . no ties."

On hearing footsteps coming along Van Buren Street, Philander backed into the depths of an unlit alleyway. A short, hefty man with a bowler hat and a cane was approaching, an easy mark, but then another appeared alongside. Two drinking companions who'd come up to street level from the last ferry boat along the river that transported folk to and from the grand fair. Philander knew never to attack two men at once, and he'd drilled Vander about this as well. He let the boisterous fairgoers pass, while his stupid brother actually tipped his hat to them! Fool.

Then Philander saw the slight figure of another person alone, not ten feet from him. He or she had a silent step and had come up along the crossroad yet to be paved in this section of town—where Dearborn met Van Buren. This waiflike figure could not see the body-thief in shadow, and so came staggering ever closer, obviously drunk or hung over. As the figure neared, Philander saw that indeed it was a woman alone . . . the perfect victim, except that she was not on the list.

Perhaps he'd have more than her wallet, he thought now. He could not remember the last time he'd been with a woman.

As she passed near, he allowed her to move on without disturbance. She absolutely reeked of alcohol, as if bathed in it. She looked the vile prostitute she was. Dirty and unkempt. Too dirty to rape, he decided, and no way to bathe her, for though her teeth appeared knocked out, and her face a mask of sourness, her body seemed lithe and curvaceous. *Odd, that.*

In a handful of additional steps she was confronted by his deformed look-alike across the street. She immediately halted, taking in his brother. The street bitch was fishing for a proposition out of the idiot, his face glowing with utter confusion under the lamplight. Philander thought it a funny sight on the whole.

The plucking of the woman for the doctor could not have been so well choreographed if he'd planned it himself, and Doc could bathe her after she was dead. Despite her not being on the list, she obviously contributed nothing to society, and if she had any ties, they must be loose tethers at best.

He saw his dummy deformed twin leap at the woman, causing her to cry out, and then he feebly put the muzzle of his unloaded gun into her ribs and ordered, "Back into the alleyway."

She instead turned and spat in Vander's face, shouting, "You go ta'ell!" while pulling forth her own pistol.

Vander was stunned, unable to respond.

"Have at it, ya bastard creature!" she shouted at the disfigured giant. "But you'll end with a bullet to yer brain! Putcha outta yer misery!"

Plucky Chicago whore, Philander thought as he moved serpent fashion to take her from behind.

"If you mean to rape me, go ahead! Make a try!" she continued to taunt Vander, waving her large pistol. Vander, frightened, his hands in the air in response to her gun, kept saying, "No ties . . . no ties . . ."

"Go on, throw down on me! You've got a gun!" she challenged.

Vander, taking her words literally, responded by throwing down his weapon. Its thud sent up a little dirt cloud at her feet, causing her to cackle witchlike, as she looked the picture of a banshee—all her teeth gone, her face a mask of wrinkles like a badly treated dollar bill.

Vander ran.

She gave a few stomps and a laugh after him, before shouting to the rooftops, "I've chased off a giant hunchbacked weasel so's people can sleep at night!"

Still laughing, smiling, when she turned, she felt the blade slice open her abdomen as her eyes met a man with a gleeful grin that showed a set of perfectly white teeth and eyes that burned with a fiery hatred. But he was no one she knew, and yet he was strangely familiar, in fact identical to the figure she'd run off, save now his features were pleasant—at least normal in shape and form.

Philander watched her eyes study him as she died, and he realized the nature of her confusion, that she hadn't the strength now to pull the trigger, the weight of the gun too much to bear. As her firearm fell to the street, her eyes said, *I'm to leave this world ciphering how the runaway weasel shape-changed into my killer.* She must think him a supernatural creature, some sort of troll capable of disappearing in one direction and reappearing instantaneously in another. "The Brothers Grimm, madam," he joked, his gravelly voice the last earthly sound she heard aside from a single long gurgling croak—her death rattle.

"Vander! Vander, get the 'ell over 'ere and help out, idiot! Bring the cart!"

Vander slowly meandered back with a four-by-four pushcart, still fearful, furtive, looking in every direction. His twin brother thought he looked every bit the weasel, just as the wench had said, regardless of his size. In fact, he looked like a Chicago wharf rat at the moment, and just as afraid. *Damn him . . . damn him to Hell . . . but he is blood . . . he is brother . . . and we are twins, regardless of the physical deformities.*

With Vander's help, Philander hefted the body onto the cart, when the revelation began to sink in. The prostitute had layers of theatrical makeup on. Spying the line about the throat, he checked her forearms—clean and smooth of wrinkles. "Jesus, she's a young woman," he said to Vander.

"Uh-huh."

"A young woman pretending to be an old street whore? What's it mean?"

He heard someone calling out, "Nell! Damn it, Nell! Where've you got offta? Nelly!"

Footsteps and a handheld police lantern approached. Two men, one a blue-suited copper.

Vander ran.

Philander opened Nell from breastbone to abdomen and began scooping out any organ he might steal before the two men searching for Nell should see him. He then began placing whole organs into the jars that the doctor'd given him for such needs. He worked quickly, experienced at this. He flashed on how he'd cut open his mother before his father's dead and bashed-in eyes.

He left Nell splayed and lying as if she'd fallen from a great height, so twisted were her limbs. The men with the lantern must trip over her, so true was their path toward her, as if they could smell the blood.

Philander rushed carefully along the stones, against the walls, at ease with the city shadows. In his ear he heard Alex whisper, "We did it. Well done, brother, well done."

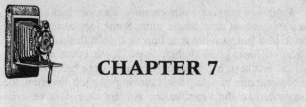

CHAPTER 7

A late night knock on a door in Chicago in 1893 was in itself cause for alarm, but nowadays Dr. Christian Fenger had a telephone, and its ringing at such an hour, on the heels of declaring the mayor of Chicago murdered by an assassin, felt doubly alarming. *Who could it be now? Not enough mischief for one night? When will I be left in peace? Damn it, I'm only one man, after all.*

However, before he could lift the receiver, someone was pounding noisily at his door as if intent on breaking in. *Someone using a cane. Alastair Ransom perhaps? At this hour? Drunk, drinking to the living, toasting to the dead, specifically the passing of the mayor?* Sure, Alastair will most certainly have raised a pint too many by now.

But the silhouette through the curtain was hardly Ransom. Whoever it was, the fellow appeared slight, dwarfish even.

Fenger got his revolver first, a six-barreled old Winchester given him by Inspector Alastair Ransom to ostensibly "hold for a time." That'd been several years before. Ransom had never come back to reclaim the revolver, so the surgeon had long since decided that he'd either forgotten about it or that the inspector had meant him to have it at his disposal for such intrusions as this.

A surgeon garners many enemies, Ransom had told him, and this was an unfortunate truth. Some foes came with the price of a bill, waving it at him as if he'd fleeced them instead of having saved their lives. Some came with their wives, brothers, big-headed, muscular, large bicuspid cousins to beat him to a pulp for "botching" the job. So often, the surgeon, like the veterinarian, got the case days or even hours before there was anything humanly possible to be done. At which time the patient died. At which time the finger of blame was leveled squarely at the doctor. As he'd told Ransom over a pint of dark ale on their last meeting, "Sometimes, but rarely, am I capable of creating gold from straw or a silk purse from a sow's ear. Hafta leave such magic to the frauds and Rumpelstiltskins of the profession."

"We're surrounded by the illiterate and unwashed," Alastair had replied, toasting to the doctor's health.

"There exists so much misunderstanding and wrongheadedness about what surgery can and cannot do."

"Still . . . at the price, some miracle is in order," joked Ransom.

The phone was ringing, and Dr. Fenger now grabbed it, only to find it dead. Whoever it'd been, they'd given up.

Again the incessant pounding at the door.

"Damn it, man! I'm coming!" Gun in hand, Fenger pulled his door wide.

On his porch, looking out over Lake Park and Lake Michigan, stood that ugly old gimp, peg-leg snitch Civil War veteran of Ransom's, Henry Bosch, aka Dot 'n' Carry. At the same time, the phone resumed its ringing.

"Mr. Bosch, what is it?"

"Aye, you've a good memory, Doctor."

"Hold here a moment. Let me answer that infernal ringing." Fenger went to the phone, lifted it, but found it dead again. "Damn thing!" he cursed, and pounded the thing back on its cradle.

Bosch had stepped into the foyer. "You're wanted o'er on Van Buren and Dearborn, Doctor. There's been a—a foul murder, sir."

"Two killings in one night? What's this city coming to, Mr. Bosch?"

"You know full well it's goin' to hell in a hand—"

"I take it Inspector Ransom sent you?"

"Indeed, sir. Says there's extra in it for you."

"Extra? Extra how?"

"Seems the victim is a Pinkerton agent."

"A Pinkerton agent, really? Is it a lunatic's night?"

"They're all mad, one and the same, in my estimation, sir."

Ransom had always said the old vet was well spoken when he wanted to draw on his education. "A Pinkerton man! Same night as the mayor's assassinated? Perhaps killed for what he knew?" A vague image of a circle of conspirators formed in Fenger's mind.

"She, sir."

"What?"

"The agent, sir, she is . . . she *was* a she, that is."

"A female Pinkerton operative? I'd not known such an *animal* existed," countered Dr. Fenger, rubbing sleep from his eyes.

"Sure, and there's Kate Warne, of course," said Henry Bosch, "but she died of consumption."

"Consumption . . . a terrible thing."

"Some say she smoked cigars till the day she died."

"Is that right?"

"She was buried in Graceland Cemetery with all the pomp old Alan Pinkerton could muster. Kate helped old Mr. Pinkerton sneak Abe Lincoln into Washington. Was her who booked the train cars, including the dummy ones. Used the rails between here and D.C. like an expert in a shell game."

"Can we get back to the here and now, Mr. Bosch?"

"Oh, *surrre.* Sure we can."

"So when did our present murder happen?"

"Within the hour, Doctor, sir. They're saying her body was still warm and bleeding yet from her wounds when her partner found her. Say the sand and very stones 'round her're still soaking up her—"

"All right, sir, you've delivered your message." Dr. Fenger tipped Ransom's snitch. "See to hailing me a cab."

"This time o'night?"

"There's extra coin in it for you."

"Right, sir, right you are."

Fenger grabbed his clothes, hastily dressed, and snatched up his medical bag just as the sound of a hansom cab filled his ears. He opened his door on horse and driver, while Dot 'n' Carry held open the carriage door. In an instant the cane-carrying peg-leg was doing battle with the driver, the two men in a scuffle over who would hold the door and extend his palm for the gentleman's tip.

Inspector Alastair Ransom had gone to his knees over Nell Hartigan, butchered by some fiend. Nell's facial makeup had been smeared to reveal her actual features beneath the rouge and eye liner. The woman's eye sockets shimmered with blood, and the killer had gutted her. "Opened her up like a fisherman handling a carp," said one of the uniformed cops standing over Ransom and the body. "And for what bloody cause? Her purse!"

"No money found on her?" asked Ransom.

"Not a dime." The officer handed Ransom Nell's empty pocketbook.

"Empty save for a few personal notes and some change," added Nell's sobbing employer, Mr. William Pinkerton. "Attacked by street toughs," mourned the private eye. "And whoever it was learned of her true identity only after the attack, hence the makeup wiped away."

"She didn't get a shot off. Gun's loaded," said Ransom, holding her weapon up to the light, a standard .38 Remington, a sidearm issued to all Pinkerton undercover agents.

"Like her to put up a fight before giving up her gun."

Something in the words or tone struck Ransom as faintly odd. An element of anger at Nell for "letting" herself become a victim perhaps, and something of a deep hurt or loss in there at the same time.

While Ransom had no reason to dislike or distrust William Pinkerton, he knew the Pinkerton reputation for holding cards close to the vest, and for bluffing well. He also knew that any operative working for the "Pinkies" was universally hated by every workingman in a union. If Nell had been infiltrating a secret society or group, she may well've been executed—a far cry from being attacked by some street thug.

Ransom had known Nell. They'd shared a beer from time to time, and she'd always urge him to end his career with the CPD and come to work for her wonderful boss, Mr. Pinkerton.

Nell's remains had the shocking appearance of an autopsy— as though her killer's level of hatred had caused the extreme mutilation. Could it be a message? A warning? An executioner's song, singing loud of "take heed all infiltrators and Pinkertons"?

The American Federation of Labor, some 250,000 strong, the Knights of Labor, now dropped to 100,000, the Brotherhood of Locomotive Engineers, 50,000, and countless others all saw a blue Pinkerton uniform as a strike-breaker, and unionists and anarchists alike considered a Pinkerton undercover operative, man or woman, a traitor to humanity as well as a grave threat to their private meetings. The Pennsylvania coal mining wars ended when Pinkertons infiltrated the ranks of the Molly McGuires and began wholesale arrests of the most violent group in the nation.

Alastair admired the Pinkertons for having broken up conspiracies all across the nation. They'd averted many anarchist plots, but their presence at a labor rally or strike nowadays only added to the powder keg. The mere sight of a Pinkerton watchman's blue uniform enraged union men in a strikebound area, and the Pinkerton watchmen were often accused of setting explosions themselves in order to gain public sympathy for management and owners. The same argument had often been leveled at the Chicago Police Department as well. Labor routinely charged that the Pinkertons fabricated evidence and saw plots everywhere simply to serve their own ends.

It was an allegation that'd become rampant since the infamous Haymarket Riot, and he had to admit that he himself continued to have niggling and persistent problems every time his scars from that riot acted up.

To date, no one could satisfy him on the point of who threw the bomb at Haymarket, and he suspected that the Pinkerton Agency had files in a secret chamber somewhere with precisely that information. However, getting at such official and semiofficial information proved a difficult proposition at best. And for this and other reasons, Ransom did not entirely trust the Pinkertons. It hadn't been so long ago that a Pinkerton and a Chicago cop were arrested for selling confiscated nitroglycerin to would-be anarchists!

Still, countless small plots to blow up trains, machine shops, and roundhouses had been foiled by undercover Pinkerton agents. The agency had amassed a fortune on strike-related assignments over the years, but in the end it was revenue they'd decided to turn their backs on. For one thing, many a Pinkerton agent had been killed or maimed for life defending the property of the Pullmans, the Vanderbilts, the Carnegies, the railroad moguls, the so-called "Robber Barons," and other leaders of manufacturing. The Pinkertons, to their credit, had simply refused to be a private army against labor any longer.

In fact, Alan Pinkerton had, for a lifetime, stood for the same principles as most labor platforms. For anyone in the know, it'd come as no surprise when the sons ended the days of Pinkerton being called on as "guns for hire" by the owners against labor. With the passing of Alan Pinkerton, who'd come to believe his agency should never have become embroiled in the labor movement on the side of big business, the two sons honored their father by never again accepting work as strikebreaking guards.

Knowing all this, Alastair was still unwilling to accept William Pinkerton's remarks hinting that Nell Hartigan had been a victim of a simple street murder, some rabid mugger after her purse, as the killer or killers had taken far more than her purse or even her life. They'd taken her *insides!*

Why?

"I think, Mr. Pinkerton, we need a serious talk," suggested Ransom.

Pinkerton disagreed, stepping away from the body and the others to step away with Ransom.

CHAPTER 8

Ransom now stood below the corner lamppost at Van Buren and Dearborn, a stone's throw from the Levy District where Nell had told Pinkerton she'd been running a scam.

"Details . . . her notes, sir? I will need both."

"Nell's one of several women operatives working for me, but she was especially keen."

"Undercover, infiltrating, you mean."

"That yes, but lately she'd gotten on to something we had no business in, and no evidence of."

"Really? Yet she proceeded?"

"Once on a scent, she was tenacious."

"Perhaps she got too close to her prey, then?"

"Perhaps."

"And perhaps you can be more specific, sir?"

"As I said, there was no credible evidence what she was working on had any merit, so what can I tell you?"

"Are you being deliberately evasive, sir?"

"I am being prudent, Inspector."

"Can you tell me in a general sense precisely what Nelly Hartigan was chasing?"

"Phantoms . . . smoke!"

"What sort of phantoms?"

Pinkerton pulled his hat from his head, gritted his teeth, and pulled a newspaper clipping from his hat, handing it to Alastair. Ransom scanned a small story, a paragraph long, someone seeking a missing sister named Flossie Widmarck, of 448 Atgeld Street, who'd simply disappeared without a trace in the span of an hour off city streets. The story ended with a diatribe on the uselessness of the Chicago Police Department in the matter, according to the outraged sister, Katrina Widmarck, who had heroically searched for her sister for months.

"Then Nell had taken up Miss Widmarck's cause?"

"Yes."

"A missing person's case?"

"Yes."

"But she'd gone against your wishes?"

"It was not a case brought to us in any formal sense. Miss Widmarck was not a client."

"I see."

"It'd been Jeff Naughton, another operative supposedly watching her back tonight. I saw to it that she not be out here without someone watching her back."

While you were home by a warm fire with your wife and kiddies, thought Ransom, wondering why this image popped into his head. "Naughton did a fine job," he replied, sarcasm dripping off each word. "It was young Naughton who discovered her murdered, right?"

"I've already raked Naughton over the coals and the spikes, but the man's already so distraught as to be unable to cope. Finding Nell in the condition she'd been left . . . well, it turned my stomach."

"I don't think it an overreaction in this case."

"She was a fine and intelligent woman," continued Pinkerton. "Very quick-witted, well-suited to the work, meticulous, a real Jack-bull for a woman, once she got on someone's heels."

"I know. I've known Nell for years. She trusted me. Why didn't she come to me about this Widmarck case?"

"I wasn't aware you two were acquainted." Pinkerton wiped his brow with his sleeve, the big man perspiring despite the cool night air.

"She was the definition of discreet. Besides, not even you can know everything about everybody."

Pinkerton nodded, accepting this.

"I knew her best when her saloon-keeper husband died, and the sleazy politicians found a way to relieve her of the well-placed property."

"Swindle, I think is the word. She had her own way of operating after that. She'd get word on a dark little operation, usually involving a Chicago politician, and she'd follow every lead . . . taking chances . . . risks."

"What about labor unrest? Anarchists? Did she think this Widmarck girl disappeared because she'd fallen out of favor with her local? Was the girl a seamstress in a sweatshop?"

"I haven't a clue about any such connection, no. Fact is, Nell had been conducting an interview with the girl's last known employer—a Dr. Mudd—last I heard. Damn her . . . "

"Damn Nell?"

"She was to work with another operative tonight, but Frederick Hake is on his back with a horrid flu."

"Damn him, then."

"She was told to stand down, but if you really knew her, then you know stubbornness personified."

Ransom nodded and lit his pipe, wondering if Pinkerton were distraught or simply dodging his questions.

"We'll get the bastard done this, the agency will," Pinkerton muttered.

"Look, William . . . can I call you William?"

"William, Bill is fine."

"You need to trust me here."

"It's not so much a matter of trust as . . . as—well, there are issues like liability and lawsuits. You know how litigious everyone is nowadays . . . and this matter is yet too sensitive and unsubstantiated, you see, and . . . "

Christian Fenger joined them, overhearing their last

words. "Mr. Pinkerton doesn't want the facts getting circulated before they are, of a certainty, *facts*, right, Bill?"

"Precisely, yes."

"What's going on, you two?" asked Ransom. "Something I know nothing about? In my city?" He folded his cane into his arm and puffed his pipe.

"It has to do with some medical school in the area, Alastair," Fenger blurted out. "Indelicate as it is, someone's going to notice soon enough, Mr. Pinkerton."

"Are we speaking of cemetery thieves, body-snatchers? Ghouls at work?"

"A new sort of ghoul," said Fenger, "one who does not require a cemetery or a shovel. Only a blade or a scalpel."

"When the second of the sisters went missing," said Pinkerton, "Nell became certain of her course."

"Murder for a person's corpse?" asked Ransom.

"It explains the missing organs," said Fenger, lighting a cigarette.

"Do you suspect this Dr. Mudd?"

"No . . . he's a mere pharmacist," said Fenger, "not a surgeon. He'd have no interest in purchasing a corpse or body parts."

"Damn it! No one catches Nell Hartigan off guard," shouted Naughton from where he sat on the curb. "It just doesn't happen."

"Obviously, it does." Ransom glanced back at the body, punctuating with pipe and a raised eyebrow. "You know, William, much as you 'operatives' would like to believe otherwise, all of us are vulnerable to one trick or another."

"I suppose you're right. Damn, if she had any family, I'd know what to do, where to go next, I mean. As is . . . what am I to do?"

"Go home and calm yourself, William," counseled Fenger. "Leave it to us. Perhaps I can say more about what happened here, and if that is the case, I'll most certainly inform you."

"Will you do that, Christian?"

"Absolutely, as soon as I know anything."

"I feared you were out of the city; called you twice and no answer."

"I am a heavy sleeper."

"A demonic hand is at work in this," predicted Pinkerton.

Dr. Fenger gave Pinkerton a brief, male hug. Ransom noted their closeness, and wondered how long standing their relationship was.

Young Naughton had climbed to his feet and coughed out, "It's surely to do with *who* she was chasing! I just know it. And had I been quick . . . "

"Easy on yourself, son," said Fenger.

" . . . quicker . . . perhaps Nell . . . perhaps I could've pre—"

"I'll want to see any notes she kept, and yours, Mr. Naughton," said Ransom.

"Not likely," replied Naughton.

Pinkerton explained. "Nell kept it all in her head. I yelled at her about this habit, that it was no good, but she gave it right back at me. Said if it's on paper, someone can get at it, but no one was getting it out of her head."

"But she reported to you. You must've kept notes, and what of you, Naughton?"

"Fred Hake's her partner. I was just filling in."

"Then by damn what of Hake's notes?"

"She'd just begun to dig on this case," said Pinkerton, shrugging, "and all reports so far were preliminary and verbal, and none whatsoever from Hake, who didn't believe in the case any more than . . . than I."

"Chalk it up to that cursed invention!" said Fenger.

"The telephone, yes," agreed Pinkerton.

"So no written record?" muttered Ransom.

"None save my own notes, but they are *cursory*."

"Cursory is better than nothing."

"Cursory is what we've just voiced."

God, this man is frustrating, Ransom thought. "All the same, bring these notes 'round to my address on Kingsbury, or to my desk at the Des Plaines station house."

"It will be done."

"Night, then, Bill, and accept my regrets over the loss of one of your own. Nell was a good woman and keen."

"Too keen to go out this way, I'd thought."

"None of this is your fault, Bill, nor even Naughton's over there. Whatever kind of butcher can carve up a woman like this is a fiend and a maniac, no less than Jack the Ripper. She was murdered, pure and simple, whether by someone she was tailing or some random act of violence—we will unearth."

Fenger repeated the words, "Random act of violence. All too common nowadays here."

"No more so than Rome in the time of the Caesars," said Ransom, defending Chicago.

"Nor London, nor Moscow, nor New York," added Pinkerton, "nor any metropolis in any time. Read your Dickens, sir." Pinkerton then took Alastair by the elbow and led him off a bit. "God attend your work, then, Alastair Ransom, to find and punish Nell's murderer." Pinkerton then rushed off, but with a heavy appearance, as if someone rode his back.

CHAPTER 9

Philo Keane, acting in his capacity as police photographer, arrived on the scene, and kneeling over the wretchedly dressed woman and the horrid wound, sleepily shouted, "Why in bloody hell've you pulled me from my bed, Ransom, for a dead prostitute? We don't go to such measures for old prostitutes."

"She's no old pro of the night, Philo," Ransom assured him. "Take a closer look."

Philo finally looked into the face smeared with makeup. "Who is she?"

"One of Bill Pinkerton's operatives, undercover."

"Incognito? Who was she? An acquaintance?"

"You've no doubt heard stories of her."

"Really?"

"Nell Hartigan."

"The saloon-keeper's wife who was robbed of her place?"

"Appears she was a magnificent actress," said Fenger, a slice of his dry wit.

"Pretense at being a harpy apparently got her killed," added Ransom, "but it may be that the man she was shadowing turned on her, or got the better of her, and this is the result."

Fenger added, "And for the moment, this is all we know."

"Butchery is your result."

"Aye, agreed," Dr. Fenger piped in again. "He took the devil's own time with her, and if you look closely, he's cut out most every major organ and carted half her weight off with him."

"God blind me at this world that a man can do such harm, and cart off a woman's insides, but why?" replied Philo, bile and alcohol threatening to send him retching.

"The papers'll make a to-do o'er it, sure," said big Mike O'Malley, who'd joined them with the intention of partnering on this case with Alastair. The two large detectives, O'Malley and Ransom, side by side, seemed like a pair of stone calves, weighty and bulky as Oriental sculpture.

"It'll be Jack the Ripper all over again, sir," bemoaned a freshly besotted Thom Carmichael, who'd somehow gotten word and crawled from his bed and his stupor. "The nasty whore-killing, evil bastard's booked passage and come to America and found *us* to terrify!"

Ransom did not know for certain when Thom had come or how long he'd been near, or what he may or may not've overheard. Thom's drinking had obviously gotten him fired from the *Herald,* which Ransom found odd. Ransom knew of no newspaperman in the city who didn't drink and drink heavily, save for the obituary fellow and perhaps the fellow who replied to the Lonely Hearts letters—but even he, Ransom suspected, was a secret drinker.

Ransom guessed that poor Thom had continued to struggle with a self-imposed guilt stemming from the "Phantom of the Fair" case, that he still believed he was somehow culpable in the death of Griffin Drimmer, Alastair's young partner. Carmichael had seen something disturbing the night of Drimmer's initial disappearance and failed to act on it. Ransom knew the pain he felt; on that same fogbound night, exhausted, he had quit the intense surveillance of the very man who'd murdered Griff. To this day, whenever he encountered fog, he saw Griffin's accusing features in it, which didn't make any more sense than Thom's guilt, but there it was, like a vigilant entity.

Not long after that awful night, Alastair achieved his final vengeance on the so-called Phantom—a ferret-faced weasel, as it turned out.

How severe a vengeance it'd been, too, but at times, when reminded how many lives had been shattered by the Phantom, Alastair believed he'd let the foul, evil creature off too easily. No one in Chicago police circles doubted that Ransom had reeked revenge and justice where all others had failed.

Still, Alastair knew that Thom or Christian or Jane, even Gabby, could as easily blame him for the killer's motives and successes. He was hardly keen in his approach. Certainly hadn't been a model investigation, certainly not one for the books. But he did privately confess to his own guilt, and the part his history as a young officer played in the deaths of all the Phantom's victims. The best that could be said of it today was that it was over.

His thoughts were interrupted by O'Malley's booming voice as Mike kneeled over Nell's remains. "Appears the work of some madman for damn sure, but if it is done for money . . . that's the worst."

"No . . . not a madman, but a cold, calculating bastard," corrected Fenger.

"How so?" asked O'Malley.

"Whoever killed her, he *harvested* her organs."

"My God." Carmichael's hand shook as he jotted this down.

"Every major organ from the thoracic area, and he attempted to pull out the uterus."

"Explains the amount of blood," Ransom dryly added.

"To what purpose? Why'd he take her organs?" asked Naughton, still highly distraught. "I loved her spirit, you know. So . . . so!"

"Take him home, O'Malley," ordered Ransom.

"I'm needed here, Rance."

"Please, Mike."

O'Malley frowned, disgruntled at such duty, but shrugging it off, he took the young man under wing, and together they left.

"You didn't answer the boy," said Philo, eyeing first Ransom and then Fenger. "What do you men think the killer's doing with the organs? Making a stew of 'em?"

"Medical reasons no doubt," said Fenger.

"Medical reasons?"

"There's money to be had from organs and cadavers sold at back doors at every medical school in the city."

"Even your own?" asked Philo.

"No, neither Rush College nor Cook County is in need of cadavers, thanks to my bargain with the city. My hospital and teaching college gets all the Jane and John Does we need."

"*Ahhh* . . . an exclusive contract with Nathan Kohler?" asked Philo.

"I assure you, Keane, it's better than the grim alternative, as you see tonight."

"Do you know who's behind it, Christian?" Alastair asked, point-blank, staring Fenger down.

"H-Harvesting people off the street?" muttered Thom. "Not so much as a pretense of burial anymore. What'd happen if there were no more wakes in Chicago? No free beer days?" Thom laughed at his own joke.

Ransom snorted. "I'll not hazard a guess. What about you, Christian? Any answers for us?"

"Like you, I can't hazard a guess."

"What 'bout your two ambulance men, Doctor? Reformed resurrection men, as if a ghoul can be reformed!"

"I assure you, Inspector Ransom, Shanks and Gwinn had nothing to do with this."

"They've alibis for one another, I'm sure."

"They're out of town, Ransom, till Monday, on holiday."

"Holidaying ghouls? Where do ghouls go to vacation?"

"The bloody Indiana Dunes, for your information."

"How happy for them."

Philo Keane had heard enough of cadavers and harvesting organs, and in fact had heard more than he wanted to know, so he went to work photographing the body from every angle, leaving Alastair to probe Christian Fenger on the bizarre subject of modern-day ghouls among them.

"There are men in the profession at every level who pay well for fresh cadavers and organs to dissect, yes." Fenger dismissed it as if to say everyone knew it and accepted it as a fact of life.

"But to murder a woman for her parts. It's positively . . . ghoulish."

"Yes, I know. The laws enacted to safeguard the dead resting in the cemeteries appears to be backfiring on the living, I'd say," replied Fenger. "Most surgeons have a scarcity of, *ahhh* . . . materials to work with."

"Great God, but to stoop to this? Outright murder?" asked Ransom.

"Men have killed for less, and you well know it. You recall just last week a man was killed in a knife fight over a melon."

"Aye . . . so I recall."

Fenger busied himself measuring the wounds with a tape measure he had to roll and unroll. It made him look like a tailor.

"Then how, Christian, do we locate the professional ghoul who murdered Nelly here?"

"Canvass the medical schools?" asked Philo.

"And hospitals, and private clinics."

"Damn, there're hundreds of doctors' offices about the city. Many in the Polish, Ukrainian, German, and Italian communities as well—doctors with little to no training and unable to speak English." Ransom leaned on his cane.

"And there're a great lot of hospitals and surgeries and schools," added Fenger.

"So . . . how do we canvass them all for fresh organs? And even as we do so," said Ransom, "how do fellows as ignorant as Mike and I know a fresh heart, say, from a feeble one?"

"It won't be beating," replied Fenger.

"Very funny."

"Look, send yourself and any detective working the case to my lab, and I will show you healthy organs alongside those that've bathed in formaldehyde for a year, as well as pickled ones from too much drink and smoke. And by the way, I thought you'd given up smoking."

"I thought you had."

The pair held up their hands to one another. "You hear that, Philo?" said Ransom to his photographer friend.

"What's that?"

"We're invited to Cook County Morgue. Be sure to take the doctor up on his promise. Get pictures of healthy and unhealthy organs."

"Duplicate the shots?"

"Enough for a squad room of police to use, yes."

"Awful how her eyes've pooled with blood," Thom said. "Did the fiend slash her eyes?" He leaned in over Nell. He was such an accomplished reporter that he became like a fly on the wall; people forgot he was on hand, absorbing every word.

Philo eased Thom aside as he moved in for a shot of Nell's bloodied retinas.

"At first, I thought it running makeup," replied Dr. Fenger, "but later determined otherwise."

"The ghoul meant to take her eyes as well?" asked Ransom, staring into the dead eyes, eyes that looked as if she'd died with a question posed to God but intercepted.

"Yes, but . . . "

"But? But what?"

" . . . but the removal is incomplete, as if . . . as if he were disturbed from going any further. As though finding the uterus too difficult or time-consuming, he thought then to take the eyes, but then he had no time even for that."

"Perhaps a passing cab frightened the monster off?" suggested Philo, still clicking away with his Night Hawk camera.

"Naughton's arrival," said Ransom.

Meanwhile, Carmichael made furious notes, drawing the detective's curiosity.

"Thom, I thought you *retired* from the *Herald*," Ransom said.

"There are twenty-six some odd papers in this town, and one of them is going to need a topnotch reporter." Carmichael kept jotting notes, quite sober now, ignoring Alastair.

"Enough here in this horrid light," muttered Fenger. "We'll need to get Nell to my morgue to learn more."

But Carmichael asked, "Are the organs, you know, surgically removed?"

"Any fool with a scalpel can surgically remove the organs in the chest, Thom," said Dr. Fenger. "But—"

"But the uterus, that's another matter," came the voice of Dr. James Phineas Tewes over them. The sound of Tewes caused the hairs on Ransom's neck to stand on end. Dr. Tewes then added, "If the killer in fact started in after the uterus, going at it through the abdomen, don't we need to ask ourselves was this a medical man at work? And how much of surgery does he know?"

"Trust me, he did not know how to remove the uterus through this route, Dr. Tewes," Fenger said. "You and I would've made short work of it, although it is no simple task. This fellow turned the uterus, but he came up short."

"So you suspect an amateur? A butcher?"

"I do, yes, perhaps having had some rudimentary lessons on how to open the chest and abdomen."

"Then we suspect a man," began Jane as Tewes, imagining the killer in her mind, "who has limited surgical skills, interrupted in the process of body theft."

Fenger calmly replied, "Nell's near detached eyes and the condition of her body say it is so, yes."

CHAPTER 10

"Who bloody asked you here, Tewes?" Alastair's voice could not mask his distaste for the man who was called a charlatan in twenty-six languages—the number of neighborhood newspapers in the city—using every word for fraud. "You don't mean to do a phrenological reading of Nell Hartigan, do you? Or attempt to conjure up her spirit, so that her dead, dangling eye there can tell us what her killer looks like, now do you?"

"I came when I heard it was a murder so close to my home. I'm here to lend what help I can."

"Which is none. Go home to your dispensary of potions and snake oils, *Doctor*." Alastair sneered the last word.

Tewes blanched, grit his teeth, and said, "If it is a ghoul's work, I know of ghouls in this city, and they never work alone."

"Nell knew this city far, far better than you, Dr. Tewes, and she would've known that . . . would've been attuned to the fact, and yet the ghouls got her. Does your magic explain that?"

"No. I profess no magic, only a divining of the human heart and head."

"Our victim has no heart, Tewes," said Dr. Fenger, following Alastair's lead. Both men had long ago given up the fight to see Jane end her charade as Dr. Tewes.

"No heart?"

"No lungs, no spleen, no entrails, no heart," replied Fenger, to which all fell silent.

"I was told only that a woman had been attacked for her uterus, which had been cut out but left behind."

"A little less than a half-truth," replied Fenger.

"Who informed you of the killing?" asked Ransom of Tewes.

"Does it matter? He was ill-informed, obviously."

Fenger knit his brow as if in deep thought. The uniformed officer who'd discovered the body in Naughton's company had stood all the while over Fenger with a police-issue lamp that could be made brighter or dimmer by pulling a lever. Fenger now asked that the officer make as much light as possible for Dr. Tewes's perusal of the gaping chest and abdominal wound. Fenger's lips then moved as if chanting a magical formula under his breath, his index finger guiding Jane's eyes to the looted thoracic area.

All could see that the woman's clothes had been ripped apart and her insides eviscerated. The flickering light cast Fenger's queerly shaped big head in silhouette, and created a dance of all their shadows only a handsbreadth away. Everyone listened to Christian Fenger's words. "There remains some element . . . a missing element as to why Nell Hartigan allowed herself to become overpowered."

"Was she . . . raped?" asked Tewes.

"It does not appear so."

"What do you mean, 'allowed' herself to become overpowered?" asked Tewes.

"She let her guard down, I suspect."

"You speak as though she contributed to her own murder."

"Go on, Doctor," said Ransom. "I gather your meaning."

"Well I don't! Explain it to me."

"How does a trained, instinctive Pinkerton operative as savvy and as streetwise as Nell Hartigan allow herself to be taken by surprise?" shouted Ransom, frustrated and fatigued.

"Unable to fire off a single shot from her concealed weapon?"

"She is stabbed deeply, a traumatic single blow with a huge carving knife, after which he sets upon his true prey—her organs," continued Fenger. "He makes quick work of the chest and stomach, followed by the female organs—and failing this, attempts the eyes."

"But he comes at the uterus through the aperture already created," added Tewes. "As a medical man might."

"Or the untrained and foolish."

"But in extracting the missing organs efficiently . . . perhaps he does know *something* of surgery. Notice the Y-incision made from each shoulder to pelvis. Classic."

"Then he is no mad slasher?" asked Alastair.

"Well yes and no, but whoever did this," replied Fenger, "he did so with calm aplomb."

"But he left the eyes and uterus," Tewes said.

"Only, I think, due to a sudden apprehension."

"Perhaps he is a failed physician," suggested Tewes.

"Or one whose license has been revoked?" asked Carmichael, still taking notes.

"Someone frustrated at being unable to practice?" asked Ransom. "So this mad surgeon goes out and carves up people out of what? Frustration, boredom?"

"Practice," said Tewes. "Perhaps he intends to stay in *practice.*"

"That's even colder."

"If it is about medical rehearsal, it may well be about medical training," added Fenger.

"Yes, if he must, absolutely must, practice and perform . . . " said Tewes, pausing. "It may well be he needs the organs for . . . dissection."

"Performances, rehearsals? Do you mean he is a practicing medical doctor, training others, like your daughter, Gabrielle?" Ransom asked Tewes.

"Hold on there, Ransom," Fenger took issue. "I am training Gabrielle Tewes."

"It's a possibility," continued Tewes, "that it is someone paid to procure the parts for a medical man."

"Gawd," groaned Philo Keane, finished with his photos and lighting a cigarette. "But why not use cats, dogs, cattle, for God's sake!"

"You are a photographer, Mr. Keane, can you understand being unable to work in your field while your camera there sits idle?" asked Tewes. "Having to sketch with pen and pencil rather than shoot pictures with a camera?"

Thom Carmichael added, "Like a journalist without a journal. I see it."

Bellowed Ransom, "But to murder a woman for one's bloody career or *practice*?"

"Please, Ransom," said Tewes, "you're about as knowledgeable of medical people as . . . as a bagpipe, I think."

"Watch your tongue, Tewes."

"Think of it, man. What obsesses any surgeon but the curiosity of cutting into flesh and revealing disease and repairing tissue?"

"So by your design, we have a mad surgeon on the loose?"

"No, not a mad surgeon but a *typical* one."

Fenger raised his eyebrow at this. "Dr. Tewes has a point we can't ignore, Alastair. However . . . "

"However?"

"My gut and my vote goes with a *procurer* of organs and bodies—one with just enough knowledge of anatomy to make quick work of it."

"You think so, Christian?"

"I do."

"You speak like a man who has seen a lotta autopsies," Carmichael said, attempting to get a laugh out of the dour-faced Dr. Fenger but failing miserably.

Silence again reigned as Fenger climbed creakily from his knees over the victim, backing the lantern-holding cop away as he did so. Around the corner there stood a bystreet with rows of freshly built brick houses and apartments, an improvement in the area to be sure. Included also were a number of storefront businesses within sight: a map engraver, an architect, a law office or two, and a number of other more obscure agencies and enterprises alongside a thriving signmaker's business.

"You're saying he got at her like a regular Jack-in-the-box, then?" Ransom asked of Fenger.

"There's no sign she got in the least struggle, not a single wound on her hands or forearms, for instance, which occurs when one is assailed and instinctively throws up the hands and arms in this fashion." Christian demonstrated for the others.

Tewes frowned and stepped away as if something disagreed in the man's bowels or as if he meant to ruthlessly disregard what Dr. Fenger had to say and wanted a change of subject.

At the same time, the waning night grudgingly gave sway to a frosty seasonal fog, looking like a great gray pale over the heavens. However, the fog found itself embattled. Battered by winds, the fog, sluicing here and drifting there, formed smaller ghostly forms of itself as if creating a regiment of spirits. As a result, Alastair and the others, all but Nell Hartigan, were treated to an array of marvelous hues and textures of twilight, for here was the darkness of evening, and there a glow of rich cream and brown and orange, like the light of some strange, ethereal conflagration.

The dismal street corner, and what they stood over, conspired with the besieged twilight to create of Van Buren and Dearborn a dark cityscape out of a nightmare Ransom often found himself inside. When it appeared for a time that the gas lamps were going out and the darkness of fog and overcast skies might win out over light, for a moment Ransom believed the reinvasion of darkness might be permanent over the earth.

That's when Shanks and Gwinn, their battered old ambulance wheels making a terrible noise like the coach driven by a battlefield banshee might, came thundering toward them. Come to take Nell back to Fenger's mortuary deep in the bowels of Cook County Hospital.

When it became apparent that it was not Shanks and Gwinn, but an equally unpleasant looking odd couple, the replacements, Ransom accepted the fact that Shanks and Gwinn were indeed out of town. Still, he would follow through to be sure. One of the replacements was a lumbering giant of a man whose back was swollen with a lump, while his partner appeared a sallow-faced, stern fellow with a furtive eye that went everywhere.

"Little more I can do for her than to sew her up for the undertaker," commented Fenger, dispelling the pall that had descended over the small party.

Riding with Shanks and Gwinn's fill-in fellows was a Dr. Hiram Hautman, Dr. Fenger's new assistant, a German surgeon who'd recently come to Chicago carrying impeccable credentials.

"I gathered the men as soon as I could," said Hautman to Fenger even before he could climb down from the wagon, recently painted a bright blue with a white cross, finally covering for good the old lurid sign that had once graced the wagon due to its previous owner: Oscar Meyer wieners in a bold arc.

"I'll see that Nell is properly handled," Fenger said to Ransom. "You needn't worry on that score. Best get some sleep, all of you."

They dispersed, rushing from the grim work of this morning. "Share a cab?" Ransom asked Tewes, surprising Carmichael, who thought the two men, inspector and phrenologist, sworn enemies.

"Don't mind if I do," replied Tewes.

Thom's note-taking hand had been stilled, and he scratched his scalp over this, but then suspected Ransom had a plan, that there must be method to his madness. Yes, as in the past.

CHAPTER 11

As the cab they shared waddled along brick streets, the fog hid in alcoves like timid souls in flight, blocking out rat-infested, damp, dingy streets just outside their windows. They passed a number of gin palaces, a low French eating house, a shop selling two-penny salads, a barber's pole, an apothecary below one of the ugliest structures in the city—meant to appear as a little European castle with turrets and multiple doors, the place instead proved a monstrosity, as each section had apparently been built by a separate contractor. The strange six-story structure had a sign above reading: H.H. HOLMES APOTHECARY & INVENTIONS. But the sign was swallowed up in the gloom and fog as dark as umber while Alastair read it.

Ransom had heard of Holmes through various dealings with Pinkerton; the man had a shady past, according to records the Pinkerton Agency had begun to amass against him. In fact, his past was riddled with scams and hoaxes, swindles and boondoggles, and there was the question of a partner in Philadelphia who had mysteriously disappeared after Holmes was named beneficiary on his will of last testament. Following this came the disappearance of the partner's wife and two children. Pinkerton was building an airtight case against the obvious villain.

As the Pinkertons were on the case, Alastair had not concerned himself with the so-called Dr. Holmes, but now he told Jane what he knew of Holmes, and when finished, he said to her, "If you are not careful, one day, the Eye that Never Sleeps—Pinkerton—will be overly interested in Dr. James Phineas Tewes as well."

"Not for murder, I can assure you!"

"Someday, Jane, one of the people you swindle with your spiritualism, someone high up—"

"Like the mayor's wife, you mean?"

"Good example. Now you see my meaning. Should Mrs. Harrison, for whatever reason, find fault with you, why next you know, the Pinkertons'll be all over Tewes if hired to do so."

"I take your meaning. Now can we drop it?"

"The man Holmes set up a booth at the fair and claims to have invented a machine that turns air into water, Jane."

"And beside him, someone has an elixir to prevent hair from turning gray, so what?" she asked. "How can you be so naive, Alastair? After all you've seen?"

"Naive?"

"Such flimflams are older than the Bible. To keep your hair from falling out, anoint your head with the blood of a black calf, but it must be one boiled in oil! Else use the fat of rattlesnakes." She laughed after this.

"Now you're being silly, mocking me."

"No . . . I am quoting from the Papyrus Ebers."

"The what?"

"Papyrus Ebers, a medical book, or rather a scroll found in Egypt and dating back to 1552 B.C."

"I see."

"It prescribes for people who're losing their hair."

"Is that so? Are you saying that you think I should read it?"

"If memory serves, you apply six fats—"

"Six fats?"

"Fat of the horse, hippopotamus, crocodile, cat, snake, and ibex, I think."

"Ibex? What's an—"

"I think the hippo hump will be the most difficult to get hold of."

"Not the ibex?"

"I suspect the hippo will cause more problems."

"Where do I find such ingredients? Your dispensary?"

"More chance with H.H. Holmes's apothecary."

"I think I'll pass."

"A special hair dressing for the queen of Egypt, called *schesh*, consisted of equal parts of the heel of an Abyssinian greyhound, date blossoms, and hooves from an ass boiled in oil."

"In other words, making an ass of the queen."

"Don't prejudge! An ass's dung took out the pain of a bee sting or a splinter." She was having fun, and he realized this. "Splinters killed our ancestors then because the cure carried a disease. The tetanus virus thrives in dung!"

"Was there anything the ancients got right?"

"Not in chemistry or medicines."

"You mean there's nothing useful in lizard blood, swine teeth, putrid meat, stinking fat, moisture from a sow's ear, goose grease, or even fly excretions?"

"They got surgery right, the Romans did, thanks to an ancient genius named Galen."

"And the point of this lecture?" he asked as the cab came to a halt before Dr. Tewes's shingle.

"What point? To pass the time of a tedious ride, and to cope with this morning's awful find."

"Nothing more? Not to defend the surgeon who may be out there paying for Nell Hartigan's remains so he can drop them in his specimen jars?"

"I don't condone it; I certainly am for advancing science, but this . . . this robbing of life in the name of giving life, no . . . this is not right in any light or angle."

"But you are a surgeon. A scientist."

"I am."

"And you understand the need, the urge to cut."

"I do. I practice every day that I can, even though—"

"Even though you have no surgical patients. So what or whom do you 'practice' on?"

"Animals and animal organs."

"And they are secured how?"

"From a connection Tewes has with a knacker at the stockyards."

"A horse butcher? You put shivers through me at times, Jane."

"Why so? Because I am a woman wielding a scalpel?"

"Because you dare associate with knackers at the yards!"

She laughed at this. "Knackers know a great deal about the anatomy of men, thanks to their skill with animals. They're not such a bad lot."

"For all we know, Jane, a poor knacker, unable to feed 'is family on what they pay at the yards, is now delivering up human organs to surgeons in the city, and in this case, Nell Hartigan's organs."

"I don't know what you want me to say further, Alastair."

"Suppose a knock came at your back door, Jane, and you—or rather, Tewes—was offered, say, a human brain, a human heart, kidneys, lungs at a price?"

"From some miscreant like your Mr. Bosch?"

"Let's say Shanks or Gwinn. What would be your response, Doctor?"

"I should shoo him off." But she'd hesitated half a second.

"Are you sure?" he asked, breaking into her thoughts.

"I . . . I am quite sure."

"You don't sound sure."

"I tell you, I would refuse it."

"Such a gift, such an opportunity to use your skills, your father's surgical tools on human flesh?"

"Damn you, Alastair, I am no part of this movement afoot in your city to have involuntary organ donation going on amid . . . amid murder and intrigue."

"It has been going on for years, curtailed only during wartime when there are always enough unidentifiable bodies and parts to fill every medical school in the land, so why should it be any different here in Chicago?"

"Science must progress at all costs," she said, climbing from the cab. "We all accept that. There is always a cost, but harvesting a living person of her organs? It's an abhorrent notion on so many levels; no, Alastair, I know of no medical people who would stoop that low."

"Or admit to it?"

She gritted her teeth at this and glared at him. "You can be so exasperating! Read my heart. I am not one of your bloody suspects."

"Who, then, in the medical community?"

"Only the most ambitious."

"No one is more ambitious in the field than is Christian Fenger."

"Don't be ridiculous. He has scruples. He's above such behavior."

"Only because he has the city to supply him with cadavers."

"Which rules him out! God, and he calls you a friend?"

"Who, then, in the city has Christian's obsession but not his access to cadavers?"

"Whom, Alastair, do you wish me to speak ill of? All those who worked so hard to keep Jane Francis out of the medical field? All those who refuse to stop killing babies and pregnant women because they fail to grasp the simplest medical wisdom? Stupidly rationalizing such practices as going from an autopsy to a birthing without use of soap and water? Or those still bleeding people because they hold firm to an idea of all disease residing in 'bad' blood rather than treating the organ?"

"Can you provide me with a list of names?"

"Don't you get it, Alastair? I suspect none of these idiots of wanton murder."

"Perhaps Christian will be more forthcoming when I interrogate him on the subject, after I get some sleep."

"Ohhh! Just how infuriating can you be!" She stomped over the boards of her porch and disappeared into the semi-darkness of her home.

"What'd I say?" he asked himself, the coachman, and the horse.

None had an answer.

CHAPTER 12

The cool morning passed reluctantly but finally gave way to a warm sun and clear skies with scattered clouds, and anyone passing the corner of Van Buren and Dearborn would never have known anything untoward had happened there, so complete had Shanks and Gwinn's replacements cleaned up after the murder.

As the cityscape changed from gloominess to brightness, the city of big shoulders shook itself awake and began to tremble with the noise of rumor, gossip, innuendo, and half-truth as the story of Nell Hartigan's unnatural death circulated. Chicago cast its jaundiced eye over the streets and over the rumor that a Pinkerton agent, and a female at that, had not only been raped and murdered, but had her unborn child ripped from her insides by some maniac who had likely sacrificed the fetus to Satan himself.

Chicagoans cast a furtive eye down every alleyway and bystreet, feeling a growing sense of unease, as if a living Devil had climbed from the sewers and walked among the population, interested in feeding on babies. Chicago looked over its big shoulders, down roads that yesterday were mud, today paved over proper thoroughfares. The meandering, amber-tinted snake called the Chicago River invited further rumor as the highway by which Satan made stealth possible with a barge from Hades that wended its way through the earthbound community, evil coming ashore, doing the deed, and returning to the safety and invisibility of the barge on the crowded waterway. Tinted, dappled green and brown, was the brow of the riverbank, the only witness to the chaotic evil along its shore. For in darkness the black ribbon of water became a sullen place for suicides and murder. And on either side of the dark waters stood monuments to the god Mammon, warehouses and businesses and brothels of export and import for all manner of goods and services. The myriad blinking gas-lit windows winking, like the million eyes of Hell's own, as wharf lights gleamed like fireflies and small beckoning hearths, flaring red and glaring yellow, summoning the naive, the destitute, the sick, poor, and addicted.

One small window acted as a shaft for an oblique green light reflected in the water and across the wharf. Endless threats to burn this place to the ground came in at police stations across the city, angry ministers and ladies' organizations, upset fathers, distraught mothers, outraged brothers, enraged sisters, and even an occasional hopping mad grandparent. This window was Madam Maude DuQuasi's brothel—the Silver Palace—a symbol of everything ugly and decadent in Chicago, and make no mistake about it, Maude, the girls who worked for her, and the clapboard shack she called the "old palace" were all three so frightfully ugly and pigsty in nature that many considered them a separate race of beings, as their surroundings and their sexual appetites were those, it was said, of apes.

This is where Newly Nightlinger found himself this morning, waking in the bed with three of the ugliest, homeliest, dirtiest, smelliest women he'd ever set eyes on. It startled him, as he could not recall the previous several days, and even now, staring at his big black hands, he felt dazed, confused, hazy in the extreme. One moment he was drinking at a tavern after a long day of work hefting feedbags off Cap'n Wakely's boat at Grathian's warehouse on the wharf, and now this, waking to such a horror, finding himself completely naked amid a snake pit of black and white-skinned pig-women! In fact, the white women here were such low creatures that a black man could not be hung for making love to them, or so it was said. In the deep South, he knew such considerations got no play—that despite the horrid look of a woman or her vile animal nature or profession, that ultimately she remained a white maiden, a *dove*—spoiled perhaps but yet a dove that his black ass had defiled. And he'd be hung at the nearest stout tree for sleeping with it. But Chicago was a progressive town.

He had lost three days and nights to a drinking binge, and he'd likely not a cent left to his name, and had surely lost his job by now. He tried to imagine a worse circumstance and could not, until he realized that he couldn't find his shirt and pants. His face must tell all, because a thin, straight, lanky white man in the hallway looking in on him asked, "Do we need help here, Mr. Nightlinger?"

He knows my name, and he calls me Mister. Must be he works here. Maybe they've laundered my pants and shirt . . .

"I sure do. Don't even know where my pants're."

"Look here, wrap yourself in this"—the stranger tossed him a grayed, stained sheet—"and follow me. I need a strong man for a day's work. Are you interested?"

"Absolutely, boss. I'm your man!"

"Climb outta there then, and come along."

Newly Nightlinger's father had been a slave in Mississippi all his life and had died before the Civil War that ended human bondage in America. His mother's name had been America, but she, too, had died a slave when, on the verge of Emancipation, she died of cholera. Newly, as a young man, traveled north and had settled in Chicago after many a ride atop a train, and he had bumped from one job to another in the city, until landing the permanent job with Captain Jeremiah Wakely, who, although a white man, treated him as damn near his equal.

Newly had seen many things, but nothing so horrid as his own behavior at this moment.

Still, he was eating well enough, and he had a good,

strong back, and he believed there was always work for a man like him, a man willing to lift any weight for any length of time so long as he was paid. But he did have his bad habits, number one being whiskey, and this followed by women. *Cigarettes and whiskey and wild-wild women, they're enough to drive ye insane*, he thought, recalling the words of an old tune. He often said that his life would make a fine, fine moaner-groaner of a blues song.

Wrapped in the sheet given him by the stranger, Newly stepped out into the hall, where he again spied the stranger, now at the end of the corridor half in shadow, idle in another doorway, his finger curled and indicating that he was to follow.

"Need you to help me carry Vander outta here, boy," the straight-backed man with sharp features said to Newly. "Hurry on!"

Don't call me boy, Newly hotly thought, but said, "What 'bout dem pants? A shirt?"

"You can have Vander's damn clothes. Come on!"

Newly tripped on the sheet, his big, awkward foot almost tearing it from his grasp. It occurred to him that he was vulnerable and naked except for the sheet, but this creeping fear was a sporadic thought and did not firmly take hold. Rather, he prized the missing pants, a shirt, and a dollar bill for helping carry out this chore named Vander—some poor fool perhaps in worse shape than he himself. These thoughts had formed solid in his mind. He had an immediate goal, and he rushed headlong toward it. Newly's normal way.

When he stepped through the door, a garish bright light hit him as if flush from heaven through the open eye of God, but then he saw the hazy outline of the window overhanging the wharf outside, and he felt a crisp, cool breeze. But the open window had momentarily blinded Newly with morning light, bathing him in it, so he failed to see any Vander. No one but the stranger, and he in silhouette like one of those black and white portraitures done at the fair. *Silhouetting with paper and scissors,* his mind told him, while simultaneously asking, *Wherebe this Vander fella?*

He did not see the man behind him. He failed even to detect the door slam behind him, his full attention on the stranger before him, oddly the same man, yet oddly different. Had the man stood hunched over before like some gargoyle ready to pounce? Then he heard the final click of the door behind him, turned to the sound. Here was the man who had beckoned him, locking the door.

Two men in the room, both standing, one locking the door and a flood of light and fresh air streaming around the hulking one who stood guard at the window.

"What's this?" muttered Newly.

The man behind said nothing. The man before him grunted. This one gave off a vague sense of deformity—*off center somehow,· maybe a hunchback, perhaps a hobbled foot.* And it grunted. Something in the eyes of the grunter, something vacant and something deviant at once, something both present and missing, eyes clearly as confused as Newly's own, like the misfiring engine on that old boat. But Newly hadn't time to cipher why the two men seemed identical yet not quite the same when he felt the other man, the straight one, take him in a full choke hold.

"You sick sons a bitches! I don't go that way! Keyrist! Let me go!"

Then Newly realized that he was saying nothing as his throat was lathered with his own blood while his brain was screaming *I'm no queer!* But nothing of sound or noise other than the sputtering and gurgling of rattling death filled the room.

Newly died looking into the eyes of the hunchbacked twin whose gaze registered a certain timid and eager horror as Newly lost consciousness.

CHAPTER 13

With the black man dead, the killer shouted at his brother. "Damn it! Do I have to do everything? Bastard! Get over here and help me wrap 'im in the sheets!"

"We don't gotta cut 'im open this time?"

"The doctor wants a whole man this time."

"But he's a black man. Doctor *won't want* no black man."

"Don't be stupid. The doc put us onto the man."

"You're smart, Philander, real smart."

"How so, Van?" He often shortened Vander to Van. Their hands worked busily to wrap the body.

"I mean . . . how did you know you could find someone here so easy?"

"Are you just stupid? This place and places like it are full of walking dead. All we have to do is harvest 'em. It's why the doc sent us here. He set it all up with Maude, and Maude pointed him out."

"That's a hard lotta cal-ca-lating, Philander." Vander never shortened his name, never used Phil. "Safer than on the street, huh?"

"We almost got caught last night when that copper came along."

"So how're we going to get this fella to the doctor now?"

The other indicated the open window. "We go out that way."

"Now? In broad daylight?"

"Who in Chicago is going to question it? We're just helping a friend out of a den of inequity to sober him up and return him to his family."

"What about the blood?"

"That's why we wrap him in the brown wool blanket. Now help me mummy 'im up."

"You're smart, brother," said the other as they finished wrapping the body.

"No one'll ever miss this Negra." Philander gave another thought to the woman they'd eviscerated only the night before. As he'd worked over her, it slowly began to dawn on him that she had the body of a much younger woman than he'd thought her to be. This came as a gradually growing shock. Her skin proved supple, her muscles taut, and her breasts firm. The killed woman simply wasn't what she'd appeared.

On closer inspection of her features, wiping away caked, oily makeup, he realized that she was no homeless old witch, but a young wench instead! Her makeup was as thick as oil paint, and he peeled it away. "Blind me, she's hardly more'n a child," he'd told his brother, who squinted in response. "She's hiding under a ton of makeup. Why?"

"I dunno," his brother'd said.

"When does a woman hide her youth below a mask of age? Queer indeed. What woman hides her beauty to become a grandmotherly street tart by comparison?"

"Dunno."

"Why does a woman present herself as more pitted and wrinkled and pickled than her years?"

"Philander, I—I—I donnnw't know."

He'd then dug for anything to help identify the real woman he had killed, but there was nothing on her. Only the handgun, which had skittered a little away when she fell. Vander had picked it up, terrifying Philander, who was sure the fool would fire it off, alerting every copper in the area. He'd snatched it from his brother and laid it aside the body.

Philander then shook it off, both the fact she was a much younger woman, and the near disaster of a gun in his brother's hands. He'd then continued to harvest organs. He most assuredly would prefer to take her entire body to the doctor—it'd mean a great deal more money, as even skeletons had a bounty on them—but this was too near a police beat and station house.

He'd gotten the major organs and was thinking he could get at the uterus when he changed in midstream to the eyes. Just as the good doctor had ordered: *I could use a good, healthy pair of eyes.* And he was about to take the eyes when the sound of firm, steady footfalls of heavy boots and the light of an approaching police lamp startled his brother, who raced off, leaving him alone with the jars and the cart.

A final glance at the accusing blue-blossom eyes that he'd begun on, and he decided they were hardly worth facing a copper over. He grabbed the pushcart and rattled off ahead of the approaching police lantern, gritting his teeth against how his dummy of a brother made him feel. Certainly, the approaching copper heard him, even if unable to see him in the gloom, as the cart and jars filled with fresh organs bumped and screamed over the cobblestones. Down the alleyway and into blackness he'd disappeared ahead of the lantern.

Even now, bumping Newly's body against the window frame, the smart one glared at the fool and wondered again what a huge liability if anyone ever got hold of the weakling and asked him three questions. The straighter of the two twins stared at his crooked other self and felt a mixture of pity, grief, guilt, and hatred all at once. But he put such thoughts on hold against the day he feared he'd be taking his brother's body to the doctor for money.

Working together, the strange twins managed to push and pull Nightlinger's body out onto the wharf and into the rented wagon standing wait. A patient, calm horse with one eye as large and as swollen as a melon looked over its shoulder at the noise made when the twins dropped the body into the rear and covered it with a canvas. The horse's eye studied the killers for a moment, then returned to the oats strapped in a canvas bag around its ears and hanging below its mouth. The ears, which had been alert, relaxed now in acceptance of the load, as if marking the significance of it all.

A shiver went through Vander, his skin rippling like that of the horse whenever Vander brushed him. Vander had named the old nag Carrie, for Carrie Nation, as a little joke, and Philander was quick to call it a very little joke.

The brothers, somewhat exhausted by their efforts, each took a side and climbed onto the seat, and with their faces shaded by hats, the sun reflecting off the water here, they and Carrie trundled off. The wagon made a terrific noise over the wooden boards of the wharf, but even this was silenced by the chaos and symphony of noise here from fishmongers to warehouse screaming machines.

"This means good money, Van."

"A—A—A job *done well* . . ."

"Well done, damn it. It's a job *well done*."

"Yeah . . . well done."

Philander blew out a long breath of air in a gesture of disgust. He let it drop and was just glad that they could now go in search of good payment to make up for the failure of the night before.

CHAPTER 14

For days and nights, Alastair Ransom made ceaseless calculations about the nature of this killer who'd dispatched Nell Hartigan, and he held no illusions about Nell's having become the only victim of this organ-harvesting ghoul. But his calculations all proved unsatisfactory in the end. It was like chasing phantoms into bottomless burr holes. He found he'd been absolutely inept and unable to establish a single bloody clue—nothing.

He had sought out his longtime friend, police photographer Philo Keane, and they hashed it out over half-decent brandy and Bach, but it had no end, this chase. Countless ghouls worked the cemeteries and streets here, but most he knew and had jailed at one time or another. Most of these crows were careful and meticulous types who left nothing of the body to be found by the lawmen. But here was a fish of another scale. Someone who didn't know enough to know that it was Nell Hartigan plying her trade as a hired operative, and not what she pretended. It told Ransom that the killer was likely new to the area, as nowadays anyone in the neighborhood could point to Nell no matter her disguise.

Conversely, Nell would've known her attacker, too, if he were a staple of the area. After all, she grew up a girl of the streets, born and bred to Chicago. It's why she made a good operative for Pinkerton in the first place and in this location. She knew the players, among them the snitches such as Bosch, but did she know her attacker? It might well be how he got the drop on her, reasoned Ransom. Human nature being what it was, a person lets her guard down if a man is the least ingratiating and solicitous. Alastair imagined fifty scenarios at once that might explain why tough little Nell might let her guard down, lower her weapon back into the folds of her petticoats, take her eye off this mystery man interested in her entrails and on the verge of pouncing.

The one who struck her down must've been an unknown, else there'd have been a trail of his blood going away. Yes, she'd have been on guard; she'd have struck back in one fashion or another. She wouldn't've taken it lying down, not Nell.

When he decided Philo was of little help in the matter, Alastair again went to confer with Christian Fenger. Their quiet discussion ended in an argument when Alastair called Shanks and Gwinn, a pair of so-called reformed Resurrection Men—grave robbers. "Those two might at any time renew their former profession." Fenger didn't want to hear it, didn't want to rehash old arguments between them about his "deliverymen," as he called the odd pair. "Besides, they're still out of the city!"

When Fenger proved a dead end, claiming he knew nothing of any doctors in the surgical field who would stoop so low as to accept the organs of a murder victim for their practice, or for the teaching of students in surgery, Alastair asked him to dig deeper for some names, and said he'd return, expecting a list, then abruptly left.

Finally, Ransom went to Jane. "Let's have dinner with you in a dress," he suggested.

"All right."

"I'm buying, but you'll have to listen to me."

"How romantic," she jibed.

"To act as a sounding board on this Hartigan matter."

"I understand you promised Mr. Pinkerton that you'd avenge Nell Hartigan."

"Damn, does a secret exist in this town?"

"None that I know of."

"You mean none that you do not know of."

"That, too."

He gritted his teeth. "How do you get your information?"

"I've cultivated *your* sources. Dot 'n' Carry for one."

"Wait, hold on. Are you saying that Bosch is now working for you?"

"He's branched out, yes."

"That weasel is *my* weasel."

"I suggest he belongs to the highest bidder."

"Damn the man."

"He came round to my—to Dr. Tewes's residence the other night—"

"To report on Nell's murder, did he?" Alastair considered the intricacies of it all. Sometime back, he'd set Bosch onto Dr. Tewes only to learn from Bosch that Tewes and Jane were one and the same. At the time, he'd chased Bosch off with rocks as a result of the impossible idea. Now Bosch, knowing Jane's secret, had made a pact with Tewes while likely holding in abeyance his knowledge of Tewes's true identity. "When?" Ransom asked Jane.

"When?"

"When did Bosch come to your doorstep?"

"I presume just after he left Dr. Fenger's. He has no phone, so it was a foot message."

"That man nearly got me killed in his wheeling and dealing and double-dealing, so if I were you, Jane—"

"I'm quite aware he knows my true identity, but it's a fact that Dr. Tewes *pays* well."

"He'll one day turn on you. It's the nature of the snitch."

"But for now," she repeated with an arched brow, "he knows I pay well for information. He'll not want it to dry up."

"But he's *my* snitch," Ransom repeated.

"He's always been anyone's snitch, Alastair. Search your memory."

"Aye, as in the time I was near shot dead by that crooked

lowlife back of the yards. It was Bosch who led me right into that ambush."

"Sure he took money to lead you there, but in the end, he did come to your rescue."

"Rescue? Him? Come to my rescue?"

"That's how he tells it."

"Damnable swine. I had to shield him and fight for my life at once, and he leapt a fence and was gone, wooden leg, cane, and all."

"But his warning shout kept you alive, as he tells it."

"I suppose, if you stretch a point, he saved me that night, yes, if—"

"If *he* tells the truth."

"I've never been satisfied that *he* was set up along with me that night."

"You suspect Nathan Kohler of it still?"

"Oh, I surely do."

"And the Haymarket Riot? Do you really believe that one man—*even Nathan Kohler*—could've planned that to come off as it did?"

"It came off badly—wrongly timed. Has Kohler's hand all over it, and one day I'll prove it."

"Or else?"

"Go to my grave trying."

"Alastair, you're a bitter man, and this obsession is beginning to cloud your judgment."

"Bitter? Perhaps so, but with good reason. Clouded, not me."

"But it poisons everything around you."

"All right, anything in excess is poisonous, I get it."

"Can't you see that this includes your every relationship?"

"I am a determined fellow! A noble, admirable quality!"

"No, you are a cynical, scarred soul."

"Is there so large a difference? Damn it, Jane, can we speak of other matters?"

"I'm not so sure I wish to have dinner with so cantankerous a man, not tonight."

"I need to talk about this case with someone."

"Someone willing to listen is what you need."

"Where's Gabby, then?"

"Leave Gabby out of this."

"She'll know of it soon enough. The papers have it."

"All the same, I don't want her in harm's way."

"I'd never put her in harm. Surely, you know that."

She relented in both position and tone. "Give me a bit to freshen up, and I'll be your guest for dinner then. You must secretly like to be told off."

"Perhaps . . . it's your wit that I love. The well-directed word, as incisive as a fencing sword."

"Good . . . good. Then there is hope for you yet."

Alastair watched this woman of substance turn and haughtily make her way to her bedroom, the same as she shared with a makeup mirror and Dr. Tewes's array of wigs and mustaches. "It's you I want to have dinner with, not him!" he shouted after, but the door closed in his face. "Wear something feminine and dainty!"

CHAPTER 15

Ransom took Jane to the Palmer House, Chicago's premier hotel and eatery, and there they saw celebrities such as Oscar Wilde, the actor Booth, the dancer and singer Sarah Bernhardt, as well as politicians and others Ransom called legitimate crooks and loan sharks: bankers and lawyers who were making a killing on Chicago's growth alongside the land speculators and developers, some of whom were former saloon keepers in the Levee District who'd exchanged commerce in drink, drugs, and lewd women for land and location.

Stepping abruptly to their table from out of this crowd was Chief of Police Nathan Kohler, who had sometime back learned that Jane was Tewes. Kohler had, in fact, used his knowledge against her for a time, until she steadfastly decided she would not be blackmailed by the likes of this man. What he had held over her head—her daughter Gabby's out of wedlock birth, and the disgraceful way that Gabby's father had died in France—Jane had chosen to impart to Gabby, defusing any power that Kohler might have had over them. But now his new threat was to expose Tewes's true identity as Dr. Jane Francis.

She had called his bluff with one of her own, telling him

in private that it was time she shed Tewes, go to work at Cook County Hospital alongside Dr. Christian Fenger—who'd repeatedly offered to help her out. In the strange relationship, she had as much on Kohler if not more, knowing of several "execution" style deaths that Kohler had been part of out at a farmstead in Evanston belonging to a certain Senator Chapman.

In her dealings with him, Jane had also learned that Kohler feared Alastair Ransom, not simply out of a sense of physicality, but from some dark long-ago mystery held between them like a rotting corpse. Something having to do with an old hurt, and from that wound a cankerous series of additional cuts and bruises characterized the pages of their respective history together; like a series of healed over scabs reopened, it seemed, each time their eyes met.

Sitting or standing between the two was no easy place to be.

"William Pinkerton called my office today, Inspector Ransom," began Kohler, sitting at their table and buttering a roll that he pawed from the centerpiece basket.

"He does have a vested interest in our case." Alastair used as few words as he could with his superior.

"Yes, I knew Nell. Knew her in the biblical sense, in fact." Kohler's laugh fell hollow.

Jane grimaced at his lack of grace.

"Not to offend you, Miss Francis, but I want to hammer home a point to your friend here that—"

"Then direct your 'hammer blows' my way, Nathan," Alastair replied.

"All right. The upshot is this, Inspector: I have a vested interest in this case along with Mr. Pinkerton, and if you go plodding along without result, as has been your style of late, then I won't hesitate to replace you. Is that understood?"

"I am sure you have an interest in any case that William Pinkerton is capable of making a stink about, Nathan."

"Then you have it clear. Results alone will save your job."

"You needn't worry unnecessarily about my future, Nathan, as I am, as they say, 'on the case.'"

"Funny . . . I see you here in the Palmer House, but you're saying you're not here, that you are 'on the case'!" He laughed and wickedly winked, giving a jerky nod toward Jane. "Now why am I *not* reassured at seeing the two of you here, Ransom?"

"Shall we find another place to dine, Alastair?" Jane asked.

"Somewhere where they are more selective about their clientele?" he asked, staring down Kohler now. Kohler, who had lit a cigar, smashed it out in the half-eaten roll, stood, and marched off.

"A most unpleasant man."

Alastair agreed. "So why isn't he the victim instead of Nell?"

"You'll have to tell me more about Nell Hartigan. Are the stories about her all true?"

"True enough. She's . . . she was a firebrand, a real . . . "

"Spitfire?"

"Aye, that she was."

They got up and left for anyplace else.

Together, they walked the downtown area under the glow of the Randolph and State Street gaslights, some sections under renovation, slowly being replaced with Mr. Edison's electric lights. "I know a place not far from here," he told her.

"In the infamous Levee District I've heard so much about?"

"You stay away from such places, whether you're Jane or James! It's no place for a lady."

For a time they were silent, Alastair's cane the only sound aside from the innocuous but rhythmic noise of the street and the hum of locusts and a low distant rumble of threatening thunder, seeming as far away as Canada.

Their shadows preceded them along the gas-lit concrete sidewalks. Concrete had changed the face of the city, from what was underfoot to what towered overhead to that new creature, the ever-growing skyline looking out over Lake Michigan, a doleful giant race of centaurs with windows for eyes.

Jane demurely asked him as he stared at his feet, "Alastair, do you think Nell's death the tip of the iceberg?"

"Depends on what she was investigating perhaps. Until I can get that information out of William Pinkerton . . . well, we may never know."

"Wasn't Pinkerton to meet with you, share his notes on what hole Nell was digging at?"

"He was, yes . . . supposed to."

"Instead he's complaining to Kohler, trying to have you removed from the case? *Ahhh* . . . and why? Do you suppose Pinkerton's not gotten back because he distrusts your remaining committed to the case?"

"Busy man. His father's agency has blossomed to cover the entire country. In fact, cases he takes on span the globe." She watched his eyes as he continued excusing Pinkerton. "The man employs countless operatives, and each one is chasing some fraud, murderer, or fiend of one kind or another as we speak."

"Yet, the man has time to talk over the case with Kohler but not you?"

"Stop it or you will have me suspecting ill of Pinkerton."

"I only mean that perhaps the case that Nell had been pursuing was and still remains so sensitive that, well, Mr. Pinkerton cannot compromise himself in the matter, yet he wants the killer brought to justice all the same."

"My God, Jane."

"What?"

"You must live inside a Ned Buntline dime novel."

"Whatever do you mean?"

"Such intrigues go on inside your head."

"Hold on. Any cynicism I have gained, I have gained by association with you."

"All the same, this is no opera we're in, my sweet dreamer."

"I resent that. I am no dreamer, but a pragmatist."

"And a liar it seems."

"How dare you!"

"Please, I know you are a *dreamer* at heart, else you'd have never reached your goal to become a surgeon."

"Ha! Reached my goal? Me? I can't practice surgery; few people trust surgery as it is, and no self-respecting, self-preserving person, man or woman, will come to a female for surgery. And they certainly wouldn't entrust a wounded or broken child to a surgeon named Jane."

"You've but to hang out your shingle," he insisted.

"No, I must go about as Tewes, called on by the highest society ladies to read tea leaves and to bring about a ghost of a loved one."

"Did your machinations in that regard help Mrs. Harrison?"

"I believe I soothed and consoled her somewhat . . . actually far more than either of those so-called theologians."

"That fool, Hobart Jabes? And Father O'Bannion?"

"At least Father O'Bannion doesn't subject a person to three-hour hell 'n' brimstone sermons."

"Jabes—a nastier man of the cloth I've never met."

"Both men make . . . a pretty living off the Golden Ones along Michigan Avenue."

"I can well imagine."

"As for surgeon Dr. Jane Francis," Jane concluded, sighing to the wind, her deep blue eyes a wine-tinted purple in the light reflecting from Marshall Fields' display window, "she has a long way to go before she can say her dreams are come true."

"Nice speech, Jane, but listen to yourself."

"How so do you mean?"

"Speaking of Jane as if she were another person instead of you, in the third person?"

"Really, it is but a manner of speaking."

"If I have learned anything from our association—from your interest in the human mind, Jane—it is that people speak volumes more than they mean to impart *between* the lines, and that a man's language . . . or a woman's speech, is her thought."

"Language and thought, yes, they are in consort, and heed me when I tell you that when interrogating one of your suspects, you can read much into his language."

"*Ahhh* . . . ever the master you are at deflecting attention away from an uncomfortable moment, when my focus is what's best for Jane."

"Really, Alastair," she began, holding her eyes on the latest Paris fashions in Mr. Field's window. They stood now below the huge iron clock at the corner of State and Dearborn.

"I suspect," he dared, "with a year of working alongside Christian Fenger, Jane, you'd be fighting off *real* patients with *real* maladies and surgical needs."

"*Ahhh*, instead of phantom-hunters and their spirits? And the dispirited deviant drecks coming and going from Dr. Tewes's clinic?" she asked.

"The phrenologically challenged?" he countered.

"It's a living," she finished, perturbed.

He chuckled and threw an arm about her. "I only worry about you, dealing with the dregs of society."

"Do not dismiss the science behind phrenology so easily, mister. Look what it's done for you."

"Your hands have done that," he snickered, "*not* the bumps on my head, but your touch!"

"Go away with that!"

They were suddenly interrupted when a street child, a boy, pulled them from their entire and complete attentiveness to one another. The little scrawny guttersnipe whispered from the alleyway they passed. "Inspector! It's me, Sam . . . Sam O'Shea," as the boy had renamed himself to have the quick and easy street name.

"Who's this, Alastair?"

"My youngest snitch, Samuel. I couldn't've ended the career of Leather Apron without the invaluable help and input of this brave young soul."

"But it's Sam O'Shea, now, Inspector, and I'm a man now." The boy was but two months older than his earlier age of ten, and the grime on his torn clothes and dirty face still marked him as what Jane was thinking: a street snipe in serious need of help along the order of Jane Addams's Hull House.

A bath and a change of clothes and a bed to call his own wouldn't do any harm, Ransom thought.

He stepped into a shadow with the boy, and their mutterings could not be heard save an occasional word, but Jane caught the name Nell Hartigan coming from the boy's lips.

"Indeed . . . well done . . . you're my boy, Sam," she heard Ransom's cryptic responses to whatever the boy imparted about the murdered Nell. The whole of it made her feel like she was in a Charles Dickens serial tale in the *Tribune* newspaper, anxiously awaiting the next chapter.

When finally Alastair emerged from the shadows, the boy having vanished so thoroughly she hadn't seen him go, he apologized for having left her standing alone under a lamp on the still busy street.

"Never mind. What did the boy have to say about Nell?"

"I rather distrust his information, so passing it on to you would be ill-advised, I think."

"If 'tis worthless, why not share it?"

"You are a curious feline, aren't you?"

"Curiosity may've killed the cat, but satisfaction brought her back. Now out with it. What did your boy have to say? And why's he not home this time o' night?"

"He has no home."

"No home?"

"None but the street, and besides, he suggested that I watch my back, that there is some collusion between William Pinkerton and my worst enemy."

"Nathan Kohler?"

"Something about there being a plot set in motion between them, having naught to do with Nell's death, but all the same, directed at me."

"Hmmm . . . sounds like a cunning little fellow at work, and a gifted gossip, this boy, Sam."

"Indeed, but he's the second voice tonight's warned me about Pinkerton's dealings with Nathan."

"Then perhaps you should pay heed, that is, if you trust the snitch and my intuition."

"I do trust both, and I will watch my back."

"But Sam had no help with who killed Nell or why?"

"Like all others on the subject, deaf and dumb, but he promises to keep an ear to the bricks."

"Appears he sleeps on the bricks. Look here, we ought to do something for that child."

"He will not have it; he's a wage earner now and likes it that way."

"He should be under the care of—"

"Addams? Her home would only vex a boy of his nature. Besides, it's overcrowded as is."

"How can you deny him an education, an upbringing? Religious training, a caring hand, Alastair? It's the cruelest kind of abuse—neglect and denial."

"I've not denied Sam anything."

"But you have! Making a mere boy your snitch!"

"Chicago's formed him, not I."

"Do you Chicagoans intend blaming this city for all the ills you perpetuate here? What sort of responsibility have you shown this child? Putting him on your payroll is not helpful."

"He eats as a result. I have helped one homeless."

"La-de-da! Pat yourself on the back, if only you could reach so far!"

"Jane, I tell you, this boy is not for your saving. He would only run away after a few hours at Hull House, and you would've wasted everyone's time and patience."

"You can be so calloused, Alastair. Sometimes I think too calloused for me to be seen with you!"

"Oh . . . please, this crusade of yours to save every homeless street urchin is an impossibility, and furthermore—" She abruptly pulled away. "Hold on! Where're you going?"

"For the closest cab stand and home, so you may argue now to your heart's content, Inspector."

It sounded like a scolding from Tewes, and in fact Jane only called him "Inspector" these days when angry. Her tone one of derision as she stretched the word between clenched teeth as in: *Innn-spec-torr*.

CHAPTER 16

"A ruined evening is it, miss?" asked a curious cabbie.

"Spoilt indeed, sir."

"Perhaps a pleasant ride along the parkway?" he suggested. "Lovely lake breeze tonight."

"No, it's to home with me! I've much to do tomorrow, and I'm in need of peace from that man!"

"Aye . . . oh yes, understand, ma'am."

Ransom leaned in at the cab's open window, his large features screwed up, sour confusion sitting squarely between his eyes in a gargoyle expression. "What have I said to anger you so, Jane? Don't go."

"I am fatigued."

"I'll make amends."

"How? By a pretense that my concerns are important to you? Never mind. Driver, push off!"

"I never meant to—it was not to you that I—*ahhh*—" Ransom near fell with his cane in hand, pulled from the cab as horse and carriage jerked forward, as in an instant. As if by some profound magic, some chicanery not of his or her making but through a strange mix of their temperaments, she'd been snatched from him.

He now stood alone on a busy stree. Inside his head, he felt like some foolish court jester, and everyone must see it and point at him. *God at play in my petty life again*, he silently mulled.

He prayed it was only a temporary tiff between them, and yet a niggling voice, like some troll beneath the bridge of his conscience, whispered, *She's forever lost to you now, fool! Besides, you never deserved her in the first place. You fraud of a human being . . .*

"Perhaps I should've told her the truth . . . " he said aloud to the horse pulling the next cab into position, "about what Samuel imparted."

He thought he heard the horse reply aloud his thoughts: *Perhaps the truth may've led to another outcome.*

The doctor ran his hands over the black man's corpse that'd been delivered to him. A black man without family or connection here in the city. "No one'll miss him," he again assured Philander as he paid him the final half of his commission.

"How kin ya be sure?" the oaf asked.

"Trust me, Vander, no one'll give a thought to his disappearance." His greater problem, as the doctor saw it, would be getting his students to work on a Negro's body without having to deal with their dull, stupid, bigoted complaints, snide comments, and outright jokes. While there was absolutely not one whit of difference in the anatomy of a black- to a white-skinned cadaver, these rustic fools coming to Chicago for surgical training actually feared getting a black man's blood and bile on their lily-white pinkies. He could only hope they'd all learned that a black cadaver was no different from a white corpse, but one of his students had even feared that his scalpel would be somehow tainted with a "black" bacterium or virus. The imbecile. *Little wonder I feel myself a gardener in charge of a weed patch at times, but it's my job. Root out ignorance; stomp it out in all its ugly forms, and if that requires the occasional sacrifice of a life, then so be it.*

Still, while the doctor felt safe in putting Mr. Nightlinger to use in this manner, it had to be of his own choosing. He did not feel secure in the knowledge that Philander and his simple-minded twin could be trusted to make such selections without his direction and help. He had wanted to turn the twins into cadavers when they'd shown up the previous night with several preserved organs from some source he knew nothing about. While he took the prizes and could use each, he scolded the brothers in no uncertain terms, telling them there must be no more freelancing.

When Philander attempted to defend himself, saying the parts were from a no account street prostitute who no one would miss, the doctor went into a rage. "You don't know that unless you do your bloody research! You can't even tell me her name!"

He had himself spent long hours stalking the black man from a boat in the Chicago River, from which he alighted to take in the metropolis. The doctor, posing as an agent of the brothels, cornered the fellow, who called himself Newly Nightlinger, in Kenna's bar and filled him first with drink and then notions and visions of beautiful women awaiting him.

"Bu-Bu-tee-ful wo-women? Me?"

"Who will anoint you, Mr. Nightlinger."

"Annoy me?"

"I said 'anoint,' not 'annoy.'"

The mark had repeated the word as if strange to his ear, "Anoint . . . me . . . "

"In fragrant oils from the East."

"Easta where?" The man was by now inebriated on free ale.

"East of you! You'll have a luxurious bath and massage before they make love to—"

"To me? They gonna make love to me?" He laughed. "By cracky!"

"To your every nook, cranny, and inch, sir."

"How much all this gonna cost me?"

"How much you got?" It was cash the doctor split between Maude and the oddly matched twins.

Nightlinger had proved an easy mark indeed, and the doctor determined early on that Newly was as good as his name—like a newborn! Furthermore, Nightlinger had no ties beyond the boat he'd stepped from; at least, none here in the Midwest, much less the city. He'd come up the Mississippi and Ohio some years before, and somehow he found himself working the Great Lakes now. He could not say how he had gotten from the Ohio to here, but he'd called it an adventure.

Most assuredly a confused adventure. The man struck the doctor as subhuman in his thought processes, as if sometime in his life he'd been dropped on his head, kicked there by a mule, or simply beaten about the cranium until his senses were loosened and distorted. The doctor's opinion had nothing to do with his being black or poor or a deckhand, as he knew that instinct and cunning had nothing to do with race or wealth or a man's chosen profession, but rather came at birth like the mark of Cain. You either had it or not, and Newly didn't have an inchworm's worth of guile or intuition or fear in him. Unfortunate for him, fortunate for the doctor. Even a fox in the forest knew when something in its nose or gut screamed danger, but Nightlinger never wavered from some deep-seated belief in his fellow man. It was the showman P.T. Barnum who was quoted in the papers as saying there was a fool born every day.

After delivering this vagabond into the care of Miss Maude DuQuasi at the brothel and paying her well, the fellow was given the ride promised, and done so in the stupor of a drunken orgy. A kind of last supper for his senses, the doctor had thought with a salacious grin.

The doctor stood in the shadows behind it all. Once he'd gotten Mr. Nightlinger ensconced for the duration of his rather useless life, he'd gone to locate the twins, telling them precisely where to find "money on the hoof," as he termed it—ready money awaiting in the form of a black named Newly. He told them to speak to Miss M. DuQuasi, the big black madam with a face broader than a yardstick, so as to be certain they had the right man. Then he showed them a photograph he had made of the black man, another invest-ment in the night's work.

Thusly armed, the twin ghouls were set on the path to lo-cate, silence, and wrap the body the doctor sought for his surgery and the edification of his students. Sometimes . . . especially at times like these, he wished he'd instead be-come a horse doctor. Nobody gave a damn about dissecting a horse.

What other choice have I, or any medical man? I'm no fiend, no more so than any man, but I must have cadavers for students if I'm to keep the surgical college afloat. Besides, how else to hone my own skills? It's for science, for the ad-vancement of mankind, in the name of learning and the fu-ture of medicine.

Thirty-something Newly Nightlinger did more good on this spinning planet now than when he was sentient, rea-soned the doctor. It helped assuage any feelings of con-science to add that the man's life was one of uselessness and idleness; that in a sense, he was not *really* using his body and brain to full potential, certainly not to the potential they were now put.

However, he knew that if his nefarious activities came to light, the names of people like Newly Nightlinger would be enshrined as model citizens long enough in the press to hang a certain surgeon and condemn the entire profession. He'd first undergo a public humiliation, a show that would not spare his wife and children; then he'd be imprisoned for some time, and most certainly excommunicated by Rever-end Jabes, and finally hanged for the transgression that hor-rified the patriarchs, the matriarchs, the gentry, and the plebian alike—*murder for the advancement of the surgical sciences—from cranial matter and sinus cavity to the three large gluteus maximus muscles that form each buttocks to the lower extremities. No one but another driven surgeon could understand the absolute need, the absolute instinctive drive toward understanding every inch of every organ, mus-cle, vein, and artery from carotid to the pinky and the toe.*

Still, the danger of his decisions made him long for a time

when graveyards were a viable alternative to harvesting people like cabbages. At one time, cemetery caretakers, grave diggers, even cops, could be counted upon to help out a doctor in need. But the politicians had to make an issue of it in the legislature. Laws already on the books against grave robbing were given more teeth and were being strongly enforced, causing a paucity of cadaverous materials to work with. Nowadays anyone conspiring with a medical man to rob a corpse of its appointed eternal rest faced hanging. As a result, the doctor's supply had entirely dried up.

This meant that perfectly fine corpses went rotting in their perfectly useless pine boxes, intact and preserved and unmolested in their eternal slumber, left to liquefy.

CHAPTER 17

The doctor had secured, cleaned, and prepared the black (and getting blacker) corpse, having removed all blood and fluids. He next filled its every vein and cavity with formaldehyde, its every cavity with cotton batting. With the stench of his work still clinging to his hair and clothes, he turned out the lights, and leaving, locked up his laboratory and teaching theater. He expected the wooden platforms encircling the body to be full with students tomorrow morning just after dawn, and to dismiss some of the idiots among them, when he would instruct young minds in the method of proper dissection and autopsy procedures.

"There is no teacher as effective and efficient as the human hand," he'd remind the young would-be doctors again and again. "And no tool yet devised by God or man that is so useful as this marvel of creation, this tentacle of the brain." He'd hold his surgeon's hands up to his students' stunned eyes, having removed the gloves he habitually wore, displaying his burn scars. "Yes, even as scarred as I am from a fire, my hands remain my best, last tool."

Mr. Nightlinger's organs would be repacked inside the thorax and his body stitched together again to be used yet another and another time, until his condition of preservation could no longer support another invasion and demonstration. Like a refrigerated cucumber, at some point the very cohesion of tissue broke down to a jellylike consistency impossible to cut even with a scalpel. The best to hope for was one excellent demonstration followed by two, possibly three fair shows. Knowing this, the doctor was already wondering where the next cadaver might come from.

The students had to get their money's worth at Glenhaven Medical School if the school were to survive in the shadow of such giants as Rush College and Northwestern University. Two institutions with a standing contractual agreement with the city to take off their unknowns. Bodies of deceased that remained unnamed and unclaimed. Bodies dissected before going to Chicago's Potters Field to be forever forgotten. Other facilities had ready-made human material to work with; he didn't unless he manufactured his own.

With this agreement among authorities and the major medical schools, even if he raided the cemetery of numbered headstones, he had no way of knowing which bodies below which sites were intact and which were not.

The doctor now called in his most promising students to give them first go at opening up Mr. Nightlinger and turning his fresh insides out. The eager young men in his classes could always count on having a fresh cadaver, and these chosen, his first wave, did not balk at working over the remains of a black man, nor a yellow, red, or green-with-moss-and-mold fellow freshly fished from the polluted waters of the Chicago River. They performed a service, keeping the river clear of floaters and the streets from the rotting corpses of winos.

"Doctor, you've done it again!" said Rucker, one of the brightest of the lads.

"Wherever do you get them?" asked Hollingsworth, not really wanting to know.

"So long as we've another opportunity to use our scalpels, what's it matter?" asked Webster.

"Indeed," added Pomeroy.

"Then have at it, you men," said the doctor. "Your results will be your quarter final grade!"

Newly Nightlinger's inert, unnamed body was jostled by the activity about it, but the supple ripples had more to do with the lighting here than with the skin tone. His body formed a final exam, and its movement mere reaction to the four frenzied scalpels going after various organs: Rucker, Hollingsworth, Webster, and Pomeroy.

From overhead now, in the viewing theater, the doctor in charge watched with avid interest at how the young interns chose to proceed. They'd obviously worked out their differences, each being assigned a separate task, and soon the organs were being removed as one single rack, attached as yet to the thoracic vertebra and rib cage they'd cut away, using heavy bone saws. On a separate table, Nightlinger's insides were then separated from one another and each organ and the lungs weighed, each number noted.

The interns only slowed to argue what might have caused the yellowing of the liver and its shriveled look, and then a handful of off-color jokes and remarks about the size of Nightlinger's penis, but for the most part the doctor's young students worked soberly and efficiently.

It was at this moment the dean of the school stepped into the theater to watch. He complimented the doctor on his obvious progress with this crop of surgeons. "And good news."

"Oh, what's that?"

"That deal I've been working on with the state penitentiary in Joliet?"

"Really? It's come through?"

"It's almost set."

"Wonderful."

"Should see results in the coming weeks."

"Takes so much off my mind. No more scrounging for cadavers. But will the inmates willingly sign over their bodies for science?"

"That's a foregone conclusion, Doctor. Ha! Most can neither read nor write. They'll affix their marks. The warden assures me."

"I can't tell you how happy that makes me."

"We in administration share your excitement, I can tell you. This will legitimize our having cadavers on hand, and no more use of those ghouls you've been paying."

"Yes, yes . . . all to the good."

"And Kenneth . . . "

"Yes, sir?"

"To be on the safe side, Kenneth, get rid of anything that could come back to haunt us."

Kenneth Mason, M.D. and surgeon of Glenhaven Medical School, glanced down at the black corpse his students worked over, and he gave thought to a handful of jars that held the remains of one Nell Hartigan. "Yes, absolutely right," he muttered.

The dean slapped him on the back. "Why so glum, Kenneth? You're getting a raise! We're onto a new day at the college, the members of the board are happy, all thanks to our *'friends'* out at the prison. Lotta inmates out there die annually."

The twins had settled in for a night of surveillance, each taking turns to watch the dapper old gent that Philander'd had his eye on for weeks. Philander believed the old fellow a perfect candidate—if not for Dr. Kenneth Mason at Glenhaven Medical, then old Doc Hogarth out at Evanston. In point of fact, Philander had simply decided he was no longer just doing it for the money. Something in him became jubilant at the notion of the hunt and elated at the kill. To feel a life draining out of another person and through his blade and by extension through him had been its own reward. The moment of the kill, as when he'd ripped open that Hartigan woman; God, but it made him feel more alive than he'd ever felt or imagined possible.

The old fellow that Philander now stalked lived alone, and he appeared to have no visitors and no friends beyond a hound. A small terrier that Philander promised to Vander. "He'll be quite easily managed," Philander assured his brother. This promise of a pet had calmed Vander.

The odd old man with warty face lived in a plush house on Gannett Street that faced the Chicago River, and it would be no difficult trick getting his body from the house and onto their little wagon, the same as had carried Newly Nightlinger from the brothel earlier in the day.

The old man seemed in fair health, save for a limp and those growths on his neck and face—which no doubt the surgeons would find intriguing. In fact, such growths upped the ante the man's body would fetch. The man's neck swung with a turkey-red goiter, and the warty-looking growths, some sort of ugly cancer, made the fellow as sure an outcast as anyone penniless and homeless. And no one seemed capable of having a conversation with the man, as they could not stand in his sight long. Most treated his malady as catching as leprosy or small pox.

An outcast in his own city.

Vander, as ugly as he was, had actually professed a sadness for old Dodge, alone in his bed, but Philander told him this man's loneliness was yet another reason to set the poor man free of this wretched life. When Vander asked what Philander meant, he shouted, "He's better off dead! Like you, maybe!"

With a bit of digging, Philander had learned from the local grocer and butcher and others bits and pieces of the man everyone called Dodge. Calvin Dodge was in some distant way related to the famous General Grenville Mullen Dodge, who'd become famous not for being shot off his horse four times and losing an arm in the Civil War, but for getting back on his horse four times in battle. The man then, after the war, became a railway builder whose Kansas railhead became a town named in his honor: Dodge City. Calvin, a so-called cousin several times removed, had created a name for himself as a banker, playing on his famous relative's name in such slogans as *Don't Dodge Before You C Dodge*, *As Safe as a Dodge*, and *Bank on a Dodge*. But Dodge's lending place had always been the back-door of a saloon.

After making more inquiries in the neighborhood about the old gentleman, the twins had learned that he called him-

self Colonel Calvin Jamison Dodge, and that he'd led men
into battle at Shiloh, or so the story went. Furthermore, he too
had been unseated from his horse by cannon fire, shrapnel
shattering his leg—in the tradition of his famous relative.

How much was true and how much nonsense, it was hard
to tell. As for his being a colonel, not two nights ago the
twins, like many in Chicago, had heard the oratory of Samuel Clemens aka Mark Twain, who'd proclaimed on the Lyceum stage, "Why . . . it's come to my typically wayward
attention that nowadays the title of 'colonel' hasn't the
slightest 'kernel' of truth to it. Why, the title's become as
commonplace as goose shit in Canada."

Feeling that he had learned enough about Calvin Dodge
to know that the old fool had no bank any longer and no one
who could stand his company any more than his warts, Philander also learned that the limp was due an old injury in
falling down a stairwell, and not won in battle.

The night of Twain's show, Philander had said to his
brother, "That man Twain pulls no punches."

"Yahhh . . . "

"Quite the funny man."

"Yahhh . . . uh-huh!"

"Sagacious, like you!"

"Yeah, sug-ga-gay-cious. Funny." Vander laughed and
spewed spittle. His color seemed a pale green like pea soup,
yellow under splotches of gaslight. His exaggerated facial
features caricatured his twin, his bulging, too wide eyes looking like Cyclops. He never blinked. Uncanny and unnerving
as it was, the blasted eyelids were held open by invisible
pinchers. The hunchback looked as always as if he carried
their third dead twin in a gunnysack over his shoulder.

The smarter of the two twins watched as Colonel Calvin
J. Dodge's lights began to flicker off in his residence; the
man was readying for bed. Still one light lingered for all of
an hour. Finally, the old fellow set aside his copy of *The
Helmut of the Sabbath* as sleep claimed him and whatever
will and righteousness and faithfulness may've moments before held his attention.

"Studying for his finals," Philander had joked, but Vander didn't laugh. Philander at first assumed that Vander was too lame in the head to get the joke, but to his chagrin, Vander had fallen asleep in the bushes outside the intended target's brownstone home.

"Wake up! Wake the devil up!" he cursed, and yanked at Vander. At once the younger twin came awake, startled.

"*Shhh!* It's me!"

"Oh . . . oh, brother, I thought it was her."

"Her who?"

"That Nell Hartigan you killed . . . come to get us back."

They had learned of Nell Hartigan's identity through the beer and ale grapevine that fed information throughout the city like lifeblood. "Don't be stupid! The dead can't touch us. You start thinking trash-thoughts like that, next you know, you'll be in Cook County Asylum. You want that? Huh, dummy, huh?"

"Can we go home now, Philander? I'm cold."

"No, damn you, look!" Philander pointed to the darkened house. "Time we pay Mr. C. J. Dodge a visit. Maybe tomorrow night."

At once, he stopped Philander cold by saying, "We maybe ought not to do to Colonel Dodge what we done to the others, Philander." Vander scratched behind his dirty ear. "Him bein' a war hero and all."

"First off, he's no colonel, not a real one, I'm told, and there're questions as to his being related to General Dodge."

"What's it mean, Philander?"

"He's an old liar!"

"But a banker can't be no liar."

"You daft fool! I'm telling you the old man's made up all that Civil War colonel bull!"

"You think so?"

"I know so."

"Is he . . . you know, goin' ta-be asleep when we do it?" asked Vander.

"Why? What's the difference, Van?"

"It's better when we don't gotta hear no pleading. I keep hearing 'em in my ears, Philander, pleading."

"Hearing who? Who you hearing?" Philander took a deep breath. *Could Alexander be speaking to Vander, too?*

"The other ones we kilt."

"Ohhh . . . but look, nobody's gonna make a sound if we do it right."

"How's-sat?"

"Suffocate him."

"Pillow to the face?"

"Easier and cheaper'n poison. Choke 'im with his own nightcap if need be."

"Why're you yellin', brother?"

"'Cause you're so stupid at times that—"

"Not nice to say—"

"Bloody idiot!"

"Philander, I'm your brother."

"Come on, we're leaving."

"But I thought we're doing it tonight."

Philander gritted his teeth. "I tol' ya, Van, tomorrow night, didn't I?"

"I guess so; I ferget."

"We don't do it without a plan, like all the others."

"Ya mean like wid Nell Hartigan?"

"Daft fool! OK, we had no plan that night."

"You said things was *des-des-per-ate*."

"We had no pig-shit way to know she was a disguised Pinkerton agent, now did we?"

Philander'd begun rushing down the street at a clip, Vander hurrying to keep up when a quick-stepping horse, drawing a carriage, almost ran into him as it came around a corner. Both twins stood gaping like men who'd wet themselves when, from the window, stared a pretty-faced woman, curious why the horse and driver had started. Next second, a younger woman poked her head out.

The two ghouls lifted their hats to the passing ladies, the bigger one lumbering into a bow, unwittingly displaying a hunchback.

CHAPTER 18

From the coach, Jane Francis Tewes and her daughter, Gabrielle, could only get a fleeting glimpse of the problem at hand. Mother and daughter were within a few blocks of home and anxious to find their beds to retire for the night. Neither one paid more than a passing interest to the strange, seedy-looking pair on the sidewalk who, together, looked like bookends, only one was a sadly misshapen creature—a hunchback straight out of that popular Victor Hugo novel set in Notre Dame. The image of an elephant man or what locals called a mule man stuck in her mind. *God's mismanagement of human flesh*, Jane thought, *wondering if surgery would ever conquer such hellish torments*.

Yet the other man, who had no disfigurement, somehow still looked like the misshapen one. About the eyes and facial features. But something beyond even this struck Jane as unusual about this odd couple.

"What is it, Mother?" asked Gabby, studying the quizzical fog that'd come over Jane's features.

Sitting opposite her daughter, Jane replied, "Odd looking chaps, yet, it's as if I've seen them somewhere at some time. So oddly . . . similar in appearance, save their size and demeanor. Frankly, I'd say it was Jekyll and Hyde come off the page, but in two bodies rather than one."

One had looked keenly and straight into Jane's eye, offering a strange smile, perhaps a lewd suggestion behind the gesture. The other had an animal-like snout and a calflike blank stare. "The one looked through me, while the other seemed to have no idea of what it was his eye fell upon," Jane added.

"Or's'if he couldn't possibly decipher the mystery of a curious woman in a coach window," said Gabby, laughing lightly as the carriage bumped along.

"Right . . . even if it took him the rest of his life, he'd never find an answer to this puzzle," agreed Jane.

"Men can be thick."

"Tell it to Ransom."

"Yesterday you were calling him handsome Ransom, and now the two of you are quarreling again. Really, you can be so churlish with one another."

Then Jane started, a look of pure light coming into her eyes.

"What is it? Something I said?"

"No, no!"

"Something you ate?"

"Something I recalled."

"*Ahhh*, 'bout Ransom, huh?"

"No, about those strange-looking fellows our coach near ran down."

"What about them?"

"I saw this odd couple before once, months ago."

"Out with the details."

"It'd been during one of my—*ahhh*, Dr. Tewes's forays to Cook County."

"Patients, were they? Begging outside the door, what?"

"Neither, as they were in the company of Shanks and Gwinn."

"Those two rat-tailed ambulance men who're in dire need of a shave, a haircut, and a bath?"

"The four of them . . . or rather three of the four had seemed in heated discussion and debate, while the bent over one played with a mouse he'd pulled from a pocket."

"A mouse? From his pocket?"

"Actually, it was this sight, the ungainly giant stroking the tiny mouse ears, that caught my attention. Otherwise, I'm quite sure I would not've begun to notice."

"Notice what exactly? What did you notice?"

"The gentleness of the bigger one, and the crudeness of the thinner one, the one in heated discussion. I'd not seen the brotherly resemblance before this moment, however. One seems most assuredly the keeper of the other . . . "

Am I my brother's keeper? Gabby mouthed but did not say.

The carriage driver had barked at the giant and his keeper, but he'd pushed on without stopping. They passed in an instant, and the images outside the window had changed with the moment like a wide-angled kaleidoscope. They'd almost instantly next rolled past the home of the eccentric Colonel Calvin Jamison Dodge, his lights out, no doubt resting comfortably from a long day of doing nothing. Jane gave a brief moment's thought, just about an eyelash in size, to ugly Calvin Dodge, who'd come to her for treatments to his face, insisting Tewes call him Cal. Nothing whatever in Jane's arsenal of concoctions collected as Dr. James Phineas Tewes could touch this man's condition, a condition killing him. He had the worst case of polyp cancer to the face and upper torso that she had ever witnessed. His case was so unique, so bizarre in fact, that she took him instantly to Dr. Fenger to ask if anything whatever might be done in a surgical way to relieve the poor man of such boils and pus-filled bulbs. Dr. Fenger had explained to them both that no surgical procedure could touch the problem.

Dodge confessed on the spot that his real name was Killough, and that his true family back in Ireland had for generations grown such ugly blossoms on their bodies. The old man had fallen into tears before the two "male" doctors, saying, "I've lived a lifetime under the curse and am not surprised it's finally overtaken me."

According to his family history, the Killough clan had been cursed by a witch put to the torch at the order of a great-great ancestor acting the cunning wise man of the village at the time but whose real purpose was to eliminate his competition for

anyone seeking medicinal cures. Ever since, according to the
old man, every family member had been afflicted. Calvin had
believed, as a young man, that he'd escaped the curse by putting an ocean between himself and Galway, but such diseases,
Jane knew, ran in families—indeed like a curse—so that no
amount of distance could have saved him from a festering
problem posited within his body, no doubt, at birth.

Calvin Killough "Dodge" was a pompous blowhard who'd
amassed a good fortune, and a man who dropped names as
others dropped coins from their pockets, all true, and yet he
was to be pitied. As he was alone, completely and absolutely, save for a son—a city alderman named Jared Killough,
as it happened—who seldom visited. The younger Killough
knew that an Irish name in Chicago politics went a great
deal further than the name of any Dodge, although the ability to dodge any question was essential for a politician's
long-term survival.

Although old Calvin spoke the names of every actor, poet,
author, artist, musician, and politician in Chicago from the
mayor down, none of these folk ever came to his door, nor
ever invited him out. This was as true of his son as it was the
actor Richard Herrick and the author Oscar Wilde. Calvin
claimed to know or have known every famous person who'd
graced the Chicago theater or walked her financial district.
Part and parcel of the disease of the mouth with Calvin, and
once he engaged a person, he spoke nonstop on the issues of
the day, the headlines, Washington D.C., the Senate, the
House, the Oval Office, not stopping for a breath, and allowing no listener to interject the least comment. And so Jane
had become fascinated on a professional level at such alacrity and ability to speak extemporaneously. She wanted to
find some pressure point on the man's cranium that might
stop his incessant tongue, if she could only hold out against
the sea of words spewing forth.

To date, she'd failed in this experiment she'd set for Dr.
Tewes's phrenological expertise. In the meantime, her own
brain had become jumbled full with Dodge/Killough nonsense layered with half-facts and half-truths. Jane learned if

she allowed Dr. Tewes to engage in conversation with "Cal," as they were fairly close neighbors, and as she'd made the crucial initial mistake of inviting him to sit for a cranial "reading," it was the devil to extract herself from this man's tidal wave of dribble.

Furthermore, Jane found it impossible to wring from him a single useful item, and it was near impossible to pull away from this verbal grappling hook once he tossed it about you, as the man talked machinelike on all manner of nontopics, from the thinness of the day's rays to the lack of ticking in his bed to the idle wisp of cobweb he could not reach with his broom

In the end, he was a sad old duffer, alone and lonely. And despite the rambling that came forth like a hydrant, Jane sensed that the colonel seemed bent on living a life of quiet desperation inside that large, dusty house of his. How he afforded his taxes and food and drink, she had no clue, as he seemed without income or checkbook or family other than the alderman.

Jane had learned that besides questionable "banking" practices, Calvin had earned what he had been living off for years from a cocaine-laced cough drop for children that made him a household name: Dodge's Throat Lozenges. But all had fallen on hard times when someone he'd lent most of his fortune to turned out to be a crooked land developer who was selling parcels of land he did not have title to in neighboring Iowa.

Now without employment, the mystery only thickened, until one day Alastair explained that the so-called colonel's income came from political funds from the city's Parks and Recreation director, who simply loved to hear the old man talk. This city worker provided for all his needs if not his wants, and kept him, so far, in his house by declaring it a Parks and Recreation structure. In the end, she decided this was all a front for money actually funneled from his son. No one could be sure of the exact particulars.

As Jane and Gabby alighted the cab that had stopped before the sign out front of their home, Jane read the deep-cut lettering in the wooden shingle: **DR. JAMES PHINEAS TEWES**.

She felt a chill that had come over her in the drafty coach

as it reached the nape of her neck again, licking animal-like at her spine.

"Are you all right, Mother?" asked Gabby as the coach rattled off from them.

"I know this feeling."

"What feeling?"

"And I know it shouldn't be ignored."

"You're tired, Mother."

"Refuses to be ignored. Something feels wrong in my bones."

"Oh, no. Here we go. It's Ransom again, isn't it?"

"Something to do with Calvin Dodge, actually."

"What about the odd duck?"

"Oh . . . I'm not sure . . . per . . . perhaps I'm just being foolish."

"Or like I said, perhaps it's the fatigue and culmination of a difficult day spent with a difficult man stuck in your head that you obviously love."

"I tell you it has naught to do with Ransom!" They remained on the porch, staring up at the half-moon together, Gabby lacing her arm through Jane's. Silence enveloped them save for the chirping crickets when they were startled by a cat that'd suddenly leapt atop a mouse.

After the fright, they laughed at their own silliness. "See, so often we fear ruinously," said Gabby, "fearing the wrong things, we human beings."

"I guess I'll then chalk it up to the spat I had with Alastair."

"And the fact he's not come 'round to apologize in all this time?" Gabby urged her mother through the door. "Get thee to a canopy bed!"

This made Jane laugh, as they'd just come from the theater and *Hamlet*, with Herrick in the lead role. Although much too old for the part, Herrick proved brilliance comes of experience.

She secretly wondered if quarreling with Alastair over Sam's circumstances had been the right thing to do.

A part of her wanted to get on the phone in the foyer to call Alastair. Another voice in her head pleaded otherwise, and she erupted with, "He made his bed, so he can just sleep in it."

CHAPTER 19

"**Good Gawd, I said I was sorry. You're right.**
Whatever it was that bothered you, about that, I mean, you
were right, Jane, *ahhh* . . . dear, sweet Jane. No, I am not
simply humoring you, Jane. Jane . . . Jane . . . I am trying, in
my way, to say . . . well, to apologize."

"Damn it, man, is't the best ya can do?" asked Philo Keane,
his Canadian accent creeping through from where he sat.
He'd pulled his plushest chair beside his gramophone, which
was softly playing a dirge so grim it would destroy the spirit
of a nightingale. From where he sat, Philo had been watching
Alastair before a full length spindle mirror practicing his apology—groveling—for Jane Francis Tewes. "You're a pitiful
poor man at saying sorry, Rance. Shall I demonstrate? Act as
your Cyrano?"

"What is that awful noise you've put on the grammie?"
Alastair asked instead.

"It's a march for a funeral, same as was played at the
mayor's turnout."

"Oh . . . and how did that go?"

"Your not being on hand, my friend, was duly noted by
your friend Kohler and others."

"No doubt he made spectacle of the fact to his superiors."

"Really, Rance, you give them more ammunition each day."

"I saw the mayor lying in state at his home. Enough good-bye for me."

"The night he was killed, sure."

"Kohler has, I suspect, put a Pinkerton agent on me."

"You mean as a partner?"

"I mean as constant bird dog."

"Are you sure?"

"I've had it from several sources now—one being Kohler himself. Fools are transparent when they open their mouths."

"Such utter, complete, pure scorn you two have for one another." Philo stood, went to a stack of "cuts" he'd recently made, fidgeted with them, studying each and frowning, up-set with the light here, the contrast there, the perspective, bullying himself about using the wrong lens or camera. Alastair saw him more an artist than a businessman, but the poor chap was in the throes of making a business of art, no easy task for anyone.

"Contempt is all I have for Kohler," replied Ransom. "Tell me, was William Pinkerton at the funeral?"

"He was."

"And did he and Kohler powwow?"

"A lotta palaver, yes, now you mention it."

"Curious." Ransom tugged at his chin stubble.

"You're like a thick-skinned scorpion, Rance."

"Whataya mean?"

"You get stepped on, look out." Philo kept his eyes on his reproductions as he spoke. "Even going down, you sting back. Is'at the plan?"

Ransom watched his friend's facial expression go from mild acceptance to prune-faced and finally to poisonously sour over the shots he'd taken of a beautiful creature, his lat-est model. At the same time as his eyes registered disdain for something he believed an error, and his countenance flashed these little telegrams to anyone bothering to notice, he chided Ransom further. "If only you and Nathan Kohler could harness the energy and passion of your hatred for one another."

"What?"

"You know, mass produce it! Like everyone's doing these days." He lifted an empty Pabst Blue Ribbon bottle to punctuate his point.

"Bottled hatred?" asked Ransom.

"Yah, and feed it to our army and navy! The U.S. would become the most powerful nation on earth—"

"It already is!"

"—and you'd be rich on the government contract for your elixir." Keane laughed aloud at his own words as if hearing a joke from another. "Think of the energy you two foes consume and expire with the level of ferocity you feel for one another." Philo lifted the print in his hand overhead and waved it with his words. "Why, it is an absolute fascination between you two—a . . . a . . . a . . . "

"Force of nature?"

"Nay, a pit the size of Hades itself."

"The Grand Canyon perhaps, but Hades?" Ransom laughed now.

"Why, it is an unholy, satanic, ultraplanetary fixation, Rance! An otherworldly obsession that will follow the two of you to Hell and beyond, so long as—"

"Enough of it!"

Philo dropped his photographs of Daphne Deland, a young protégé of a well-known stage actor. The young thing appeared bent on becoming an actress in her own right at any costs, and apparently, from all that Philo had told Ransom of Miss Deland, she paid well. Philo's singular thick brow lifted devilishly when he used the phrase "paid well."

"The kettle calls the pot black," muttered Ransom.

"What's'at?"

"Apparently, you've learned nothing of controlling your own passions when it comes to *commerce* with beautiful women, despite—" Ransom stopped in mid-sentence, realizing what he was about to say could only hurt his friend. "Why don't you put on some Wagner, something lighter, uplifting. I'm sick of that dirge."

"Despite what?" asked Philo, not allowing him free of the subject he'd started on. "The tragic death of the woman who took my soul to the grave with her?"

"Stop that or you'll make Emily Bronte's Heathcliff blush," joked Ransom.

"My soul match, she was."

"All true in your head. The woman could neither hear nor speak."

"Making her my perfect match. *Ahhh* . . . Miss Mandor. How awful that such beauty should die at the hands of a fiendish monster."

Ransom held up his brandy glass. "To the end of the Phantom of the Fair."

"Killed my fair lady." Philo dropped his photos and slumped into his chair. The dirge now played for Miss Chesley Mandor.

If Philo slowed enough to be self-observant, Ransom knew he might acknowledge the small part he'd played in the lady's death, a horrible murder that Keane'd been falsely accused of and arrested and jailed for.

But such was, although mere months ago, ancient history to such a mind as Philo's, Ransom decided, as obviously he was up to his old tricks. Ransom loved Philo as much as one man might another, and he'd do anything for him, but he also knew how fickle and short Keane's memory and alliances with women were. His professing love and passion for this soul mate now dead was more drama at this point than anything Alastair had ever seen off the Lyceum stage. Philo changed women as he did socks.

Philo quickly changed the subject on Ransom. "What've you uncovered in the Nell Hartigan case?"

"Precious little."

"Nothing more come of Dr. Fenger's autopsy?"

"She took a huge, nasty knife to the gut, which he's sure was the first blow. By all accounts, she was taken by surprise, else she knew her attacker and didn't expect or see it coming."

"I didn't know her personally, but her reputation makes her out both sharp and tough."

"She was both."

"Odd that she'd be working for Pinkerton."

"Not really. Women prove excellent spies, and basically what Pinkerton agents do is infiltrate and report. They learn the lay of the land and who the players are, as in who is heading up a proposed strike and where dynamite or nitro or the bodies are buried, or all three."

"I see."

"It's how countless strikes were put to bed before they began. Pinkerton, hired by the company, learned who the leaders were, and this information was handed over to police, and we made all manner of excuse, but we took them off the street."

"Isn't that somewhat illegal? Unconstitutional even?"

Ransom rubbed the bridge of his nose and forehead. "The labor wars got us all bending rules."

"Is that your term for the Constitution? Rules? Don't answer that, just tell me, you ever feel like a hired gun?"

Ransom dropped his gaze. "I did often, yes, back then."

"During Haymarket, sure. Whataya got lately to fatten your dossier on Haymarket?"

"Lost . . . all gone . . . a burglary."

"This is the first I've heard!"

"It's OK . . . it's my cover for where my files are kept—nowhere, Nothingville."

"*Ahhh . . . I see.*" *And little more than nothing in 'em*, Philo imagined.

"It's the bloody truth."

"Sorry if I am having trouble determining what is and what is not the truth coming from your direction," Philo said with a frown.

Alastair cleared his throat. "All of us in uniform were, in essence, working for the establishment. It's how the Chicago PD was formed—to protect the interest of big business."

"Civic lessons I got never touched on it," Philo said, smirking. "Hasn't changed much either, has it?"

"Some . . . we've had some important labor laws enacted, for instance."

"So you've skirted my question about the dead Pinkerton lady."

"Got damn little to go on in Nell's murder, but I have feelers out."

"Your little army of snitches?"

"My own operatives, yes."

"And so far? Nothing?"

"Nothing." Ransom stood and paced, fidgeting with his cane, shining the wolf's head with a handkerchief, and next toying with his pipe while staring out the window. He next tugged on his pocket watch, the gold fob shinning, checked the time, and then let it slip back into his vest pocket.

Finally, Keane asked, "Why do you think her organs were harvested?"

"Some medical purpose, I suspect."

"Ghouls! Do you mean to say . . . harvesting the living now? Not enough bodies in the cemeteries?"

"That or else someone is making a strange bisque somewhere."

"I wonder which of the two possibilities is worse?"

"Ghouls, I think the worse by far."

"How do you make that assessment?"

"Ghouls barter in bodies and body parts, while a cannibal at least is feeding a need."

"A perverse joke, Alastair."

"Doing it for money is the more perverse."

"You've known a few cannibals and ghouls," replied Philo. "You ought to know."

"A few cannibals, yes." He stopped to consider the horrid memory of having been attacked by a family of such fiends. "Shanks and Gwinn are supposedly reformed ghouls, a perfect pair to run that meat wagon of Fenger's up and down the street."

"The ambulance chaps? Once ghouls?"

"No one's ever proven it, and somehow Dr. Fenger got them off and employed them. Part of their deal is that they answer to Dr. Fenger."

"I see. I had no idea."

"Few do . . . believe me, and perhaps they have associates still active in their old profession."

"But will they be cooperative . . . with you in particular?"

"No. For some unaccountable reason, they dislike me."

"I can't imagine why."

The men laughed together. Each thought of the time when a wounded Alastair had kicked out the boards from the inside, locked as he was in the closed wagon they'd thrown him into, the wagon used to transport the injured and the dead to Cook County Hospital and Morgue.

"I must go see Pinkerton about those records. Thank you for the brandy, not sure about the music. You listen long enough to that dirge, Philo, and you'll become a sot."

Philo stopped the music, stood and walked Alastair to the door, where they warmly parted. After Ransom had gone, Philo toasted the air, chanting Miss Mandor's Christian name, Chesley . . . Chesley. He switched the dirge back on and sat in the grim aloneness within himself.

"I can't do this," he said aloud after long moments of reflection. He'd visited Chesley's grave every opportunity since she'd been so horribly mutilated. She was the only dead person he talked to, or ever had talked to. He got up and returned to his photographs and quickly, compulsively, forced his entire being to focus on the work and not his dead lover.

CHAPTER 20

Once again on the street, Alastair made his rounds. He was not foolish enough to keep regular or meticulous rounds, but rather, to mix them up so no one knew he had a routine. No one knew better than he that a routine could get a cop—even a detective—killed.

He caught a ride to an area of the city where, at this time of morning, he imagined Henry Bosch was sitting about a cracker barrel, pontificating on the virtues and vices of the Civil War generals Grant and Sherman, both of whom he'd formed lasting and firm opinions of during his days as a private in the big blue monster called the Federal Army.

When Alastair arrived, he was not disappointed, finding Bosch at Reach's corner grocery, bait and tackle, laundry and bathhouse. Old Mr. Bowman was known as Reach, as there was nothing that exceeded his reach in the city should it be requested of him. Reach Bowman said once of his clapboard establishment with his apartments overhead that a man could find everything but liquor and loose women on the premises, and he meant to keep it that way. He'd been among the teetotalers who'd marched on Little Chicago and helped burn out "that rabble" a decade before. Now he hobbled about with one hand on his back, the other on his Shalala, the crooked cane as gnarled as the crusty old shopkeeper. Reach and others huddled around the storyteller Bosch politely acknowledged Alastair as he came through the door, but Bosch paid no heed, continuing with his tale of Sherman.

"Swear . . . never seen a pair of eyes more striking."

"Striking in what manner?"

"Mad . . . fierce as flame . . . burn right through a man. He couldn't find a uniform to suit his scrawny, sickly frame, that General Sherman, and being as he was a general in the Federalist Army, he saw to having a tailor come to his tent to fashion a perfect uniform for his build and peculiar measurements, 'cause fellas, I am here to tell youse there was nothing on the man that matched its counterpart. One arm seemed longer'n the other, one hand bigger. Sure his face was cockeyed and off center, but so was his whole body."

"So he got himself a custom outfit at the army's expense?" asked one old duffer, tamping his pipe, his face as puckered and wrinkled as a raisin.

"He did indeed, and ordered several so as he could keep a cleaner appearance than Grant, which in fact was not hard for any soldier to do." Bosch paused, awaiting a laugh from his audience, but it did not come. "You see, when Grant saw himself in the mirror or in a photograph, he only saw what he wanted to see, and was pretty satisfied with the results, but ol' William Tecumseh Sherman, he'd seen a photograph of himself, taken with one collar up, one down, his stern face turned to an odd angle, and those wild unsettled eyes cut him to the quick. The image scared even him!" This got a laugh. "He looked every bit the reincarnated madman John Brown, he did."

Ransom leaned against the counter alongside Reach Bowman, taking a moment to hear Bosch out.

Bosch didn't skip a beat. "Sherman, he liked to tell folks he was a nice fella, a good fella."

"Was he affable off the battlefield?" asked one of the men.

"Oh, yes! An affable man, but a practical man as well. It was him put the bug in Grant's ear that this prisoner exchange business must stop!"

"Is'at so?"

"I never knowed that!"

"Thought it was Grant's idée."

"Thought it was Abe Lincoln's notion."

"They mighta said it was them," continued Bosch, "but it first come from Sherman. I tell you, the man was tough like a Jack Bull terrier, and smart like a fox. Some say that if he'd been in charge instead of Grant, the war woulda been won a year ahead."

"Think so?"

"I know so!" finished Bosch, turning in his seat to face Ransom. "Sherman was a lot like Inspector Ransom here. He generally got exactly what he wanted when he wanted."

"Like a set of custom uniforms," commented Bowman.

"Every one of his uniforms were shot to hell soon enough, though, smudged, torn, creased by gunfire. Why, once his coat was smoking, and then by cracky, he damn sure looked the part of Satan, just like the Georgians say."

This made them all laugh, and even Alastair joined in. "No one got a picture of that, heh, Bosch?" Alastair pushed off the counter.

"Not for lack of trying!" countered Bosch, standing and jamming his peg leg in tight and snug. "Sherman-the-German didn't take to the camera at all. Not many photos of 'im to be found, to my knowing, no."

"We need to talk privately," Alastair finally said, indicating a back room. Bowman nodded, and the general store crowd thinned, each man deciding he had something to attend to or somewhere to be. The bell on the door rang out repeatedly as Bosch's audience filed out.

"You sure can clear a room," Bosch said a little sadly.

"What? Those loafers? Bowman, did a man jack of them buy a single item this morning?"

Reach frowned and slowly shook his head to say no.

"Then I'd say the place needed a good clearing out!" Ransom indicated with a single finger that Bosch was to follow him.

* * *

In a moment Alastair was alone with Bosch. He got right to the point. "What news have you about Nell Hartigan's murder?"

"None that I can strictly attest to, just rumors."

"Then rumor away."

Money exchanged hands.

"Rumor has it there's a medical man who's working with Madam DuQuasi. She liquors a man up, the doctor arranges for his disappearance, and it's all a totem pole. Everyone being paid off to keep mum."

"How then did you come by the information?"

"One of Maude DuQuasi's girls."

"Why did she tell you this?"

"That old bitch DuQuasi put her out on the street for reasons she would not say."

"Then your informant has reason to lie, now, doesn't she?"

"I know when a common whore is telling me the truth and when she's lying, Inspector."

"Do you now?"

"She'd be wringing her petticoat or her hands if she were lying, and she'd be unable to look me long in the eye."

All techniques Alastair himself used in questioning a suspect. "All right then, let's assume she is telling the truth. Who is the doctor in question?"

"She didn't know his name, but she knows 'im by sight."

"I see." Alastair considered how he could use this information and possibly the prostitute to uncover the identity of this phantom doctor said to be harvesting people for his clinic. "There're hundreds of surgeons in the city."

"Your man, he's one of 'em, sure."

The ghoul theory was taking firmer shape in Alastair's head, as much as he wanted it to be untrue. "When and where did you meet with this lady of the night?"

"Early this A.M. She was wandering my alleyway just outside my window. She was in tears. I inquired from my basement window, and she dropped to sit, to get a better look at me and my place before agreeing to come down my stairwell and inside for warm bread and coffee."

"So you're now keeping a woman?"

"I am." Bosch beamed with pride in being able to convey this fact to Ransom. "I am." He thrust out his chest like a bandy rooster.

"You are some fool, Bosch! She likely's told you precisely what she thought you wanted to hear." Ransom snatched for the bill he'd handed Bosch, but Dot 'n' Carry, as he was called, reared back on his peg leg and jabbed Ransom in the gut with his cane. "I tell ya, the lass knows what she's talking about."

"The lass? How old is she?"

"No telling, maybe forty."

"Forty?"

"A good sight younger than myself, and so she's a lass. A spoiled dove, to be sure, but my spoiled dove."

For a half second Ransom gave a thought to his Polly, a reformed prostitute, dead now because she'd become his woman, a ready target for the Phantom killer of the fair, a maniac who'd do anything to hurt him. The bastard had succeeded at it, too.

"I'll want to talk to this spoiled dove of yours direct."

"Oh, no!"

"Bosch!"

"She's not going under no interrogation by the likes of you, Inspector."

"I'll be gentle with her."

"You mean you'll only singe her fingers and you won't burn off her eyebrows?"

"You know damn well I'll not harm her."

"People learn she's talked to you, she could wind up dead."

"What of you, Bosch? Why isn't that a worry for you, then?"

"It is a worry for me!"

"Oh? I hadn't noticed. I pay you, and you're at the races again, chasing a four-legged dream."

"One of these days, a six-legged horse, a creature of beauty like some flying unicorn, is gonna be born! That'd take the race, wouldn't it?" Bosch's eyes sparkled and his broken teeth shone whenever he spoke of the ponies.

"You ought to save up for the day they run a six-legged animal!" Ransom chuckled.

"But it's true, Inspector. I gotta be looking over my shoulder every second, even out at the racing meadow."

"Set up a meeting with the woman, Bosch."

"Where?"

"Where no one'll know or see or overhear."

"It'll cost you double, for her and for me."

"Done, just do it."

"All right, you needn't yell."

"You deaf old codger, how else am I to be heard?"

From Reach Bowman's place, Alastair made his way to the downtown headquarters of the Pinkerton Detective Agency, where he meant to locate William Pinkerton, son of the now famous Eye that Never Sleeps, now in perpetual sleep— Alan Pinkerton. Brothers William and Robert Pinkerton had inherited the old man's business on Alan's death in the spring of '84. These Chicago offices were housed in an old brownstone off Michigan Avenue in what amounted to a discreet building that might be taken for a bank except that a huge sign overhead shouted: THE PINKERTON AGENCY: WE NEVER SLEEP. The trademark eye stared down from the center of the wording.

In the 1880s, bank robberies were normally the work of what Ransom and Pinkerton called "yeggs." These yeggs hadn't the sense or ingenuity or finesse of criminals that gained the headlines, like Charley Bullard or Max Shinburn. They came out of hobo yards, the jungle of the disenchanted and the disenfranchised. Tramps often in desperate circumstances, they moved at night, selecting banks in small communities with few police if any. They used nitroglycerine or black powder on safes, and often with no criminal associates, they disappeared into the grim bleak world they'd stepped from. They proved near impossible to trace.

As a result of the rash of bank robberies popping up everywhere, Alan Pinkerton and his sons began their notion of charging banks for protection and placing their Eye Never Sleeps seal prominently in the window of any bank that paid for their services. Their guarantee of a centralized agency acting for all banks proved a powerful persuader. They took out ads and made it clear that they would run to ground *anyone* foolish enough to rob a Pinkerton Agency protected bank. And they had lived up to their word, their record most impressive. They were so successful, in fact, that soon banks without Pinkerton Agency representation became the softer targets and were robbed at a far more alarming rate. There were even stories of thieves returning money after the fact on learning the bank they stole from was a Pinkerton associated bank.

Ransom entered the Pinkerton building and found the elevator going up. He continued his reverie of Pinkerton accomplishments as he did so. Another profit business for the most famous private eye firm in the world was supplying watchmen for strikebound plants, rail yards, mines, and corporations like Pullman City. The notion longstanding was that in such matters as labor disputes, the law and government protect the lives and property of the owners and non-union workers against the "anarchist" horde. If local law failed to do so, owners called in private armies for protection. Since 1859 the Pinkertons had hired men at an enticing five dollars a day to stand and protect property and people, and depending on the size of the plant, this could range from twenty to three hundred hired guards. In seventy-seven strikes in all those years, only three strikers were killed by Pinkerton agents.

William Pinkerton, however, once confided in Ransom, "We never looked for any strike work."

"No, really?" Ransom asked at the time.

"It's just something that was thrust upon us, kinda grown around us."

"You've a remarkable record nonetheless," said Ransom.

In 1888, only five years before, the Pinkertons played a

major role in the great CB&Q—Chicago-Burlington &
Quincy—railroad strike, one of the most stubbornly con-
tested battles in the history of the labor struggles. The president of the Knights of Labor, much later at a Senate hearing
on the matter, charged the Pinkerton operatives with incit-
ing riots, murdering strikers, and setting dynamite charges,
only to blame workers. Ransom had done an investigation
of the charges for the senator from Illinois and found the
charges leveled at the Pinkertons completely fabricated and
unfounded—*at least in this case*.

"We act as watchmen," Pinkerton had told the Senate during hearings, "guards only, and never has a Pinkerton ever
sat down at a striker's job and done the work of a striker. We
are not in the business of taking jobs and food out of the
mouths of the workingman. In that sense, we are not strike
breakers but mere policemen."

Ransom knew the Pinkerton policy. Before they would
send a single man into the danger zone, the local sheriff or
high authority must swear every man jack-of-'em in as dep-
uties, as the local peacekeepers. It was a stroke of genius.
"For now we could," as William had testified, "conduct ourselves in a lawful way."

The elevator opened on a hallway and a door facing him,
again with the big single eye staring him down.

On the inside, once Ransom finally found his way to the
hefty William Pinkerton's office, he received a cool recep-
tion from everyone on the floor, including an Italian courier
leaving with a sealed envelope, a lunch counterman carrying
in sandwiches, and the black janitor with mop and bucket.
Alastair nervously realized that any one of them—courier,
counterman, janitor—could be incognito as a Pinkerton
eye.

CHAPTER 21

Ransom had told Pinkerton that he'd want records on Nell's current cases, to understand why she was on the street the night she was fated to die. But now, standing in Pinkerton's line of fire, leaning in the doorway as Pinkerton paid the sandwich man, Ransom thought the look on his face was one of an animal caught off his territory, yet the man was in his office!

"I wasn't expecting you," he said.

"Oh, but it's been two days and nights, and having not heard from you, sir—"

"But I was told you'd been taken off the case; that they needed you for more pressing matters."

"Odd . . . no one's told me so."

"*Ahhh* . . . I suppose I was being soaped then by someone."

"I'd say so."

"Still . . . so soon, Inspector," he said.

"The sooner I see those records, the sooner I may find a lead and uncover who is behind Nell Hartigan's murder."

"We all want that, yes, of course . . ." Pinkerton hesitated, coughing into a handkerchief, complaining of being under the weather. He stood, paced to the window, pulled a sash tight, tying it off, and next opened a window, jammed his hands out into the air and rubbed them together, nervously looking out, back in, around the room, until he spied a crooked picture and began fidgeting with this. It was a picture of his thick-bearded father, founder of the agency, beside a separate autographed photo of Abraham Lincoln with the American flag as backdrop.

"Mr. Pinkerton, is there something troubling you?"

"Why, no!" He put on a disingenuous smile before dropping back into his seat. "It's just that the records you want . . . there is a sensitive matter attached, you see, and I can't have just anyone privy to—"

"I am not just anyone," interrupted Ransom.

"Of course not. You are perfectly right, sir."

"Where, then, are the records? Nell's notes on her current cases?"

"They've . . . quite frankly . . . It—It's embarrassing, but they've disappeared."

"Disappeared?"

"Like smoke, yes, quite the mystery."

"Did you have a break-in? Were the notes stolen along with other files? Did you report it?"

"No, nothing like that. Look, every agent has his or her own method of working, and Nell was known for working not out of the office but out of her head. Was a joke around here. Nell worked 'outta her head'—get it?"

"Funny." But Ransom returned to the file. "An inside job, you think? Are you interrogating your people?"

"I am, yes."

"Sounds like any 'notes' will go to Nell's grave with her."

"We believe, that is, it's possible she never filed reports on her current case, else it's clerical error and in time they will surface."

"Clerical error?"

He shrugged. "Wrong file, and if you look around, you see the extent of our files."

"The file is lost in the files?"

"If it exists at all, yes. I'm sorry."

"Then speak to me. Tell me what's in her notes. What was she working on when she died?"

"All right, I'll tell you what little I know, but first, you of all people, you must know it is both a boring and a precarious life, being a detective."

"What's that got to do with—"

"Nell did countless, countless jobs for us; I can't begin to enumerate the many midwestern holes she traveled to where she infiltrated, living in the boardinghouse, playacting as a penniless drifter, having the occasional drink with strikers, learning their plans, usually with Frederick or another operative playing pool at the billiard table. She had never compromised her cover, not once. The chief duty of an undercover operative is to act as part of an intelligence group gathering information. She was in the early, early stages of this case, and pretty much on her own."

"Too premature to write down? Is that what you're saying?"

"Exactly."

"But you must have some inkling of what she was working on, right?"

"*Ahhh* . . . yes and no."

It seemed another hedge. *Why isn't Pinkerton leveling with me?* he wondered. "Then just tell me as much as you know of her footsteps," suggested Ransom, his frustration rising like a tide.

"OK . . . all right . . . but you are sworn to secrecy."

"My right hand to the Bible, my sainted mother's curse on my head if you wish."

"All right, but this can't get out to the papers or the street."

"You have my word. Go on." *This better be good*, Ransom thought.

"Nell was on to a couple of interesting threads. . . . *ahhh,* leads. She was watching closely the firemen and the switchmen, expecting a strike any day."

"Firemen? Switchmen? They are a pretty settled group since the CB&Q settlement, aren't they?"

"There's always discord with some groups."

Ransom jotted notes to himself. "You said she was on to a few leads. Anything else?"

"She thought she was on to a series of strange disappearances."

"Really? Strange disappearances?"

"People vanishing off the street, yes, but her partner, Frederick Hake, a good man with more experience, counted the so-called disappearances as simply disenchanted folk who had moved on, gone west."

"I see." Gone west was a street term for gone south—six feet under south. "Do go on."

"Well . . . from all accounts, these were people not missed."

"Not missed?"

Pinkerton pointedly replied, "*Not-missed-by-anyone-whatsoever.*"

"If that were the case, Nell, Fred, you—now me—none of us would be speaking of them, now would we?" Ransom pointedly asked.

"See Webster's dictionary for derelict," Pinkerton said with a smirk.

"All of them derelicts?"

"And strays."

"Deviants, perverts?"

"Exactly."

"The sort who're invisible to City Hall and most of the population?"

"Precisely."

"And the police commissioner? And Chief of Police Nathan Kohler? Do they know about this?" Ransom watched closely for any sign of Pinkerton's reaction to the name, but either Pinkerton was cool or he had no hidden agenda involving Kohler.

"I know of your difficulties with your chief, Inspector, that there is bad blood between you."

"Spilt blood is more apt, but that wasn't the question."

"You have my word as a gentleman and a professional, sir, that I will not get between the two of you."

"Is that what you told Kohler?"

"In more words and with more passion, yes. But he relates some horror stories about you, I must say."

Ransom wondered if this were the reason for Pinkerton's extreme nervousness, but it did not fit with the man's reputation to show the least fear. "You've something of a reputation yourself, William."

"I do, yes."

"Your having personally overseen that case out in Aurora, unearthing a huge cache of explosives meant to destroy tracks, bridges, and blow engines off the rails."

Pinkerton smiled for a brief moment. "Don't leave out the kegs 'pon kegs of illegal whiskey!" He laughed raucously. "My, but I miss my time in the field, I do. I envy you that kind of . . . freedom."

"You put those bastards away for two years in Joliet." Ransom continued to butter up the other man.

"I did that, yes, and all the while the labor people charging us with fabricating the whole thing, of planting evidence!"

"You were cleared of all the nonsense charges. Even the men you arrested testified on your behalf, that you got them fair and square."

"All true, but it didn't stop the next rumor, that those men were paid to be complimentary. Then it *evolved* that they were in fact Pinkerton operatives paid to do jail time!"

"Ridiculous the conspiracy theories that float 'round here."

"Hey, it is Chicago."

A long moment of silence settled between them. Pinkerton finally stopped tapping his desk with a pencil and said, "The worst thing on earth for a man like you and me is to be saddled to a desk all day. Where's the success and freedom in that? Where's the reward?"

The man is as slippery as a wet eel, Ransom thought. Hard to pin down to specifics, for sure. Pinkerton had successfully avoided his more serious questions, and then the private eye had the audacity to ask, "Is it true that you doused a man with kerosene during a secret interrogation? An anarchist?"

"That much is true."

"Then set the man afire?"

"That's the lie."

"OK, I can accept that, but more recently, did you literally drop a suspected garroter into that lake out there to drown alive?"

"Wild speculation."

"Your chief has a vivid imagination?"

"And a memory that picks and chooses amid the truth. It amounts to half-truth, and outright lie."

"Nothing substantial, heh? Nothing to hold up in a court of law?"

"Look, I could ask you why there's so much blood on the banks of the Monongahela, huh? But I won't."

Pinkerton blanched white at the mention of last year's botched strike job, the one that had made up the collective Pinkerton mind to once and for all get out of the strike-breaking business, thereby honoring his father's last wish.

"But I rather doubt," continued Ransom, "you want to talk about that."

"Robert and I gave in our testimony and opened our records to the Senate and were cross-examined by the subcommittee. Homestead is over and so is our ever again hiring out watchmen in such a situation."

"Sounds like everyone at Homestead learned his lesson, but it takes cases that blow up in your face to prove the need for good records—detailed, written records."

"I doubt you could understand the depth of this agency's sorrow over Monongahela. Why, we lost more operatives that day than in all our history."

"So . . . getting back to Nell's project here in Chicago?"

"Good call, 'project.' She chose to work on it against my wishes, against Fred's judgment as well, on her own time."

Finally . . . a break in the man's armor.

CHAPTER 22

Ransom paced about William Pinkerton's office now, taking in the historic photos lining Pinkerton's walls. "I have a photographer friend who would find these shots of great interest."

"Bring him 'round sometime."

Chummy all of a sudden. *The man is hiding something,* Ransom decided. "I take it Nell's pet project didn't bring in any revenue?"

"None whatever."

"And your agency, is it paid, in certain instances, to look the other way?"

"To remain in business in Chicago—any business—you know that is par for the course, that the city is for sale and all its services are for sale, including City Hall, or perhaps because the sales stem from the top."

"Then you are paying tithes to City Hall to operate out of here?"

"Aren't we all? Your paycheck, Inspector, where does it derive from? Graft is the heart's blood of Chicago just as surely as New York."

"But Nell wanted to investigate anyway—after you gave her this or a similar lecture?"

"You're an astute man, Inspector."

"But you didn't think she'd get far with it before you'd swamp her with directed work."

"But she surprised me, yes. Tenacious little Nell. Like a big cat on the scent."

"You had strong feelings for her?"

"I did."

"Did those feelings translate into actions?"

"That's really none of your business, sir."

"In a murder investigation, sir, not answering a question speaks volumes."

"Yes, I suppose I know that."

"Tells me enough that I can surmise."

"All right, yes, I was secretly seeing her, but my family cannot know of it, do you understand?"

Another layer of worry on the man, thought Ransom. "I do understand the need for discretion, and they'll not hear it from me, but by the same token, we need to trust one another, Mr. Pinkerton, if we're to be an effective team. I won't harm you, your reputation, or your family, and you won't go behind my back to Nathan Kohler."

"A fair deal, then, we've struck."

"Done. Now, tell me what Nell Hartigan was working on so . . . so diligently."

"And blindly," he added.

"You're still saying nothing. Look, William—you asked me to find and put away Nell's killer, but you tie my hands."

"As we discussed, th-the victims, she theorized, were of lowliest standing."

"I got that."

"Not only did they go unnoticed, even by law enforcement people like yourself, Inspector, but missed by no one."

"Ahhh . . . the sort of vermin no one wants in the city to—"

"To begin with."

"—to begin with." They finished in unison. "But William—Bill—you're not of that opinion, are you?"

"Of course not, but then again, are you going to stand here and tell me, Inspector, that you've never wished the . . . the vermin away?"

"Is there some sort of involvement here between surgeons, ghouls who supply them with fresh cadavers, and . . . and City Hall? That Carter Harrison knew of these shenanigans along with others?"

"Absolutely not! That is to say City Hall looks the other way on such matters, and . . . "

"And like God, hasn't time for details?"

"It's not a conspiracy toward genocide or racial cleansing as in the time of the Romans!"

"And your agency, you were asked to pay no attention to the needs of the medical community here?"

His silence was his answer. Alastair remained on the attack, pursuing this line of questioning. "But your own Nell strongly disagreed?"

"That's the gist of it, yes."

"I see, and you tried to get her to stop snooping into this matter?"

"I threatened to fire her, yes, if she didn't cease and desist."

"Looks like someone made sure she did—cease and desist, I mean." Ransom thought of how often now he'd tried to convince Jane to end her Tewes act, and how resistant she'd become as a result. The more he argued, the more entrenched she'd become on the subject. Was it a woman thing? Was it like this between Pinkerton and Hartigan?

"I'm committed to finding those responsible for Nell's death," Bill Pinkerton said. "Rest assured. I'm no longer taking payoffs on behalf of the city doctors or anyone else."

"That's got to be a comfort to Nell." It was a mean thing to say, and Ransom wished he'd snatched it back before it got said, but too late. The words floated between them, and William Pinkerton's eyes glazed over with wet tears he now dabbed at. Ransom sensed his tears genuine. "I want a list of the doctors you had an arrangement with."

"You know," he sadly said, "I loved her, but if this gets out, a lot of lives are ruined, and—"

"I understand. Seems to me you've been influenced heavily to believe in the scientific need here—"

"The advancement of science at all cost, yes! Isn't it what that entire World's Fair was about? The advancement of man's knowledge, skills, tools, industry, medicine?"

"Too bad it paid so little heed to our failure to advance in morality and the warding off of evil." Ransom didn't know what else to say; he understood how the man must feel over the loss of Nell. Alastair recalled how he'd himself fallen apart on seeing his Polly murdered by a fiendish monster when the big fair was hardly under way. But all he could offer the grieving William Pinkerton was, "By all accounts, she was a fine example of womanhood, Nell was."

Pinkerton began jotting down words on a pad of paper. "She was. Had substance. But I'm a married man . . . with children."

"Say no more on it. More important to me are your impressions and feelings surrounding her case. Who did she have in her gun sight?"

"Here's a list of names you may wish to pursue."

Ransom accepted the handwritten note, a mere list that Pinkerton had quickly scribbled. "Good, at last . . . getting somewhere."

"The last I know, she'd been pursuing this strange little fellow Tewes and Insbruckton."

The list was long, extensive, and ridiculous. Half the names, Ransom knew to be honorable men, and one an honorable woman. Even Dr. Christian Fenger was on the list. When Ransom called Pinkerton on this, citing that Fenger had no lack of fresh cadavers to work with, Pinkerton snatched the list from him and scratched the name off, muttering, "Somewhat dated list. Dictated to me by Nell over the phone. Sorry."

"Dr. Raymond Ian Benson Sutherland? No way anyone connected with Northwestern University has a problem getting honest cadavers donated to that institution. Hell, the alumni are known for giving their last penny and their hides."

Again the name was marked off.

"Anyone else?"

Ransom called out six more, and all were scratched from the list without the slightest hesitation on Pinkerton's part. Those remaining, aside from Tewes and a Dr. White Insbruckton of the Oaklawn-Holyhoke and Insbruckton Institute of Surgical Medicine, were:

> Dr. Morris Brashler, GP and Surgeon, private clinic
> Dr. Stanislaus Czerniuk, a Bohemian doctor, private
>   clinic
> Dr. James Phineas Tewes, magnetic healing, Phrenolo-
>   gist, sometime surgeon, private clinic
> Dr. Albert J. Sikking, surgeon, Chicago Pediatric Hospital
> Dr. Kenneth Mason, surgeon & instructor, Glenhaven
>   Medical School
> Dr. and Dean Nehemmia Conklin, Mason's dean at
>   Glenhaven

"We can mark off Dean Nehemmia Conklin and Dr. Kenneth Mason now as well," said Pinkerton.

"Oh, how so? Isn't Glenhaven a struggling upstart of a school out West?"

"It is, but they've brokered a deal with Joliet for bodies."

"The prison?"

"Yes, you don't get bodies from City Hall."

"Are you intentionally making me laugh? Is this even legal? Are the prisoners involved willingly signing over their bodies?"

The two experienced lawmen exchanged a knowing grin once Pinkerton fully realized what Ransom had hinted at, that convicts were easily coerced.

Ransom added, "In the end, it's the legislature that must decide this issue of consigning over prisoner remains to medical schools."

"All the same, a deal's been struck, and our views are no matter. Don't waste your time here. Mason and Conklin are no longer a concern."

Ransom relented, saying, "No longer in your collective *eye*, heh?"

"Exactly," and Pinkerton drew a line through these two names. "This leaves only a handful that Nell had her roving eye on."

"Until she was murdered."

"I'd urge you to look first at Insbruckton," repeated Pinkerton. "Rather a queer fellow in my estimation, but then again . . . there's something not quite square with this Tewes chap either."

"You don't say. So Nell suspected a doctor named White Insbruckton and perhaps this mentalist and fraud Tewes?"

"Tewes is on more than one of our lists here. We suspect him of a double life."

"What? What do you mean?"

"Like that fellow Holmes, we suspect Tewes is an alias of some sort."

"Have you any proof?"

"Fellow's cagey, but no. Not yet. Still, Tewes strikes me as being in a category with Holmes."

"That pharmacist who claims to be a doctor?"

"We suspect that Holmes is an alias for Mudd, his real name, but so far we've not been able to conclusively connect the names." Pinkerton sighed heavily at this. "I have a bad feeling about that man."

"Then why isn't Holmes on this list?"

"Every operative we've sent into that place, including one as a plumber, insists there are no operating tables or slabs on which to carve bodies up."

"Hmmm . . . I see, but there are such facilities at the other private clinics?"

"Yes . . . yes there are."

"*Hmmm* . . . I've been in Tewes's clinic and I saw nothing whatever in the way of an operating room."

"Basement, we suspect."

"Really. It would seem a dirty place to operate on a man."

"But not on a corpse."

"Hmmm . . . will have to be more vigilant there."

"No one was more vigilant than Nell. Be careful."

"And Insbruckton? Never heard of him."

"Do you know every surgeon in the city?"

"I guess not."

"He operates a school southwest of downtown, on Ashland Avenue."

"Far out."

"He's trying to compete with the majors and finding his chances dismal. Northwestern, Cook County, Fenger's school—Rush College. The big medical schools outstrip any school that comes up against 'em; they attract the best students, and they have a far better money base and business sense."

"It doesn't hurt County and Rush to have Fenger on staff," added Ransom. "The man is legend."

"Understand he's managed to keep you alive more than once."

"True . . . quite true."

"The deal he cut with the police department for cadavers, unclaimed victims, well, it was a stroke of genius."

"Some say every scalpel stroke he takes is genius."

"So I've heard. Fortunately, I've never required his services."

"So Nell had her eye on this fellow Insbruckton."

"Nell kept most of it in her head. She left scant few details."

"Then I'll amass what I can on Insbruckton and hope we can do her memory justice."

"And what is justice for you, sir?"

Ransom met the other man's eyes, and he knew that if left to his own devices, William Pinkerton would take out his own brand of justice on Nell's butcher.

Pinkerton had taken a liking to Ransom after their talk, and so it being just past noon, he talked Alastair into having lunch with him in his office. "The counterman's brought up enough for six hefty fellows," he'd said. When Ransom declined and tried to pull away, Pinkerton insisted so strongly that he'd relented. Once lunch was finished, Ransom stood to go.

"I wish you well, and of course, all of us at the agency want to see Nell's killer caught, tried, and hung."

Alastair reached across Pinkerton's desk and nameplate and briskly shook the famous detective's hand, each man's grip rivaling the other. Alastair had a great deal of respect for the Pinkerton dynasty. They had ended the careers of untold criminals of every stripe, from rapists and murderers to con men and embezzlers and bank and train robbers. They'd made life hell for such desperados as Jesse and Frank James, and Butch Cassidy and his Hole in the Wall gang, so much so that their reward on Jesse James's head had gotten him killed, and Frank James had given himself up, while Butch Cassidy with Harry the "Sundance Kid" Longbaugh had left the continent for South America, where they'd reportedly been killed in a gun battle with Federales.

"You think or you know that Nell followed Insbruckton that night?"

"She claimed . . . that is, she felt that she was getting close, yes."

"I'll pick up where she left off," he again assured Pinkerton.

"Careful, then. If Nell didn't see that knife coming, no one could, Ransom. Not even you. Whoever Insbruckton is—as it could be an assumed name—and whoever he has working for him, that man is deadly and as fast as a viper."

"Thanks for the warning."

"Of course, if we learn any more in the meantime, I'll keep you apprised."

Like you've done so far? wondered Alastair, still sensing that Pinkerton was holding back. Something in the eyes, the speech, the way he moved, told Alastair's trained sense and experience that the man was hiding *something*. Strange, he thought, if he so loved the woman, then why was he holding back? And what was he holding back? Ransom instantly believed Nathan Kohler was somehow involved, along with large sums of money. All speculation, but speculation based on years of know-how when it came to interrogating suspects—not that this had been an interrogation or that Bill Pinkerton could be construed at the moment as a suspect in

Nell's death, but Ransom also knew that a chasm of guilt had come of this man's passion. He himself had been there; he understood it completely.

Did Pinkerton simply feel guilty in losing a valued partner in the business of the hunt, his operative, as he had lost his partner Griffin Drimmer sometime back? And if so, was it based on Pinkerton's not backing her a hundred percent in her clandestine endeavor to uncover this man Insbruckton? Or was there more to Pinkerton's guilt? As there had been more to Philo's and his own guilt in the death of Chesley Mandor and Polly Pete at the hands of the Phantom last spring? Murdered in large part to cripple him, Ransom knew. Could there be a similar situation at heart in Nell's murder? Had someone done her in to hurt William Pinkerton, knowing of his fondness for Nell? To bring the man in line? To terrify him and control him?

Blackmail by murder?

All these thoughts bulleted through Ransom's head as he again shook Pinkerton's hand and made for the door. He could not put such devilish acts past Chief Kohler; the man was without remorse, knew nothing of regret, and had no association with pity, yet his mother's name must be *Guile*— a cunning, deceitful, treacherous man born of Guile, who had particular skill in plunging the tender hooks into a man—even a man of William Pinkerton's stature, or perhaps because of his social rank and standing. That was Nathan Kohler. The man had perfected his cleverness to a magician's trick, and Ransom had seen him, on occasion, take a dislike to an officer under his command and reduce the poor fellow to a quivering mass of nerves.

While Pinkerton outwardly did not appear a quivering fish on a hook, the moment Ransom closed the private eye's door, he decided that fat William had somehow become pinned butterfly fashion on Nathan's wall. He had to know, what Kohler used for leverage against the detective.

In the meantime, he'd go in search of a certain Dr. White Insbruckton.

CHAPTER 23

Before going to see Dr. White Insbruckton, Ransom paid a visit to Frederick Hake, Nell's partner, who had stood out as absent in all this affair. It took Ransom all of two sentences to determine that Hake was no friend of Nell's or the agency, as he'd been fired for not being at her back that night. Disgruntled and upset, all the man had to offer were a fistful of insults for all involved. "Curb your tongue and tone it down, sir, or I'll have you run in for public indecency," Ransom told him.

"Public indecency? You? I've seen the file they have on you over at the agency! Ha! You arrest me for pub—"

Ransom handcuffed the man to the steam pipe in his apartment. "I'll leave you here to burn if you fail to answer me straight."

"All right . . . all right! What's it you wanna know about Nell and Pinkerton and her little pet project?"

"I know all about that! Damn you, man! What's this about a file Pinkerton has on me?"

"Pinkerton's got a file on everyone. It's no big secret."

"Why is he gunning for me?"

"He's got a payroll to make, and bringing down a dirty

cop . . . well, let's just say that City Hall and your superiors'd love to see it."

"Bastards. Are they tailing me routinely?"

"You're a hard man to tail."

"How do you know?"

"I was put on your scent like a bird dog for days."

"When?"

"When they feared you'd find a way to murder that Phantom of the Fair guy. Frankly, I didn't care for the duty."

"And before the Phantom case? Anything?"

"No, they come to us after that lad you killed disappeared."

"What evidence do you have, Hake, that I killed anybody while on duty?"

"None. We came up empty-bloody-handed."

"Off duty, then?"

"Won't ya now unchain me and turn off the damn heat?"

The moment the man relaxed, he got a burn.

"Off duty!"

"None! Nothing, I tell you."

"Yet they're running a dossier on me?"

"Your boss—"

"Kohler, yeah, I smelled the rat in this infestation."

"He won't let up; he keeps coming back at Pinkerton, throwing more and more money at him. And you throw a little my way, and I'm your Pinkerton agent here out, Inspector."

"What good can you do me, Hake? A man who couldn't back up his own partner?"

"How's this? I know the money Kohler is throwing at Pinkerton is coming from another source."

"Really?"

"A sawbuck and I'll give you my thoughts on it, but damn it, man, pull me loose from here!"

"How do I trust a thing you say?"

"Henry Bosch!"

"What's Bosch to do with it?"

"He'll vouch for me! He'll recommend me. We've talked about it."

"Lying roach bastard."

"What?"

"Bosch isn't in the habit of sharing funds with anyone, and you being on my payroll would only cut into his habit money."

"Horses is how we hooked up! We're thick as . . . that is, we're going into business together. He's got respect for a retired Pinkerton agent."

Ransom remained dubious. "I want to hear this money man's name, and if it is who I suspect, then we have us a deal, Mr. Hake."

"Excellent, Inspector, excellent."

"Say it; speak the name."

Ransom meant to kick the man's teeth in if it were the wrong name, say Tewes or the deputy mayor, both of whom he trusted, or something equally ridiculous such as Philo Keane or Dr. Christian Fenger.

"The moneybags is Senator Chapman."

It was the name he expected. "We're in business, Mr. Hake, and from here out, you are watching my back, but ever I should suspect you of pointing a gun to my back, you can count yourself among all those you've heard that I have sent to the deep."

It stood to reason, Senator Chapman and Chief Kohler, both of whom Ransom knew to be murderers in their own right. Ransom had seen the results of Chapman's rage and vengeance in his stables out in Evanston, but he'd no way of proving it so long after the fact now, even though Jane had been with him at the time. However, it appeared that both Nathan and Chapman weren't sleeping nights, worrying that one day Alastair Ransom and Jane Francis Tewes would find a way to indict them on murder in the Leather Apron affair.

To this end the cold blooded pair had hired the "Eye that Never Sleeps" to watch over Ransom's every move. Fortunately, that eye had been the bumbling stick of a man, Frederick Hake, the cut of his jib so common that he could, with his guile, fit into any street, alleyway, or wharf scene and never be seen. Perhaps, one day, Hake now on his side, dangerous as that might be, Ransom thought he might well find a good use for him. God knows Nell had none the night she was butchered. Hake, unlike Bosch in so many ways, expressed no sorrow or regret whatsoever over Nell, and Ransom guessed him the sort of man who could feel little and perhaps naught at all. Such a fellow could be called on in a pinch to do the dirtiest of jobs, but could he be trusted to keep his mouth shut?

For now, Ransom told him, dig up all you can on a Dr. White Insbruckton and deliver it to me tonight at Moose Muldoon's, last seat at the rear.

"I know." It was the creepiest *I know* Ransom had ever heard, realizing that this piece of human vomit had been at his back for some time now. "Told Nell we need to focus on you, not some fool notion about street vermin disappearing for cadavers."

"What'd she say to that?"

"She fought tooth and nail with Pinkerton for his having taken on your case, but the money was good, very good."

"I can imagine." And Alastair did imagine. He made a mental list of all those in Chicago who'd like to see Inspector A. Ransom dragged into a courtroom, pronounced guilty of heinous crimes of murder, and sentenced to die.

Dr. W. Insbruckton proved a cagey fellow. He gave Ransom a full tour of his school and labs and operating theater. Something about the man gave Ransom an instant dislike, and while he could not put his finger on the cause of this extreme and immediate reaction to Dr. White Insbruckton, he felt it as strongly as a wall of exuding odors emanating from a public toilet that he had encountered at the Chicago World's Fair one night. Except that the overwhelming odor of urine was replaced by formaldehyde and certain tinctures that, even with his experience, Ransom could not place.

Insbruckton struck a calm and calculated pose. He'd instantly taken to Alastair, saying, "I am so pleased the distinguished local constable should visit us at Oaklawn Hospital, way out here. Always a comfort to know," he added, "that an organized force of constables, such as yourself, sir, operate in the district, yes . . . yes, indeed. You must meet my assistant, Dr. Robert Weinberg, our orderlies, our students."

Bullshit, thought Ransom.

"So good of you to take an interest in our struggling, young surgical school. Of course, we are extremely conscious of the need for law and order here, and sir, be assured if ever there is any way that Holyhoke Hospital of Oaklawn can repay your going out of your way for our benefit, rest assured, the rewards can be great."

"I see you've familiarized yourself with our ways, here in Chicago," said Ransom, not missing a beat at the man's clumsy suggestion of a bribe.

"Adapt or die, as they say; adaptation is the name of the game, isn't it, Constable?"

"Inspector . . . Inspector Ransom."

"Of course, and you've come to 'inspect' us."

He pushed a rolled stack of bills into Ransom's hand. Alastair did not decline or balk, realizing he must go along to ingratiate himself with the good doctor, who now expected him to disappear.

"I'd like to see your morgue, sir. Where you keep the cadavers."

"Really?"

"Yes."

"It's like any other morgue."

"You've taken to refrigeration compartments? How adequate is your space? Are you being careful that disease cannot be spread here? What precautions are you taking to safeguard the health of your students, not to mention staff and yourself, Doctor?"

"You really are an inspector, aren't you, sir?"

"That I am."

He went for deeper pockets, bringing out his wallet.

"No, no more money . . . not now," said Ransom. "Part of my report has to be on your facilities. It's necessary that I see everything."

"Everything?"

"The kitchen sink, everything, yes."

"You realize we've not been in business long."

"I'm not interested in shutting you down, Doc. I shut you down, I get no more scratch, right?"

"Of course, of course."

"Besides, I am not an unreasonable, unfeeling chap. I know I've got to give a thought to your lads."

"Lads?"

"Your students, that is. All things considered, what I've seen so far has impressed me."

"Really?"

"As have you, sir."

"I see."

"Now how's about a look at the morgue, and where do you keep the spare parts, you know, organs and such?"

"Ahhh . . . this way."

The doctor led him into the bowels of the labyrinthine brownstone that'd been converted into Oaklawn-Holyhoke Hospital and the Insbruckton Institute for the Advancement of Surgical Medicine on Holyhoke Street. Ransom could smell the decay long before they arrived at the morgue.

"You really ought to keep it cooler down here," he calmly remarked while his mind screamed. Finally, he added, "A bit rancid, wouldn't you say, Doc?"

"We've had some problems with the refrigeration unit, but that's been repaired. How . . . how often do you intend on inspecting, Inspector?"

"Once, maybe twice a month. My family hasn't had a vacation in some time," lied Ransom.

"I see." Ransom thought he heard the man gulp.

Inside the morgue, Ransom looked at each face on each cadaver. All of them had been surgically worked over far too many times. Not one face was recognizable as a result; in fact, each looked as if made of caked mud, straw, and leather.

No eyes remained in the blackened pruney-looking faces that'd fallen in on themselves like spoilt fruit. Only empty eye sockets filled with the void of death looked back at Ransom. These corpses had not an inch of suppleness remaining of the skin and frame. If it were not for the skeletal centers, they would not be intact at all. Each felt to the touch like long dried tobacco leaves and as brittle as ancient parchment. Limbs were set in all manner of impossible poses, as time after time each cadaver had been used up by successive waves of surgical students.

"Have you not one or two fresh corpses to work with?"

"No one wants to donate his corpse to science. Getting raw material is our most difficult task."

"The slaughterhouse doesn't lack for raw materials."

"It's not the same, dissecting a sheep or a goat," Insbruckton complained. "That's child's play."

"Hmmm . . . yeah, seem to remember cutting up a chicken myself once to see what made it tick—when I was a kid, that is."

"From what I hear of your reputation, sir, you've carved up a few men in your day, too."

"Gossip, idle talk," but he said it in such a tone that the doctor had to believe it or else. Ransom then erupted with, "Look, you must be in need here of fresher meat." He put it on the table. "How much would you pay for say one or two bodies no one'll miss?"

"Can you do that? Do you have access?"

"We load bodies to Cook County every day and night," Ransom replied. "I see no reason they should get *all* the rejects."

"I'd pay top dollar to get my hands on some . . . some fresh ahhh . . . meat," the doctor confessed.

"But I'm not going into competition with anyone. If you've got a procurer already, I'm out."

"But I don't."

"Don't what?"

"Have a procurer."

"No? Really? Tell me no lies, man. I want to help you, but I have to know the entire extent of your current operation."

"Operation?"

"Business. Do you do business say with Shanks and Gwinn from time to time?"

"Only in the past. They're out of the business."

"Then who is it you are currently working with? Who brought you these specimens?" Ransom pointed to the three desiccated bodies on the slabs here.

"Why, these were purchased at auction, bought at fair price from the pool of John and Jane Does that go unclaimed."

"All those go direct to Rush College and Cook County now."

"Precisely why we haven't a single fresh cadaver! Short of digging up a fresh grave, what am I to do?"

"You've made no other arrangement with anyone, then?"

"None whatever."

"Can I trust you are telling the truth?" Oddly, Ransom believed the man. Something in his manner. Cagey, yes, but his body and features hid nothing. In fact, he'd proven far more forthcoming than had Pinkerton, who seemed bent on his beginning with Insbruckton before moving on to the mysterious Dr. Tewes. But if this were so, why was Nell targeting Insbruckton?

"I tell you, I am destitute, and I fear my school doomed," Insbruckton was saying as if to himself, walking about in a small circle.

"Doc, show me what you have in the way of organs in jars."

Insbruckton's rabbitlike manner and demeanor annoyed Ransom. His little pinched nose, bifocals perched there, the beady eyes so rodentlike, the demure and unmoving lips as he spoke, all conspired to irritate Ransom. The man simply annoyed, and he tried to picture him before a class explaining the intricacies of a surgical maneuver. He imagined the boredom of the man's students. Then he began to suspect that perhaps it was not Insbruckton at all Nell shadowed but one or more of the surgeon's students, who, out of sheer hellish boredom and frustration over the lack of a good cadaver to work on, simply began their own side studies by helping themselves to a citizen or two. He imagined a number of such bored lads. Boredom led to crime as surely as a river fed its banks.

Was it possible? After what he had seen in his city, the perversions and cannibalism and blood-taking, anything could happen here, he told himself.

Insbruckton showed him a collection of withered limbs and organs in jars, the most powerful to assault Ransom's senses being an unborn child.

"How is it you came by this?"

"An abortion. Mother's life was in jeopardy, and if you look closely at the head, you'll see the child had encephalitis."

The head looked normal to Ransom. All the same, there were no fresh hearts, lungs, kidneys, or livers. The whole of the place seemed a sad museum of lost souls, and nowhere could the word "vital" or "fresh" be found.

"You have no other rooms down here?"

"None. You've seen all save my private quarters and the half-dozen rooms for the surgical students."

"Have you a half-dozen students?"

"I have five using the residence hall. One left me. Others arrive from off campus."

"I'd like to see any records kept on the five on hand."

"Records?"

"Yes, including the one that got 'way."

"I keep them in my office."

"I will be discreet."

"But why do you need to know about our young men?"

Ransom handed Insbruckton back his money. Startled, the man looked into Alastair's eyes, his amazement like an enormous question mark sitting atop his head. "I'm not interested in working for you, Dr. Insbruckton."

"But the bodies you promised!"

"I came here as a police detective, Doctor, in search of—"

"Murdered men!"

"And now a woman, yes."

"My God, and you . . . you suspect me?"

"Your name came up in conversations."

"Horrible to think that someone could imagine that I . . . I could be any part of what I'm reading about in the papers! The very idea that someone was murdered in order to provide a cadaver for study appalls me."

"It's why I must see your records, rule out your boys, sir."

"Rule out, yes. There is not a lad among them who'd stoop so low, I can attest."

"Including the one who left you?"

"Including Michael, yes."

"Let me at the records, and I will be the judge of it, sir."

He nodded and led Ransom back up the winding stairs, Alastair glad to escape the odors here. They passed the doctor's operating theater where yet another overripe, overcut cadaver lay in wait for the A.M. class.

Somehow Ransom's nose, pores, and brain became frozen against the musty odors of this so-called surgical school and Dr. White Insbruckton's river of endless words. The man blabbed nonstop as to his reasons for "setting up shop," as he put it, in the "Prairie City," as there could be nothing but growth in its future. No doubt the man's palaver covered for an inward nervousness, almost to distraction. *Tewes's hands, that's what the man needs, if there was any hope for him at all.* Certainly, he had a rubber mouth and mind as each continuously flexed, and neither had a shut off valve.

The entire time Insbruckton talked, Ransom tried to determine if there was an inkling whatsoever that any of his current students could be construed as a murderer. The doctor talked ceaselessly without the ability to edit or come to the end of a thought without leaping to another and another.

When Ransom finally left Insbruckton, who stood waving from the top stair like a grandmother saying good-bye to a child she'd never again see, Alastair filled his lungs with a Chicago breeze. He'd been too long inside there, and he felt as if he'd been through a bizarre nightmarish sauna of sorts in that place over his shoulder. In fact, he'd been *saturated* with meaningless words that'd rained down in an incessant storm. Besides this, he'd had to deal with his own perspiration over a useless effort, alongside a clinging decay.

"God damn Bill Pinkerton . . . sending me to this caterwauling idiot, thinking I'd be kept busy, sidetracked. Sending me on a wild goose chase! But why? What reason had he? You'd think *him* guilty of killing Nell."

CHAPTER 24

Alastair hadn't time to get back to Pinkerton before reporting into headquarters on Des Plaines Street, as it had been a long while since last he reported in. However, the moment he stepped inside the noisy, bustling station house, he had to rush out again, as Hogan, the desk sergeant, advised him, "Chief Kohler wants you at the home of Calvin Dodge, 178 Belmont."

This was close to Jane's place, and Dodge was a local character Ransom knew well enough to avoid. Alastair's alarm only showed in a quick flare of the eyes and a tick about the jaw. "What's happened?"

"Dodge's son says he's gone missing."

"Missing?"

"Vanished."

"Damn . . . perhaps he hurt himself, became disoriented, and wandered off."

"There's that possibility," replied Hogan, nodding. "Still, what with all that's been going on, maybe there's more to it. Enough to get the chief out."

Ransom wondered why the chief had so quickly gotten involved in so low level a matter, until he recalled that old

Dodge's son, who went by his real name, Jared Killough, was a politico with some clout.

"So Kohler's personal touch, this is . . . "

"Payback." Hogan was born and raised a cop.

Ransom tried to picture the scene. Nathan Kohler couldn't ignore Dodge's disappearing from his bed if the son had called, distraught.

"I'll get right over there. If the chief calls, tell 'im I'm on my way."

"Will do, Inspector."

When Ransom arrived at the supposed scene of the crime, he felt an immediate sense of violation—some voice deep within telling him that whoever had come and gone with the old man didn't have the best interest of the "Colonel" at heart. Most glaring, aside from the bright blood against the pillowcasing and sheets, were the turned out drawers and opened cabinets. A botched robbery, was Ransom's first impulse. A second story man working catlike around the old duffer as he slept, but something awoke Dodge, perhaps an opened music box, a single clumsy move on the part of the burglar? Awake now, Dodge posed a threat. He might've reached for a gun kept at his bedside, but no reports of gunshots had been made.

The odor of blood wafted to Alastair's nostrils, and the blood on the old man's pillow was an unmistakable giveaway of some violence having occurred here. This was no nosebleed. Most certainly, Dodge had met with a bad end.

Ransom took immediate charge, saying, "Alderman Killough, your father didn't walk off of his own volition."

"Are you sure?"

"The blood on the pillowcase and sheets tells me so, and for my money, the old man wouldn't't've left without his slippers or shoes, not if some benign fellow lifted him to a carriage and made off to hospital."

Killough gasped at the unspoken suggestion from Ransom. Kohler shook his head, frowning. "We can't know it was foul play. He may've cut himself shaving for all we—"

But Ransom pointed to the neatly placed slippers and shoes tucked at the foot of the bed as if awaiting the old man.

"He's a tidy old fellow, so?" asked Kohler, his doughy face pinched in thought.

"In addition," continued Ransom, "there's no bloody tracks whatsoever. If he harmed himself, why he'd be going to the lavatory, and it's odd but there's no blood trail anywhere in the room." He pointed to the rug at his feet, a dark paisley. The others hadn't noticed the stain against the burgundy. Ransom dropped a white handkerchief over it, and they watched the white cloth turn to a brackish red wine stain. "Felt it the moment I entered," he said.

"My God, Nathan," said Killough, "we've been standing in his blood the whole time! And Father was keen on cleanliness next to godliness, all that."

Chief Kohler assured Killough, "It's most likely your father's simply wandered off, perhaps in a daze. I have officers canvassing the neighborhood for any sign."

Never make a promise you can't keep to a politician and a grieving family member all rolled into one, thought Ransom, but he kept his mouth shut and his thoughts to himself.

"We've got our best man on it now, just as you requested," Nathan told the son, indicating Alastair.

"Word's been sent all 'round the neighborhood for people to be on the lookout for Mr. Dodge," added Mike O'Malley, who'd come in from the hallway and into the bedroom to assume a position beside Ransom, "but no one's seen him since last evening."

"We'll find him," Kohler chanted. "With any luck at all, we'll find him."

Ransom exchanged a look with O'Malley, both men fearing otherwise. "Has anything been touched in here, Mike?" Alastair asked him.

"Everything was left just as we found it, Rance, till you could get here."

"You call for Philo Keane? Dr. Fenger?"

"Mr. Keane, yes, Dr. Fenger, no."

"Really?"

"With no body to look over, we figured Dr. Fenger wouldn't take too kindly to—"

"To his being called out. So, we call for a neighborhood doctor instead."

"Already done so, Rance."

"So where is the sonofa—"

"That'd be me," said Dr. James Phineas Tewes, now standing in the doorway. "Came as soon's I got word."

"All of us have changed since that train station murder, the Phantom's doing," said Nathan Kohler, trying to smooth over the moment as Ransom glared at Tewes. "I mean Mike here is out of the blue uniform, now a full inspector. Our good Dr. Tewes has earned a reputation as a caring medical professional, and Inspector Ransom has . . . has . . . "

"Has defied evolution and change," said Tewes.

This made Mike and even Kohler laugh, while Killough didn't find anything funny.

"All right, enough with the niceties," said a frowning Alastair. "Take a good look at your neighbor's bedside and floor, and you tell me, Dr. Tewes, what you think has gone on here."

"A man was abducted from his bed . . . or rather, forced."

Dodge's son gasped and Kohler frowned at this pronouncement.

"How very astute," Ransom said with a shake of the head. "If he'd wandered off as you suggest, Chief," Ransom muttered, "he'd have left footprints in blood from the throw rug."

"Makes sense," said O'Malley.

Dr. Tewes had kneeled to examine the wine-colored handkerchief that'd revealed the blood soaked into the carpet.

"There was a second rug," said the son. "A larger one at the foot of the bed."

"Gone?" asked Kohler.

"What's it mean, Inspector?" Killough turned to Ransom for an answer.

"Means the man didn't walk out of here, but was rolled up

in the larger rug and carried out through the balcony window and down the fire escape."

"Good God! Then you think he's dead?"

"Met with foul play, sir, yes. My best estimate."

"And you, Dr. Tewes?" asked Killough. "Do you concur?"

"If the man walked out of here, you'd've bloody prints to follow, but if a rug soaked up the blood . . . "

No one said another word. There was a long silence as each mind summed up what might've happened. Dodge's habitual brandy toddy remained intact alongside a half-eaten slice of zucchini bread. Nothing on the nightstand was a-kilter, making the scene all the more disturbing.

"I must agree," said O'Malley, who'd come now to unconsciously stand with Ransom and Tewes on the subject. "We have to begin our investigation as practical men here."

"Meaning?" asked Killough, standing alongside Kohler.

Tewes cleared his throat and added, "Not likely old Dodge slid down to the end of the bed without leaving a second trail of blood."

"And it is strange," continued Ransom, "an entire carpet gone along with him."

An eerie breeze lifted a sash in the room, as if a spirit revisited the bed. The soft contours of the shadowy wind sifting through the sash and hovering about the bed, a shy whisper of an echo, made a shiver run down their collective spines. It was as if Dodge's spirit cried out, *I am dead! You may leave it at that, and damn you all!*

"Was he in the habit of sleeping with his windows cast open?" asked Ransom.

"No . . . it is another mystery atop the mystery that the balcony window was open when we got here."

Ransom considered the younger man's pain. It was evident in his face that he felt great regret over the loss of his father.

"Put it to me straight, Inspector Ransom. What is your truthful assessment of this room?"

"The man's bedroom was routinely locked, his windows

routinely locked, and yet someone entered and attacked him."

"But who?"

"Did your father have any enemies?" pressed Ransom.

"A city full, yes, an absolute city full."

"That narrows it down considerably."

"His company left him poor, but it also left a lot of others poorer still."

"Shareholders? You think one could have killed him?" Ransom kept at the younger man.

"No . . . none I know would murder him and rob his body."

"I think the operative questions here might well be," began Tewes in that irritatingly high-pitched voice of his, "who would rob his body? Who would have need of it? Who'd consider it worth anything?"

"There'll surface a ransom note," Kohler suggested. "Killough here has money, and whoever's behind this, they know it!"

"A ransom note's not going to surface," countered Ransom.

"You've no way to know that."

"Did we see a note left on Nell Hartigan's eyes?" asked Ransom. "For her organs?"

"What's this got to do with that Pinkerton woman?" asked Killough, panic in his voice.

Tewes, Mike, Ransom, and Kohler all exchanged a knowing glance. Ransom finally said, "I fear there'll be no ransom notes!"

"Why do you say so?" Killough grew frantic now.

"People don't as a rule ransom the dead except to medical men."

"Please tell me it can't be! My father on a dissecting table? No, neveeer, neveeeer."

"Dodge couldn't've—of his own volition and will—gotten up and stepped off from this much blood loss, gone out to that balcony and down a fire escape, and not left evidence of his having wandered off."

"If you'll allow me to finish," said Tewes, putting a hand up to Ransom. "He, Dodge, attempted to fight off his attackers, but he took a nasty wound, obviously."

"Perhaps stabbed like Nell Hartigan," suggested O'Malley.

"Bled out until . . . until . . . "

"Until they wrapped him in that missing carpet," said Ransom. "And carried him out through the balcony and down to the street."

"And my father . . . dead or dying inside that Persian carpet."

"Persian was it?" asked O'Malley, jotting the detail in his notes.

"Authentic, yes. Bought it at the Istanbul exhibit at the fair."

"We're all very sorry, sir, but yes, this is essentially how I read it. There are the pillows thrown asunder, as if an attempt to suffocate the man was made; when that failed, he was stabbed—most likely fatally."

"If it's any consolation, sir," added Tewes, "I'd say your father put up a worthy fight, forcing his way up to a standing position here when the blade found him."

"Father was strong for his age," said Killough.

"I warrant it's the work of the same man who murdered Nell," said O'Malley.

"On the surface that might look the case," began Ransom, "but that makes a helluva leap, Mike, as we have no proof of it."

"Whoever's responsible, I want him caught, and I want to sit front row at his execution," said Killough. "Do you understand? All of you? And there's a handsome profit in it for you all if you do a thorough and speedy job of it. I want this monster who creeps into an old man's home and kills him in his bed caught and punished!"

"We will do everything in our power, Jared, to take steps to do exactly that," said Kohler, placing an arm over his political friend's shoulder. "You can count on my people. Right, Inspector Ransom?"

"Absolutely, Mr. Killough. Even if we must go by instinct alone, you may rely on the Chicago Police Department."

"But not a one of you holds a hope, not a sliver of it, that my father is yet of this earth?"

At that moment, Philo Keane came nosily up the stairs and through the door, asking, "Where's the body? I'm here to photograph a body, so where've they taken it?"

"That we'd all like to know," Ransom replied.

"No body?"

"None."

"So what am I here for?"

"Photograph the condition of the room, particularly the bedside area and the blood splatters," instructed Ransom. "And the pillows where they lay. And the open window. And the broken lock, necessary to get into the room, and this." Ransom held up the now saturated red handkerchief, and Philo, using his quick flash Night Hawk, shot it.

"Anything else, Inspector?"

"Yes, take a shot from the balcony to the alleyway below, bottom of the fire escape," suggested Tewes.

Ransom exchanged a glance with Jane. "Yeah, what *he* said, Philo, add to your repertoire."

"Why am I shooting a dirty alleyway?"

"Just do it." Ransom looked around like a bear in search of its next meal but saw only expectant faces staring back at him. Oddly enough, everyone had gone along with Jane's alias as Tewes. Big Mike O'Malley and Jared Killough proved the only two in the room who didn't know of it.

Jane had stepped out on the balcony to take in the view of the fair in the distance, where men worked day and night under harsh lights to disassemble the monster buildings and pavilions, Grecian statues, and Mr. Ferris's two-hundred-and-sixty-foot-high wheel.

"Seems a sad end to the fair," she said in Ransom's ear.

"Good riddance, I say. That fair took the life of Mayor Harrison, and how many others?"

"It's not the fair that killed anyone, not even progress or science or industry, you big oaf. It's like blaming our woes on God. God doesn't build shabby houses that burn or crumble under the wind, and God does not tell us to stand on a precipice and fall. We humans do a fine job of getting ourselves killed without God's interference one way or the other."

"Jane . . . I want to come back to you . . . back to your bed."

She said nothing.

"Tonight . . . now. I need you."

"Well . . . I don't need you. I don't need *any* man!"

"Alastair!" It was O'Malley below them in the alley entrance off the fire escape. "I've found something!"

"What have you, Mike?"

"A pair of spectacles, broken and bloodstained, I think."

"Did Dodge wear glasses?" asked Ransom of his son.

"For reading in bed at night, yes."

Again Mike shouted from the street. "And a book, Ransom, a holy book."

"Bible?"

"No but close enough."

"God hadn't a hand in it, heh?" Ransom quietly said to Tewes.

CHAPTER 25

Little else remained to be done at the Dodge
home, and while the man's son had become increasingly on
edge and apparently guilt-ridden over what had happened,
Ransom felt a need to flee and to take Tewes with him. With
Nathan escorting Killough home, with Mike O'Malley taking what little evidence they had to lock up, and with Philo
long gone to develop the photographs, Alastair escorted Jane
Francis to street level, to peer down the alleyway where
Mike had discovered pieces of the puzzle.

"A sure place for a waiting wagon or other transport," said
Jane, speaking in her own voice and dropping Tewes's.

"I'm thinking it's the same creeps who got Nell, the
ghouls."

"Only this time they had the privacy and time to get the
whole body and not piecemeal."

"There're still other possibilities. You heard the son. The
man had angered a lot of people. It could be a simple matter
of murder."

"Nothing about murder strikes me as simple," Jane said.

"Straightforward, then. Poor choice of words. I meant
mundane, usual, typical murder coming out of a typical mo-
tive like love, hate, vengeance, money, greed, food."

"*Ahhh* . . . look for the white elephant or pink alligator, you mean?"

"At least rule out the usual and obvious first."

"Or jump on it and foolishly ignore the unusual? Isn't that how you've cracked your most bizarre and satanic crimes? The weird and unthinkable gets ignored until enough bodies are racked up that—"

"OK . . . I take your meaning."

"Besides, Alastair, how many simple murders have you investigated where the body is disposed of?"

"A few. True, not many, but some."

"*Mafioso* hits most likely."

"They know how to cover their tracks, yes."

"Apparently you do, too."

"You give me too much credit."

"This city ought to erect a statue to you!"

He laughed at this. "Not enough brass."

They'd begun to stroll toward her house below the gaslights of Belmont. "But Alastair, the old man had no dealing with the Italian gangs."

"Anyone can hire an Italian assassin."

"All the same, Alastair, just last night on my way home . . . "

"Yes? Go on."

"Take me to Muldoon's. Buy me a pint of ale," she countered.

"If it'll help, sure."

They walked to Muldoon's instead of Jane going home. For a moment outside the tavern, under the dull light of lamps, the last line of this day's horizon blinked and died forever. They'd been in and around Dodge's home for over an hour and a half, a long time to stand over a bloodstain.

Over red ale, Jane told Alastair of the strange pair she'd seen standing on the street outside Dodge's home the night before. "And I had such an odd, inexplicable feeling come over me."

"An odd feeling? Really."

"Don't mock!"

"You know very well I can't arrest and interrogate two men on a feeling."

"The hell you say! You do it all the time!"

"On my cop's sense, yes, but not on a feeling you or Dr. Tewes might have."

"Where is the difference?"

"Experience, know-how, instinct."

"I tell you, these two did not *belong* on that street. I tell you, they were up to no good."

"But you never saw them before?"

"Never," she lied now, thinking he'd get no more from her with his attitude of superiority.

"Do you think you might recognize them if you encountered them again?"

"I do."

"Then come down to the Des Plaines station house."

"What for?"

"To examine our rogues gallery of rats that've taken up residence here."

"Photos?"

"Yes."

"It could be a waste of time if you don't have them in your books."

"Yes, but on the other hand, you might be surprised."

"I'll try to get around."

"Don't try. Do it."

"All right, sometime soon."

"Yes, soon."

They drank a second round, and he walked her back to her place, where, standing on the porch, he said good night while hoping she'd invite him in, but she failed to do so; still stinging from their previous disagreement over Samuel, he imagined.

When Ransom rounded his block, having decided to walk from Jane's to his residence, a goodly distance and a brisk exercise, he saw a man in shadow up ahead. Shadows along

Kingsbury Street fell into the category of black holes, and when the figure stepped in and out of each cut of light made by the lamppost, Ransom made out a lanky, sinewy, tall man with bones for a frame: Hake.

Although Alastair had hoped to see Frederick Hake, and by all rights ought to've expected him, he felt such an uneasiness with the entire Pinkerton organization by now that it still came as a surprise to find Hake at his doorstep. *Just how closely am I being watched?* he wondered.

Did Hake come bearing information or a wild-hair notion to get back at him? Was he a courier of news that might help, or had he come with a knife or a gun in hand?

Ransom immediately let the dangerous, nervous fellow know that he'd seen him at a distance, calling out his name, "Hake! Is it you there? Step out where I can see you, man! And show me your hands are empty!"

Ransom had already torn his .38 from its sheath—a shoulder holster beneath his coat. Hake hesitated only a moment before stepping back out into the light.

"We need to agree not to use my name," he said, coming closer. "Don't want nobody to know I'm working for you, do you?"

"Probably a good plan. So how shall I refer to you?"

"Ohhh . . . dunno . . . have always fancied the name Reginald, though."

"So it is, Reginald. What've you got for me?"

"I dared not carry it with me, but I know you'll want to pay well for it."

"What is it?"

"It is a dossier."

"Nell's notes?"

"Forget about Nell's notes. She kept no notes, and if you ever see Nell's notes, know that they're phony."

"Well then, what is this dossier?"

"It's on you."

"Are you sure?"

"I am indeed. They're building a case for your having

murdered that fellow you suspected of being the Phantom of the Fair."

"Suspected? Has there been a single garroting murder since the bloody suspect disappeared?"

"You needn't convince me of it."

"A jury'd laugh 'em outta the courtroom. Don't know a Chicago judge who'd entertain the notion either."

"That might change if they get to someone, someone talks . . . least that's what Kohler has Pinkerton chipping away at—your friends, so-called."

"How'd you come by the file?"

"How do you imagine?"

"I imagine Pinkerton hired you in the first place because of your felicity with locks and your history as a second-story man."

"I've given up burglary, Inspector, except as a means to an end, as in this end, to work for you."

"Be sure then that you keep your nose clean. Look here, when Pinkerton learns this file on me has been stolen, he's likely to become a bit upset. Make yourself scarce for a while but not before you place the dossier in my hands."

"I'll need some travelin' funds. Wouldn't mind going to see my sister in Cincy."

"I didn't know you had a sister."

"Everybody needs one."

Ransom doled out twenty dollars to Hake. "When can you get it to me?"

"Twenty won't get me far."

"You'll have twenty more when you turn over this so-called file."

"*Ahhh* . . . it's a careful man you are, Inspector. Good. I am a careful man as well."

"The file?"

Hake looked about, as if expecting to be shot at any moment. "Caught a fellow following me earlier. Could be a Pinkerton operative . . . "

"Or the man you owe money to?"

"Or him, yeah . . . "

"Get the file to me."

"I'll come 'round three in the morning. Have that twenty ready."

"Knock three times on my window," suggested Ransom. "So I know it is you and not someone else."

"Window?"

"Back of the place, my sleeping quarters."

"See you then."

"Don't come back empty-handed, Hake."

"You have me word."

Hake slipped back from sight into the deep cut blackness of an alleyway as sure-footed as one of the cat-sized river rats Ransom had often seen along the wharves. He could not help but wonder if this man was not working both sides, accepting payment from Pinkerton as well as him. He had no doubt that Hake had ransomed his soul more than once. Three A.M. was a time of dark consequences. *What was it Twain said of the hour? That we are all a little crazy at three in the morning.*

Ransom knew he must expect a setup and a possible attack either from Hake or others.

CHAPTER 26

Jane Francis Tewes could not sit still, her mind racing with questions swirling about her ears, questions about the two men she'd seen outside old Dodge's place two nights before, and now Dodge was missing, blood spatters discoloring the rug beside the old man's bed. Something untoward had happened, and it appeared his place had been ransacked for jewels, money, bonds, and keepsakes. The intruder or intruders had gotten away with it during the night, and Jane could not get those two faces out of her head. She instinctively knew that these "associates" of Shanks and Gwinn had had something, if not all, to do with her missing neighbor and items from that house.

For this reason, she went slumming as Dr. Tewes. She'd grown to like red ale, and it had become Dr. James Tewes's favorite libation. She had gone first to Cook County Hospital, certain she must do this on her own and tell no one, not Dr. Fenger, and certainly not Alastair. Either or both would put an immediate stop to her plan.

It was a simple plan: closely watch the off-duty activities of Shanks and Gwinn. See if they might lead her to the strange pair she'd spied from the coach the other night. Her reasoning was neither heroic nor intelligent, she knew. Her motivation was, in fact, money. Everyone had heard what Alderman Killough said about remuneration to those who solved his father's murder and who determined where his body might be. Why shouldn't Dr. Tewes benefit from this situation? She could certainly use the money toward Gabby's education, and perhaps with some left over for another donation to Hull House, her pet charity.

And so she went down to Cook County the following late afternoon, not to watch Dr. Fenger operate, and not to learn her craft, but to tail Shanks and Gwinn, and to hope that their paths would again cross those of the strange couple whom she feared had killed Dodge not so much for his money or material things, but for his body and organs, his head and brain.

She timed it well, getting to County just as Shanks and Gwinn stepped off duty. The two had gotten paid, and just as she suspected, they went on a spending and drinking binge. She tried to keep up without their noticing.

It turned into a whirlwind of travel across Chicago's underbelly and through Chicago's darkest holes, from Hair Trigger Block to Chinatown; however, despite her tenacity, Jane did not once encounter the odd pair she sought.

Meanwhile, with each ale that Dr. James Phineas Tewes consumed, Jane Francis Tewes felt an increasing personal and bodily risk, finding herself balking at the bawdy house where Shanks and Gwinn ended up. She'd had to struggle the harder as the evening wore on to set aside that portion of her brain sending an insistent code to herself that screamed: *not another alcoholic drink!*

Three A.M. came and went, the clock ticking on to 3:05 . . . and Ransom dozing . . . then three-ten and Ransom opening one eye to see . . . then three-fifteen, at which time both eyes shot open wide as the doorbell rang. The thing sounded like a two-alarm at the firehouse.

In his nightshirt, gun in hand, Ransom inched toward the door, fully expecting that Nathan Kohler and Pinkerton, having decided that collecting dirt on him had proved a slow process with few results, had devised an assassination plot instead, using Hake as their decoy.

As he came within inches of the curtained doorway, he saw the silhouette in shadow not of a tall, lanky Hake but of a small boy.

The boy snitch, Samuel, rang his bell again. For half a second Ransom wondered if the men aligned against him had gotten the boy to come in on their side and were using him. Samuel's disheveled and even beaten appearance might attest to this onerous suspicion. Were they using the boy? Would Ransom feel the scorching fire of a bullet ripping through him the moment he opened the door to Samuel? But Sam had grit, and he honored his friendships. It didn't fit.

Ransom tore open the door in a show of defiance to the blackness all round. "Samuel? You alone? It's after three in the morning."

"I need your . . . your help," the boy weakly said.

The boy had been beaten, his clothes strewn about him as if he'd hastily dressed, there were blood spatters here and there, and his nose was caked with dried blood. Through the curtain, Alaistair'd had an inkling of the boy's distress, still, he was stunned to see just how shaken and beaten was this boy standing on his doorstep.

"What's happened to you, son?"

"I—I—I—*ahhh* . . . "

Looking about for any movement in and around the street, Ransom hustled Sam inside his dark home, which to the boy, he knew, must look like a cave dwelling built into a mountainside. It was a first floor flat, a rental, but Ransom had made it his own, surrounding himself with leather, wood, and books. "Sam . . . what're you doing here, and what's happened?" he repeated to the silent little fellow.

"I got beat good."

"I can see that much! Well, we'll get you fixed up!" He had been dozing when Sam rang his bell, but the sight of the boy cleared his head. Half listening still for Hake's three knocks at his window, which likely were not coming, Ransom imagined two things: One, he was out twenty dollars for nothing, and two, his young snitch had gotten into a street fight he'd lost.

"He beat me good this time, but I got 'im back, I did."

"Sam, who did this?"

"Father."

"Father? You told me you had no family."

"He's not any father of mine! Not—Not no more."

"And what's his name?" Ransom worked to gather warm water, soap, and a hot washcloth. He was soon cleaning the boy's wounds as he spoke—wounds that ranged from red welts, blue bruising, a black eye, and a missing front tooth, along with a nasty red choker. "Where's he live? Where can I find him?" He began pacing before Samuel. "Where can I find him?" repeated Ransom, agitated, moving about the darkness like a cave-dwelling creature. He grumbled while looking for his clothes, shoes, and cane, and he realized only now that Sam was reluctant to say any more. "Sam, at the very least, this creep needs a good talking to!"

"You'll kill him."

"No, I won't kill him. Where's he live?"

"St. Peter's."

Ransom froze. "The church? My church?" While Alastair had not been inside St. Peter's since he was Sam's age, he still considered it his church. He'd been a choirboy before he tired of the pomp and circumstance.

"He's a—a—a priest at the church," stuttered Sam, "a-a-and he's a bad man."

"Why . . . why would he beat you, Sam?"

"He thought he could do to me what he's done to Tommie, Jonas, and some other boys."

"Done what? Tell me!"

"He wanted me . . . that is . . . wanted me—"

"Spit it out, Sam, like a man!"

"But I ain't no man!" he cried out.

Ransom pulled the boy into him, hugging him. "Whatever it is, we can deal with it together then, Sam . . . Sam?"

"The bastard . . . he wanted to put his . . . his thing in my mouth. At first, he just wanted to rub it against me, then for me to hold it, and next . . . well."

"I get the picture, Sam, and you're right, this priest is a bastard."

"Tol' 'im I'd be damned in Hell before I would!"

"That how he put it to you? That your everlasting soul was at stake?"

"Said . . . said it was a good, holy act I'd be doing."

"Sin-ofabitch! Sin-ofabitch!"

"Said it was a sign of good penance to do anything—*anything*—to make a priest's hard life better."

"Said that, did he?"

"Said a boy's gotta do whatever a priest tells 'im, he says."

"Bastard."

"I put up a fight."

"Good for you, Sam!"

"Hit him with a big cross."

"Really?" Ransom lightly laughed.

"Pulled it off his wall and smacked 'im good! Bloodied his head, I did."

"Good, Sam."

"Bloodied his head with it, I did," Sam repeated, relishing the moment.

"Hold on! He had you in his private quarters?"

"That's where he's done other boys; that's where he gets ya."

"Calls himself a priest," muttered Ransom. "Look, why were you there to begin with?"

"Not for what he wanted! They give us boys free soup and bread."

"No such thing as a free lunch, Sam. You'll learn that in time."

"It was for acting as a choirboy, he told me."

"Choirboy, huh? That's what he called it? Acting as a choirboy?"

"He never said a bad word ever."

Euphemisms, Ransom thought. *The degenerate wraps himself in religious euphemisms.* "Father Frank, isn't it?"

"Yeah . . . how'd you know? Oh, yeah, you're a detective. Think I wanna be an inspector some day, sir. Father Frank. What'll you do to him, sir?"

"What do you think I oughta do, Sam? Say the word."

"I couldn't say, sir. I guess . . . whatever comes to you, I s'pose."

"Good, I'm glad we can agree on that."

Ransom gave the boy a towel, a huge new bar of Nelson's fragrant soap, and Eddy's shampoo, and pointed out the indoor shower, but Sam stood gaping, not knowing how to work the controls, having never seen indoor plumbing before. So Alastair demonstrated, turning on the shower and flushing the toilet. Both actions made the battered boy gleefully laugh, and this reaction hurt his injured eye and cheek where the man of God had hit him. Ransom then left Sam to his privacy.

Soon, when Sam came out of his shower wrapped in the towel, Ransom saw his face for the first time without any smudges or grime. He hadn't any idea how handsome the little fellow was until that moment.

Outrage over what'd happened to "his boy" sent a red cloud of anger coursing through Alastair's head, and he feared one of his major headaches might follow. The red he could feel, even smell, where it sat behind his eyes, smoldering like a fiery dye racing through his brain, but he struggled to remain calm for the boy's sake. "Bet you're hungry," he said, as he thought: *How could some sick priest—an adult sworn to the work of the Lord—take advantage of so innocent a face or person?*

"I truly am starved," replied Sam, seemingly unaware of the battle raging within Ransom. "But I don't expect no charity. I'll work it off. I'll find word on that murdered Pinkerton agent lady for you."

"Good man, Sam."

Ransom went about feeding the boy bread and a leftover

stew. The whole while, his mind turned over the event that
had chased Samuel to him. In fact, molesting a child sexually was the one crime he had terrible difficulty understanding. He could not fathom it. While he could place himself
into the shoes of a desperate man who breaks and enters, a
thief who robs at gunpoint, a train robber, bank robber, a
murderer even, he simply could not do the same with what
Dr. Fenger called the "lowest form of life, below that of the
grave robber, the man who robbed a child of his or her innocence." Nor a mother or father who kills their own off-
spring, or raises their children as criminal vermin or
murderers. Often out of a deep evil seed embedded in some
undiscovered island of the human mind. And too often, these
child molesters and child killers were found in the end hugging a Bible or other religious tract, like Father Frank Jurgen.

Fenger had hinted that Shanks and Gwinn had both been
raised in a horrible manner and were abused as children
years before they found one another and gained some modicum of love from one another. Ransom had joked at the notion, saying, "I guess even toads can feel love in some
perverted form."

Fenger had lost his temper with him, shouting, "The two
take care of one another, watch one another's backs, give
one another moral support and love, Rance, perhaps something you can't understand. Most married couples don't do
near that much for one another these days!" It was Christian's final word on why he'd gone so far out of his way to
help the two reformed resurrection men.

Samuel ate heartily and the stew disappeared in huge
gulps, as though it were some exotic food he'd never before
tasted. "Minds me of rabbit stew my mum made when I was
a little kid," the nine-year-old finally said, mopping up the
last vestige of stew with his bread.

Ransom asked, "Whatever became of your ma and your
da, Sam?" His mind kept rolling over the notion of this damnable priest blackening the good name of the church he still
thought of as his. The man disgraced his robes over a driving

need to demonstrate complete domination over a weaker person—not unlike an animal in a cage that must dominate all the others sharing that space. Ransom could find some thimble full of understanding for all the deviants and perverts he'd known, but not for the man who crossed the sexual line with a child. Try as he might, he could never get a reasonable explanation out of such a man, and he could not, as a result, understand the mental chaos, the sexual confusion, or the demoralized heart. Ransom simply could not fathom a being who could ruin a child for a handful of euphoria. It was all just so disgusting for him to contemplate that even attempting to understand it proved painful.

His final conclusion was one any farmer would do with a perverted animal on the farm—*castration*. Then throw such perverts into prisons and asylums without their jewels, and by all means keep them away from children. One such fiend had told Ransom during an interrogation that "a child has no idea whatsoever the *power* it holds over me, Inspector."

"Power over you? A child?"

"The child . . . how it attracts me . . . like a childhood memory of a place I love."

"You mean a child attracts you like a moth to flame?" Ransom had asked the degenerate.

"Yes, although the flame has no intention of harming the moth, and you got it backwards, Inspector."

"How so?"

"I'm the one destroyed. The child is the flame that ignites me, and I the moth burning and out of control."

"So it's the child's fault you attack her?"

"She attacks me! With her being, with her flame that I must have."

"So she's at fault, not you?"

"Yes!"

"For being a child . . . for being childish?"

"Yes, damn you! Yes! Now you've got it right."

"So we should let you go as the injured party?"

"Yes, Inspector, yes."

Ransom only knew it as a horrid and putrid crime. A

crime to make every man ashamed of his species. A crime that no one wanted to think about it, much less speak of, and so it remained a *buried* crime. Even when such a crime reached the courts, judges were quick to close down their chambers and deal with it behind closed doors. As obviously the church—his church—had done.

"Get some sleep, Sam," he told the boy. "Use the settee."

"What about Father Jurgen?"

"I'll pay him a visit, Sam. You don't have to go back there."

"Really? Thanks, Mr. Ransom." Sam ran across the room and curled up beneath the wool blanket that Ransom had laid out for him, his head hitting the pillow, his eyes closing.

He looked the epitome of the wounded angel. The whole scenario recalled to Ransom's mind a painting he'd once viewed at the Chicago Art Institute of a wounded angel being found in a heap by a pair of grimy-faced children.

CHAPTER 27

Ransom dressed, leaving tie and collar off, grabbing his cane and pacing bearlike before a snoring Sam. Once he felt certain that Sam was out for the night and that Hake was a no-show, he left.

Outside, the street was deserted save for the vermin and the homeless. He yanked his coat collar up against the chill night air as a stray dog overturned someone's trash can. As he walked, his cane beating to his step, Alastair imagined that Frederick Hake was a slacker and a liar, and the information he supposedly had a fiction as well. He imagined he'd been taken for twenty bucks, enough for Hake to put down a useful bet on a horse or to get into a crap-shooting game.

"You'd think I'd've learned by now," he muttered against a brash, Chicago wind coming against him. The good news was the unlikelihood of a dossier on him sitting somewhere in Pinkerton's office. Still, it would explain why Bill Pinkerton had been so jumpy and nervous when he appeared at his desk.

He'd have to give it more thought; he'd have to run Hake down as he had so often run down Bosch. Find him in one of his lairs or his favorite gambling den. At the moment, however, to hell with Hake, and Pinkerton, and Kohler. He had an evil as sin priest to deal with.

Alastair moved swiftly for a man his size, cutting through familiar gangways and backyards to half his trip and time. Sunup wouldn't help in the business he had in mind.

It galled him that he was forced into this—on such an unholy errand to the church that he'd once called his second home, where he meant to bash this man's teeth down his throat or do worse harm. It galled him in so many ways, not the least being that St. Pete's was and had always been the one place in the city where he thought Sam and his generation safe. A refuge, it was supposed to be a place of comfort where angels held one out of the storm called the human condition long enough for respite and relief. But due to this priest, this special, magical place failed to keep the storm out for Sam, and God alone knew how many others his age.

Ransom knew St. Peter's well, and he knew what the young priest, Jurgen, looked like. It was now just a matter of finding him and "laying on of hands."

Alastair traversed the distance in short order, as St. Peter's was not far from his residence. While unsure precisely how he would handle the matter, he felt his anger rising with each step that took him closer to Father O'Bannion's cathedral. Soon the spiraling pinnacles of the place came into view. All the pomp and circumstance, all the marble blocks, all the stone statues and gargoyles amid the turrets of this place, every symbol down to the wafer and the wine, all took a major pounding due to this hypocrite priest Jurgen. A priest unable to resist a prurient urge to touch and be touched by some angelic child. A priest who'd tonight madly beaten Sam when the boy refused the adult's deviant lies and advances.

The huge double doors of the church, some fourteen feet high, had enormous knobs and locks, but the church was never locked. Its doors were always open to the needy, and Ransom always felt this place a sanctuary to the homeless and children like Samuel. Now this.

A hundred different scenarios played out in his head. Who outside himself would believe Samuel? If he arrested the priest in proper style, Father Jurgen'd be released immediately, and all would be turned on him, instead, as some sort of villainous atheist to do such a thing; yes, it would become twisted and turned on him and Sam. And Samuel would be unable to prove it didn't happen another way entirely. That perhaps Samuel solicited the behavior himself. Worse yet, the thing could easily become a kind of twisted fodder for Chief Kohler to destroy Alastair's reputation by putting forth witnesses to say the boy had been beaten and attacked in his home tonight, and most certainly *not* in the house of God.

So how do I proceed? Alastair asked himself as he pushed through the door and stepped into the huge pew-filled church. Blinded by the brightly lit backdrop of the pulpit flanked on either side by Mary and Child, and by Jesus on the Cross, Ransom realized this was too public for what he contemplated; he began backpedaling out as a feeling of panic and claustrophobia enveloped him here in the huge, open room filled with stained-glass offerings of scenes from the lives of the saints. The claustrophobia took on the feel of a dark huge beast creeping over him just below his skin. His heart rate had increased, a cold sweat lathered his brow and neck, his scalp felt afire with ants, and his perspiring palms wrapped tighter about his cane. He couldn't do what he'd come to do. Not here, not in this place. Not even to Father Franklin Jurgen.

Ransom had made one stop on his way here, and that was at his friend Philo's home, disturbing Philo from a deep slumber.

"Do you still have possession of those farm implements that Montgomery Ward had you photographing for their new catalog?" he'd asked Philo.

"They refused the return post, expecting me to pay for it!"

"So you have them back?"

"I do, but why? And what's got you in such heats?"

"I want those castrating scissors they use on horses. Do you have them?"

"Rance, what in the world have you in mind? And are you *sure* about this?"

"Fool, it's not for me!"

"A horse, then?" he asked.

"No, not a horse."

"You mean to . . . to castrate a man? God, Rance, isn't your reputation already beyond repair?"

"No one'll ever know it was me. When I'm through with this bastard priest, he won't be talking to anyone."

"Priest!"

"He's molested Sam."

"Nooo! A man of the cloth, sworn to abstinence?"

"A man of the lie more so than the cloth. Now where are those bloody pinchers?"

"Are you sure, Alastair, that this is how you want to proceed? This gets out, it could end your career."

"Where're the damn pinchers?" Ransom pushed past his friend, who stood in his nightshirt.

"All right, all right. But they must never ever be traced back here, you understand?"

"Not by me."

And now Ransom was standing in the church foyer, one hand on his cane, the other fingering the horse-neutering pliers held beneath his great coat. In fact, he cut his finger on the razor sharp edge.

He'd never felt comfortable in the house of God, not as a child and certainly no longer. What made him think he could take out his revenge for Sam on Father Jurgen here, now, tonight, in such a place? Perhaps Philo was right; perhaps it'd be too cruel and inhumane to butcher a man this way? Not even be sure to go through with it, he thought when footfalls interrupted him.

"Can I help you, my son?" called out an old priest who looked as if he'd torn himself from a hoary grave, his white hair wispy and lifting with the wind from the door that Ransom held open.

The thing sitting on Ransom's chest—like some dark incubus of nightmare—made it difficult to speak, but he croaked out his lie. "Sorry, Father O'Bannion. I just stepped in to throw off a fellow I'm tailing."

Ransom made the mistake of meeting the old man's incisive, cutting glare. "Is that right now? Using the Church to further your career? It'd be a headline if it got out, Alastair."

Ransom instantly knew he was caught in a lie. Damn the priest.

O'Bannion was an institution in Chicago, a priest with the reputation that made Irish priests uncomplicated and complex at once. He had been a boxer few men could defeat in the ring, and a minister no one doubted. A big and tall man in his prime, he looked to be what a child imagined God to look like, and Alastair had never known him to be without a gray beard. He had ministered to the poor in this parish for over fifty years with little or nothing to work with and even less reward.

Despite all odds, Father O had somehow kept a soup kitchen open. He had begun a school in an adjoining building whose owners he'd convinced to donate to the church. He personally kept the books, somehow keeping it all revolving in the air like a trick cyclist with multiple plates on the end of countless thin rods.

"Are you sure, Alastair?" probed O'Bannion.

"Sure . . . sure, yes, I'm sure."

"I could always tell when you lied, even as a boy."

"All right, I came to have a talk with—*ahhh . . .*"

"Father Jurgen, I suspect."

"Then you know what happened with Samuel, the boy?"

"I've heard Father Jurgen's side of it."

Ransom snorted, his hidden hand tightening around the pinchers. "And I'm sure it's a fine rationalization, too."

"Father Jurgen was to take over here. He's made a series of . . . let's say bad choices."

"I'll say he has."

"And his punishment is already great."

"Great enough that he won't harm another child?"

"That is my estimation."

"Then you didn't fall for his rationalizing this away?"

The priest led Alastair toward the altar and the candles. "I've been concerned about Father Jurgen's, *ahhh . . .* "

"Activities?" Ransom supplied a neutral word for it.

"Activities, yes?" Not even the tough-talking old bird of a priest could find words for this kind of crime. No one wanted to acknowledge that such things existed in the world, in nature, in society, in the things men conceived of, and certainly not the churches or the schools. Ransom's neutral word fed right into the *faux* politeness.

The two men stood before the candles, and Father O lit one, saying, "We should pray for Father Jurgen . . . will you light a candle for him?"

The old chess player had outmaneuvered Alastair. He could not light a candle without giving away what he hid beneath his coat. Ransom ignored the question, saying, "Then these activities have been going on for how long, Father O?" The old priest happily allowed people to refer to him as Father O as an endearment.

"For . . . let's say, some time, but the offense has only recently come to my attention through a series of unfortunate events."

"I see. Then why not turn me loose on him?"

"I've already taken him to great task, Alastair."

"Great task? How? With words?"

"In my younger days, I'd have made him get in the ring with me, and I'd've bloodied him good before he got out," said O'Bannion.

"That could be arranged with me opposite Jurgen."

"Perhaps it could."

"But it'd hardly be enough punishment."

"I certainly understand your rage and anger, Alastair. Had to find my own center of calm myself. But at my age, I fear that climbing into the ring against a younger man would only flatten me!" O'Bannion laughed at his own remark, but a glint of nervous electricity fired in his eye. "Let it go, Alastair. The Church deals with its own, dirty laundry and all. We don't any of us want a scandal. A thing like this spread across the headlines—"

"By God, put me in the ring with 'im!"

O'Bannion took hold of his arm. "I can't have 'im killed, now can I?" The old priest tried smoothing it over with a smile and a hand on Alastair's back.

"Just point out his room to me, then!"

"You won't find him here."

"Where, then? Don't tell me you've castrated him down at the butcher shop."

O'Bannion laughed again. "No . . . no, he's been *transferred*. No longer my worry, and no concern of yours, son."

"Transferred?"

"Sent to another parish."

"Another parish? Where he can attack other small boys?"

"Hold on!"

"What kind of punishment is that?"

"His new parish is in Greenland." He said it as if the word "Greenland" meant the last word on the subject.

"But he's still in robes? Still dealing with children?"

"He's been reprimanded, and he has shown how contrite and horrified he is at his own behavior. Something you should perhaps try sometime, Alastair."

Ransom turned and rushed back up the aisle for the door, believing the old priest as to Jurgen's having already vacated St. Peter's.

O'Bannion rushed after him, moving surprisingly fast for his age to close the distance between them, wishing the conversation to remain muffled. "I can assure you—"

"Assure me?" interrupted the cop, turning on the priest. "The man's obviously ballyhooed you, old man! Damn you! What about the children in that parish in Greenland?"

"Franklin has sought out help and received counsel."

"What help? What counsel?" Alastair's words dripped with contempt.

"My counsel, and God's counsel, Alastair! Do you think *your* counsel is above God's or mine?"

"Sure . . . sure, the *weasel-snake-creep* spouts off apologies to you and to God, but not a word to Sam or his other victims, yet Jurgen's somehow the better for it?"

"He's a changed man, much better."

"You arranged for this transfer?"

"I did."

"And this parish in Greenland? Will Jurgen be head man there?"

"He is, yes, and that responsibility will curtail any future offenses, you see. A heavy responsibility can cure a man of such ills."

Ransom pulled away. "He's molested boys here, and— and you're sending him someplace where no one knows him or what he is capable of do—"

"In order for him to begin anew! We must help heal Father Jurgen."

"Heal him! What about Sam?"

"The boy is young, and children are capable of remarkable strength."

"You rewarded the guy! Gave him his own parish, a place where he is in charge. Would you put the devil in charge?"

"Hold your tongue, man!"

"You don't give a drunk the keys to the liquor cabinet!"

"I tell you the demon has been exorcised from Father Jurgen!"

"Did you personally absolve him to this new height of redemption?"

"Do not mock the practices and teachings of Christ and his Church."

"So you performed an exorcism on him?"

"I cast out his demons. Look, the lad is like a son to me! I know his nature!"

"Your fool's charity and religious fervor have left you blind, Father."

"I am not so blind as I can't see your shortcomings, Inspector, nor that your soul is on the precipice."

"Get off me, Father, and onto Jurgen. I've not molested innocent children!"

"Some of those so-called innocent children are not so innocent in all this, Alastair. Get your facts straight before you—"

"Ahhh . . . I see, Father Jurgen's convinced you that he's the victim here, that these evil urchins like Sam lured him into it. That's classic . . . just typical, standard characteristic bullshit from a man who pets boys! You should've reported this crime against the children and had your junior arrested, Father."

"I chose to handle the matter as discreetly as—"

"How many times have you seen me go past these doors, knowing a crime was being committed here?"

Their eyes locked.

"Just go!" O'Bannion pleaded. "Go now before I have you arrested!" Ransom knew his last remarks cut deep.

Still on the attack, Ransom replied, "You're being as unreasonable and totalitarian as . . . as the Pope in this, aren't you?"

"I handed him over to God!"

"Good God!"

"Rather than subjecting him to the humiliation and agony of men like you!"

"Excellent, Father, 'cause you just handed this child molester license to do it again."

"Never!"

"Handed him more power than ever such a fevered brain can handle!"

"The decision's been made, Alastair. Calling me names and casting blame on me will change nothing."

"I'm sorry, Father, but my estimation of you has fallen like a bag of bricks from one of those twenty-story buildings on Michigan Avenue. I'd heard that cops, firemen, lawyers, cover for one another, but I hadn't thought it possible that priests were as prone to lies."

"How dare you! I've just told you the *truth!* Confided a confidence between a man and his spiritual advisor, and you have the temerity, the unmitigated gall, to stand in my church and dictate—"

Ransom pushed through the doors and rushed down the stone steps, while O'Bannion shouted after him from the top stair, "Pray for Father Jurgen! Pray for the man and his soul!"

Ransom heard the plea on the wind as a gust from off the lake nudged him along in his flight from St. Peter's. He'd heard a threat in O'Bannion's tone. He shook inside at the turn of events and having to swallow his anger when indeed a stout wind came off the lake to snatch at him, to pull him and his cane apart from one another as he muttered, "Yeah, sure, I'll pray for him all right; I'll praaaaaaaay Ransom fashion."

"And pray for yourself, Alastair!" the old man's final parting salvo reached his ear as if O'Bannion somehow could send his voice on the wind.

"Not in your catechism, O'Bannion!" he shouted back, certain only the alley wags, the yeggs, and the homeless digging in trash cans heard his response.

Ransom's fingers wrapped about the concealed "weapon" he'd kept out of O'Bannion's sight. He could not recall a time when he'd been more furious, frustrated, and disappointed all at once.

CHAPTER 28

While Ransom busied himself with how best to get vengeance for Sam, Jane Francis, acting as Dr. Tewes, made the rounds so important to the nightlife of one Shanks and Gwinn. Two more deplorable people she could hardly imagine. They spent their money as fast as they received it; spent it on horse racing and other forms of gambling, spent it on liquor of every sort imaginable, and spent it on loose women of low stature and lower morals. They spent much of their time at Madame DuQuasi's on the river in the ill-reputed Levee District where painted women and red lights abounded.

Their other passion took them to the opium dens. Jane quickly came to the conclusion that the now somewhat re-spected Dr. James Phineas Tewes's already besmirched rep-utation could not withstand a charge stemming from this night's travels. Dr. Tewes simply could not be seen in or around such places as Maude DuQuasi's on the wharf. Not to mention an outright fear of contracting some horrid dis-ease from leaning against a wall here. She decided this after tailing the reformed resurrection men this second night—which had felt more like an entire weekend.

Shanks and Gwinn seemed bent on living life to its fullest

every moment, as if their daily working with the dead dictated such a policy. This lifestyle said they must completely immerse themselves in Sin City—the city within the city—to enjoy life in the here and now, and to go out of this world having spent every dime they'd ever earned.

During their riotous and raucous bouts with the bottle, Shanks and Gwinn had seemed to share a kind of fright, a look of fear coming over each man. Like a pair of animals who know they are being stalked, they sometimes looked over their shoulders in tandem, as if of one mind, and as if at any moment someone or some thing would lurch from the shadows to swallow them up.

At first Jane thought they sensed her shadowing them, but their behavior was more complicated than any concern so mundane as learning that Dr. Tewes was watching. Whatever was stalking these two, it was greater, larger, and far more threatening than a small doctor.

Jane Francis as a man saw a side of Chicago that Ransom had only hinted at. She felt a sense of hedonism in the dark dens where she drank ale at a distance, watching Shanks and Gwinn, hoping to see them meet with the strange couple she'd seen outside Calvin Dodge's home the night her coach almost ran them down.

She could not help but think of the real James Tewes, Gabby's father, who, in France, had succumbed to such places as this. Men acted like pigs at a trough in such places. The only good coming of her surveillance effort appeared that she'd not run into Alastair or anyone else she respected in these dens.

Jane did not go into the brothel on the water. She drew the line at the wharf, and she felt extremely vulnerable here. Alone, a small person, she could easily be a target for a mugger or worse.

She bid Shanks and Gwinn a silent good-bye and good luck in their madcap search for whatever it was they sought. She'd never witnessed men so bent on self-destruction as these two since her first love, the real Dr. James Tewes, who'd died in a French jail.

When James came to mind, Jane knew she'd seen enough.

She sought out a cab and quickly made her way home, disappointed that her evening as a private eye had been a bust. Once safely in the cab, allowing herself some feeing of relief, she swore to never repeat this attempt again.

Her lonely ride home was filled with sadness and thoughts of the slow, unsteady march of evolution, the mental disorders of men in need of perversity and of perversely harming themselves. As a medical woman, Dr. Jane Francis wondered if there were some seed or seat in the brain where all things wicked resided like a dark god, luring men and sometimes women into a kind of euphoria that held sway until they wallowed in sin, became enveloped in it, enamored to it, lapping it up like a dog at the filthy river's edge.

She guessed now that it was death itself; that the two men, in order to cover their fear of the dead that they'd had no respect for, the dead they had desecrated—no matter their reform—stalked them in the nature of spirits, and not spirits of the sort bottled and labeled and competing for a ribbon at the fair, but spirits looming large inside their heads.

"Yes," she quietly said to the sound of the cobblestone beneath the hooves outside her cab, "such men fear themselves, can't abide themselves, hate themselves and fight being alone with themselves." So they hid inside noise and laughter and delusion and drink and the life of the flesh and materialism, she mused. They expected at any moment to be revealed as frauds, and to have their cushy new lives as Dr. Fenger's aides torn asunder. Little wonder that they feared and hated Alastair Ransom. He might take their new life from them, but worse still than Ransom was their own history. This past as ghouls must feed on their current lives! And their livers, and their hearts, and surely their souls that'd long ago fallen into all those open graves they'd left in their wake. *In a nightmare, how many open graves did it take to create the abyss?*

"They fear that after their own deaths, someone will steal their bodies and sell them to a medical school. That one day they'd feel the ripping out of their own organs." Foolish as this sounded when she spoke it aloud, to her medical mind, somehow Jane knew the truth of it. Superstition remained the coin of the day, far more so than religion with promises of penance and redemption. Oddly, the pair acted in sync, as if of one mind, and together they suffered a fear beyond reason, despite their outward appearance of happiness.

It reminded Jane of something her father had instilled in her. He would say, "Success is getting what you want, Jane, but it's happiness that is illusive. Happiness is wanting what your success has won. Happiness is seldom established and firm and finally within your grasp. Happiness drives men insane."

She gave a prayer to the now long dead, real Dr. James Tewes, a man who'd swept her up, a man whom she'd believed in need of her, and a man quite worth fixing, like Ransom now. If only there were such an animal; it never worked, going into a relationship believing you could fix another person. *If he needs fixing, he's no good for you. Run like hell,* she screamed silently inside the cab. She didn't want to be around when Alastair Ransom decided to destroy himself as James had.

Tears filled Jane's eyes.

It made her think of the passion and happiness she'd found with Alastair, and how damnably illusive it had proven to be. She gave a passing thought to all the promises they'd made to one another, or rather, all her promises, as he had been far more reserved. In fact, as the coach arrived at her home, she realized that it had all been rather one-sided, that she'd made a fool of herself over him, whispering all those sweet *nothings* in his ear there in bed, while he had literally kept mum. Alastair had whispered *nothing* in return.

Ransom found Hake the next day at Hake's filthy apartment, sleeping amid racing forms, spoiled food, dirty sheets, and an even dirtier woman. Ransom pulled him to his feet and instantly regretted it. Hake's scream sent horrid odors from his fetid throat into Alastair's nostrils. "God, man, you got drunk and you passed out! You were supposed to find me last night! Three A.M., remember? Something about a file that likely doesn't exist!"

"I give it to yer boy!"

"What?"

"I got there a bit late, but I give it to the boy. Samuel, said he was yours. Nothing in the file about you having a kid."

"He's a house guest, not my son! Damn you, Hake! You gave that file to Sam!" Ransom let the man slide back to his bed sheets and his woman.

"What 'bout the payment? Twenty more, you said."

"The boy and the file are gone, fool! And I've no idea where."

"You mean the kid'll sell it to the highest bidder?"

"What's the matter, Hake? You upset you didn't think of it first?"

"I got no love loss for Pinkerton."

Ransom frowned at the man. It was obvious he wasn't going to his sister's, if he had one, and that he'd long ago spent all he had on the booze and the broad.

Ransom threw a twenty at him and said, "You find that boy, you give me a call."

"Sure . . . sure. Sorry, I took him for—"

"And next time you assume I'm a father, let me know in advance, OK, so when we go to visit Dr. Fenger at Cook County, we can do it up right."

"Cook County . . . Fenger? Hospital?"

"So they can get my foot out of your ass."

"Look here!" shouted Hake's scar-faced woman. "Who do you think you are?" She was shit-faced drunk, too.

"Shut up, Dorcas! That's the man!"

She slapped Hake hard for his disrespectful tone.

Hake hauled off and slapped her back.

She hit him again, and he returned the favor as Ransom rushed for the door. As Ransom turned to pull it shut behind him, he saw that the two besotted souls had fallen into one another's arms and began renewing their passion.

He closed the door on the "lovers" and wondered where in the city Samuel might be at that moment with the file.

CHAPTER 29

Scattered leaves intermingled with discarded leftovers, fish heads, and other leavings conspired to stink up the Chicago wharves where boats and ships of every size, flag, stripe, and kind took up space like so many dinosaurs afloat. Amid the rubble and beneath the half-light of a world that might well've been conceived by Dante Alighieri in his *Divine Comedy*'s Inferno, an old, wretched, bent-at-the-hip man collected bottles, rags, fish parts, often fighting off cats, seagulls, and wharf rats as he went, arguing with them in a loud brogue, arms flailing. Amid the squalor, the old man occasionally found something that delighted him, and he'd begin to hum and laugh aloud at his good fortune over a particular trinket or found coin. The old man looked up at one point to stare into a dirty, warped window at his reflection, taking it in as if his visage and appearance were that of a stranger. Then he stared into his reflected eyes and found himself—deep in the irises.

Just as he was about to turn from his reflection, another face, grotesquely distorted by the warped window, was beside the old man, and this big fellow with a hunchback grabbed onto the old man, holding him, pinning his arms, when a second man stepped from the shadows, a man who looked peculiarly like the gargoyle seen in the reflection, but this fellow's features were not distorted.

"You two fools!" shouted the old man.

"Shut up!" cried the cleaner of the two, holding up a large blade. The blade itself shone like a third mugger, it was that large.

"Do we gotta do it?" asked the man who'd pinned the old man against the boards.

His thin partner replied, "We're going to take what we want from you, old man!"

"I got nothing but me rags and bottles to sell!"

"Oh, but you do have your rotten old flesh!"

Ransom, in disguise as the bottle and ragman, stomped hard on the foot of the man holding him, causing a pain so severe that he was instantly set loose. He snatched his revolver, but the knife man came at him so suddenly, he fumbled the blue-burnished steel .38 as he backed off, dropping it and watching it go over the side and into the Chicago River.

Ransom instantly brought up the large tool for castrating horses, which he'd kept hidden beneath the ratty clothes he wore. With all his might, he swung the cast iron pinchers, striking the knifer in the temple, sending him reeling back.

"Oooh, no!" cried the bigger one, going to the thinner one, concerned for his partner's bleeding temple.

"You damn fools! You're trying to mug a Chicago cop! Damn fools! I'm a CPD inspector!"

The lean one threw his knife at Ransom. It struck Ransom's thick coat and belt—all part of his disguise—but the blade did not penetrate. Instead, the knife fell away, chasing Ransom's gun into the dirty river. At this point the knifer raced off, leaving his accomplice behind.

Ransom stomped and shouted as he approached the dumb animal before him. The big man turned, grunted, and raced after his partner.

"Bastards! SOBs!" Ransom shouted after the pair. Few people on the darkened wharf took notice or wanted to be involved in any manner.

Ransom, as the ragman, went on his way, toward the destination he'd planned. As he did so, he again tucked the farm instrument beneath his coat.

He had bigger fish to fry than a pair of thugs.

Eventually Alastair got two of the three things he wanted that night. In fact, earlier in the day he'd gotten a lead on another strange doctor, a man who might be accepting body parts and whole bodies for dissection, paying ghouls at his back door. It was information he found in Nell Hartigan's cursory notes, notes that previously hadn't existed and were finally located and turned over via courier from William Pinkerton's office. The man was a Dr. Kenneth Mason. A check against the list Pinkerton had originally provided showed Mason crossed off.

Second, this night Ransom had learned that Father Franklin Jurgen was booked on a ship leaving from Lake Michigan to travel through the Great Lakes, up the St. Lawrence to Catskill Bay and the Atlantic, and finally on to Boston. There, Jurgen had passage on a ship crossing the Atlantic, a cushy, expensive berth on the Cunard shipping line, all paid for by the Church in its effort to relocate him and rehabilitate their man. Alastair had paid dearly for this information from Father O'Bannion's new secretary, who seemed to have caught an inkling of his keen interest in Father Jurgen and called him for a secret meeting. The bribe cost Ransom almost his entire month's pay, but he believed it well worth it—if the information proved true and timely.

The third thing he'd wanted so much to have but failed to achieve had been Jane's forgiveness. Alastair had gone to see her, but somehow bungled the whole apology. It began well enough, but she kept pouring on the guilt until he lost his calm, and it was all she needed to hear when he reminded her of her pillow talk.

"What happened to 'the world can call me a fool, but I've got to be right with you?' and—and, 'No matter what it is you want, I'll never say no to you,' and—and—"

That's when Jane slammed her door in his face—a loud "Ohhh!" escaping her lungs; the ultimate act of an angry woman at a loss for words.

Tonight it was first things first; he had to meet the ship taking Father Jurgen out of Chicago, else lose any chance to confront the skulking creep and exact some modicum of justice. So he'd put his personal problems on hold, along with any thoughts of going to see the private surgeon, Dr. Kenneth Mason and his dean, Dr. Nehemmia Conklin, names Pinkerton had crossed off the list—something about their having a contract for bodies of prisoners from the Joliet Penitentiary.

Nell's targeted ghoul-employer. Conklin kept coming up in Nell's notes, but Jurgen kept coming up in Ransom's brain. One thing at a time . . . first things first . . .

So here he lurked in disguise.

When he wreaked vengeance on the so-called man of God, he didn't want to be recognized. He had to act quickly without thinking, and to this end he'd been practicing all day with the heavy iron pinchers. The tool was a prong with powerful razor-sharp jaws that cut through metal cans in an instant. Flesh should be a quick zip-zip.

He gave a momentary thought to what Jane and Gabby might think of his level of anger and what he contemplated for the child-molesting priest. He gave a moment's thought to sleeping on it, but he knew by then the priest would be out of the city, untouchable.

More time passed with no sign of the priest or anyone from the church.

Ransom continued his tiresome lurking about the wharves, listening to the constant clatter of rigging against masts under a vigorous wind, which became monotonous and sleep-inducing. He had the ship under surveillance, and every passenger arriving by private or public coach. It still bothered him to know that Father O'Bannion was protecting this monster in vestments. And such thoughts kept his eyes open.

Soon he began to wonder if his information was worthless after all.

Ransom was not certain precisely how he would arrange for Father Franklin Jurgen's castration, but he'd figure it out as he went. He imagined that thinking too long and too seriously on the procedure would only hamper quick action. Like a mugging, he knew it must be done swiftly and with alacrity, without a moment's hesitation. He knew that fast action was good action, and that any bringing of this robed priest before a judge would be worse than useless, worse than slow, amounting to no action whatsoever brought against the perverse priest, this cretin.

At the moment only he and O'Bannion, along with Samuel, knew that he meant to personally mete out justice in this case, and O'Bannion could only surmise it as a possibility. So it must be done in such a manner that neither O'Bannion nor Samuel might be targeted as witnesses against him. He certainly didn't want Sam picked up for questioning or mixed up in any way with the disfiguring and maiming of a priest.

To this end, Ransom had donned one of his many disguises. Few people knew of his closet full with disguises, and fewer still knew of his habit of going about the city as someone else in order to gain and gather information, a foothold in an area, or simply to protect himself or a snitch.

"Where the hell're those priests?" he muttered, tiring of the wait, assuming O'Bannion would be on hand to be certain his man got aboard the *Lucienta Maria*, the ship Jurgen was supposedly booked on.

Again Ransom wondered at the quality of the report he'd paid so dearly for. Perhaps it'd been a ruse all along by O'Bannion; perhaps Father Jurgen was on a train for Boston—long gone. The thought made Ransom grit his teeth when he saw sailors come alive on the *Lucienta Maria*, making early preparations for a sunrise departure.

"Damn!" he cursed. "I've been buffaloed by O'Bannion!" Instead of getting the revenge he'd paid for, he had made a donation to the church.

Angry with himself, angry with O'Bannion and the little secretary who played her part so well, Alastair raised his large right fist to the ship when he saw a man smoking a cigar and walking the planked deck, a man in the robes of a priest—Father Franklin Jurgen.

He'd been on board the whole time.

Ransom knew he had but minutes to get aboard, grab the man, excise his jewels using the horse pinchers, and get off the ship, or become stranded on Lake Michigan with the man he'd attacked and a boatful of Portuguese sailors.

Was it a sign he should forget about his rash plan? Was it the wiser to leave the man, as O'Bannion had pleaded, to God?

Twilight would soon be overtaking the wharf. A handful of the men had come down the walkway, still loading a few crates and bundles of cargo and supplies. Without further hesitation, Ransom made his way to the gangplank before it would be removed by the crew. As he slipped past these fellows, he found himself face-to-face with a young-looking first mate who demanded, "You, old man! Get down outta here! Off the ship."

Alastair grunted and said, "Was mugged. Hurt."

"We've no room for the likes of you, old man! No free rides! Off, off!"

As Ransom was contemplating knocking out the young fool standing in his way, the priest turned at the shouting and rushed to the old man's aide, saying, "Mr. Tate, sir, even though this poor retch has no money for passage, you must treat a fellow human with the love and dignity of his Maker. Charity, my friend—charity of language and deed is ever rewarded."

The man named Tate rolled his eyes and replied, "This isn't the Salvation Army, Father."

Father Jurgen looked long into Ransom's bloodshot eyes and disheveled features, a patronizing smile on his face. Jurgen then said in the softest, warmest voice Ransom could imagine, "Now tell me, old sir, are you in need of bread?"

Using his old man's voice, Ransom replied, "I've gone today now three day and night sir without food, save for the discarded cabbage and raw fish heads I find an' boil up."

"Cabbage 'n' fish heads?"

"Some meat right 'round the jawbones."

"Have we not time to feed this poor man, Mr. Tianetto?" asked Jurgen of another man who appeared—the captain. Jurgen's eyes widened with his good deed. Ransom summed him up as one of those people whose "good deeds" convinced him of his "goodness" no matter his most vile actions against the innocent.

Helping an old man to a meal straightened his halo.

An annoyed captain replied, "I am still not comfortable with you on board, Mr. Jurgen."

"It's *Father* Jurgen, and I was put on this ship here and now in order to help this man!" He pointed to Ransom, unaware of the horse pinchers stitched to his inner lining.

"Ohhh, I suppose, all right," replied Captain Tianetto, "but you must see he gets off the ship in ten minutes."

"Ample time for gruel and bread in the galley!" Jurgen took firm hold of Alastair and led him toward a ladder going down into the bowels of the cramped ship. *It must be fate*, Ransom thought, *fate that had Franklin Jurgen step out on deck for a walk about, to stretch and to have a smoke.*

Condescending to the aged man, Jurgen guided Ransom to the ship's galley, noticing for the first time his cane and limp. He remarked on it.

"The one item I've not had to hock yet," said Ransom in his most gravelly voice. "'Twas given me by a dear departed one."

They passed other men, some sleeping in hammocks, some playing at cards, some scraping toes with huge knives, battling fungi and bunions, some chewing tobacco, while others sucked on lemons. The deeper into the hull he went with the priest, the surer Ransom felt it'd be impossible to escape or find the deck after he took care of Jurgen.

Finally, they came to a causeway, and overhead Ransom saw moonlight filtering through a hatch. A short ladder dangled here—a quick way abovedecks. A voice of experience and instinct shouted in Ransom's head: *Now!*

Alastair instantly grabbed the unsuspecting priest who

meant to assuage his guilt and sin by feeding a homeless man. With one quick blow of the wrought iron grapplers given him by Philo, he opened up a gash in Jurgen's head. Blood painted his scalp and forehead and he went down in a daze. Ransom tore at the robes, having to lift them, tore away the man's underwear, and in the darkness of this hole, feeling like a mad incubi or gargoyle, perched over the priest, he applied the horse tool.

All Ransom had left to do was apply the pressure of his hands at the end of the monster mechanism.

He hesitated, swallowed hard, and realized that perspiration poured from him.

Jurgen cried out, "What in the name of God!"

Calling on God this way only made Ransom surer of what he'd contemplated. "In the name of the children you've molested!" he shouted in response.

Several of the sailors poured into the small area, hearing the final exchange before Jurgen's horrid, pained scream, coming with the realization of what the old man intended as the cold steel of the pinchers telegraphed the old man's desire. "Please, please! No!"

Alastair realized something, too, at this moment; he realized he couldn't go through with it. He instead lifted the huge pinchers overhead and brought them down hard between the priest's legs.

The priest thought himself castrated, and out of his lungs came the scream of a wounded animal. The sound filled the belowdecks, lifted to the surface, and wafted like the echoing cry of a bobcat out over the water.

Ransom immediately pulled himself up the ladder to the half-moon peeking through the open hatch. As he did so, he felt someone grab onto his leg in an attempt to pull him down into the black cargo hold. A quick kick sent this fellow hurtling over the screaming priest and his bloody robes.

Ransom climbed like a big-shouldered beast from the hold, struggling as his shoulders caught on the small hatchway. The ship's captain and his young first mate rushed at him and the sound of Jurgen's cries.

"What'd you do, old man!" shouted Tianetto as Jurgen's continued wail cut into everyone's bones.

"That priest you have aboard is an imposter!" shouted Ransom.

"Imposter how?"

"He is a bloody child molester!"

"That's an awful charge!"

"And a grandfather has just taken revenge for the boys he's so badly used."

"If that's true, you may be sure the authorities will handle the matter. Now hand over yourself to me, ship's custody, and we'll sort this out."

"I'm no stranger to the law here. Chicago will bury me in a cell, and they'll make a hero of that ugly man you have below."

"From the sound of him, he's likely to die."

"I only gave him a head wound. A surgeon can sew him up. He won't die. In the meantime, I am walking off this ship."

The first mate pulled his pistol and pointed it at Ransom. "You'll do what Captain Tianetto decides and nothing else."

Ransom saw a man in nightshirt and cap standing on the bridge—the ship's doctor. The screams aboard had awakened him. "Bring all injured parties to my chambers!" he shouted with authority.

Ransom stood like a bull opposite Captain Tianetto, a Portuguese man with dark features. He sensed from the man's very posture the type of self-inflated, self-important little captain he was. Captains aboard these small ships that plied the Great Lakes tended to enjoy holding court and typically loved applying maritime law. He half imagined himself being tied to the mast and flogged until his skin had been peeled off as "just punishment" for his crime, or worse, that they would turn his weapon of choice, the pinchers, on him! Regardless of the fact he hadn't gone through with his plans.

"All right, I'm sure your captain's a fair man," began Ransom, speaking to Tate, the English-speaking first mate, "and—and perhaps he has children? Grandchildren perhaps? Little ones, and that he must guard against deviant toads like Jurgen who'd molest them?"

"He has many children, he's fair, but quite the Catholic," warned the younger man, his gun pointed.

One of the sailors came up the ladder with the castrating pliers in his outstretched hand, blood still dripping from them. "The priest, he . . . he cut himself . . . badly!"

"You mean he castrated himself?" asked Ransom.

"We thought you did it," replied the sailor.

Alastair believed this was going very bad very quickly, and with the speed of a viper, he reached out and wrenched the horse grippers out of the sailor's hands, striking the first mate in the jaw, sending him and his gun skidding across the deck.

Instantly, three other sailors leapt at Ransom and a brawl ensued. Ransom's cane brought one down, his fist wrapped around the iron pinchers slammed into another. The third man decided he hadn't enough invested in the priest, so he backed off, his hands going up in the air. The ferocity of Ransom's fighting had instilled a fear in all three, and so unchallenged further, he made for the gangplank when, inches from his hand, a gunshot splintered the wood. Ransom looked over his shoulder and his eyes met those of the white-bearded ship's doctor, who, no doubt, had been well paid to safeguard Jurgen.

"I left the bastard unharmed!" Ransom cried out.

Ransom then turned his back on the unarmed, shocked Captain Tianetto and walked slowly down the remainder of the gangplank, disregarding the captain's cries to stop and the doctor's threats of again firing.

It was a gamble, and Ransom inwardly flinched, half expecting to feel a bullet rip through him. But he gambled that the captain would prefer a quick, clean end to this matter; that Tianetto didn't want his departure held up by an inquest, one in which he'd have to explain the entry wound in Ransom's back. Shooting a man in the back, even in a situation like this, remained an act of cowardice in the collective mind. It would not serve the captain well to read about himself as a back shooter in the Chicago press.

Jurgen's screams and the gunshot had brought people out, and the wharves were suddenly busy with onlookers, so the captain must know there'd be multiple witnesses to anyone aboard shooting him in the back. The gamble worked.

Cane in hand, the old man moved unmolested by anyone, and Ransom hurriedly disappeared in the gloom of night beyond the lights of the wharf, but only after tossing the Montgomery Ward's castration pliers into the Chicago River.

CHAPTER 30

The following day, Samuel could be found nowhere, and the newspapers had eyewitness accounts and sketches of the old man who had, in a maniacal and unprovoked attack, "disfigured a priest who'd merely extended a helping hand to the beggar." The exact nature of the disfigurement could not be openly discussed in the papers for fear of scandalizing ladies and all refined gentlemen—so shocking, horrifying, and horrendous was the mutilation. Women in particular would be outraged, and one reporter feared that if he described the extent of Father Jurgen's injuries, people might faint outright.

The Chicago Police Department chief, Nathan Kohler, swore that he would put his best people on the case, and that the CPD would not rest until the fiend who'd mutilated this poor man of God was apprehended and punished to the full extent of the law. He finished by saying that every witness and anyone who'd come into contact with the mystery man who'd attacked Jurgen were being questioned for every detail, and as they'd pieced the event together, a clear picture emerged of an insane white-bearded, heavyset maniac in their midst, a madman who might strike again at any citizen of the city.

The papers did describe the weapon that had been used on the priest—the horse grippers. In fact, a sidebar described the instrument in detail, virtually trumping the story itself and making clear the nature of the injuries to Father Franklin Jurgen.

The thinking went that if the attacker could find fault with a saintly priest, God forbid he should ever attack a guilty man—meaning no one was safe—man, woman, or child in the city. Therefore, anyone who might've seen the old rag and bottle collector hanging about the wharf, wolfing down raw fish heads, was asked to contact police and come in for a statement.

When Alastair read about the circumstances and that Father Jurgen had been rushed to Cook County Hospital for surgery, he wondered who among the crew had reason to hate the priest or want him dead.

He thought of the two muggers who'd accosted him with a knife. As he folded the morning paper and had his coffee and pastry at the shop he frequented most mornings, he quietly chuckled at the notion of all the wharf rats showing up on Kohler's doorstep to assist in the investigation, and to collect a reward for doing a civic duty.

Just then a shadow blotted out all light across Alastair's table, and he looked up to find Philo Keane staring wide-eyed at him, slapping a hand against the paper he held. "*You* bloody did it!"

"*Shhh* . . . sit and calm down!"

"And you used my pinchers."

"Technically, the *item* belongs to Montgomery Ward, and secondly, I didn't do it."

"Somehow, Rance, your saying so doesn't ease my mind."

Ransom shook his head in disbelief. It never failed to amaze him that the truth was so often harder to believe than a lie. "Sit and have some coffee."

Philo dropped into the seat opposite him. "I never imagined you'd actually go through with it."

"I didn't."

"I thought you'd threaten him, terrify him, but Rance, this . . . this is unbelievable."

"Again, I tell you I did not go through with it, and no one can trace the weapon—someone else used on the priest—back to you, so stop blubbering."

"I see. So that's how we will play it. Where is *the weapon*?"

"The river."

"Thanks for that much. Nothing goes in there ever comes out."

"Are you calmed down?" Alastair asked. "Look, my friend, no one's going to put it together, and honestly, I failed to go through with it in the end."

"How can you be so sure no one will piece it together?"

"All right, no one's likely to put it together."

Philo said it slower, enunciating each word as he would to a dote. "How-can-you-be-so-sure?"

"No one saw me. They saw old Jack Ketchum."

"Your favorite disguise. How sweetly ironic . . . so Jack did it, and you couldn't. That's how you live with it? Rationalizing it away as the work of Ketchum?"

"Weathered ol' Ketchum didn't do it either, but he's gone to rest eternal now."

"Yes, he must forever remain dead and gone if you are to survive this! The fervor gotten up in the press, if old Jack were caught, he'd be burned at the stake."

"Not before they castrated him," teased Alastair, smirking.

"I'm glad you can joke about this! And aye, for what you did to a spiritual leader, if they catch Jack or you, you might be castrated."

"Sad old Jack comes out the pervert instead of the pervert coming out the pervert."

"Be smug and jolly 'bout it, but just suppose Nathan Kohler were to put it together, Alastair? He knows your disguises, and he knows you're after Nell's killer, that you could well've been on that wharf as Ketchum. And if he puts it together, Rance, you can kiss your real self good-bye."

A waiter entered Philo's peripheral vision, asking for his order.

"Coffee, black, with a Danish."

"Yes, sir. And you, Inspector? Anything else?"

"Another coffee, yes."

"How did you do it?" Philo asked after the waiter moved away. "And why aboard the ship?"

"I'd like to share the details of every moment with you, but Philo, I suspect you and I are both safer if I keep it *entirely* to myself."

Philo pouted. "Are you implying that you can't trust me, your confidant and best friend?"

Ransom glared at him, realizing how backward this entire conversation was. "It's not that I don't trust you, Philo."

"After all we've meant to one a—"

"I've seen you wilt under interrogation, remember?" Ransom said, cutting Philo off. "Besides, drink loosens your tongue."

Philo sat back in his chair. "*Hmmmpf* . . . I see."

"Don't give me that look. You know full well I'm right."

"And the boy, Samuel, when he learns of all this?" Philo jammed his index finger into the newspaper lying between them. "How tight-lipped do you think he'll be when he gets among his fellows?"

"He's a good kid. Reminds me of me."

"That's a horrid thought."

"He'll do as I say and acquit himself well."

"If he doesn't come under Kohler's thumb! Or if he doesn't get it in his head to collect a reward."

"He'll do neither." Ransom shook his head. "Have you no trust in human nature left, Philo?"

"Bosch does sometime work for Kohler."

"I'm aware of Bosch's burning both ends."

"At the very least, the kid'll want to brag to his friends how Inspector Ransom did him a good turn."

The waiter returned with Danish and a coffeepot. After a moment, Philo sipped at his steaming coffee and tore into his pastry. "It's human nature that I worry about; it's natural the boy would want to talk about you, his hero."

Ransom, for the moment, worried more about what Samuel was planning with that Pinkerton dossier. But he calmly replied, "You always fret over the wrong things, Philo."

"A boy his age can hardly keep this to himself and not drop your name. If you're not careful, you'll find yourself behind bars, facing a judge on charges of—"

"All right, point taken. Enough. You're like a washerwoman sometimes!" But Alastair thought how right Philo was; that in fact Philo had no idea just how right he was.

The waiter returned with more coffee and something on his mind. The thin, sallow man in an apron looked jaundiced from years of drink and his voice was gruff. "Horrible isn't it?" he said to the seated gentlemen, jabbing an index finger at the headline lying between them. "How even a priest in this city can be targeted by a maniac. First the mayor, and now a priest! This city's going the way of Sodom and Gomorrah."

"Yeah . . . whataya going to do?" asked Ransom.

"What're you coppers gonna do, Inspector?" asked the waiter. "A mayor and a lady Pinkerton agent killed, and now a priest castrated, and what's done about it? Nothing's done about it."

The sallow-faced waiter made his way back to the counter, picked up a rag and began wiping down. Philo commented, "The prevailing belief from the man on the street, Ransom. So what are you going to do about Nell's murder, now that you've got this other *matter* out of your way?"

"Ever hear of a surgeon named Conklin? Dr. Nehemmia Conklin?"

"No, can't say I have, but this city has as many surgeons as pigeons."

"Nell had the fellow under watch."

"*Ahhh* . . . then you've finally gotten some cooperation out of Pinkerton?"

"Bill Pinkerton, yes." He chose not to mention Hake.

"And are you going to hammer Conklin . . . or cut his nuts off?"

"*Shhh* . . . Philo, do you want me hauled in for ending the career of a child molesting rat when in fact I did not carry through with it?"

"All right . . . all right, you'll not hear another word of it from me, but I fear, Rance, that one day this action of yours will come back to haunt you or bite you in that big arse of yours."

"Thanks for your advice, my friend, and for agreeing to speak of it no more."

"Rance, the man wound up in Cook County."

"Under whose care?"

"Dr. Fenger's care."

"Fenger, heh?"

"Yes, but there was little he could do but close the wound and hand the priest his testicles in a formaldehyde-filled jar."

"Perhaps Jurgen can make money showing the jar at a traveling carnival," quipped Ransom.

"Would make a helluva an exhibit, all right, as in exhibit number one in the case against you, if you're not careful."

"I thought we agreed to end talk of it, since I did not clip the man's jewels."

"We did agree, but you asked about Fenger's involvement."

"I did, didn't I?"

"Fenger, too, has condemned the man who could do this to another man. Called him a bestial creature likely from Hades itself, likely with horns and a bifurcated tail, complete with pitchfork."

"He said all that?"

"I had to take pictures of the man's mutilated parts, Rance. Hardest thing I've had to photograph since . . . since Chelsey's murder."

"You feel pity for this disgusting pig?"

"Here, damn you!" Philo discreetly pulled forth a photo he'd made. "Your handiwork. Take a good look."

The shot of the mutilated center of the attack made Ransom turn his eyes away. "All the same, Philo, for the last time, I didn't do this to the man. I came damn near it, but I couldn't."

"Are you serious? Are you really innocent this go round?"

"Innocent, yes."

"Rance, crimes against children—"

"Just get thrown out of court. Kids don't vote; they've no rights!"

"OK, you're right," replied Philo. "We both know it."

"Just would've been swept under and tossed out had I gone through the system. No one wants to deal with this particular societal cancer."

"All right . . . end of discussion." Philo lifted and put away the bloody crotch photo. "Just be careful. Kohler gets wind of the truth, whatever it is, you've had it."

Just then the shop doorbell rang, its lilting sound announcing Mike O'Malley, who stood near the door, scanning the room. When he saw Ransom and Philo Keane huddled over a photo, he rushed toward them, waving.

"Mike!" said Ransom

Philo secured the photo.

"Ahhh . . . I see Mr. Keane's shown you that awful photo!" Mike replied, pulling up a seat.

For Ransom, looking at young Mike O'Malley amounted to looking back through time at himself twenty years earlier. "What's the word, Mike? You looking for me?" he asked.

"Matter of fact, yes. Kohler sent me to locate you."

"Really?"

"Wants me to haul your ass in," Mike said, laughing.

"Haul 'im in?" asked Philo.

"What does that balding blowhard want, Mike?"

"He wants you to head up the investigation."

"But *I am* heading up the investigation. Where've you been, Mike?"

"No, not the Hartigan case, the Jurgen case!"

"The Jurgen case? Me?"

"Yes, wants you to locate and put the collar on the man who attacked the good priest."

"Why Inspector Ransom?" asked Philo, amazed.

"How ducky," said Ransom. "Why is it that Nell's case is

taking a back seat to this attack on a priest? Why do you think, Mike? What lesson does it send?"

"Ahhh . . . Kohler's conscious of the media attention given the priest as opposed to Nell?"

"Exactly. Anybody ask why this old man attacked the priest to begin with?"

Mike shrugged. "Witnesses say some sort of sudden loss of control. The priest offered him bread and drink, and he just, for no reason at all, attacked Father Jurgen."

"Anyone question Father Jurgen yet?"

"I did, yes." Mike ordered a coffee.

"And what was Father Jurgen's explanation?" Ransom made the word "Father" sound like a sneer. While Mike failed to notice, Philo rolled his eyes.

"He says the attack came when he asked the man to pray with him."

"Really?"

"To help a stranger overcome vile, inner demons, he said."

"He said all that after being castrated?"

"Word for word."

"Wonder who's to help Jurgen overcome his demons?"

"Well, Father O'Bannion's sitting with him."

Ransom and Philo exchanged a look, Alastair enjoying the irony of his being put on a case in which he'd literally be in pursuit of himself as the number one suspect. "Frankly, Mike, I can almost guarantee that we'll never locate this insane old madman who attacked Jurgen."

"Why not?" asked the kid.

"Yeah, why not?" asked Keane, curious how Ransom would answer.

Philo downed his coffee as Ransom slowly replied, "He's a yegg, a transient, described as an old man with a cane, a limp, and an ungodly pair of horse castrators! No doubt once a farmer who lost his place, now bummin' about, all he owns on his stooped back."

"You make 'im sound like he's the victim," said Philo.

"Kinda sad, really, the old duffer losin' his farm."

"And so," added Philo, "this miscreant yegg has likely hopped a freight and's many hundreds of miles from Chicago by now?"

Opening his pocket watch and staring at the time, Ransom exploded. "Oh, my! Gotta go. It's late. But that is a fine assessment of the situation, Mr. Keane. You have it right, no doubt!"

"Yeah," agreed Mike, "if he's a yegg, he's on the move for sure."

"Perhaps, Inspector O'Malley, you should head up this ballsy investigation."

"I've not your experience, Rance."

Philo piped in with, "Besides, Rance, you have the knack of *cutting* to the chase."

"But Mike here's got the stamina. He's young and will stay on the scent."

"Quit putting me on, Rance," replied Mike.

Philo added, "But you'll have to look under every rock, Mike!"

"Yeah," agreed the young inspector, "Kohler expects results or else."

"Or else what?" asked Ransom.

"Heads'll roll, he says. He made promises to Father O'Bannion and Jurgen at his hospital bed before newspaper reporters."

Ransom flinched at the name O'Bannion. "Kohler always knows a photo opportunity when he sees it."

"Come, man," said Philo, "the sensationalism alone of someone accosting a priest equates to front page news, but to mutilate the privates of a man of the cloth! Surely, you don't think Kohler can control such news."

"I suppose you're right again Philo."

"I know."

"Mike, you'll learn that Philo here knows everything, and I know the rest," Ransom teased.

"Stop it with that!" Philo chastised, and turned to Mike. "Inspector Ransom is joking—mimicking Mark Twain's stage words on Kipling and himself."

"*Ahhh*, a performance I missed."

"Sounds like I am up for my own performance before Kohler and O'Bannion," said Alastair, getting up to go.

Philo stood and placed a hand on Ransom's shoulder. "Take all due care, my friend, that your performance go well."

Lifting his wolf's head cane in salute, Ransom departed with Mike at his side. In his wake, Ransom left the shop bell atop the door ringing as if it would never stop.

Remaining at the table, having another cup of coffee, Philo Keane pulled out the photo and stared once more at what he feared his friend Ransom capable of, even if he did push it off on an alias. In the back of his mind he began plotting out a course of action of how best to whisk Alastair from Chicago and into Canada against the day he must flee, a wanted man.

CHAPTER 31

Early in the day, news had gotten out that Dr. Christian Fenger would be performing an extremely delicate and highly unusual operation. Dr. Fenger had made a call specifically to inform Jane Francis Tewes that while no female medical personnel could be on hand at the request of the man being operated on—a Father Franklin Jurgen—he, Christian, saw no reason why a certain Dr. James Phineas Tewes could not be on hand.

In other words, be there, she thought, and she had been on hand to watch Fenger perform his surgical magic.

As a result, Jane had seen firsthand the awful result of mutilation done to the priest, and she'd wondered what kind of world was it that brought about such suffering. Thank God for Christian Fenger. While he could not reattach that which had been severed, he could sew the man up and ease his pain.

The greatest problem Jane had in viewing the ghastly wound and procedure was keeping her breakfast down, as she'd been up the previous night.

She had, as Tewes, begun to get more and more work at Cook County, and it never ceased to amaze her the bizarre and wild cases that walked in the door or were carted in by Shanks and Gwinn.

She needed sleep now, and to that end had returned home. Waiting in the empty lot amid the birds and the bushes, however, crouched Henry Dot 'n' Carry Bosch. She'd used Henry Bosch's dubious services in the past, and now she had set him loose on her problem of the strange pair that seemed known only to Shanks and Gwinn. Instead of attempting to tail the ambulance men any further, she'd hired Bosch to do her slumming and report back.

"What've you got for me, Mr. Bosch?" she asked from the swing on her porch, still in her Tewes getup, as Bosch had long before informed her that he'd learned of her dual identity before anyone else. The little wrinkled man had taken great pride in his determination. In fact, it'd been Bosch, the ferreting snoop, who first informed Alastair of this fact, at a time when Ransom had refused to believe it, so certain was the inspector that Tewes was Tewes and Jane was Jane.

"I know where that pair you're looking for lives. I got that much!"

"You have an address on them?"

"Did I not tell ya I'm good at what I do?"

"Have you written down the address for me?"

"I have, ma'am." He passed a crumpled, dirty piece of torn paper through the bars of her porch fence, and she passed him several bills in response. When she looked again, Bosch was gone as if he'd slipped below her porch, a regular leprechaun.

She read the note in Bosch's tight little script:

> 400 Atgeld Avenue, go to back apartment, first fl.
> Names are Vander and Philander Rolsky.

"They're related?" she asked the night.

"Cousins perhaps?" Bosch was back as if by magic.

"Maybe uncle and nephew?" she offered.

"Could e'en be brothers . . . can't say for sure."

"Determine the relationship, Mr. Bosch, and I'll pay you more," she replied, but no way Bosch could hear, as now she saw him and his stick rushing off down the alleyway. Even with a wooden leg, the man moved as swift as any four-legged creature.

Now that she had this information, she wondered if it might not be prudent to share it with Alastair. Perhaps it was time to get help on this matter, share her suspicions of these two men named Rolsky.

"Was it that vile little man Bosch again?" asked Gabby the moment Jane stepped through the door. "And, Mother, you look extremely fatigued."

"You can see that even in Dr. Tewes?"

"I can. You'd best get some sleep."

"But I have patients beginning at ten." The clock read 9:10 A.M.

"Wow, Mother, do you really mean to give yourself a whole half hour, fifteen minutes maybe?" Gabby's facetious reply was not lost on her mother. "Look, I know a few things. I'll take care of Tewes's patients today. I'll give 'em what they want to hear, sell them a bottle or two of Tewes's Terrific Tonic—the cocaine-laced stuff that makes everyone feel better, and I'll send 'em on their way with a promise to see you tomorrow!"

"Got it all covered, do you?"

"I do."

"They'll insist on seeing a man—me . . . *ahhh,* Dr. Tewes."

"And I will insist it is impossible. Go to bed, Mother! Now!"

Jane, who needed no second telling, had taken Gabby's suggestion and gone to her room, where she now lay in Tewes's clothes across the bed, seeking a brief respite from the world. Closing her eyes, her mind played over the difficult surgery of the religious man, and she could see Fenger's every cut to make the jagged edges as clean as possible. She relived every stitch, realizing that she could well have done the surgery herself.

The operation itself was a success, but as with any surgery, infection could set in as rampant as a swarm of locusts. For this reason, Jane feared poor Father Jurgen might well find himself in the hospital for weeks, and months should his wound become abscessed. If so, he'd need round the clock, constant care and the vigilance of someone, perhaps Dr. Tewes, to stave off death.

Sadly or mercifully, Jurgen had slipped into a coma. According to Father O'Bannion, on hand at the bedside, the injured priest would be unable to take charge as head priest over a church in Greenland, of all places. "Such dedication," she'd said, "to go to such a desolate place to give of himself."

"Yes . . . yes," O'Bannion had replied, clearly unhappy with the turn of events.

"What kind of a fiend could do such a thing?" Tewes had asked Father O'Bannion.

"A misguided man, someone who thinks himself capable of doing the work of God, I suppose."

This unexpected reply confused her. "Of God? Don't you mean Satan?"

"Yes, Satan, of course Satan."

With her eyes still closed, Jane said a silent prayer for the injured priest, and the condition of the world flowed from her thoughts moments before she fell asleep.

When Alastair and Mike arrived at the Des Plaines station house out of which he normally worked, a waiting sergeant ushered them into Nathan Kohler's second floor office. There, Ransom came face-to-face with Father O'Bannion. "I understand you two know one another, Inspector Ransom," said Kohler. "Father O'Bannion's brought me a disturbing report."

Alastair raised his chin and with his eyes focused on O'Bannion asked, "And what might that be, Chief?"

"Inspector Ransom," began Kohler, unclenching his teeth, "Is it true that—"

"That I threatened Father Jurgen the night before he was attacked?"

"What?" asked Mike, confused. If his wide eyes were any indication, his mind raced with strange scenarios.

"Then you don't deny showing up intoxicated at St. Pete's and looking to harm the priest, and that O'Bannion here sent you away?" Kohler's eyes pinned him like daggers.

"All true, except that I wasn't drinking."

"You only deny being intoxicated?" pressed Kohler.

"I was intoxicated on anger, not liquor."

"He was drunk, I tell you, and threatening," O'Bannion firmly said.

"I was soberly angry," countered Ransom.

"All right, even sober, you're confessing that you were upset enough to harm Father Jurgen?" Nathan led with his next question.

"I was pretty damned angry, yes."

"So when Father O'Bannion heard that I meant to put you in charge of locating and punishing the man guilty of this atrocious attack, he naturally came to me."

"To protest my leading up the investigation?"

"Exactly."

"I will step aside for Mike here, or for any other detective of Father O'Bannion's choosing. Will that please one and all?"

"That's a first step. Care to explain *why* you were looking to crack the father's skull with that cane of yours?"

"Actually, it had to do with a gambling debt," Alastair lied.

"Do priests gamble?" asked Mike.

O'Bannion frowned at this.

"Father O'Bannion tells another story," countered Kohler, ignoring Mike. "Says you accused his priest of molesting boys in his care. Is there any truth to these, *ahhh* . . . allegations?"

"All right. I was trying to be tasteful, keep such filth out of the press."

"You mean when you attacked Father Jurgen?" asked Kohler point-blank, and it became immediately clear to Ransom that the chief had already made up his mind.

"That's preposterous!" shouted Mike.

"I'll handle this, Mike," said Ransom, putting up a hand

to calm the junior detective. "You know me well enough, Nathan, to know that *had* I attacked this lowlife bastard hiding behind robes in order to manhandle and fondle children, he would not have come away alive."

"We're all familiar with your notions of justice and retribution, Alastair," returned Kohler, getting to his feet. "Eye for an eye, tooth for a tooth—"

"And in this case?" Ransom asked. "Do you really think me foolish enough to risk my position and career on a man of such low character once I calmed down?"

"Besides which," put in Mike, "all the witnesses agree it was an old man in rags."

"An old fellow, yes, with a wolf's head cane," said Kohler, indicating Ransom's cane.

"That's a bald-face lie!" objected Alastair, knowing he'd not used the distinctive cane the night of the incident aboard the *Lucienta*.

"An old man with the strength and agility of a much younger man, it would seem"—Kohler didn't skip a beat—"taking on three or four burly sailors at once. Sounds to me like a *bear* of a man."

"Some older guys are tough as nails," offered Ransom.

"Why, me own grandfather could beat that wharf rabble any day," added Mike.

"Wore one of your disguises, did you, Alastair?" asked Kohler. "Perhaps the Jack Ketchum get up?"

"If you think it so, then I will stand a lineup with four other men in similar garb, and if I am picked from among them, you may hang me as you see fit from the nearest bloody flagpole!" It was a challenge and a bluff.

"Quite the poker face." Kohler rose to the bluff. "Arrange it, O'Malley."

A red-faced Mike shouted, "But, Chief, sir, such a step is a slap in the face of every detective on your force!"

"Damn you, man! Arrange it!"

Mike seethed a moment, Alastair nudged him, and finally he nodded, saying, "All right, but this will win you no points with the lads, sir."

"Are *you* satisfied with this arrangement, Father O'Bannion?" asked Alastair.

"Well . . . yes then."

"In the meantime, with all this wasted effort," began Alastair, picking at lint on his coat, "the real culprit is likely sitting in a boxcar on his way to parts unknown as we play games."

"And Father Jurgen fights for his life in a wretched state, and if and when he comes to, God knows how he will react to the realization that he's been . . . that his, *ahhh* . . . "

"Dick is in a jar?" asked Alastair.

"No, his penis is intact," countered O'Bannion.

"You mean . . . " began Mike, "whoever did this knew precisely to take the testicles alone?"

"And was the cut precise?" asked Alastair.

"Quite . . . precise, yes."

"Then we should be seeking someone who's had experience at this sort of thing," shouted Mike. "Experience . . . and the right *tools*, say a—a pig farmer, or a horse knacker from the yards."

"A slaughter man?" shouted Kohler, facetiously adding, "Of course, he'd be another Leather Apron killer on the loose? Hey, Alastair?"

Ransom raised his hands in a gesture of defeat. "Look, sirs, Mike makes complete sense, and he's ahead of all of us on the case. Just listen to him! I nominate Inspector O'Malley as lead investigator since all my energy and focus is at the moment on the Hartigan murder."

"I'm honored that you'd entrust it to me, Inspector Ransom," said Mike.

"O'Malley!" exploded Nathan. "Ransom hasn't yet gained the authority to give you anything of the sort!"

"But it makes sense!" shouted Ransom.

Meanwhile, Mike's Irish white face blanched red with passion.

"No one said this job has to make sense," countered Kohler.

"God forbid it should," replied Ransom. "Perhaps, Father

O," he continued, turning to O'Bannion, "your giving a blessing over the investigation might help, and one for Nell Hartigan while you're at it."

"Both of you out, and O'Malley, arrange for the lineup that your senior partner proposes, and once done, you're to head up the investigation into who slashed Father Jurgen and why."

"Start with the parents and grandparents of each choirboy," suggested Ransom. "And for the sake of propriety, for goodness sakes, don't let the press get wind of the *why*."

CHAPTER 32

The lineup arranged at the Des Plaines Street station proved something of an embarrassment for Alastair when he learned that Gabrielle Tewes, Jane's daughter, had done all the clerical work to make it happen. He tugged at Mike's arm when they brought him and the others in, whispering, "What's Gabby doing here?"

"Kohler's idea. He put her on it."

"Bastard," muttered Ransom.

More and more, Gabby had gotten involved in police work and at as many levels as she could manage to breach. She'd been instrumental in the final phases of ending the career of the Phantom of the Fair. She was an anomaly, and her being headquartered at the Des Plaines station was not without friction. Still, the situation, at least in her mind, seemed to be working out just swimmingly. She had an eye for detail, and alongside her medical schoolwork, and working with Dr. Christian Fenger as his special assistant to the police, she'd shown herself capable. Gabby meant to become his mentored replacement someday—a full-fledged autopsy expert, rather than what her mother had hoped—a surgeon to the living.

Ransom had watched her growth, and he'd taken great

pride in her, like a father, as it'd been his urging early on that
resulted in Gabby's having taken a leap into this man's
world.

But he didn't figure on Gabby being on hand for the bluff
he was carrying out against Kohler. It was the most outrageous card that Nathan could pull from his deck—putting
her on this unctuous duty.

Four other ragged men who'd been snatched from the alleyways of the neighborhood, aged men with beards, gray
and white hair, now stood beside Ransom in his Jack Ketchum disguise. With Alastair dressed in wig, mustache,
beard, and rags, perched directly in the middle, the others
appeared shaky, some with the DT's, looking confusedly
about the unfamiliar circumstances. Each was now told to
hold up a number. This further confused one and all.

"What?"

"How high?"

"I'm no number . . . I'm a man."

"Where's me money you promised?"

Mike and Gabby had to deal with this confusion before
they might allow the so-called eyewitnesses through the
door one at a time. Anyone with any experience working
such a detail knew never to place eyewitnesses in a room
together, as typically a disagreement or even a fight broke
out over their testimony. The disagreement and level of con-
tradiction between people who claimed to have seen a crime
in progress was legend among police, and knowing this,
Alastair's bluff rode on the twin chariots of ambiguity and
inconsistency.

This truth proved at work among the sailors who'd struggled with Ransom hand-to-hand, including the injured first
mate and his captain. All of whom Ransom had supposed
long gone by now, as the *Lucienta Maria* had, after all, been
preparing to depart when he had boarded. Apparently, the
crusty old lake captain had delayed departing, Kohler having
impounded the ship and crew in his effort to get Inspector
Ransom.

Still, none of the sailors, including Tianetto, could conclusively identify Ransom from among the five derelicts. In fact, only the first mate called out number three as the culprit, while each of the others, taken in turn, claimed it was the man on his right or left. When First Mate Tate was told by the lovely young Gabby that he'd picked out a Chicago police detective in disguise, he blushed red and quickly recanted and selected number four instead. By this time, Mr. Tate was far more interested in Gabrielle Tewes than in righting a wrong.

Just when Ransom thought it over, O'Malley escorted in another man, a hulking hunchback who looked familiar from the moment Ransom spied him. A kind of tall Quasimodo, he was one of the pair who'd tried to mug him on the wharf the night before, but he knew that to say so now would only further incriminate him.

For a moment Alastair thought he'd be found out and punished, ironically, for something he hadn't done, while a nagging voice in his head, sounding strangely like Jane's, declared it fitting justice. A fair deal for all the crimes he'd committed in the name of lawful expediency.

The lumbering, freakish-looking man brought in to ID Ransom kept wiping away spittle that seemed uncontrollable, and his nose was runny and red with a cold or some worse malady. He coughed into a raggedy red paisley handkerchief, and his dumb stare—as vacuous as the eyes of a kewpie doll—came along with bloodshot irises. He breathed so heavily and nasally, he seemed a queer monster to be curious of and cautious of at once. At the same time, he looked the part of a giant sapped of strength, and definitely a man who belonged abed. All the same, Ransom felt a twinge of fear from this man with whom he'd locked eyes the night of the incident.

Staring at the lineup, the man Gabby called Mr. Rolsky could not say which of the five might be the man he saw on the wharf that night, but if he must guess, it would be number one.

"Why number one?" asked Mike.

"'Cause number one's staring back at me so hard."

"I see."

"He looks guilty?" asked the slow, lumbering sloth of a man.

From his darkened corner, Nathan Kohler, standing alongside Father O'Bannion, curtly said, "Get 'im outta here, O'Malley!"

"Thank you, Mr. Rolsky, for coming forward and doing your civic duty," Gabby said, showing him the door.

"Where do I get my money for coming in?" he asked.

"Go along with the officer," she gently informed him.

She then said to Mike loud enough for everyone's ears, "This is ridiculous, the whole thing a sham just to play Russian roulette with Inspector Ransom's life. Just to implicate him any way you can."

"We've got one more witness," said Mike, calming her. "Mr. Rolsky's brother, so let's just get through this, OK, Miss Tewes?"

"Yeah . . . right."

"Bring 'im in!" shouted Kohler, ignoring Gabby's outburst.

Mike escorted in the man Ransom imagined most likely to finger him. This fellow was the knife-wielder of the evening before, the man who'd cost him his gun over the side of the wharf, and this sallow-eyed fellow proved an opposite of his dote of a partner, despite similarities in their appearance, masked only by the misshapen features of his brother. This one had steel for a spine—to come forward like this, straight in Ransom's own precinct. *Arrogant impunity on spindly legs,* Ransom intoned in his head.

He watched this particular Mr. Rolsky size up the room the way a cougar might, determining who was a threat and who was not, and quite likely who was the weakest animal in his sights. When finished sizing up the authorities, he sized up the motley crew forming a lineup, studying each with great care and a critical eye. A kind of clinical detachment to his manner, like a doctor puzzling over a necrotic organ. Ransom felt as if this Rolsky could see straight through him. He felt on the verge of arrest for the suffering priest.

Ransom took the bull by the horns, stepping out of character and leaping off the lineup stage to confront this Rolsky fellow. "I've had enough of this nonsense! This man is a known criminal, a mugger and quite possibly a murderer for all we know!"

"It's him! This is the man!" declared Philander. "He even told us—my brother and me—that he was a Chicago cop! Ask Vander! Bring him back and put it to my brother."

"This whole matter's botched!" cried out Alastair. "You can't possibly take the word of a known criminal in a lineup. Paying these men is corrupting enough of the process, but hiring wharf rats like this!"

"I'll show you who's a wharf rat!" Rolsky had snatched his newly acquired blade and held it out before Ransom's eyes.

Ransom grabbed his wrists and squeezed until the man shouted in pain and the knife dropped to the floor.

O'Malley jumped Philander and quickly handcuffed him, leaving him lying on the floor, his hands behind him, his knife confiscated. Then Ransom put his face close to Rolsky's and muttered, "You're really lousy with a knife, you know that?" He then yanked him to his feet.

Mike slapped the man on the back of the head and said, "Gabrielle, take his measurements and check'm against the Bertillon system, see what we have on this gutter scum's measurements and characteristics, if anything."

Ransom added, "And for heaven's sakes, take his prints. When the devil's fingerprinting going to be a matter of course around here?"

The innovation of fingerprinting criminals and fugitives for evidentiary purposes, while in vogue in England for sometime now, and used for centuries in commercial transactions in Asia and India, was still meeting resistance in American police circles. The cumbersome and questionable Bertillon file cards continued to hold sway in the minds of most police authorities.

"Sure, we'll take finger and hand prints," Gabby enthusiastically replied.

"Just get this roach out of my sight." Ransom sighed, knowing that no one, including Kohler and the courts, understood fingerprint evidence, and that it might take another World's Fair and another scientific awakening. It maddened him that the same scientific fact written about in Mark Twain's *Puddin'head Wilson* in '47 was still treated as fiction and fantasy.

"I tell you this is your man!" shouted Rolsky, struggling against the cuffs and Mike's grip on him, spitting and kicking.

"How can you be sure it's Inspector Ransom?" shouted Nathan Kohler, now in the man's face. "How can you know?"

"His voice . . . it was his voice . . . and—and his eyes!"

"Now that'll be the day you convict a man in a court of law based on his voice or his eyes!" Ransom laughed at the notion.

Kohler considered this and had to agree. "Take him to booking, Mike, Gabrielle," he said. Turning to Ransom, with O'Bannion grinding his old teeth, he added, "You win this one, Alastair."

"But what about his guilt? What about my word?" exploded O'Bannion. "I have no reason to lie."

"Afraid it's not enough, Father. Your word against his, and you saw him in a rage the night before the incident. You think he may have been hiding some sort of weapon beneath his coat, but you saw nothing, and you were nowhere near the ship where Father Jurgen was attacked."

Ransom gave a thought to O'Bannion's secretary, who had not been called as a witness. Another bullet dodged.

O'Bannion's rage showed in every feature. He looked about to spew forth a long list of profanities. Instead, he gritted his teeth. "Force the inspector here to Father Jurgen's bedside. *He* will tell you it was this man who viciously attacked him."

Ransom imagined the younger priest might well believe it had indeed been his hand on those pinchers at the crucial moment. Or had Jurgen punished himself?

"It's my understanding that your junior priest is in a coma at this time," Kohler countered. "Perhaps when he comes 'round we can indeed arrange it." He turned to Ransom. "That suit you, Inspector?"

"I'd like nothing better than to clear my name of this cruel allegation."

O'Bannion's red face seethed with thoughts of vengeance of his own, it seemed, as he turned and pushed through the door, rushing out, calling down a strong and effective Christian curse with a Gaelic twist: "May your bones turn to ash, Alastair Ransom, and be swept into Satan's waste bin!"

"And a pleasant evening to you, too, Father!" Ransom shouted after the retreating O'Bannion.

Inconclusive as the lineup was, Nathan Kohler still believed that Alastair Ransom had something to do with castrating the young priest, but he hadn't the proof. His score of witnesses had proven useless. Ransom believed that his expensive wolf's head cane, which he'd held throughout the lineup proceedings, had in its way marked him as *not* the culprit. *A stroke of genius on my part*, he told himself.

Meanwhile, the man who now twice accosted him with a knife was being booked for attempted assault on an officer. The idiot had done so not only in front of witnesses and cops, but in his own *house*! The man would now spend time in lockup until a judge adjudicated his case. It only proved to Ransom what he'd concluded long ago about criminals—*that crime made one stupid*, and the criminal urge was, for so many, a natural state of being.

Down the hall from the room used for lineups, Ransom found Gabby trying to calm the other Rolsky brother, the giant one with the pushed-in Pekinese face and the unfortunate hunchback. The big fellow was distraught on learning his brother was not leaving the jailhouse police station with him. "This ain't right . . . this is wrong! What am I gonna do without Philander? He keeps me outta trouble. He tells me what to do."

It was painfully clear that the big man, brother to Philander Rolsky, had the intelligence of a child. He stood pacing in pure panic, fear wrapping about him with each passing thought about spending a moment—much less a day and a night—without his brother beside him.

"You keep this up," Mike O'Malley said to him, "and you'll be locked up right alongside your brother."

"Can you do that? I wanna be with Philander."

Gabby pleaded, "Why don't you just go home and wait for your brother? He'll find you there after he's seen the judge."

Her voice seemed to calm the big fellow, who was a head taller than Ransom. When he saw Ransom, he exploded toward him, his hands extended as if to choke the life from Alastair. Side-stepping, Alastair tripped Vander Rolsky with his cane, sending the huge man sprawling across the boards, his head coming to rest at the steps going down. "Go home, Mr. Rolsky!" he shouted. "Take Miss Tewes's advice! Now!"

The command in Ransom's voice often proved enough to break up a riot, and the change that came over Vander on hearing the orders barked at him seemed remarkable indeed. He suddenly became a cowed creature, and he slinked down the stairwell and out into the street like a dog with its hind legs hiding its tail. Once more Ransom marked the red, bloodshot eyes, black and beady at their centers.

"Poor brute," said Gabby. "Reminds me of Shelley's *Frankenstein* for some reason."

"Don't waste your time or sympathy on 'im!" said Mike, losing points with Gabby.

Ransom added, "So far as I can tell, he and his brother work as a team along the wharves, accosting people for money and jewelry and anything they can turn a profit on."

She turned on Ransom, a fire in her eyes reminiscent of Jane when riled up. "Being callous to the retarded among us does not become either of you gentlemen! It's obvious he does whatever his brother puts him up to. And why not? He's learned to trust no one else."

"Yeah . . . like a monkey grinder's pet," said Mike, a snicker escaping.

"Or any trained animal," added Ransom. "Recalls to mind an A. E. Poe story I caught in *Harper's* about an ape trained to murder in a Paris neighborhood."

"The two indeed make a strange pair, but we're speaking of a human being here, not an animal." Gabby remained calm despite her punctuating this with a stomp.

"All right, say his brother is the ringleader of their little street carnival," began Ransom. "If this dote kills someone on his brother's say-so, it doesn't make him any less guilty of murder."

"Perhaps not, but then . . . " She hesitated. " . . . perhaps it should."

"You'd rather see him in Cook County Asylum than prison?" asked Mike.

"He would receive more humane treatment and medical care."

"Have you taken the time to see that asylum?" Mike argued.

"Trust me, Gabby," added Ransom, "that asylum needs major reforms. The kind that not even Christian Fenger or the love of Christ has put a dent into. People still treat the mad as a leprosy they don't want to know about, hear about, or speak about. Result—it's no place for any man."

"Neither is Vander likely to last long in Joliet." Gabby's eyes had gone wide with her passion. "So there's not a damn place in all the world for people like Vander." She stalked off.

"Fiery when she gets her hackles up, isn't she?" asked O'Malley.

"Yes . . . like someone else I know."

Mike asked, "How do you want us to proceed with this Rolsky fellow in lockup?"

"Full background check, any records we might have on him, previous arrests, time spent and where, talk to his landlord, the neighbors."

"Will do, and Rance . . . "

"Yes?"

"Congratulations."

"On the lineup, you mean?"

"On beating Chief Kohler at his own game."

"Wasn't hard to do."

They laughed, winning the stares of others coming and going. "Imagine Kohler thinking you cut off a priest's nuts." Mike's laugh filled the station house.

"Did make an ass of himself, didn't he?" Ransom joined in the laughter, and it felt good. After all it was justice. A rare commodity these days.

Alastair gave a wonder to who had harmed the priest with the weapon he'd carried aboard the *Lucienta* that night. Was it the crewman who'd come up the ladder brandishing the horse pinchers? Was it another down below, someone who owed Father Jurgen money, or whom the priest owed a debt? A lot of gambling went on aboard a ship. They'd just reached the entryway to the galley where Jurgen had proposed to feed the shabby old Jack Ketchum when Alastair had made his move. The nature of the attack on the priest begged the question of who meant to wreak such vengeance on Jurgen other than himself?

And there was the sudden disappearance of his boy snitch, Samuel. Could it be possible that the boy had followed him, shadowed him somehow?

Or might it be another boy, a boy aboard the ship the whole time in close proximity to the pandering Jurgen? Every ship had a cabin boy and a galley boy. Child labor was alive and well in maritime circles.

Alastair concluded it must be so. Perhaps the likely suspect was a nameless, faceless, defenseless—until he saw the pinchers—galley boy. Whoever it'd been, he'd done the deed in the presence of other sailors, mates who'd shielded him. Perhaps it would remain one of those frustrating unsolved mysteries without end. Quite fitting perhaps.

CHAPTER 33

"It was perfectly sad, Mother," Gabby told Jane over breakfast the next morning. She'd gone into detail about Ransom's trouble with having been literally accused of the awful attack on Father Franklin Jurgen, who now lay in a coma, fighting a gangrenous infection in his private parts. Jane listened intently, allowing her daughter to go on as she described how Father O'Bannion and Kohler had done all in their power to lay it at Alastair's doorstep, this heinous crime.

"How absolutely mad Nathan Kohler must be!" Jane said of the allegation.

"I know!"

"It's just as I've warned Alastair time and again. Nathan's hatred of Alastair is beyond reason."

"It's clearer every day," agreed Gabby.

"Put nothing—nothing—past Kohler."

"I'll remember that. But, Mother, there was this sad, sad giant showed up at the lineup."

"Giant?"

"With a hunchback, yes. Name's Vander, and how he clung to his brother, when the brother was thrown into jail for coming at Alastair with a knife."

"My God, and you in harm's way at that place! Was Alastair hurt?"

"I was never in any danger, and Alastair was masterful the way he took the knife from the other man."

Jane frowned at this. "But why would Father O'Bannion suspect Ransom in this hideous affair?" This Jane could not fathom. Kohler, yes; Father O'Bannion, no. This felt like a bona fide mystery.

"Apparently, Alastair had gone looking for Father Jurgen the night before, and was quite upset with him."

"Upset with a priest, Ransom? For what reason?"

"At first I heard gambling debt, but in fact it was something far worse, Mother, an allegation of wrongdoing."

"Worse how? Wrongdoing? Be direct, dear."

"Alastair claimed he'd gotten information that Father Jurgen had been . . . that is . . . was . . . "

"Out with it!"

"Petting children."

"Petting children?"

"All right, playing with children."

"Playing with children, how? Like St. Francis of Assisi?"

"Oh, Mother, you can be so dense for an educated woman."

"Oh, my God, you're saying Father Jurgen has touched children inappropriately?"

"Molested, yes—but we've no real proof."

Jane stepped off and moved about the small house and clinic, her heart racing. She imagined an enraged bull named Ransom going after a man, any man, who harmed a child. Then she shook off the thought that he could possibly have castrated a priest. "I saw the man's wound, and I must agree with Dr. Fenger. Whoever mutilated Jurgen was sending a message."

"A message meaning what?" Gabby asked.

"A message of let the punishment fit the crime."

"Chicago justice? The sort Inspector Ransom might mete out," Gabby mused aloud.

"There's no proof of his involvement, is there?"

"None, and he stood a lineup in that old man's disguise of his and passed."

"I see. But we don't have evidence of Father Jurgen's crime either, now do we?"

"Only hearsay."

"What sort of hearsay?"

"Well . . . rumors are flying, but I hate to pass along a—a—"

"Pass it!"

"I only heard it by accident."

"Overheard, yes, yes . . . I know you do not engage in idle gossip. What did you over—"

"That Father Jurgen had indeed molested a child, and that the child's grandfather had stalked the priest to the ship, and this old fellow bided his time, and the moment he got the least close, he—he exacted his terrible revenge for his grandson."

"A priest molesting a young boy? It's too horrible to contemplate." Yet she'd read lurid accounts of priests in cloisters and monasteries going mad and attacking nuns, or nuns doing likewise, some attacking children.

She recalled the horrible case popularly called the Devils of Loudun, France. Descartes had written about it in some vague attempt to quantify evil. She'd also seen it written up in a medical journal, the author an obscure German medical man who attempted to understand the psychology of temperance and abstinence, and the role that religious political fervor played in the case. The Loudun, France, incident was generations ago, in 1635, during the Renaissance.

Perhaps such horrors occurred more often than anyone imagined and were kept quiet—secrets of the Church hardly being a new concept.

Still, Jane's mind, seemingly independent of her, wanted quickly to reject the notion. Priests were sworn to serve man through the love of Christ, to walk this Earth as His angels, to care for the poor, the destitute, the ill and infirm, and especially to administer to children, and to harm not so much as a mockingbird. This accusation against Father Jurgen simply could not be.

And yet, who maims a priest in such a way without cause? And if there is cause, there is affect. Cause meant reaction to an action. Was this mystery grandfather reacting to something imagined or real? How much horrid truth might come of Gabby's rumor?

Gabby continued with her tale of all that'd happened at the station house, although Jane's thoughts had gone astray. "You'd've been so proud of Alastair, Mother."

"Ohhh, and why is that?"

"The way he just took charge."

"He has that quality about him, yes."

"I mean when he leapt from the stage so . . . so—"

"Melodramatic?"

"Dramatically, yes! Tearing away his wig and beard, revealing himself to his accuser."

"Sounds rather like pure theater, dear."

"I don't mean to say he was playacting, only that he was, well, dashing."

"Swashbuckling, heh? Well, it is a brash fool who wields a knife in Alastair's face."

"Yes, Alastair said, and I quote: 'I'll not stand here and be judged by the likes of this wharf scum!'"

"*Ahhh*, an apt line. I can hear it rolling off his tongue myself."

"The man with the knife turned out to be the giant's brother, also addressed as Mr. Rolsky," she continued. "Although one of the pair is deformed, their features are uncannily similar. And Mother, recall the pair we saw that night milling about the street near Colonel Dodge's place?"

"Of course, brothers! One misshapen, a growth on his back?"

"Yes, like I said, Vander."

"Vander? And the other one, Philander?"

"Yes, but how did you know his name?"

"And the one appears normal, he orders the deformed one about like his dog, doesn't he?"

"Yes. How did—"

"I must interview these two men."

"What? Whatever are you talking about?" Gabby's eyes had grown wider each time her mother spoke.

"I'm, *ahhh* . . . conducting a study."

"A study?"

"A medical study of criminal families . . . and this pair certainly sound as if they are familiar with crime. Their anecdotes might be of help." Jane watched Gabby's features to see if the lie had taken hold or had failed.

"A mental study of criminal families, really? How fascinating."

"Yes, fascinating."

"*Ahhh* . . . something Dr. Fenger set you to doing, isn't it?"

"Yes, and it pays well." Jane latched onto the explanation.

"He's a great one for doling out studies for others to do." Gabby paced, looking a bit hurt now. "But why didn't he put me on to it?"

"Perhaps he feared you've enough on your plate. In the meantime, I'm finding it an intriguing and absorbing study, dear. Do you think I might gain entry to the cell where this Mr. Rolsky is being held, you know, to conduct a proper interview?"

"I can get you in."

"Wonderful. Today? This morning?"

"Today? Now?"

"Dr. Fenger is a taskmaster."

"Why not speak to the retarded one first; he's likely to be home, and if I go with you, he'll remember I was kind to him at the station. He might open up."

"Then later, will you get me in to see his brother?"

"Absolutely."

"All right, then that's how we'll proceed. I merely have to do my disguise."

"You needn't see either of them as Tewes, Mother! Go as yourself. Assert yourself. After all, you have a medical degree. Besides, Vander's sure to know nothing of Tewes, and he responds, I think, far better to women."

"All right, I rather fancy the idea, but the final study will have Dr. James Phineas Tewes's signature on it."

"Whatever makes you happy, but I for one am so fatigued over this business of your dual personality. And if I am, so you must be."

"Frankly, dear, there are so many advantages to walking out there"—she pointed to the window—"as a man than as a woman, I've rather become fond of being Dr. J. P. Tewes."

"That's become increasingly obvious, and scary, Mother, and it has put a strain on everyone around you, including me . . . including Alastair. And it'd go a long way in helping you two make up."

"There'll come a time when Mr. Ransom learns how to apologize, I'm sure. Now let's make our way to see your gentle giant, Vander. I need a good talk with this fellow."

"Well . . . I'm not sure where exactly he lives."

"I'll get that information quickly enough," replied Jane, taking her purse and herself to the phone, finding a pencil and pad while simultaneously cranking the phone. In a moment she made a show of talking to Alastair, saying she and Gabby wanted to visit Vander Rolsky, adding loudly, "We mean to bring the poor dote an urn of soup and bread, and to sit and pray with him, and to educate him as to his many options here in the city that cares."

Feeling famished, Gabby only half heard the one-sided conversation as she scrounged about the kitchen for a slice of cheese and crackers for herself. But then she clearly heard Jane pronounce the street and address they required.

"Telephone's such a marvelous invention," said Jane, returning to the sitting room where she shared the block of cheese and soda crackers that Gabby had placed on the table.

"You might've asked Alastair how he is faring." Gabby munched at her food. "It must be awful . . . his having to endure such godawful accusations. Why do people hate him so?"

"Well for my part, I didn't want him to think I had a single thought in my head of his being capable of such a horrid act!"

"I see . . . so you said not a word of it. *Hmmm* . . . perhaps being prudent on the subject is the right approach."

"Shall we go see Mr. Vander Rolsky?"

"What about that soup and bread?"

"On second thought, it is rather presumptuous of us to assume the poor man has nothing in his cupboard."

"Ahhh yes, Mother, but I think in this case it's a fair assumption."

Jane smiled at her bright daughter. "You are so wise."

"And you, Mother, are so caring."

"And no doubt your concern for the man at the police station won favor. So yes, let's take the time to gather that soup and bread. It could be our Trojan horse."

"All right. Better to be presumptuous than unprepared."

"Hey, I rather like that phrase."

Gabby smiled at this. "Perhaps it could be useful at our next rally."

"Oh please, don't you have enough to do without carrying on in the streets with those bloomer girls?"

"Suffragette sisters, Mother. For heavens sake, New York ladies run their undies up a pole, and we're all branded as fools. Besides, I'm just saying it'd make a nice banner."

"I'm sure that men everywhere will appreciate it more than bloomer-waving flags."

"I'm afraid too many men prefer the bloomers."

Jane laughed and added, "And sadly, fewer still can read."

"I'm sure that's true in the case of this Vander Rolsky."

"Yes, from what little I know of him, I am quite sure he'll appreciate the food over the slogan. And in that spirit"— Jane worked her way around the kitchen as she spoke— "it does a heart good to do for others. Man the cooking utensils!"

"Yes . . . yes, it does a heart good." Gabby followed her mother's lead. "If more people would discover that joy, I think we'd have a far better world."

While Jane consulted her raggedy cookbook, Gabby began cutting up vegetables for the stew. Mother and daughter went about cheerfully fulfilling an old recipe. In the midst of this preparation, Jane telephoned the Bryce Hansom Carriage Company for transportation to the Atgeld Avenue address where the two suspected ghouls made their home in the first floor flat at the rear. Information she'd gleaned from Henry Dot 'n' Carry Bosch. By this time a fresh loaf of bread was rising in the oven.

CHAPTER 34

When they finally got to the Atgeld address of the Rolsky brothers, it was mid-morning. The Tewes ladies held the cab at a distance for most of a half hour while uniformed police, directed by Mike O'Malley, went in and out of the residence, carrying out various items and storing these into a paddy wagon.

Jane feared they were too late, that the giant Gabby had spoken of would be arrested and hauled off to join his brother, but that was not the case. O'Malley and the others left on the police wagon with some clothing, a rug, and a box, the contents of which might be anything. She suspected the box and its contents were likely headed directly to Chief Nathan Kohler's office and lockup, pending a trial that would put Philander Rolsky away for a lifetime or until he was hung.

However, they hadn't arrested Vander Rolsky. The big man sat hunched over on his stone doorstep, head in hands, quaking, looking a bit like an abandoned child or a stone gargoyle, depending on one's attitude.

"Perhaps we should return tomorrow," suggested Gabby.

"Whatever for?"

"I'm sure Mr. Rolsky has had enough turbulence for one day."

CITY OF THE ABSENT

"But we are hardly turbulence; besides, his soup and bread belongs to him."

"All right, Mother, if you're sure, but I worry."

"Worry?"

"About what O'Malley carried out of the apartment."

"No doubt Nathan or Alastair Ransom sent him to search for anything incriminating against Vander's brother to keep him behind bars."

"Suppose they find something truly incriminating and that poor wretched soul sitting on his stoop is left for a year or even several years without his brother to take care of him? What then?"

"You're predicting an awful future for the man. Why not a good future?"

"I fear there can be none for him. Mother, he's like a stray dog in need of . . . of a farm place where he can just be himself and have the run of the place and be left in peace and no one taking advantage of him."

Their eyes met on this note. Jane had held the same fearful opinion of the big man's future. "Enough with such grim thoughts, child."

"I tell you, Chicago eats people like Vander alive."

"And it is equally as possible that some Chicagoans, such as ourselves, can find a place for the fellow."

"All right, touché, but Mother, what if—"

"Come, let's keep a cheerful faith, shall we, dear?" Jane opened the slot overhead and ordered the coachman, "Carry on. Drop us across from 400 Atgeld." She paid him well for his time, pressing a bill through the slot.

In a moment the ladies, dressed in their wide-brimmed hats and flowered, casual prints, one yellow, the other pink, climbed from the coach with the gifts they bore for Vander. "I want you to let me do the talking, Gabby."

"Why so? Mother, what's going on inside your head?"

"The study I am doing requires no interruptions, coaching on your part, or insertions from outsiders," she lied again. "Understood?"

"I see. I'm on hand for introductions only."

"Exactly, to break the ice."

The cabbie having been paid, the hansom pulled away, over the cobblestones. The ladies stood across the street from Vander's place, and they saw the last of him moving like a meandering, confused buffalo around the outside of the building.

Urn of soup and loaf of bread in hand, the ladies made haste to catch Vander before he should disappear completely. To this end, they made their way to the run-down, ramshackle apartment house, an obvious, blatant monument to typical Chicago graft, as it screamed fire violation multiple times over. On approach, in fact, as they closed on the edifice, Jane saw the clinging wood fire escape and the stacked porches and landings rising alongside a stripped apple tree. The closer one got, the more obvious was the firetrap nature of the place.

"This place should be condemned," said Gabby.

Jane laughed nervously. "I suspect it has been, many times over."

"*Ahhh* . . . and approved many times over on account of promised repairs?"

"Money talks."

"Meanwhile lives are at risk."

"The way of it, I'm afraid."

They walked to the rear of the building and found it looked the same, only here was a court with a pair of trees, box elders, rising to the top of the building in search of more light.

It was a simple matter to find Vander Rolsky, as he'd returned to a kind of sitting fetal position on his back stoop. Fewer prying eyes here. Neighbors and the curious had earlier watched the police activity, but they'd all gone back to their own concerns now. The police had made Vander a public figure for fifteen minutes as they'd tagged his home as worthy of a search and seizure operation.

Vander lifted his gaze from the dirty stone steps when their combined shadows and the smell of bread and soup caught his attention. He instantly recognized Gabby from the police station. "Oh . . . it's you."

"We brought you something, Vander," she replied.

"I'm Jane, Gabby's mother." Jane held out the soup urn while Gabby extended the wrapped bread.

Gabby, seeing how Vander wanted the food, suggested, "Why don't we go inside where you can eat in peace?"

"And where we can talk in private," added Jane.

Vander hesitated only a moment, his desire for the food overcoming him. He nodded and lumbered to his feet, and the three of them retired to Vander's apartment.

Deep inside the firetrap now, Vander pushed through an interior door and went directly for a small table. Here he sat like the proverbial giant of "Jack and the Beanstalk." Wasting no time, he began slurping his soup and dipping his bread.

"Thought you might like some home cooking," said Gabby.

His eyes registered his pleasure over the gifts they'd brought. He remained astonished. "Really good," he muttered. "Nobody ever done such a kindness."

"Yes, really good home cooking." Gabby smiled across at Vander.

Jane asked, "Can I talk to you, Mr. Rolsky, about you and your brother, about how you work together, that is?"

"Philander don't let me talk to nobody. 'Specially not about work."

"I got that impression at the station," replied Gabby.

"Says I shouldn't talk to strangers or people—*never.*"

"Yes, but we're not strangers," said Gabby. "You know me now. We're, *ahhh,* friends."

"Friends?"

"Besides," added Jane, "we can bring more gifts for you, Vander. You like gifts, don't you?"

"Yeah, I do." He gobbled down more of the bread loaf, and a sad look passed across his features on realizing the soup had gone cold.

"All homemade, just like from mama's kitchen," said Jane.

"I didn't hurt Mama."

This sent a chill through Jane and Gabby—right along their spines as they exchanged a look of confusion. "What happened to your mama, Vander?" asked Jane.

"Mama and Papa was bo'f bad to us. Me and Philander."

"*Ahhh* . . . bad how?" asked Jane. "I mean how bad?"

"They beat on us a lot. Didn't hardly hurt me, 'cause I got thick skin and a thick head, but Philander, he got hurt bad."

"Beaten by his father?"

"And Ma, too."

"I want to ask you, Vander, did you and your brother ever hurt anyone else, other than your father and mother."

"I said . . . I—I—I didn't hurt Ma and Pa."

"OK . . . OK, I believe you, but have you and Philander ever harmed anyone *together*?"

"Mother—" began Gabby, but Jane gave her an upturned hand and a stern look, silencing her.

"Vander, I am a medical doctor," said Jane, "and my daughter Gabby is soon going to be a doctor as well."

"Really?"

"Really," replied Gabby.

"And so we doctors are doing a study of families that are prone to violence, you see?"

"You're really doctors?" Vander asked Gabby, his eyes and body coming to life with curiosity. "I never known no woman doctor, and now I got two at my house?"

"We are rare, Vander, but then so are all of us," replied Gabby, "unique and rare."

"Philander calls me rare. A rare specimen, he says. Also calls me stupid . . . says I'm an idiot . . . an em-em-embar-embar-rass-ment."

"Well I think your brother needs to work on his manners," said Jane.

"And his temper," added Gabby. "He tried to knife Inspector Ransom."

"Twice," said Vander.

"No, just once," corrected Gabby.

"Philander tried to cut him the night before when—when we saw him on the wharf."

Jane and Gabby exchanged another curious look, each wondering anew about Alastair's whereabouts the night Father Jurgen was attacked. Gabby shrugged.

Jane produced a small but distinct photograph of Calvin Dodge, then asked Vander, "Have you ever seen this man before?"

Vander shook as if cold water had been thrown on him, his skin rippling like that of a horse experiencing a chill. His strangely handsome yet disfigured face made one want to stare all the more at his unfortunate features, and the curious hunchback only added to his bizarre yet alluring look. He might have been the Cyclops if he covered one eye, or Goliath of biblical infamy. Yet his nature was little more than that of a child.

"Gabby and I saw you and your brother, Vander, outside Mr. Dodge's house the night before he disappeared."

"There's no medical study, is there, Mother?" asked Gabby, but Jane ignored this, her eyes boring into Vander, awaiting an answer.

"Uh-huh. It was youse two in the carriage!" he gleefully realized, proud at being able to recall the incident.

"Yes, it was us. But Vander—"

"Yeah?"

"Did you and your brother harm Mr. Dodge and carry him out of his home in a rug?"

"Philander made me clean the rug. Said it'd bring us money, too."

Gabby pulled her mother away, and beneath a naked overhanging gas lantern, she said, "God, he'd be so easy to get a confession from, but he's harmless. He couldn't've killed Dodge."

"He and his brother work as a team. I don't know how much blood is on his hands, but I suspect his brother uses him for his strength. Dodge wouldn't have a chance against a man of this size and strength."

"Then you suspect the brothers of having killed Nell Hartigan as well?"

"And who knows how many nameless, faceless people in the city?"

"The study for Fenger, all a ruse?" pressed Gabby.

"Yes, I'm sorry about that."

"Forget it, but your conclusions are a big leap, and how do we prove them?" Gabby had become excited at the prospect of mother and daughter cracking this unbelievable case. But it seemed too easy, too pat.

"Imagine it . . . " began Jane, pacing, "you see these brothers who, on the one hand, look alike, and yet do not look alike."

"Due to the big one's deformities, yes."

"Imagine you're Nell Hartigan or Calvin Dodge and in the dark with this, you're seeing a circus act."

"You do a double-take."

"Double-take is right. And in that moment of hesitation the knife-wielding brother has your guts in his hands."

"He snatched that knife out against Alastair like a snake attacking; it was so fast. Like a reflex."

"It could explain a great deal."

"As in how an experienced Pinkerton agent could be overpowered?"

"Before she could get off a shot."

Gabby nodded at the suppositions when Vander groaned and complained that his soup had gone cold.

The simpleton sat dunking his bread and chewing. "Good . . . good . . . " he chanted, "but soup's cold."

"I'll put it on the stove to warm," replied Gabby, taking the urn to the stove and lighting the gas.

"Vander," began Jane, "your brother's telling the cops that *you* are the one who murdered Nell Hartigan and Calvin Dodge."

"What?"

"Isn't it true?"

"Philander is telling people *I* did it?"

"Yes."

"Well . . . then . . . he must know."

"Must know?" asked Gabby.

"Know what?" asked Jane.

"Philander, he knows *everything*."

"I see," piped in Jane.

"He says so himself."

"Really?"

"Ahhh, all the time. He says, 'Van' . . . he calls me Van sometimes . . . he says, 'I know all there is *you* need to know, so you don't need to know *nothing,* 'cause I know.' You see what I mean?"

"You believe him when he says you killed that woman?"

"She was s'pose to be a prostitute, and Philander says prostitutes don't deserve to be livin'."

"He . . . he said that?"

Gabby began jotting notes on a pad for the day when a jury needed this to hang Philander.

"Says the world's better off with all the prostitutes dead," continued Vander.

"He says that, and he knows all, but she wasn't a prostitute, Vander, now was she?" asked Jane calmly, her voice soothing.

Vander could not wrap his mind around this nonsensical notion that his brother was imperfect, fallible.

"And what about Mr. Dodge? Huh?" persisted Jane, in pursuit of his mind. "Is the world better off with him dead and gone?"

"Philander says so, yes. Said he was a liar, a crook, and said it was the only way to shut him up."

"Mother, we've got to get Vander back to the police station. Get an official statement, and besides, Ransom should hear this."

"You're right. But, Vander, first tell me, would you kill me or my daughter here if Philander asked—"

"Philander don't ask . . . he tells!" Vander laughed, the sound a hollow mirth.

"OK . . . if Philander *told* you that Gabby was a worthless piece of human trash, and that I was a street slut, and that the world'd be a better place with us gone, Vander, would you harm us?"

"I—I—I like Gabby . . . and I—I like you, too."

"Thank you, Vander, but that isn't answering the question."

"Mother, your tone."

Jane persisted. "Would you kill *me* if Philander asked you to?"

A voice from behind them replied, "Vander will do whatever he's told, so long as it's me doing the tellin'!" The voice belonged to Philander, somehow here, somehow out of jail. Had he somehow escaped?

"We were just leaving," said Jane.

"Pity that!" Philander advanced on them. "I so wanted your company, the both of you dear ladies."

"Don't you come near us!" shouted Gabby, startled, shaking.

Philander shouted, "Grab her, Vander!" as he took hold of Jane. "Tie them up until we can decide how to take care of this matter!"

Vander hesitated to grab hold of Gabby, saying, "But they've been real nice to me. Brought me soup and bread, they did!"

Jane kicked out at Philander in an attempt to free herself, and at once Gabby picked up a lamp and hit Philander square on the head.

At this point, an agitated Vander grabbed up Gabby. Both women were screaming until Philander knocked Jane senseless and Vander cupped his hand over Gabby's mouth—his hand so large that it covered her nostrils as well, choking off her air until she fell faint.

CHAPTER 35

Alastair Ransom hadn't any idea of the whereabouts of Jane or Gabby as he repeatedly rang their annoying doorbell, its light, airy tinkle certainly not enough to be heard at the back of the house and perhaps not from the clinic run by the infamous Dr. Tewes either. Why weren't they answering his insistent ringing?

Then he wondered if the bell mightn't be malfunctioning. He had awful luck with mechanical devices. Suspecting this might be the case, using his cane, Ransom instead began pounding on the door, rattling the windows. "That oughta get some attention." He rapped again.

Anyone seeing him at the door might make him out a bear that'd strayed in from the surrounding countryside, somehow confused and running amok in the city. Reverend Jabes from two doors down at the Episcopal church thought so when he stuck his head out the parsonage window and shouted, "What is that ungodly noise?"

Ransom stepped around to face the minister, giving the man a slight nod and a wave of his silver wolf's head cane. "In need of Dr. Tewes down at the station house again," he lied to the minister.

"Don't know where the doctor's got off to!" Jabes shouted

back, making Ransom wonder if the man might be deaf, the way he shouted at everyone and everything. He had heard of the man's sermons. In fact, the man's preachings were legend in the neighborhood as the most zealous ever pounded out at a pulpit.

To the usual, run-of-the mill good Christian, Jabes had earned a reputation as one who lived up to his name far too much—jabbing at people with his tongue. The minister lashed out at sin and sinners, of whom there were many; in fact, Jabes found them at every turn, and his multiple-hour single sermons had earned him the nickname of Jabberwocky Jabes.

"What of Dr. Tewes's womenfolk? Why isn't someone home?" Alastair dared ask.

"At least *they* come to church on occasion!" he retorted. "Can't say the same of Dr. Tewes. He seems to have an aversion for the Lord's word and house—not unlike *yourself*, Inspector."

"A cop in a city like ours, Mr. Jabes, he doesn't have much time for niceties like—"

"Niceties, is it? Is that what you call answering to the Lord?"

"Well no, I didn't mean to say—"

"Yet you find time for drinking and brawls and womanizing and gambling, I understand."

"As I said, a cop in Chicago leads a full life, sir." Ransom inwardly smiled at his own remark. "So you have no notion where the ladies may've got off to?"

"I did see them take a coach."

"The two of 'em?"

"Southbound is all I know."

"Did they happen to say anything at all?"

"Said they'd try to make my sermon Sunday."

"Oh, I see. Anything else?"

"I recall nothing further."

"Hmmm . . ." Alastair imagined they'd gone shopping, either at the market or one of the huge department stores on State Street.

"Except . . ." muttered Jabes.

"Except? Yes, except what?"

"It was somewhat garbled. The younger one asked if they shouldn't call you, sir, before embarking."

"Call me?" *Not to advise them on shopping,* he thought. "Nothing of their destination?"

"Sorry . . . no, but their hands were full with food. I suspect they were going to visit some shut-in perhaps."

"Thanks all the same."

The thin-faced, beak-nosed, goggle-eyed minister in spectacles replied, "Do come by Sunday, and let's work on reclaiming and restoring your good soul, Inspector, to God and Christ and the Holy Ghost."

"'Fraid, sir, they'll all have to get in line."

"In line? You mean as in to *stand* a lineup?"

Ransom glared at the minister. "News travels fast."

"Especially among the clergy."

"O'Bannion's spreading lies, Mr. Jabes."

"He holds you responsible for the unfortunate affair with Father Jurgen."

"I tell you, I had nothing to do with it." Not entirely true, as he'd brought the weapon.

"True or not, your reputation comes back to haunt you, and being what it is, cultivated as it has been, people will quite willingly give this news a nod."

"I'm aware of that." *Painfully so,* he thought.

"Certainly few will dispute it, but if you make your confession to me, I will hold it in confidence or counter O'Bannion's opinion, depending on your wish, Inspector."

"I'll take it under advisement, sir."

With that, Ransom rushed off, wondering how many citizens of the town had it on bad authority that he'd laid Jurgen low with those horse pinchers. Obviously, Father O'Bannion was busily spreading the word, setting public opinion clearly against him.

Unsure how to locate Jane Francis, Ransom was scanning Belmont Street for any approaching cabs when he saw Samuel and Bosch, both his snitches, coming toward him, waving him down.

The three found a nook near a livery stable and in shadow began to talk. "Samuel, I thought you'd vacated the city, poof! Gone."

"No sir, just lying low."

"With something that belongs to me."

"Sorry, sir. Yes, I took the file, but only so's to keep it from falling into the wrong hands."

"What hands?"

"Some men came after Hake and the file. I ran."

Likely Bill Pinkerton, Ransom thought. The private detective had caught on to his dealings with Frederick Hake. "Learning from Bosch here, are you?"

"He's a fast leaner," said Bosch, smiling like a doting teacher over a prized pupil.

"You two planning extortion? To blackmail me?"

"Now that's an awful thing to suspect of the boy and me," replied Bosch.

"Tell me, then, what's got you two working in consort?" asked Ransom. "Gotta be that Pinkerton file."

Bosch's features pinched into a huge question mark, while Sam made not a sound.

"Inspector," began Henry Bosch, "we're here to inform you that Miss Jane's been seeking information about the fellow you arrested earlier today, that Rolsky fellow, and his brother."

"What're you talking about?"

Sam blurted out, "Miss Jane's been seeking help in locating that pair of strange fellas who might be body snatchers."

"Ghouls, they are!" Bosch added. "Go ahead and say it, Sam. The word won't turn you into no pumpkin." Bosch laughed until the laugh turned into a coughing fit.

Ransom grabbed the wizened Bosch by both shoulders, stilling him. "Damn you, Bosch, why didn't you tell me about Jane's getting so involved!"

"I didn't for the longest time know what she suspected of the two! Or why she wanted information on 'em. I just did me job and got paid. Since when do I ask questions of a client?"

"I ought to flay your skin off, old man!"

"But why?"

"For not coming to me with this sooner!"

"Do so, then. Beat me into tomorrow if it'll please you. J-Just don't, you know, go for my privates."

"Not you, too? And Sam, do you believe I'm guilty of castrating Father Jurgen?"

Sam bit his lower lip. "You was pretty mad, sir."

"Damn it, I didn't do it."

"The news has everyone fearful tenfold of you, son," said Bosch. "Your reputation is intact. True or not, it's good for the bear."

Ransom gritted his teeth while his thoughts ran amok. *If everyone believes that I attacked Jurgen with the pinchers, then what are Gabby and Jane thinking about now?* "Never mind about my reputation, Bosch! What information about the Rolskys did you supply Jane Francis?"

"Just their names and address is all, and she pays a damn sight better'n you, and I need the—"

"What address, fool! Spit it out!"

"I writ it down but I give it to her. And my memory isn't so good these days, but I recall the name Rolsky, two brothers, and the address was something like 1400 Atgeld."

Ransom's jaw was set so hard now it hurt. "These men are dangerous scoundrels, Bosch."

"They're a strange pair," said Samuel. "I had a run-in with 'em once."

"You did?"

"The big one seems harmless as a child, friendly even, but his brother, he's cold and mean. Said he'd as soon kill a man as share bread with 'im."

"You heard him say this?"

"I did," replied Sam.

"Gabby and Jane went to the address on Atgeld?" Alastair asked.

"They're likely there now, yes," replied Bosch.

"They have no notion Philander—the more dangerous of the two—made bail already."

"He's out?" asked Sam, eyes wide.

"How'd Rolsky get set free?" asked Bosch.

"Find out for me, Henry," replied Alastair. "Who stood his bail."

"It'll be anonymous."

"Find out! Someone's got to know."

Ransom wondered if the answer might not lead to Rolsky's boss, the one who held his chain. All he knew was what O'Malley had told him over the phone: "When I got back to the station house from 400 Atgeld with evidence that could nail the bastard for murder and ghoulish activities, I learned he made bail."

Ransom had been flabbergasted and angry to learn of Rolsky having gone free. He'd asked O'Malley about the nature of the items he found in the apartment. Mike had itemized and logged in the evidence, now safely in lockup. It pointed to Philander as the man behind Dodge's disappearance and perhaps Nell Hartigan's murder. The level of involvement on the retarded brother's part remained in question. And now this awful turn of events—Ransom's two ladies gone to Rolsky's lair.

"You going to get over to 1400 Atgeld?" asked Bosch.

"Fool, it's the 400 block of Atgeld! I had O'Malley search the place. On a warrant, he found specimen jars, wrapping sheets stained with blood, a Persian rug, jewelry, and a box of cash."

"Then why wasn't the man rearrested?"

"This has all occurred within the hour. I just learned the miscreant is roaming free."

"Four hundred block's pretty near where I had a run-in with 'em, sir," added Sam.

Ransom found a police call box, opened it with his key, and studied the dial. What should he press? Murder, rape, abduction? There was a button for each and for every sort of crime known to these streets. He opted for abducted as it was as close to "missing" as he could find. By pressing the abducted lever, and winding the phone, and getting the closest precinct, he was guaranteed a police wagon and some two dozen uniformed men who'd answer to him. He and his army of twenty-four could fan out and cover every entry and exit where the Rolsky brothers might choose to crawl.

"You, Samuel!" Ransom called out. "You come with me! We've got some palavering to do."

"What 'bout me, boss?" asked Bosch.

"This doesn't concern you any further, Henry. Besides, I need you to learn the identity of the man who posted Rolsky's bail."

Bosch frowned and put out a hand for money. Ransom dropped two dollars into his palm. "There'll be more, but at the moment it's all I've got!" Then he snatched Sam, and together they rushed to find a cab. They'd meet the police wagon at the Atgeld address.

In the meantime, Alastair prayed that nothing bad had happened to Jane or Gabby or both.

On the cab ride to Atgeld, Ransom began explaining what he had not done to Father Jurgen, and he felt that his plea of innocence had been accepted by Samuel. Finally, someone who knew the details and facts as he knew them, and believed. He then suggested that another young person aboard the ship had done the actual operation after Alastair had left Jurgen in one piece. "Still, Sam, you're the only person in this city who can finger me for it, son, and so I'm at your mercy. So how much do you want for the file?"

"How much for the file?"

"The dossier that Hake dropped off at my house that night he rapped on the bedroom window."

"I almost wasn't going to open the window, 'cause I thought him a desperate-looking fellow, but he made promises that he was your friend and that I was to give this file to you."

"All right, so you took the file through the window."

The boy swallowed hard. "Laid it across the bed, and a photo of you holding a dead man's head in your hands fell out."

Ransom recalled the photo taken by Philo at the train station the past spring while he was investigating the third garroting murder in the Phantom of the Fair case. "Then you read the file?"

"I did and I'm sorry."

"Sorry you did it, or sorry over what you learned about me?"

"Sorry I did it."

"Well now you know the half-truths and lies my enemies are willing to tell to put me away at any cost."

"I didn't understand it all. I don't read so good."

"Do you think me a heartless murderer now, Sam?"

"They couldn't prove it by me."

"What'd you do with the file?"

"Burned it, I did."

"Burned it? Yet Bosch is trying to make a buck on it anyway?"

"He's an enterprising duffer."

Ransom smiled at this.

"Burned it as lies, I did, and—and I scattered the ashes over your partner's grave."

"My partner's grave? Griffin Drimmer?"

"May he rest in peace. The file said you got him killed."

"Another lie . . . or rather, half-truth. If I'd had stayed with him that night, who knows." Ransom thought of the grave site in Mount Carmel, the headstone he'd personally paid for, and he gave a thought to Drimmer's little family, the wife and children somewhere now back East near Boston—a civilized place, she'd called it between sobs as Ransom had held her close.

"I thought burning the file the right thing, Inspector."

"Did the reports have the eye on them?"

"The big eye of the Pinkerton Agency, yes, sir. That is, most pages did."

"Then it's true. Pinkerton's joined forces with Kohler."

"They didn't have nothing that they could prove, lotta words about suppose this and maybe that and perhaps here and could be's and would be's and such."

"Surrounding what?"

"Your interrogation of a man who got burned to death, for one."

"Haymarket days. Old news, and it wasn't me torched the man."

"I never believed it, as many times as I've heard it told."

"What else?"

"Something about a shootout, you killing a man."

"Self-defense pure and simple, and a setup to boot."

"Bosch told me 'bout that one."

"What else?"

"Some notion you may've killed some lady named Polly Pete. Said you may've made it look like the work of the Phantom."

"Fairy tales. Nonsense. What else?"

"Something about dropping a man kicking and screaming to the bottom of the lake."

"They're reaching."

"Still, I'd be careful of who you call a friend at the fire-house."

"Meaning?"

"They had a statement from Mr. Harry Stratemeyer, the fire investigator . . . "

"Harry, no. What must they have on Harry?"

"Says he helped you dispose of a body out on the lake, the body of the supposed Phantom of the Fair."

"Sounds like you read well enough, Sam."

"Is it true?"

"What?"

"Is it true you dropped him alive into the lake?"

"Samuel, you saw what he did to Griffin, to Polly, to others, and the law—Kohler—let him go for lack of evidence."

"Mostly heard secondhand about it. Met you sometime later . . . on the Leather Apron case, sir."

"What else did you see in the file?"

"They had statements against you for what happened to both your partners, Drimmer and another you worked with on Leather Apron . . . Logan."

"Bastards blame me for Logan's death, as if I don't blame myself."

"And another thing they're keen on what wasn't in the file, but Bosch says it's so."

"What's that, Sam?"

"Getting you for what happened to Father Jurgen."

"Father indeed, the man doesn't deserve the title, so let's just call 'im the pervert he is. They can't make that stick."

"They're on the lookout for me," Sam replied.

"You?"

"Figure to shake me down, pay me off, do whatever's necessary to break me and make me talk ill of you, to stand in witness 'gainst ya."

"And if it came to that, Sam?"

"I didn't witness nothing, and you never told me nothing, so I won't make a witness for 'im."

"That's easier said than done. If these men get you in their hands and sweat you, Samuel, they're professionals; they know how to break grown men."

"They won't break me!" he determinedly said.

"That leaves Philo, then," muttered Ransom. "Anything in the file on Philo Keane as . . . as a known associate?"

"Tons, sir . . . just loads."

Pinkerton's targeted Philo. This is not good, Ransom thought. "Look, Sam, I'm going to ask you to leave the city for a while, and here're the funds to do it with." He held out two fifty dollar bills.

"Leave Chicago?"

"Just for a month or so, till I know which way the wind is blowing."

"Wind's always blowing off the lake, south-southeast."

"You know what I mean."

"I got no place to go."

"Go to the Dunes in Indiana, the Dells in Wisconsin, to a hunting lodge, I don't care, but get out of the city till this nonsense blows over. Can't imagine why they're defending a sicko-deviant pervert in the first place, from O'Bannion down, and disappoints me that Bill Pinkerton's been taken in by guile or money or both."

"Somebody stamped in big letters across most everything in the file the words: 'Questionable as Evidence.'"

"Take the money and get on a train, Sam."

Sam took the bills.

"When we get to our destination on Atgeld, Sam, stay back."

"But I wanna stay with you, sir." He pushed the money back on Ransom.

Ransom refused to take it. "No, you can't! Please, take the cab a block off. Kohler has spies among the coppers I'm meeting, for sure. And if they've been told to get hold of you, well . . . I don't want to think of you in one of their interrogation rooms or lockup."

"I still want to stay with you."

"Damn it, son. If one of Kohler's men sees you, you'll be run to ground, Sam, like a dog."

"I know every squirrel hole and burrow in the city, Inspector. There's not a copper who can catch me 'less I want 'im to."

"*Ahhh* . . . the Artful Dodger! Still, my young friend, take the hundred and leave this city, and if you never come back, Sam, it may well be in your stars to find happiness elsewhere."

"Then tell me the truth before I go."

"What truth is that, Sam?"

"Did you really not do it to the priest?"

"I swear on my mother's grave, Samuel, that I've never lied to you in the past, and I am telling the truth now. Did you lie to me when you said you accepted my plea of innocence in the Jurgen affair?"

"Guess I did, but I believe you now, Inspector."

"Means a great deal that you do, Samuel."

CHAPTER 36

Alastair had immediately climbed from the cab with his cane in hand and quickly closed the door to conceal Samuel, and then he tipped the driver to move on. The commandeered hansom cab hurried away, giving Ransom breathing room but not much. In fact, he'd alighted from his cab to find the paddy wagon he'd called careening around the final corner.

Then Ransom realized that a second paddy wagon followed on the wheels of the first. But who were these men? Who'd called out a second wagon?

The bells and whistles of two paddy wagons were a common enough occurrence all across Chicago these days, but Alastair feared the Rolsky brothers had been alerted, despite the fact that brothels, taverns, gambling dens, and opium dens peppered this part of the city. Locals had come to expect periodic raids in the area.

All the same, Ransom knew that Rolsky could be at any window and could be drawing a bead—either his eye or his gun—on him at this moment where he stood in the street, attempting to choreograph this raid. Alastair made a large target, waving down the noisy others, gesticulating for them to cut the bells and whistles while at it. But no one aboard either wagon read his hand signals properly, as instead they ratcheted up the noise.

A crowd began immediately to gather about the commotion even before the cops had a chance to climb down from the two wagons. The sudden appearance of this forty-eight man swarm of uniformed cops had surely alerted Philander. Ransom imagined one thing on the criminal's mind—escape; it could also cause him to panic and kill Jane and Gabby, if they were indeed in his clutches yet alive. At this point anything might be true. Anything could happen. Or not. The possibilities, Ransom realized, all walked a high wire strung by Rolsky, but he, too, had hold of one end of that wire, as did the mystery person who'd bailed Philander out—possibly the surgeon who most benefited from the grim work of the Rolsky brothers.

In the back of his mind, along with his fear for Jane and Gabby, Alastair dreaded the mystery surgeon, a man who ordered up death as others might an omelet. He feared this nameless, faceless monster might well escape any form of justice should the brothers be shot and killed in an altercation with police. Clever, cunning bastard. Perhaps the mystery doctor counted on this scenario playing out. That he knew that police would descend on Vander and Philander like locusts out for blood.

And again, who called for the second paddy wagon?

He considered how orchestrated the whole unsteady untenable affair appeared—and how much Chief Nathan Kohler knew and when he knew it. Kohler was known for being cold and calculating. Furthermore, the men climbing from the second wagon had come prepared with high-powered scoped rifles; snipers.

"Need I even ask who called in police sharpshooters?" Alastair questioned himself.

To get him at all cost, Ransom knew that Nathan would sell his soul. And could William Pinkerton have unwittingly provided ammunition for Kohler? Could Nathan Kohler have worked a deal with the deadly doctor or doctors behind the ghouls? Had they ties to Senator Chapman? *Are all the principal players in a bloody conspiracy or am I reaching?* Alastair wondered. If it were so—and he could put nothing past Chapman and Kohler—this was larger and more insidious than any secrets the two harbored about the Haymarket bomb or the Leather Apron case.

It all had come to a head here and now outside the building where two Rolskys lived. All culminating in this standoff today instead of a courtroom into which Alastair might have been led in chains had Nathan gotten his way.

If fate is the hunter, Ransom now thought, *it had hunted him in his tracks, and fate now threatened Jane and Gabby as well.*

As the first police wagon came to a halt before Ransom and the suspect building, and officers in blue leapt off the horse-drawn, covered wagon, some shouted, "Where's the fire?"

Others shouted, "Are we too late?"

"Lads! I need you one and all!" replied Ransom in his most commanding voice, but those in wagon number two fanned out and located positions from which they might fire their deadly and accurate weapons. "There may be two ladies of Chicago being held against their will inside here! Hold your fire!"

"Ladies?"

"Womenfolk?"

"To be saved?"

Ransom realized it was every man's fantasy to rescue a damsel in distress, be kissed by the saved angel, fall in love, marry, and live happily ever after. He intentionally turned loose the fuel that stoked this fire of adolescent dream.

The captain in charge of the wagon Ransom had called for, a barrel-chested man named Benjamin Shorendorf, wore a crestfallen face that looked the part of an angry bulldog that'd lost a fight over a bone. Shorendorf shouted back, "Who precisely are we arresting? Who's been murdered?"

Ransom gathered the uniformed men to him. "We're looking for a pair of brothers," he began, "one a giant of a man and slow-witted to be sure, and the other his keeper! The names are Vander and Philander Rolsky, which may be an alias."

"It's that Italian ferret-faced guy we had in lockup over at Des Plaines, isn't it?" asked Shorendorf. "Why was he let go in the first damn place?"

"Not sure he's Italian, more likely Polish, but yes, same man."

"Why'd you let him go?"

"Bailed out! But I've secured a warrant for his rearrest," Ransom lied, though O'Malley was at the courthouse at that moment seeking the arrest warrant.

"Why'd you ever let him outta your sight then, Inspector?" Captain Shorendorf sounded angry at Alastair. "Now you say he's holding two women inside?"

"Rolsky was released on bond put up by someone I have as yet to identify, Ben. No one consulted me!"

"But he is Italian, right?"

"If it helps you to take him down, yes, he's Italian. But we need these two brothers alive to sweat information outta them, understood? And look, I fear Rolsky may have hostages."

"Hostages?"

"Miss Jane Francis and our Gabby Tewes."

"You don't say! Those kind ladies! The bastards! Hear that boys?" Shorendorf asked his men. "These Rolsky fiends who killed Nell Hartigan 'ave snatched two more of our women!"

"For the carvers?" asked an astonished young copper.

"The surgeons, yes," replied Ransom.

"I don't care if you break down every door!" shouted Captain Shorendorf. "Get into position and shoot to kill."

"Whoa, hold on!" shouted Ransom.

"What is it?"

"I want these monsters apprehended, Ben! For questioning! And I don't want the women harmed."

"I have me orders, Alastair."

"Whatya mean? You're called out by me, you take orders from me!"

"My orders come from a higher power! Now shove off or help, either one, Inspector, but let go'a my arm!"

"Who gave you a shoot order?"

"Chief Kohler!"

"How'd he hear of it?"

"Dunno, but he called just after you and give me the order, shoot to kill any armed and dangerous, and that means these ghouls!"

"But I want to learn who's behind it all! I want to interrogate these men! Learn who is paying for bodies! Who bailed Rolsky out. All of it!" If so, Ransom reasoned, he might even implicate Kohler in a conspiracy here. Was Nathan covering up for others in high society?

Or was Kohler himself being used in this unholy affair? Fate, in a sense, was being doled out to all of them from some unknown source. How much did Pinkerton know? How much did Nathan Kohler know? But at the moment, Ransom's fear was for Jane and Gabby. Yet fate had a human hand and face in this city, and possibly in this instance. If Kohler could side with O'Bannion and Jurgen on the matter of sexual deviance against children, then siding with ghouls and their degreed patrons was child's play for the manipulative chief.

Ben Shorendorf began deploying his men. Ransom hustled to stay with him. He shouted in his ear, "Tell me the truth! It's Kohler, isn't it?"

"I told you the order to shoot came from him, yes!"

"No, it's more than just a shoot to kill order."

Ben turned on him. "What're you talking about?"

"Kohler . . . Kohler is somehow behind the whole bleak, bloody business," he replied as he and Ben picked their way through a causeway in search of any local residents or rats who might speak English. The neighborhood was largely a mix of Polish and Italian immigrants, most of whom only knew the rudiments of English and got by largely through Pidgin English and hand gestures. Most such immigrants avoided uniformed men of any kind, and today was no exception, but Shorendorf spoke German and enough Polish to get by.

"According to neighbors, the brothers are inside. No one knows anything about women inside."

Each moment of the process drove a deeper stake into Ransom's heart as he contemplated life without Jane and Gabby. He hated his mind for even suggesting his fear: *They might well already be dead and on dissecting tables in some remote medical facility.*

He struggled mightily against the horrid idea.

CHAPTER 37

At the same time that Alastair and Captain Shorendorf were jockeying for who was in command, and discussing how to disperse the men, Jane came to, woozy and dazed from Rolsky's having struck her, but her initial concern was for Gabby. She screamed out at the men who hovered over Gabrielle as if determining how best to transport her body, and Jane screamed anew at the thought that Gabby was dead.

Her screams filled the small, dank apartment and filtered out through the cracks at the windows and the single door that led out into the hallway and two stairwells, one leading to the front of the building, another to the courtyard.

"Shut up, woman!" shouted Philander, coming at her with a raised knife, a knife he'd been holding over Gabby moments before but Jane hadn't seen till now. Gabby had told her in the coach coming over that the man was in custody, his knife confiscated. Gabby had in fact sent the knife to Dr. Fenger to compare against Nell Hartigan's wounds, as Nell's body had remained on ice. Apparently, the man's first thoughts were to arm himself with this kitchen knife that now hovered huge over Jane.

I'm going to die like Nell Hartigan and Gabby before me,

she thought. *This butcher's going to sell our bodies to the highest bidder.*

Then she heard Gabby coughing.

With Gabby alive, Jane knew she must free herself and her daughter from these men and this place.

"Vander!" stormed his brother. "Do like I damn well tol' ya, you idiot! Kill the little bitch before she starts screaming, too! *Now*, dummy!"

Jane took the moment's hesitation on Philander's part as he chastised Vander to grab what remained of the hot soup now boiling on the stove. She snatched it up and hurled it into Philander's face, and when he cried out and cringed, she slammed the cast iron urn into his temple, sending him reeling but still holding tight to his knife as if it were a lifeline. Temporarily blinded, Philander called his brother to stop the woman. "Kill them! Kill 'em both, now!"

Vander's eyes remained on Gabrielle, however, and he did not look as if he could harm her. "It ain't right, Philander . . . they come to help me is all. Ain't right!"

"Kill 'em, damn you! Damn you to cursed hell!"

Vander stood, stepping away from the still prone Gabby. She had tried to pull herself up, but Vander kept his weight on her, pinning her. But now she pulled herself to her elbows.

"You've got to get out of here, Gabby. Hurry!" Jane shouted across to her daughter, but Gabby, unsteady and groggy, only climbed to her knees, choking, yet gasping for air. "Come on, baby!"

"Stop her, Van!"

"I don't wanna hurt no more women, Philander."

"They're police! They can hang us, you freak!"

"No, Gabby and Jane wouldn't do that."

"You imbecile! You ant-brained moron!"

"Stop calling me names, Philander!"

"Then do what the hell I tell ya!"

"No!"

Philander's blind rage sent the knife up and deep into Vander's gut, the big man instantly going into trauma, the shakes taking hold of him. He appeared in a near epileptic seizure, and when Jane got Gabby through the door, she looked back to see that Vander's powerful right hand had seized on Philander's throat.

"I—I never wanna hear you call me bad names ever 'gain, Phil-an-der. You understand me?"

Jane only heard the choked inaudible reply, as Vander had already broken his brother's neck, quite by accident. While Philander remained alive, he lay paralyzed, unable to speak or to move, both of which disturbed Vander greatly, agitating the big man. Vander began sputtering, slavering, pleading with his brother, asking, "What do I do now, Philander? Philander? What'll I do now? Tell me what to do!"

"He . . . he can't answer you, Vander," Jane near whispered, and Vander's eyes widened at the voiced fact.

"He's gotta be fixed! You said you were a doctor! Fix him! Fix him!"

"His injury is not fixable, Vander, and he's dying."

"Dying? No . . . he can't do that. He can't leave me."

Philander's head lolled to one side, his tongue wagging like that of a lapdog in confused anxiety.

Jane instructed Gabby, "Take Vander out into the courtyard and keep him calm."

"What're you going to do?" Gabby asked.

"Put this wretch out of his misery."

"Perhaps you should at least wait, Mother, until we can get hold of Ransom. He may want to make that decision."

"It's a medical decision that's needed here."

"That monster didn't show any mercy to his victims," Gabby countered. "So why should we show him any special consideration?"

"The consideration you'd give an animal in pain is all I am doing."

"Even so, why should we?"

"Because we are better human beings than he is? Because we are medically trained? Because we took an oath?"

Gabby offered Vander her left hand as she took charge of the knife with her right hand. Vander allowed her to guide him like the child he was. At the door, Gabby wondered aloud, "What about Vander? What kind of consideration do you think a Chicago judge and a jury will show him?"

"The laws against executing the insane and the infirm of mind will safeguard Vander."

"Will they, you think?"

"Yes, if upheld."

"If . . . yes, if they're upheld. But many will want to see him hang."

Vander stood stolid, a child without comprehension and still in shock over his brother's condition and the fear of being alone while ignoring his own wound and pain. It was difficult to say which fear won out over the other as Gabby finally led him from the apartment.

Jane located what she expected to find in the cupboard—morphine and heroine-laced pills sold at any apothecary in the city. She quickly mixed the contents of the capsules she found with water and returned to Philander. The drugs would end his suffering fairly quickly, although they might kill him in the bargain, as the dosage was largely guesswork.

She lifted Philander's head to the cup, about to pour the barbiturates down his throat when suddenly the injured Philander grabbed her wrist and forced her to drop the cup and its contents. With her free hand, Jane rummaged about for anything she might use against this attack, as the moment he made her drop the cup, his one movable, griddle-sized hand wrapped about her throat and he squeezed hard, sending a shooting pain throughout Jane's body. She tried to scream out for Gabby, for help, but her air was completely choked off in a matter of seconds. His grip was a powerful vise, and Jane could feel the bruising as it was happening, and she imagined in a moment her vocal cords would be permanently damaged and her hyoid bone crushed, as she meanwhile brought up the butcher knife that Gabby had thrown to the floor. Using the knife, she tore at the ghoul's hand.

The knife cut deep and repeatedly across the hand locked on her throat, and a couple of swipes came dangerously close to her own skin and jugular vein, nicking her. Jane's blood mingled with the killer's own, spilling over his hand and onto his cold inert eyes, until finally Gabby brought down a heavy chair pulled from a corner atop the dying man, smashing his face in.

Jane fell back, gasping for air, her throat painted in blood smears so messily that Gabby thought her bleeding profusely. Jane had to quell Gabby's bawling cries, gasping out, "I'm all right . . . uncut really. Just need catch my . . . *ahhh* . . . breath . . . "

Gabby grabbed her arms, the ladies holding firm to one another on the filthy floor when Alastair Ransom, followed by several policemen, rushed in and took charge.

"Damn it to high heaven, Jane!" Alastair shouted. "You might've been killed! Whatever possessed the two of you to come into this lair?"

"It's a long story, Alastair," she managed between gasps.

"Where's the other one?" he asked, staring down at the inert body of Philander Rolsky.

"He's outside, sitting on the stairwell near the elder trees. Left him only a moment ago," said Gabby.

"Get on it, men!" shouted Shorendorf. "The big dumb one's escaped!"

"Vander is the only reason we're alive!" Gabby stood now toe-to-toe with Ransom. "You mustn't hurt him!"

"He's half of a murder team!" shouted Shorendorf.

"He's got the mind of a child," countered Jane, who, with Ransom's help, opened a window for air.

"Mind of a child or not, he's a killer," continued Shorendorf.

"A woman killer at that," said William Pinkerton, now at the door alongside Chief Nathan Kohler. Obviously, Ransom's call for help had indeed been intercepted.

"We suspect Vander only followed orders," said Ransom firmly, searching out the back window for any sign of the hunchbacked giant.

"He's still a murderer for having followed murderous orders," shouted Kohler.

"No, he could not harm us," said Jane. "Said he would not

do to us what Philander did to the other woman, Nell. They also spoke of Colonel Dodge."

"Damn it all, we still don't know who was purchasing bodies from this pair of ghouls," said Ransom. "Do we, Mr. Pinkerton, Nathan?" Ransom's question to the two men was pointed, as if there were some hidden agenda between these men.

"I hope you're not suggesting that either Nathan or I have all along known the name of doctors who've a covenant with such men as these crazed brothers."

"Imagine it," said Gabby, "bartering in body parts."

"We need that big boy alive to lead us to the doctor or doctors benefiting from their murderous activities," Ransom continued. "You get the word out, Captain Shorendorf. We need Vander Rolsky alive, and he shouldn't be hard to spot— the size and mentality of a rhinoceros."

"Understood, Inspector. I'll order my men to take him alive, but he could be dangerous, and I won't order my men to lay down for him."

"Do your best, Captain," said Kohler. "That's all anyone can ask of you. I'm going to personally join this manhunt. I'll call out every man jack of the force. There isn't a hole big enough for this fellow to crawl into."

"It'd be like hunting down a five-year-old, I tell you!" shouted Jane. But none of the men were having any of it. No one was about to mollycoddle Vander Rolsky.

"Damn it, Inspector!" shouted Gabby as the men filed out. "He's like a frightened animal! When you find him, let us talk to him before something just awful happens." She said it as if she knew something horrible was inevitable.

"You need him!" shouted Jane. "You need that boy alive, so he can lead you to the truly guilty in all this, Ransom! Ransom!"

But the small army that had failed to rescue Jane and Gabby had disappeared in search of the monster. Jane was reminded of the cliché of the typical villagers taking up pitchforks and torches and trailing off into the black forest to slay the dragon.

CHAPTER 38

Ransom heard the echoing pleas of the two women he most loved and respected in the world, but he knew he had to stay close to Pinkerton and Kohler. He suspected the two of them in some sort of collusion, and in order to keep his eyes on them, he must keep up. Still, it looked like he and all the men were of one mind: Locate and execute Vander on the spot.

Gabby had said the giant was left sitting on the back stairwell below a pair of trees in the courtyard; she'd hinted at his being distraught. Had he simply wandered off? Or had he made a dash for freedom?

The nearby train yards might well be a place a man like Vander would gravitate to, and knowing the area well, Ransom allowed the others to go ahead of him over back fences, searching the Atgeld neighborhood.

Ransom instead made a beeline for the train yard, cutting through alleyways and between buildings, soon emerging at the spot he'd contemplated.

Jane and Gabby followed Ransom. He heard them behind, shouting for him to wait up. He slowed, as he wanted an explanation from Jane as to what she had been doing in Rolsky's place.

"What the deuce were you two thinking?"

"It's a long story but—"

"A fool's tale is what it is! You could've been killed, and you place your daughter in danger?"

"Hold on," said Gabby, "I went with mother of my own free will."

"You, young lady . . . I'd've thought you smarter than—"

"We had every reason to believe Philander locked away in a cell!" Gabby said, ending the discussion.

"There he is! It's Vander!" Jane pointed to the huge, hulking figure in the distance. A Chicago gray sky now, threatening rain, painted the entire area in a grim and uncaring hue here in the train yard. Vander moved through this landscape like a creature out of time.

Gabby and Jane began shouting his name in unison, asking him to stop and to come with them.

Then Ransom saw the small figure holding onto Vander's hand. It was the boy, Samuel. How Sam had gotten in the middle of this, Ransom hadn't a clue, but he imagined the boy had led Vander off, hoping to get him out of harm's way.

Ransom bellowed for Samuel, saying, "Trust me, Sam! Vander's best off giving himself up to me!"

Sam and Vander seemed in discussion, but they were too far away for the others to hear, when it became apparent that they had made up their minds. The boy and the giant, hand in hand, turned and took steps toward Ransom and the ladies.

Moments later, the cry of a bullet from a sniper's rifle exploded through the air. Vander dropped to his knees and, still alive, covered Samuel, blocking any harm coming to him. To Jane's and Gabby's screams, Vander then keeled over, dead.

Gabby raced for Vander, hoping against hope that he was not fatally wounded. Jane rushed after her. Ransom followed. In the distance, from across the train yard, Captain Ben Shorendorf and his men appeared, all of them having fanned out in their search for the fugitive from justice, now lying on the railroad tracks and bleeding from a gunshot wound.

Ransom, his own weapon drawn now, could not ascertain the source of the gunfire, and as he attempted to do so, Kohler and Pinkerton came from a third direction.

Suddenly, Sam buried his tearstained face into Ransom's coat, and he quaked with sobs for Vander.

When all parties arrived to stand over the dead man, Jane Francis condemned them all. "You men! All you know is to maim, kill, and destroy! Bastards, all of you!"

"Who fired that shot?" Ransom demanded of the assembled men. "Rolsky was unarmed and giving himself up to my protection! Who ordered him shot, Nathan?"

"I thought he was about to harm the boy," said Benjamin Shorendorf, eyes downcast. "I felt it necessary."

"Ben? You fired that shot?"

"I did, and I stand by my actions."

"Who gave the order, Ben?"

"No one. I took it upon myself."

"You disappoint me, Ben." Ransom's angry eyes moved from Shorendorf to Pinkerton and then to Kohler. "You all disappoint me."

It was raining now, as people from the surrounding houses converged on the train yard and the body despite the downpour, the sky as dark as night. At the same time, busy trains lumbered slowly about them like animals disinterested in human concerns. In the distance, the tall buildings of downtown Chicago looked on, lighted windows like blinking eyes. The lamps that lit Chicago streets by night came on in answer to the darkness. The train yards were lit up, casting long shadows of those standing around the slumped-over body of the giant, Vander.

Captain Shorendorf, a rifle at his side, said to Ransom, "When I saw the big man's hand go up over that wee lad's head, it appeared he had murder in mind."

"A righteous shooting, I'd say," added Nathan.

"What move did he make?" demanded Gabby.

"I saw no threatening movement either!" shouted Jane.

"Don't you get it, Jane?" asked Ransom. "These fellows had to shut Vander down at any cost."

"Hold on, Inspector!" Kohler warned. "There'll be no wild allegations or speculations, and I'll not stand here and be defamed by you, Inspector."

"And you, Mr. Pinkerton?" said Ransom, turning to the private eye. "I'd expected better of you, sir. What's Kohler got on you?"

"I am here, sir, merely as a courtesy."

"A courtesy? What courtesy is murder?"

"I did not murder the man!" shouted Ben Shorendorf. "I shot to protect the lad!"

"All at once, people are concerned about your welfare, Samuel," said Ransom. "How's that for a twist?"

A rain-soaked Samuel instantly snatched Ransom's cane and began pounding Ben Shorendorf with it until some of his men grabbed the boy and threw him to the stones.

Ransom turned to Kohler, his jaw tight. "Thanks to your shoot-to-kill order, it's a safe bet we'll never know the names of the doctors who traded in bodies with Vander and his brother."

"It was a good and necessary call on the captain's part, Alastair." Kohler stood beneath an umbrella rushed to him by his aide. "Two women at risk of life and limb at the hands of a pair of murderers, right, Pinkerton?"

Pinkerton said nothing in reply. Instead, he pulled forth an envelope stuffed to overflowing with cash and jammed it into Kohler's hand. "I did not sign on to be your stooge, Nathan." Then Pinkerton briskly walked off, his long coat lifting about his ankles to a Chicago sleet there in the train yard.

"He was just a child himself, Captain Shorendorf!" Gabby called out from where she'd gone to her knees over the dead Vander, his chest a mass of blood where the heart had exploded in response to the strike of the high velocity bullet that'd killed him.

"The girl is distraught!" shouted Kohler. "She can't possibly be responsible for her emotional state, Captain Shorendorf. You did your duty and that's that. And I for one am satisfied we have Nell Hartigan's and Colonel Dodge's killers, and I say end of case."

"But it doesn't touch the doctors!" countered Ransom, angry and frustrated.

"Nothing ever touches the doctors, Alastair," said Jane, standing alongside him now. "That's why they are doctors. Correct, Nathan?"

Kohler stared at the pair, Ransom and Jane Francis. "You two make a handsome couple. You really ought to make an honest woman of her, Alastair, perhaps retire from the force while you're at it. You could oversee the clinic, work for Dr. Tewes. Now as I said, I am done with this affair, and with these two deviants dead, I say Chicago and justice have been served."

"Kohler's justice, you mean," muttered Jane.

"It's time the CPD devote itself to more pressing matters," continued Kohler, ignoring her remark.

"Meanwhile, the doctors bartering with the Rolsky brothers go scot-free?" asked Jane.

"I will waste no more manpower or time on it. Nor will you, Inspector Ransom! That is an order."

Ransom watched Chief Kohler and Captain Shorendorf and all the blue-uniformed men under their command turn and walk away.

"I'll call in Christian Fenger, Nathan!" Ransom shouted after him. "There'll be an inquest! This man was unarmed and there're witnesses!" But he knew his words to be useless, empty, untrue. He'd shouted them in as much bravado as he could muster, but it was merely show for the ladies and Samuel. He knew that neither Nathan nor his stooge Shorendorf could be touched for killing Vander—an escaping refugee and suspected murderer.

Ransom knew he'd been defeated, and some voice deep within said it couldn't get any worse than this, to be humiliated and beaten by Nathan Kohler in front of the two women he loved.

CHAPTER 39

The next day, things got worse for Alastair when more loaded fate came literally knocking at his door. Captain Benjamin Shorendorf dressed in his cleanest uniform stood on Alastair's doorstep alongside a dumbfounded Mike O'Malley and several other strong-armed cops. Mike kept apologizing while Shorendorf read the arrest warrant.

Ransom only heard the last portion. "'... for the murder of Father Franklin Jurgen, who overnight died in Cook County Hospital of complications of his wounds.'"

"They're saying they have new evidence pointing to you, Rance," said Mike, "but I don't for a moment believe it."

"That's good of you, Mike, but apparently everyone else is all too willing to believe the worst of me."

"Will you come along quietly, Inspector?" asked Shorendorf.

"And what about you, Captain?" asked Ransom.

"What about me?"

"Shouldn't you be getting some sort of commendation for that perfect shot through the heart of that big fellow yesterday who was on the verge of harming a child?"

"I only did my duty as I saw it."

"*Hmmm* . . . lot of that going around."

Shorendorf held up the wrist cuffs and a second officer held up the ankle chains.

"Don't be ridiculous, you men!" shouted O'Malley. "You don't take a fellow Chicago police officer into custody in chains on a whim."

"It's no whim! I have orders!" countered Shorendorf.

"Tell me something, Ben," Ransom said, extending his wrists, "how safe are you and for how long, once Kohler decides *you* are a liability?"

Shorendorf's eyes gave him away, going temporarily wide before he shouted, "Get 'im into the paddy wagon, now!"

"Yeah . . . treat me as just another Paddy, Ben. Go right ahead, but one day it'll come back on you."

The ankle chains snapped around him, and Ransom was led off amid the inquiring eyes of his neighbors. Only two people might hurt him and badly, he reasoned, and they'd never testify against him. He'd already anticipated getting each out of town.

Moments before the wagon door was closed and locked, Alastair saw Frederick Hake lurking about the shadows, watching the arrest with great interest. Had Hake come to warn him too late? Or had Hake come to gloat? Was Hake set up to lie on the stand? Would William Pinkerton lie on the stand? After all, there was nothing innocent about his actions the night someone had disfigured Father Jurgen, a disfigurement that ultimately led to the man's death.

"Damn it, I didn't do it," he muttered in the pitch-dark wagon.

"Sure you didn't, Inspector . . . and this is the result!" It was Bosch, beaten and thrown into a black corner of the wagon.

"Henry, what've they done to you?"

"Beat a confession from me, they did."

"What confession?"

"That I led you to Father Jurgen, and that you had a nasty large pair of pincers the whole time."

"Not that you saw me use these so-called pincers on Jurgen?"

"They stopped pushin' when I fainted out the third time."

"Sorry this had to happen to you, old-timer, very sorry."

"You and me both." Bosch could hardly speak. "How much've they got on you, Inspector?"

"I'm told the Pinkerton's've amassed a regular dossier."

"Un-g'damn-believable that it should end like this. You and me, good, stouthearted fellows, our good turns and kind natures turned against us." He paused to spit blood. "T-Turned on us like the twisting head of a snake. Just not fittin' nor right nor proper."

"It isn't over yet, Henry; we still have our day in court. And we hold onto our dignity."

"Dignity, ha! You perhaps. Me . . . I couldn't take it when they started on me in earnest."

Ransom lit a match from a box yet in his pocket. The light illuminated Bosch's ashen and bloodied face and head.

"Shorendorf worked you over badly, but I saw no bruised knuckles."

"Used his brass knuckles, he did. Did a thorough job of it. I'm spittin' teeth."

"You only made the one lie, Bosch?"

"That I guided you to that boat, yeah. Hell, I didn't even know the name of the tub till they supplied it."

"What about Samuel?" asked Ransom. "You think he's OK?"

Bosch's eyes lit up. "Is he the reason you're in this fix? I knew no good could come of it, paying that boy same wage as me!"

"Is he in harm's way?"

"He might've been, but no. Seems your lady friend got him over to Hull House, where he stole a bundle from the kitty and hopped a freight outta town. 'Least that's the story."

"And a great story it is, too."

"Plain, simple truth no matter how hard to swallow." Bosch was having trouble gulping and breathing. He was too aged a man to take such a beating without its taking a great toll.

"It's good he's out of the city."

"You knew Kohler would—" Bosch's words were punctuated and interrupted by coughing. "—that Kohler'd put the Pinkertons on to you, so why in hell'd you not skedaddled yourself?"

"Too late for regrets now."

"They mean to hang you for murder."

"Then damn them, they've a fight on their hands."

"Why do you suppose they put us both in here together, Inspector? Answer that, you're so smart?"

"They likely expect me to kill you just so they can bolster their flimsy warrant."

"My sentiments exactly." Bosch's laughter turned into a gut-wrenching cough. "So are you?"

"Am I what?"

"Going to kill me?"

"Convert you, perhaps; kill you, no."

"Thank you, Inspector, for sparing me. Now tell me . . . for my own edification . . . did you really cut off a priest's privates?"

"Do they really believe for a moment that I'm going to give up a jailhouse confession to the likes of you, Bosch? Or anyone else for that matter?"

"I heard you say, 'I didn't do it,' when you believed yourself alone."

"Give me something I can use, Bosch."

"I have nothing."

"Tell me you have the information I asked you to find."

Outside, they heard the muffled toll of a bell and men shouting. Both men inside the closed, windowless wagon wondered why the commotion and to what precinct were they being carted.

"Sounds like a funeral dirge out there," remarked Bosch.

"Forget about that. Listen, Bosch, now you, of all people, know the truth of my innocence in this affair with the priest."

"Yes, I know . . . for what it's worth." Bosch's bashed-in face shone purple in the darkness here. Outside, the bell tolled again. "They say the truth sets a man free, but in your case, who'd believe it? 'Fraid you're a victim of your own making. That reputation of yours, how you handled the Phantom of the Fair . . . all of it is come back to—"

"Roost, I know."

"Haunt ya is what I was 'bout to say." The wagon jostled over a pothole. "There go my dentures," joked Bosch. "Wh-What's left of 'em."

"Sorry you had to take such a beating, Henry. How do you afford dentures?"

"P-Paid for by the ponies."

"Damn it, Henry. Tell me you learned who 'twas bailed out Philander Rolsky? Tell me you're holding out on me for a better deal."

"Rance, I'm sorry. They got me by the short hairs before I could learn anything."

"Then we might never know who put up bail for that murd'rin' Rolsky."

"I shoulda acted faster. Thought I had time, you see."

"No blame falling on you, Bosch, but when you're set free, do me a kindness, will you?"

"Whatever I can, yes. We've been partners a long time, Inspector."

Hardly partners, Ransom thought, but said, "Get word to Jane Francis Tewes as to what's happened, and without telling another soul. And don't be followed by that creep Frederick—"

"Hake, yes, I mean no! I know his hand is in this business somehow. Evil bastard'd sell his own mother to the butchers."

"Also get to Mr. Philo Keane at his studio, and if he's not already gone from the city, tell him to get out of Chicago until all this blows over." Ransom knew that Philo would never survive a Chicago police interrogation room.

"If it blows over." Bosch sat silent a moment, and again came the tolling bell and the muffled shouts of men outside the wagon. "What the deuce is all that noise for?" Bosch finally asked.

"Can't quite make it out, but I suspect they're wasting no time in drumming up public opinion against me."

"Is that legal?"

"It probably is in Chicago."

"Damn them but I think they have you checkmated, Inspector."

"It's never occurred to me," he half joked.

"The charges are not frivolous or slight, but the sort that'll incite press and public against you."

"I'm sure I'm already hung in the first edition."

"I'll talk to Carmichael, tell him your side—your suspicions."

"I fear Carmichael useless."

"Why do you say so?"

"He's washed up, on the sauce, and I fear he's too far gone."

"Somehow, then, we've lost."

"The only leverage I have is public record, and not even that if it's been falsified."

"Aye, someone may've altered the books."

"Someone paid cash to see Rolsky walk. The who of it could lead to some answers as to why Nell Hartigan was killed, and why Pinkerton threw up so many hurdles."

"A cover-up?"

"Of the case she was investigating, yes."

"And you say it is Pinkerton, do you? Once again working for the establishment?"

"Possibly. Damn but I need a lawyer. Listen, again, once they release you—"

"They'll only do so if I tell them what they want to hear, Inspector, and that will seal your fate."

"Then tell them."

"Tell them what?"

"What they want to hear. I need you on the outside."

"But when they call me to court, what then?"

"Then tell the truth."

"Or skip bail?"

"Or skip bail. But not before you contact Malachi Quintin McCumbler for me, Henry."

"The lawyer, yes, the one I can ill afford."

"He's worth his salt, and McCumbler'll know, or by God find out who posted bail for Rolsky."

"You'll need him for trial at any rate."

"Exactly."

"I'll get to him if at all possible."

"Shrewd fellow is McCumbler."

"Still, it's all wishful thinking. Suppose they don't let me go, Ransom?"

"You strike your deal with 'em; they'll let you walk until the day you're called to testify."

"Yes, but e'en so, Mr. McCumbler's not likely to listen to a clothespin like me!" He smacked his peg leg as he said this.

Ransom's eyes had adjusted to the dim light. "Tell Malachi what we've discussed. He'll know what steps to take."

"Hope you've a plan. Hope you can beat this thing," said the old snitch, ending with a coughing jag.

The wagon came to a sudden halt, men shouting at animals. Then came the reverberation of lock and chain being snatched away, and the doors were flung open on a gunmetal gray sky, framed in the iron bars, all mirroring Alastair's mood. Ransom stepped out to find himself staring at the Des Plaines Street station house. They'd taken a leisurely, long route to get here, tolling a bell as they did so and spreading word of his arrest along their route. This had been all the noise that'd kept him and Bosch curious and nervous at once. All a display to embarrass him on his home territory.

"Damn it, Ben," he swore at Shorendorf, indicating the Des Plaines station. "We gotta do this at *my* house?"

"Orders . . . just fol—"

"Following orders, sure, Ben, sure. And when I make bail, I may follow some dictates of my own."

"I am assured you'll never make bail, but hold on here! Are you threatening me? You wanna add threatening an of-

ficer to the list of complaints against you, Inspector? Trust
me, the list is long enough."

"You used to be a good cop, Ben, till they got their hooks
into ya."

"Shut your blatherin' mouth, Ransom."

"Go ahead, rough me up! Do me like you did poor Bosch
in there cowering in the corner! Bastards, all of ya!"

Bringing his billy club over Ransom's head, Shorendorf
struck in the flash of an eye, and Alastair fell, bleeding, to
the ground, his body sliding up under the paddy wagon.

Mike O'Malley, who'd stood nearby, rushed Shorendorf
and yanked the club from him before he could strike a second blow. "The man's in chains! What the hell was that
for?" Mike looked as if he might slam Shorendorf with the
club, but he was grabbed by Shorendorf's men.

"Resisting arrest!" replied Shorendorf, regaining his club.
"You all saw it."

Mike, shoving away the men holding him, shouted, "The
ill treatment of the prisoner'll go in my report, Captain. You
can bet on that."

"Look, we're all cops here, all professionals, but a man like
this"—he pointed to Alastair, who unsuccessfully struggled
to regain his feet—"he brings us all down in the eyes of the
public. I've no mercy for him, and neither will the courts!"

Alastair sat beside the paddy wagon, still dazed. He half
heard Mike's words defending him. "Ransom's the best detective on the force. Sure, maybe he's somewhat unortho-
dox, but this time, perhaps he just got too close to the truth
to suit some people. Hey, Captain?"

Bleeding and blinking blood from his eyes, Ransom saw
from where he sat a regular fop of a man parting the cops—a
man so obsessed with modern fashion and so vain about his
own appearance that he'd become a ridiculous caricature,
except that it was not a man. It was Jane as Dr. Tewes, and
Gabby Tewes directly beside her. The ladies fought past
Mike and the others. "Leave him alone! Get back!"

Jane had her black medical bag with her, and she stooped
beside Alastair, hurrying to bandage his bleeding head.

Gabby continued embarrassing the men in blue, calling them all barbarians.

"I told you, Jane," Ransom whispered to her. "Told you all there'd come a day when you'd need to distance yourself from me. Now it's come."

"I'm not turning my back on you, Alastair."

"Nor I, Inspector!" shouted Gabby, now kneeling on the other side of Ransom.

"Nor I, Inspector," repeated Mike O'Malley, who'd overheard.

"Don't be fools!" shouted Ransom, blood streaking his face. "Go to the Devil, the lot of ya! But get as far from me as you can."

"Are you confessing?" asked Shorendorf. "Hold on! I'll get a stenographer out here! Somebody get a stenographer!"

"Shut up, Ben! I'm confessing nothing!"

Gabby regained her feet, and she now pummeled Shorendorf, shouting, "Haven't you done enough damage?"

"This man needs more medical attention than I can give him here!" shouted Dr. Tewes. "He should be transported to Cook Country immediately."

Then Bosch crawled from the shadows deep within the wagon, and everyone gasped at his appearance. "I c-c-c-could use a few b-b-bandages myself, heh-heh."

"What in the name of Solomon is going on here?" demanded Nathan Kohler, rushing into the foray. "Shorendorf! Take charge of your prisoners and get them to where they belong—under lock and key. There'll be no hospital stays for these two brigands."

Cook County was notorious among criminals and police as a stopover before an escape.

"You've got me on my knees, Nathan," said Ransom, who'd remained on one knee, Tewes and Gabby holding onto him. "Win at all costs, even if you have to lie, cheat, steal, and protect Senator Chapman?" Ransom rose to his full height as he spoke until his eyes were level with Chief Kohler's.

"You brought this all on yourself Alastair." Kohler tore

Ransom's gold shield from his disheveled clothing. "Consider yourself a citizen in need of a lawyer in the suspicious death of one Father Franklin Jurgen, and the questionable disappearance of one Waldo Denton."

"Father Jurgen?" asked Jane, her voice cracking.

"We have solid evidence now that Ransom here castrated Father Jurgen, which led to his death by infectious complications."

"Murder? Murder of a priest? It's a bogus charge!" Jane could not fathom it.

"The only proof you have is the proof of lies," added Ransom, nose-to-nose with Kohler now. "Fabricated lies that you may convince others of, but no thinking person, Nathan."

"We have your own snitch here, the veteran of the great war, Mr. Henry Bosch, confessing knowledge of the crime."

"A confession beaten from him by your thugs."

"And we have your associate, Mr. Philo Keane, making a statement as we speak."

"No doubt coerced!"

"Regarding the day after, when you discussed the matter with him at a coffee shop, witnessed by O'Malley here!"

Mike stood shaking his head. "I heard no such confession, ever."

Kohler was not slowed by this. "And . . . and we have a witness who places you at the scene, Alastair."

"A witness can't exist to a crime that wasn't committed."

Kohler smiled like a snake. "You know better than that, Alastair."

"All you have are lies and half-truths." Ransom prayed the so-called witness was not Samuel.

"Captain, take your prisoner into lockup!" ordered Kohler.

"Hold on! Who's your witness?" asked a commanding voice from back of the crowd. It was the lawyer, Malachi Q. McCumbler. "I have been retained to represent Inspector Ransom in this matter, and we expect that a list of his accusers be presented to us immediately." McCumbler came to the forefront, a man without the slightest idea of fashion, his crookedly perched eyeglasses his trademark. He held a small box camera in hand. He took several photographic shots of Henry Bosch and Alastair in their current condition while Nathan Kohler and Ben Shorendorf looked on. While photographing, McCumbler said to Alastair, "Dr. Tewes retained me on your behalf the moment he learned of this series of unfortunate events."

"Called McCumbler when I learned what the tolling of the bells meant," added Jane.

Jane's eyes met Alastair's and the two exchanged a troubled, wane smile. Alastair wanted to explain in detail every minute of that night, and he began with, "I didn't do what they say, Jane. I wanted to . . . came close to it, but—"

"Not another word, Inspector," ordered McCumbler. "If you wish to beat back these heinous charges against you, sir, from here out you speak only through me and only to me. Understood?"

"Understood, but this frame-up is looking—"

"Zip it, Inspector."

"Understood." Ransom's mind raced with all that he wanted to tell Jane and Gabby; he didn't care what others thought, but he desperately needed these two to believe him.

"Now go peacefully with Captain Shorendorf, Inspector," finished McCumbler. "And I will be along shortly."

Alastair did so, but he yelled over his shoulder for Gabby and Jane to believe in him. "They'll never prove these outlandish charges."

"Zip it!" shouted McCumbler as Shorendorf and his men escorted Alastair inside for booking and lockup.

McCumbler proved true to his word. He was quickly inside after a few whispered words to Jane and Gabby. He now accompanied Ransom, step for step, through the process, and at one point he said in Alastair's ear, "They have your friend, the photographer Keane, Ransom, and they're taking his statement this moment. How much can it hurt us?"

Ransom gritted his teeth. "As you might recall when I retained you to help him last spring, Philo doesn't do well with pain and the sort of interrogation techniques that go on inside here."

"Yes, I recall, but we beat the ridiculous charge against him."

"Still, Philo might tell them anything if they sweat him long enough."

As Ransom was marched off to a cell, his mind played tiddledywinks with the dire and strained possibilities lying ahead.

For a moment he heard Bosch's words echoing inside his head. . . . *reputation come back to haunt you . . . checkmate.*

CHAPTER 40

Shortly, the efficient lawyer, McCumbler, had arranged for privacy with the most infamous client he'd ever represented aside from a certain private eye and once a certain senator. McCumbler came straight to the point, leaping right into this "unfortunate state of affairs," as he called the circumstances Alastair found himself in: charged with murdering a priest and possibly a harmless hack driver at an earlier time.

"I wish to God we could prove that Waldo Denton is alive and well and living someplace, so we might at least dispense with that charge."

"They've no proof I harmed a hair on his head."

"The fire chief, Stratemeyer, might say otherwise." McCumbler pushed the witness list across the table at Ransom. Alastair read the names in solemnity:

Father O'Bannion
Frederick Hake
Samuel O'Shea (not yet located)
Philo Keane
Henry Bosch
Dr. Christian Fenger

CFD Chief Harry Stratemeyer
William Pinkerton
CPD Chief Nathan Kohler

"Just before you were arrested, I managed to get a name of my own," said McCumbler with a grin, his thick glasses lifting with his cheeks.

"Hold on . . . whataya mean *before* I was arrested?"

"My services were drafted, sir, on the day before Father Jurgen died."

Ransom's face pinched in confusion. "Who hired you? I was under the impression it was Dr. Tewes." *Jane Francis*, he thought. "And that it was *after* my arrest."

"Dr. Tewes did approach me after your arrest, yes, but I was hired before then by someone else."

"Who retained you, sir? I have a right to know."

"Miss Gabrielle Tewes."

"Gabby indeed." He thought about why Jane's daughter would have hired McCumbler when she did. She'd anticipated his arrest for what'd happened to Jurgen. Gabby saw it coming. She had foresight. Else, she'd hired McCumbler to investigate him. God, how many people were investigating him? "And so you've been investigating the death of Jurgen since Miss Tewes hired you, then?"

"I have, sir, and I must say I was beginning to believe you guilty as sin until I came across a certain bit of evidence that might exonerate you, Inspector."

"The name you mentioned?"

"Yes."

"Father Jurgen's true killer?"

"I wish, but nothing so dramatic. I don't believe we can count on a confession from anyone else."

"Then who? What name is it?"

"Norman Vincent Freemantle."

Ransom grimaced. The name meant nothing whatsoever to him. He could only stare at McCumbler's glasses reflecting a gray haze about his wrinkled eyelids. "Do you know the man?"

"I've known of him for years. He's a personal secretary."

"That doesn't help me, sir."

"Secretary to an old friend of yours, Inspector."

"Quit playing games, man!"

"Normal Vincent Freemantle does the bidding of Senator Chapman."

The sudden silence in the bare lockup meeting room made Ransom's ears ring. "Harold J. Chapman . . . the *senator* put up bail for a ghoulish killer?"

"He did."

"But why?"

"Perhaps the senator has a stake in this matter? And has all along?"

"His secretary put up bail for—"

"Freemantle used an alias to throw everyone off, but yes, he did."

"And someone tipped you off?" Ransom leaned in over the table, close to McCumbler's face, studying his inscrutable features, wondering if the lawyer knew what he was talking about.

"Some two persons tipped me off."

"Two? Then I have two—"

"Witnesses for the defense, yes, but I fear one is a most unreliable sort. The sort who could get himself killed before a trial date is even set."

"Who is he?"

"And a second fellow who is far more reliable a person, not likely to flee the jurisdiction or to get himself killed in a bar fight."

"Two men corroborating the evidence for our side? Who are they?"

"Frederick Hake, who wants to see William Pinkerton's reputation tarnished—rather obsessive about it, actually— and the other man—"

"Pinkerton himself?"

Malachi McCumbler smiled at Alastair's beating him to it. "Clever of you, Inspector."

"And you, sir, are full of surprises. But hold on." Alastair jabbed his index finger onto the paper lying between them. "Both these men, Hake and Pinkerton, are on the prosecution's witness list."

"The one man secretly wishes to drag the other through the mud for his having fired him, while Pinkerton himself secretly held, *ahhh* . . . let us say genuine feelings for Ms. Hartigan."

"I knew there was fire there, but I thought him too entangled, shall we say, to pursue her killers to wherever the trail might lead."

"On that score, you were right, but he's had time to have, shall we say, a change of heart."

"His word carries a lot of weight."

"Inspector, Pinkerton admires you. Apparently has for some time, but particularly for your bull terrier attitude in pursuing Nell's killer, for pursuing those he has had a reluctance to pursue—for obvious reasons."

"Not so obvious to me."

"Chapman has been a Pinkerton client for decades."

"I still want to know why Bill Pinkerton has a sudden conscience."

"Let's just say he does, and while the prosecution thinks him a star witness . . . well, he and I have other plans, as does Mr. Hake and I."

"Then you've discussed the coming testimony with both men?"

"We've had separate conversations, yes."

"And you feel no compunction of setting these dogs against one another? No attorney-client privilege problems? All that?"

"It doesn't hold. They have not hired me. I am your client and yours alone in this matter."

"You're a genius, McCumbler. You persuaded Pinkerton to go down this path, didn't you?"

The man frowned. "No, no, no. I'm just a prairie city lawyer with a passion for justice, and I've known you long enough to know you've been framed."

"Pinkerton didn't hire you on my behalf?"

"I told you. It was Miss Gabby Tewes."

"By way of Pinkerton?"

"All right, all right, so what if Pinkerton put her up to it?"

"I like to know where I stand, Malachi, and with whom."

"Why hell, Pinkerton knows that Nathan Kohler has been after your skin for how many years now?" He laughed loud and long. "Pinkerton and I would love to get Kohler and Chapman, and we think it's time to blow the lid off their dirty secrets."

"You've never held any love for either man, have you?"

"Together, Inspector, I believe one day you and I will prove it was a plan hatched by Chapman that convinced Kohler to throw that bomb at Haymarket Square."

Ransom thought of his scarred leg and the six police officers killed that day, and the execution of seven suspected anarchists. Kohler's plan to stir up sentiment against the workers had backfired. The police had been sent in too soon by a Sergeant Ben Shorendorf.

"How much do you know of it?" Alastair asked McCumbler.

"I've done some digging, but that is for another time. Right now we concentrate on keeping you from the gallows."

"Deal . . . agreed." It was the first glimmer of hope in learning the truth of Haymarket that Ransom had had in several years.

"So it was through both Hake and Pinkerton that you learned of this man Freemantle?"

"This is how I learned who bailed out Rolsky, yes."

"Pinkerton wanted a different outcome, apparently. What alias did Freemantle use?"

"Frederick Hake, of course! Who ostensibly had been working for you, you see, at the time."

"*Ahhh* . . . I see, meant to be another nail in my coffin. What a tangled web, heh?"

"Now you catch on. Quite a web of deceit. One that may unravel if and when we have an opportunity to cross-examine the state's witnesses, and to examine the senator himself."

"That would be something. To see Chapman grilled under oath, not that he'd do anything but lie his heart out." Ransom recalled how vicious Chapman had been toward those he suspected of murdering his granddaughter during the Leather Apron case. "The man is himself a multiple murderer. I'm duty bound to warn you, Malachi."

"To be forewarned is to be armed."

"McCumbler, do you know just how shark-infested these waters are?"

"Take me through the shoals, Alastair."

Ransom recounted all he knew of Chapman's heinous crimes and what he'd seen firsthand at the Chapman estate in Evanston, Illinois.

Once he finished, the aged lawyer calmly said, "I represented the man in an action once. He is a frightening adversary, but if someone doesn't nail him soon for one or more of his crimes, he'll die quietly in his sleep at that bloody estate of his. I'd like to be the man who brings him down. How about you?"

"And with him Nathan Kohler?"

"Perhaps . . . but let's not get ahead of ourselves. In proving your innocence, many another man will be looking guilty of collusion, Kohler included."

"Then let's have at it."

"Easy, my friend. In legal matters, the tortoise wins the day."

Ransom nodded. "I place myself in your hands."

"Yes, one step at a time. No rock left unturned, all that. Now tell me, will you attest to everything you saw at the Chapman estate that day? And what about Jane Francis Tewes, since you say she was with you there?"

Ransom recalled the man's huge pigs that'd fed on the remains of the senator's enemies—both real and imagined. After detailing every death on the senator's estate that he knew of, with McCumbler taking notes, he balked at the lawyer's question about Jane.

"We must keep Jane out of this at all costs, Mr. McCumbler."

McCumbler looked up at Ransom and shook his head, hardly able to believe it. Still he said, "Truth . . . stranger than fiction. You and she are intimately involved, aren't you?"

"Keep her out of it."

"If it can be helped, of course."

"Promise you'll keep Jane and Gabby Tewes off the stand at all cost."

"I'll do all in my power."

"Either you do or I plead guilty."

The lawyer grimaced and gritted his teeth. "You tie my hands, Alastair, and—and we've not even got to court yet."

"The ladies're to stay out of it and above the dirt, understood?"

"But the ladies think they are paying my fee."

"Not any longer. Return any payment either has made you."

McCumbler shook his head, stood and paced. "All right, we have a deal."

"Now back on point. If Freemantle acted on Chapman's behalf to get Rolsky out of lockup, and I presume out of the city . . ."

"Then the senator has some connection with the medical people who hired the Rolsky brothers."

Ransom nodded, his smile wry. "And if so, little wonder Bill Pinkerton and Nathan Kohler did all they could to dissuade me from following up on Nell's case, you see?"

"I see. Indeed, I see."

"Nell was onto this same trail, perhaps tailing Rolsky when . . . and had she blown the case open . . . had it hit the *Tribune*'s pages, it would've indicted the senator."

"And possibly those who'd looked the other way."

"And no doubt Chapman's a shareholder in a medical school."

"And I suspect it means a tidy sum. Look, Inspector, I've many leads yet to follow. I've learned that Senator Chapman is in fact a trustee of a school."

"Which school are you referring to?" Ransom thought

of how Pinkerton had stirred him toward Insbruckton's institute.

"You know very well which school. The one Pinkerton did his best to stir you *away* from."

"The one supposedly has an agreement with Joliet Prison?"

"Which I've learned via a phone call to Joliet is a lie. The so-called deal fell through."

"Little wonder Pinkerton wants to extricate his agency from these dealings, heh?"

"Bingo! While nothing was ever finalized with the prison, Chapman was pushing for legislation that would free up John and Jane Doe and inmate bodies from every prison in the state. This much is public record."

"You've done your homework, Malachi."

"My motto—be prepared."

"Begins to all make sense now. Say, are you also representing Pinkerton?"

"He's cooperating with us, so we protect him any way we can."

"And Hake?"

"The same plus expenses."

"Careful. He will bleed you."

"It's why our defense will open with Hake, before he bleeds us too much."

A week later

Each time he spoke with his efficient, capable lawyer, Alastair Ransom came away feeling better and better about his chances of acquittal on the basis of reasonable doubt. Still, in the night and during those lonely interim days behind locked bars, as the hours ticked away, he began to question how they could possibly prove a single countercharge against Senator Chapman, Freemantle, Shorendorf, or Nathan Kohler. McCumbler kept up a constant reassurance that they would, at very least, prove his innocence in the death of

Father Jurgen and, without a body for the prosecution to point at, Waldo Denton.

Still he paced. Still he worried.

How many times had he asked McCumbler the same questions: What jury in the city will stand with me against Father O'Bannion, the pillar of society, versus Alastair Ransom, the bane of the police department's existence? Won't throwing me to the wolves be as simple to a Chicago jury as repealing the Sunday drinking laws? Who'd blink? And who'll remember, and will past service to the city mean nothing? A man's record, a man's lifetime of commitment, mean nothing?

McCumbler's stock answer had become a mantra. "Quit making my case out to be so bloody awful! It's not awful."

"And it's not your life on the line is it, Malachi?" This, as Alastair wondered, *Can I trust even this man? Suppose the senator's money has reached out to him?*

And so it went, and so he paced day after day, awaiting trial here in what'd always been his second home, the station house he'd worked out of for so many years. Seeing it from a cell was not a new experience. He'd been thrown in the drunk tank before. However, awaiting this ordeal for his life while caged and staring through a barred window at the dreary rain-swollen Chicago clouds had converted this place into a bleak, bleak house indeed.

When Alastair slept, fitfully if at all, he recalled stolen moments with Jane. He'd lie half awake, recalling all she'd whispered in his ear. How she'd said, *Alastair, I have been* Ransomed *and hope to be again.*

Now Ransom wondered at the odd, unfamiliar schoolgirl behavior, her silliness, her abandon and giddiness in those intimate moments. Yet it'd felt good to see her with no guard up, to experience her truly; to know her feelings, even though her zeal frightened him off that night the world had been upended when Mayor Carter Harrison was murdered.

He recalled how Jane had voiced a desire to be his completely. Still, this abandon had come on the heels of their lovemaking, when all else save the thrum of the city outside

Jane's window had fallen silent. She'd made amazing pronouncements then, all of which had stuck in his head these many days. Words no flesh and blood woman could possibly live up to. *What in hell was she thinking?* he silently asked the empty cell now.

In Ransom's head, her melodic voice and words played again, a kind of sonata; the kind of unfettered, unconditional song a man of his bearing, nature, and sensibilities had never heard in life. Yet deep within, it amounted to words he'd always secretly longed to hear from a loved one.

What was that she whispered? *The world be damned, Alastair, if things aren't all right with me and you . . .*

Could things ever be right with them again? he wondered now, lying on his back in this cell. *Could he come out on the other side of this trial a free man, declared innocent by a jury or by a judge or by decree or blackmail?*

The latter might well be his only hope, but at least he was not without hope.

Along with McCumbler, who claimed to have more than mere hope on his side, along with Jane's and Gabby's belief in him, perhaps he could indeed beat the charge and bring down his worst enemies in the bargain.

"And why not?" he roared like a bear, disturbing others in cells around him, mostly derelicts and petty thieves. He stood out as the star inmate here.

His bare hands and cell walls were beginning to take on the same color and texture before his eyes, and he found his hands trembling at times. They trembled now as Jane and Gabby were led in to see him, guided by Mike O'Malley.

"I told you, Alastair," began a tearful Jane, "that Nathan Kohler would one day have your head."

Mike quickly vacated to give them a moment and to guard the entryway.

Alastair had come off his bunk like a man propelled, and he took Jane's hands in his through the bars. "And I'm telling you two that McCumbler and I have a few heads to chop off ourselves, Nathan's among them."

"And if McCumbler is gone before the trial?"

"What're you saying?"

"He's in Cook County Hospital."

"No, how? What's happened?"

"Christian says a bad case of food poisoning, but I suspect simple poisoning."

"Poisoned how?"

"Impossible to say, but he very nearly died."

"But he can't die. I need him."

Gabby piped in, "I've no doubt they tried to eliminate Mr. McCumbler. He's been through a shocking night. But to be safe, we've hired a private guard around him twenty-four hours a day."

"It may take that. This means he's frightened them; means we do have enough to counter their lies and slanders." Ransom paced his cage now, looking like a trapped animal.

"We've hired an outside lawyer, an Indianapolis fellow that McCumbler respects. They're catching up now at the hospital."

"Backup . . . in case they get to Malachi next time."

"All manner of people die around you, Alastair," accused Jane, her eyes boring into him, "but this time I mean to keep those helping you alive."

"I believe we can win in this case and cast serious light on Chapman and Kohler's dealings."

"So do I, dear. So do I."

"Mother means we," added Gabby. "So do we."

"You will hear all manner of vicious attacks against me at trial," Ransom assured them.

Through the bars, Jane clasped his hands in hers. "*Ahhh,* but we know the true man within the bear."

"With you and Gabby at my side, Jane, I know I'll win. I will."

AUTHOR'S NOTE

Once upon a time . . . in the gaslight era of the
1800s, well before television and the advent of technological
wonders that've changed our relationship with the written
word . . . the written word was God. An exacting god for both
reader and writer. A sense of passion for language pervaded
all written documents. In all media, people expressed themselves with such force, flare, pomp and circumstance, even in
the lowly area of advertisements and "throwaway" brochures
like the one below, handed to every ticket holder at the
Chicago World's Fair or Columbian Exposition of 1893.

A quick glance backward in time is what we have here.

While this paper "tour" guides us to and through the
highlights of the great fair, it also evokes a time when the
written word created a wonderful dialogue and closeness
between writer and reader, as did live lecture houses, theaters,
and later the radio. As an author and wordsmith all my life,
I've so marveled at Mark Twain's time period; on how well
written the magazines and newspapers were. These were
the TVs, iPods, BlackBerries, and Palm pilots of the day—
Collier's, Harper's Weekly, all the *Heralds* and *Tribunes.* In
fact, a simple glance at the language of the day is found in
this exquisitely written "throwaway" document.

Furthermore, the eloquent, unknown author of this lost brochure fills this current day author with wonder. I invite you to join me in this stroll down the lanes lit by Thomas Edison's amazing street lamps. It is so worth the time, and it will fill you with wonder as well. The size, scope, and fascination of Chicago's celebrated White City cannot be overstated nor comprehended so well without the coffee table photographs, but in this brochure a thousand words are worth a photograph or two. Besides, Inspector Alastair Ransom most certainly would ask you to read the brochure or face the consequences . . .

Visitor's Guide to the World's Columbian Exposition

In the City of Chicago, State of Illinois,
May 1 to October 26, 1893.

BY AUTHORITY OF THE UNITED STATES OF AMERICA.

~~~~~~

Issued under Authority of the World's
Columbian Exposition
[HAND BOOK EDITION.]

~~~~~~

CHICAGO

Ten Suggestions for Visitors

1. Before leaving home arrange for lodgings either by addressing the "Bureau of Public Comfort, Jackson Park, Chicago, Ill.," or through information from friends or from hotels mentioned in this guide.

2. As there are accommodations for feeding 60,000 persons per hour within the Exposition grounds, and hundreds of thousands outside the grounds, it will be found, as a rule, more convenient and economical not to include board in advance arrangements. Meals may be had at time and place as desired at cost from twenty-five cents upward.

3. The visitor would be wise not to attempt to see the entire fair in a single day. Indeed, the Manufactures and Liberal Arts Building alone could take up a single day or more by itself, if the visitor is sufficiently interested. Use the map to plan what area of the grounds to visit each day. A typical five-day itinerary might include two days for the Court of Honor, one day for the Southern Court, one day for the Northern, and one day for the Midway.

4. Jackson Park, the site of the Exposition, is about seven miles from the downtown railway depots and may be reached by street car or elevated railway for 5 cents; by Illinois Central railroad, round trip, 20 cents; or by steamboat from the foot of Van Buren Street, round trip, 25 cents.

5. The State buildings can serve as a clubhouse for visitors from that state, wherein you can find friendly advice, gain information about other exhibits presented by your state throughout the fair, and meet friends and

family from your state who are visiting the fair at the same time.

6. Many exhibits in the Agriculture Building hand out free food samples during lunchtime.

7. There is a newspaper printed on the grounds, the *Daily Columbian*. It is eight pages in length, consisting of the first pages of the *Times*, *Tribune*, *Inter Ocean*, *Herald* and *Record*. The other three pages contain official orders, programs, prices of transportation, daily events, classified ads, and notices.

8. An abundance of drinking water is supplied free of cost. "Hygeia" Waukesha water may be had at 1 cent per glass.

9. Admission tickets may be had at 22 ticket booths in the business portion of Chicago, aside from the booths at the Exposition grounds.

10. Admission to Exposition, 50 cents. Children under six years of age free. Ticket admits to every attraction on the grounds, excepting the Esquimaux and Cliff Dwellers' exhibits. Midway Plaisance attractions are not part of the World's Columbian Exposition. Consult the Bureau of Public Comfort on the grounds in relation to all matters; advice and assistance will be given cheerfully and without charge.

The Main Exposition Buildings

These structures cover twice the area and represent twice the cost of those of the Paris Exposition of 1889. The plans were prepared by the best architects in America, and several structures exhibit the highest achievements of American architecture. The work of construction was from the first to close under the general supervision of Director of Works, Daniel H. Burnham, and to him, perhaps, more than to any other one man is due the daring conception of the whole and the general harmony of design.

Inside, they house exhibits from more nations than ever before assembled in one location. Seventeen thousand horsepower for electric lighting is provided. This is three times the electric lighting power in use in Chicago. There is 9,000 horsepower for incandescent lights, 5,000 for arc lights, and 3,000 for machinery power.

Electricity Building

Here are located the most novel and brilliant exhibits of the Exposition. The south front is on the great Quadrangle or Court of Honor; the north front faces the lagoon. For the first time in the history of International Expositions, a great structure has been set aside for electrical exhibits. Many of the exhibits are illustrations of the commercial and economic uses of electricity, and show the latest inventions for creating the three great economic commodities—light, heat, and power. The exhibitors here are all private corporations or firms, and in most cases, they are vigorous commercial rivals. Within the walls of the building, special demonstrations and experiments are made for the benefit of the visitor. Among the most unique exhibits is the new kinetograph, which transmits scenes to the eye as well as sounds to the ear. The inventor Edison was granted a concession to make a special exhibit of this invention. Architects: Van Brunt & Howe.

Hall of Mines and Mining

Located at the southern extremity of the lagoon, and between the Electricity and Transportation buildings, the Mines building has a length of 700 feet and a width of 350 feet. Its architecture has its inspiration in early Italian Renaissance, with which sufficient liberty is taken to invest the building with the animation that should characterize a great general exposition. In no other department of the World's Columbian Exposition, perhaps, is seen a greater diversity of exhibits than in that of Mines and Mining. A dazzling display of diamonds, opals, emeralds, and other gems, and of the precious metals, has for its setting a most extensive collection of iron, copper, lead, and other ores, and of their products, of coal, granite, marble, sandstone; of soils, salt, petroleum, and, indeed, of everything useful or beautiful in the mineral kingdom. Architect: S. S. Beman.

Transportation Building

The leading architectural characteristics of this building disclose simplicity of design, harmonious structural effects and dignity of proportion, relieved by richly ornate details. The grand portal on the east front, facing the lagoon, consists of a series of receding arches entirely overlaid with gold leaf. This department fully presents the origin, growth, and development of the various methods of transportation used in all ages and in all parts of the world. As far as possible, the means and appliances of barbarous and semi-civilized tribes are shown by specimen vehicles; of wheeled vehicles from the first inception of the idea of the wheel, to their present seeming perfection; and of the greatest of all means of transportation—the railway—there are specimens of the engines and passenger cars themselves. Architect: Adler & Sullivan.

U.S. Government Building

This building is most attractively located. Its architecture, the central figure of which is a huge dome, is classic and bears a strong resemblance to the National Museum and other government buildings at Washington and elsewhere. The building is devoted to exhibits from various government agencies, including the Post-office Department, Treasury Department, Department of Agriculture, and the Smithsonian Institute. Architects: Windrim, succeeded by W. J. Edbrooke.

Woman's Building

Woman has been from the first a most important factor in the World's Columbian Exposition. The Act of Congress creating the Exposition provided for a Board of Lady Managers, and in the administration of affairs, lady commissioners have been actively at work in every State of the Union, and in every foreign country. The Woman's Building is a great museum or exhibition of everything that woman in the past has contributed, or is contributing toward the common stock of knowledge and material progress. They show that women are capable, in almost every department of human activity, of competing with men. Architect: Sophia G. Hayden.

Sculpture on the Grounds

Throughout the grounds, the visitor finds himself in the company of sculptural pieces of acknowledged artistic merit. Many of them are connected with the great buildings. Others, however, are to be found in the State group, while others are met with upon bridges and viaducts, or among the trees, or on the Wooded Island. Native wild animals of America are illustrated in sculpture by Edward Kemeys and A. P. Proctor, prominent among them being a male and female puma, a buffalo cow and bull, a brown and black bear, a polar and grizzly bear, an elk, and a moose. Many of these are repeated. Three distinctive pieces of work, however, stand out in bold relief.

The Columbia Fountain

This beautiful creation, sometimes spoken of as the MacMonnies Fountain from the name of its sculptor, is located directly in front of the Administration Building, at the western end of the Grand Basin which forms a gateway of the Exposition, and around which is located the group of buildings which form what is known as the Court of Honor. The sculptor Frederick MacMonnies is an American by birth, and scarcely thirty years of age. The central idea of the fountain is that of an apotheosis of modern liberty—Columbia enthroned on a triumphal barge, guided by Time, heralded by Fame, and rowed by eight standing figures, representing on one side the Arts, and on the other Science, Industry, Agriculture, and Commerce. The barge is preceded by eight sea horses, forming a circle directly in front and mounted by eight young men as outriders representing modern commerce. The smallest figure is about twelve feet in height, and the largest twenty feet. At night, the sculpture is illuminated by electricity, after the principle employed in the fountains in the Champ de Mars.

The Statue of the "Republic"

Looking eastwardly from the MacMonnies fountain, the eyes of the visitor rest upon the great statue of the Republic, the largest ever made in America, which faces the Administration Building from the eastern end of the waterway. This figure is sixty-five feet tall, is perfect in symmetry, and was designed by Daniel C. French of New York. The arms and hands are upraised toward the head. In her right hand she holds a globe on which an eagle rests with outspread wings, the left hand grasping a pole on top of which is a liberty cap, the globe and eagle symbolizing the invitation of liberty to the nations of the Earth. Between it and the Statue of Liberty which stands in New York harbor there is a striking resemblance. There is a stairway through the inside of the figure, and the man who attends to the electric lights in the diadem clambers up a ladder through the neck and out through a doorway in the crown of the head.

The Columbian Quadriga

This group, representing Columbus as he appeared in the triumphal fete given in his honor on his return from his first voyage, has for its central figure the great discoverer standing in a four-horse chariot, leaning lightly on a bejeweled admiral's sword. The figure, fourteen feet high, is poised firmly on its feet, the head thrown back proudly as an indication of the daring determination of the bold navigator. The horses drawing the chariot are led by women, whose attitude expresses strength and energy. Their light drapery flies in the wind, and the mounted horses are prancing impatiently. A mounted herald on either side completes the group. D. C. French and E. C. Potter are the sculptors and designers.

The Midway

The Midway Plaisance: the summer playground of nations, where all the serious business of life seems to be laid aside, and all peoples, tongues, nations, and languages have assembled for a summer holiday. Some have said the Midway Plaisance affords a grand opportunity for ethnological study, and as being an equivalent for foreign travel—a place where one can study the peculiarities and customs of the various nations represented, as if under their own vine and fig tree. On the other hand, some have spoken of the immoralities and vulgarities of this unique pleasure-ground. One should not make the mistake of adopting either extreme of opinion. The people of the Midway are typical only to a certain extent. They represent some phases of foreign life, but it is life in its most whimsical aspect, and it would be as unfair to take them as representatives of their respective nations as to take Buffalo Bill's "Wild West" show as typical of American life.

The strip of land which holds this heterogeneous collection of races is 600 feet broad and contains eighty acres. It was formerly a popular shaded driveway connecting Jackson and Washington parks. Now it is the temporary and peaceful abode of people who, centuries ago, had they chanced to meet, would have challenged each other to mortal combat. Let us make a tour of this motley world. Walking down the cosmopolitan avenue, jostled by men of every race, color, and creed, with quaint faces and quainter costumes, we are attracted first to a Javanese village.

The village consists of a picturesque collection of twenty bamboo houses, set in the midst of tropical palm trees. The strange and varying noises of the gong-orchestra invite the visitor to enter the theater, where he will be entertained with jugglery, dancing, fencing, wrestling, and snake-charming. The "wajang-wong" or Javanese dance consists of a succession of graceful poses, forming a pantomime, which is part of a continuous story.

Nearby, in the street of "Old Cairo," may be seen a perfect representation of the narrow roadway, and picturesque architecture of the old Egyptian city, with its balconied houses and curious ornamentation of open woodwork. Many curiosities and antiquities are offered for sale in the bazaar. Hideous dances and exhibitions of jugglery are carried on at almost every corner, accompanied by ear-torturing music. We are not sorry to leave Old Cairo, nor do we care to tarry along among the natives of Algeria, where may be seen the shocking brutalities of the torture dance, performed to the deafening clang of cymbals.

At last, we find ourselves in the shadow of the wonderful Ferris wheel, from the top of which, 260 feet above terra firma, we may view the counterfeit presentment of "all the kingdoms of the world and the glory of them." Literally, we can see from this lofty lookout the whole of Jackson Park, Chicago with its suburbs, miles and miles of the blue expanse of Lake Michigan, the states of Wisconsin, Michigan, and Indiana, and far into the interior of Illinois. Moving on, we find entertainment in watching the marvelous tricks and performances of Hagenbeck's trained animals. A visit to the Libbey and Venetian glass works completes our experiences on the Plaisance. We leave behind us without regret this fantastical conglomeration of strange people, with their antipodal customs, dress, and amusements.

—MARION SHAW, Special Correspondent
for *The Fargo Argus*.

General Exposition Information

Boats:
The interior waterways of the grounds are equipped with speedy small boats for pleasure and transportation purposes, driven by steam and electric power. Every principal building on the grounds is reached by water, and there is an

ornamental landing for each. In the service is a fleet of 40 electric launches, with a capacity of 45 people each, known as "omnibus boats," making round trips of the waterways and touching at each landing. A fleet of 50-foot steam launches ply in Lake Michigan, entering the grounds at the upper and lower inlets to the interior waterways. On the interior waterway also is a fleet of gondolas, manned by picturesque Venetians. These boats may be hailed at any point for time service, similar to the street cab. Patrol Launch: A patrol launch patrols the waters of the Exposition as a life-preserving or precautionary device.

Intramural Railway:
Trains on the Intramural Line travel between stations at a rate of about 12 miles per hour. The loops are south of the Convent of La Rabida, and over the lagoon north of the Fisheries Building. This is the first elevated electric railway ever built anywhere. A complete circuit of the Exposition grounds may be made in twenty minutes.

Movable Sidewalk:
A mechanical contrivance which carries passengers from the steamship landing on the pier into the Casino. It is a continuous double platform, half of which moves at the rate of three miles an hour, and the other half at the rate of six miles.

All of the boats from the city land at the pier which juts beyond the Peristyle, and twenty turnstyles for the sale of tickets of admission to the grounds are located here.

Pavilions:
Numerous pavilions are scattered throughout the grounds, among the most notable being those east of the Manufactures Building, near the Peri-

style. These pavilions were erected by concessionaires, among them being the VanHouten & Co., Walter Baker & Co., and others.

Children's Building:

Location, between Woman's and Horticultural Buildings. Erected by contributions from the Exposition management, the States of the Union, foreign governments, and private individuals. General plan beautiful though simple; two stories high, with roof as a playground. Everything likely to instruct or amuse children is found in this building. Children may be left here by the hour or by the day in the charge of careful nurses.

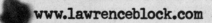